Hawk's Property

AN INSURGENTS MC ROMANCE

Chiah Wilder

I love hearing from my readers. You can email me at chiahwilder@gmail.com.

Sign up for my newsletter to receive updates on new books, special sales, free short stories, and ARC opportunities at http://eepurl.com/bACCL1.

Visit me on facebook at facebook.com/Chiah-Wilder-1625397261063989

Description

From the first time Hawk saw her, he knew he wanted to do dirty things to her in his bed.

Hawk, the muscled, tatted, badass Vice President of the Insurgents Motorcycle Club, sees women as bed warmers, nothing more. He never stays with the same woman, and although there are plenty of women who want to be his old lady, he wants none of that.

He doesn't date.

He doesn't let chicks ride on the back of his bike.

He doesn't fall in love.

And that suits him just fine until he meets her whose eyes light a fire in him. Problem is she's not so easy to get into his bed. Hawk wants her. And when Hawk wants something he takes it.

Cara Minelli doesn't want to go to the biker bar, but her friend talks her into it. Swearing off men since she caught her fiancé cheating on her right before her wedding, she has buried herself in her career not wanting a man in her life. Until she sees him. He is sexy, rough, crude, and oh so very wrong for her. So why can't she stop thinking of all the nasty things he'll do to her if she relents and lets him in her bed?

Then a vicious killer who has been strangling women in the area focuses on Cara. Police think bikers are involved. Can Cara set aside her trust issues and let Hawk into her life?

Hawk sees it as his job to protect what is his...and Cara is very much his even if she doesn't know it yet. Cara keeps her heart guarded, but when danger comes calling, their lives collide. Hawk will stop at nothing to keep Cara safe and make her "Property of Hawk".

The Insurgents MC series are standalone romance novels. This is Hawk and Cara's love story. This book contains violence, strong language, and steamy sexual scenes. HEA. No cliffhangers! The book is intended for readers over the age of 18.

Titles in the Series:

Hawk's Property: Insurgents Motorcycle Club Book 1
Jax's Dilemma: Insurgents Motorcycle Club Book 2
Chas's Fervor: Insurgents Motorcycle Club Book 3
Axe's Fall: Insurgents Motorcycle Club Book 4

PROLOGUE

HE STOOD IN the corner of the empty, concrete warehouse barely breathing, the anticipation of what was to come taking hold of him. Time seemed to stand still as he waited for the roar of the bikes, the vibrations of their powerful engines. They would arrive soon, bringing a sexy treat with them, then the desire clenching his cock would be satiated.

The four motorcycles roared to a stop in front of the building. The lead biker pulled his passenger off his bike. A trembling girl with platinum blonde hair stood in front of him, appearing awkward in her too-high heels and her tight-fitting spandex skirt, her cropped, red top barely covering the underside of her small breasts.

Dragging her behind him as he entered the warehouse, the biker said, "Hey, I gotcha somethin' extra special." His voice bounced off the metal walls.

From the shadows, the man appeared. The girl stood in the middle of the room with crossed arms. Her lips and chin quivered. A smile broke out over his face and he whistled softly under his breath, nodding in approval. "You did good. She's perfect."

"We know you like 'em young and tasty." The biker shoved the girl in front of him.

Moving toward the girl, the man said to the biker, "I will take care of you, as promised."

"Fuck yeah, man. You take care of us, and we'll take care of you. There ain't no shortage of pretty young things. Have fun."

The warehouse door clanged shut and the girl flinched at the motorcycles' roaring engines. She and the man stood, listening to the bikes as they disappeared into the night.

"What's your name, little one?"

Looking down, she said in a low voice, "Nadyia."

"Well, Nahdeeah, you and I are going to have a real good time. You treat me right, and I'll treat you right, okay?"

Nodding slowly, Nadyia tugged her top down. Watching her shift from one foot to another, his eyes took in her petite figure. When he touched her hair, a glimmer of hatred shone in her eyes.

"Don't you like me doing that?" he whispered.

"No very good English," she mumbled.

"You from Russia?"

"Slovakia."

"How do you like the US of A?"

"Excuse me?"

"USA, you like?"

"No, not what I want."

"I can give you what you want, sweet one." He moved closer to her. "Tell me what you want."

She glanced quickly at him then turned away. "I was to be model. I come here for job as model. I come to make money to send to my family."

"Are all the women in your family pretty like you?"

Shrugging, Nadyia picked at her cuticles. "I want to make much money, pretty clothes, and beautiful home. I want to be women I see in *Good Housekeeping* magazines."

He laughed. "Sorry to disappoint you, but you look more like the women in *Playboy*."

Redness brushed across her cheeks as she yanked her top down again, trying in vain to cover her midriff. "No, *Good Housekeeping*. You know, where kitchens is modern, husbands nice-looking, everyone has straight, white teeth."

"You're such a luscious angel." A thread of danger wove through his thick voice.

"I no understand what you say to me."

"It doesn't matter. Hell, I'm nice-looking and I've got straight white teeth. This is your lucky night."

"You make me do dirty things I no want to?" Her voice shook.

"Come over here, little one."

Avoiding eye contact, Nadyia moved toward him. He grabbed her arms and slammed her into his tall, slender frame. Moving his hands down her face, to her neck and shoulders, he cupped her breasts, squeezing them hard. Nadyia winced. He squeezed them harder until she cried out. He panted heavily as he tore off her top, exposing her chest. Licking his lips, he continued squeezing and hitting her breasts. He twisted her nipples and she stifled a cry. Putting his mouth on her nipple, he bit down. Hard. Very hard. Nadyia screamed. He kept biting. Her screams pierced the stillness of the night.

A FEW HOURS later, in the darkness of the early hours, the man threw Nadyia's battered, lifeless body into the newly dug grave behind the warehouse. She was nude except for the too-high heels on her small feet. He planned to keep her top and skirt so he could relive the excitement, the rush, this pretty angel gave him. This was one of the better fucks he had experienced in a while. Those asshole bikers outdid themselves on this one. They gave him a bonus—a virgin. He hadn't had a virgin in a long time. He was so damned excited he fucked her in every hole, and the more she screamed, the harder he fucked and punished her. Just thinking about it and seeing her darling body in front of him gave him a hard-on. Shit, he needed her again, but he liked fucking them alive, not dead. After all, he wasn't a sick bastard.

He laughed aloud as he covered her body with dirt. He'd have to get another luscious angel soon.

CHAPTER ONE

"WHY ARE WE here again?" Cara looked around the dark, smoky bar. Leather-clad men gawked at her.

"I have a crush on the bartender," Sherrie said, jerking her head in the direction of a muscular, thirty-something guy behind the bar.

"But a biker bar... *really*? How did you even find out about this place?"

"Friend of mine who likes it wild parties with different bikers. She said this place was fun. I've been here a few times, and I've totally fallen for the bartender. His name is Patsy. Don't you think he's hot?" Sherrie threw back her shot of scotch and motioned the bartender for another one.

"Not my type. Has he fallen for you?"

"He flirts with me, but he does that with all the girls. I figure if I keep coming, he's bound to want to know me better. We're kinda at the 'checking out my ass and boobs' stage."

Cara rolled her eyes. "Well, I don't think you should put your love life on hold for too much longer."

Shrugging, Sherrie threw back her newly delivered shot. "You still sipping your first drink? Damn, girl, you're taking it slow."

"Yeah, I guess I am, but this vodka tonic is so damn strong. I'm feeling a little lightheaded already. I guess I should've eaten before we went out. Speaking of, you better slow down with those shots. You're on your fourth, and there's no way I want to be the only sober one tonight, especially in this place."

Looking at Cara with slightly unfocused eyes, Sherrie turned around on her bar stool, trying to get the bartender's attention. Cara watched the various patrons as they came up to order their drinks. The majority of them were men, and the few women in the bar were dressed in provocative clothing: short skirts, barely-there tops, skin-tight jeans, and spandex dresses. Her blue jeans and sleeveless, knit black top made her look like the poster woman for prim and proper. Sherrie, dressed in a tight black dress with silver studs and buckles, had told her to "slut it up a bit," but Cara didn't feel comfortable wearing anything too revealing in a biker bar. Seeing all the women strutting their stuff, she realized she stuck out like a sore thumb. She jumped when the entrance door slammed, making Sherrie laugh.

"God, you're nervous."

"These aren't the type of people I usually hang with." Cara looked toward the door and watched a tall guy heading toward the bar. She gasped when he came into full view.

Her first impression was of raw power and sex. He was gorgeous, with shoulder-length black hair tied back in a ponytail. Sporting a nice build—muscular, but not bodybuilder-like—he wore two earrings in his right ear, jeans which fit him snugly around his legs and crotch, and a t-shirt that molded over his sculpted abs. A black leather jacket hung over his broad shoulders and gleaming silver chains hung down from his jeans' pocket. He was definitely all male.

Cara raised her eyes from his body to his face, and a strange shiver slid up her spine, making her scalp tighten and her hands tingle. His ocean blue eyes stared at her from below perfectly shaped dark brows and above a slightly Roman nose. Full lips twitched in a half-smile, making her lick her own while widening her eyes. Hard, angular planes, a strong jaw, and a five o'clock shadow lent to his blatant sexiness. Swallowing hard, Cara glanced down again at his crotch, transfixed by the big mound against his zipper.

Looking up once again, she met his blue eyes, smoldering with intensity. Her cheeks turned crimson and she glanced away. In the mirror behind the bar, she saw him smirking at her as he leaned against the end of the counter.

"Hey, Hawk, what's your vice?" the bartender asked him.

"A bottle of Coors." His deep, smooth voice stroked Cara's senses like silk. He jerked his head toward her. "Do you know her?"

"She's a friend of the blonde who's been coming here for two weeks chasing me. Damn, her friend's so nervous and outta place. It looks like she's never been to a biker bar."

"Yeah, she doesn't exactly fit in. Fuck, she's hot, though."

Cara's whole body tensed as her face heated, and she crossed her hands on the bar while he flagrantly assessed her. She averted her eyes and stared at the scratched markings on the wooden bar, running her fingers over the grooves, while she wondered if she should be livid at his vulgarity or flattered that he thought she was hot.

Patsy, the bartender, laughed. "I know you're checking out her big rack."

"You know me, man. A stacked bitch does it for me every time. I'd love to have my mouth around those soft tits. Her curves aren't too shabby, either."

Cara pretended to be engrossed in conversation with an inebriated Sherrie. Her face was turned toward her friend, but her ears were glued to the biker's conversation. She couldn't help herself; she was repulsed, yet titillated by his crudeness.

"You horny bastard." Patsy chuckled.

"No argument there. She's one sexy woman."

Her cheeks flushed as the men continued to talk about her. She was tempted to grab her friend's arm and yank her out of the dive at any second.

"Damn, girl, that guy is really checking you out. He's totally hot." Sherrie nudged her, tilting her head in Hawk's direction.

"He's being rude, and I'm not flattered." Unable to resist, Cara glanced at Hawk sideways. Every time she looked at him, he was staring back at her, his gaze lingering on her mouth. His piercing stare made her stomach flutter. *These drinks must really be strong.* She was ogling a complete stranger decked out in leather and chains, picturing his lips on hers, his tongue probing her mouth. Fanning herself with her hand, she swore not to have another drink.

"I'd do anything to have Patsy look at me the way that badass is looking at you. Maybe if my boobs were bigger? What do you think, Car?"

"Yeah, I think you're right."

"You do? You mean my boobs aren't big enough for Patsy?"

"What? Oh, yeah, I mean no. Sorry, Sherrie, I didn't really hear you," Cara admitted.

Sherrie, beyond tipsy, swayed on her bar stool. "Men always like the big boobs. Hey, Patsy man, give me another."

Patsy came over and put two drinks in front of them. "Excuse me, but I didn't order another one. Only my friend did," Cara said.

"Drinks are compliments from the two guys coming your way, ladies." He smiled wide.

"Isn't he cute, Car? Shit, Patsy's hot." Sherrie stared at Patsy's ass as he bent over the ice machine.

Cara looked around to see who'd ordered the drinks. Two bearded men with slight potbellies were coming their way. She turned away. "Don't look now, but we have some not-so-hot admirers coming our way. Ugh! Why did I let you talk me into coming here?"

"Admirers? Where? I'll show Patsy man that I don't need his hard ass," Sherrie slurred, turning around.

Wishing she could slip away unnoticed, Cara kept her head down, hoping it would make her somehow invisible. No chance. "Hi, pretty lady," a whiskey breath said in her ear.

Crap. Cara turned toward the voice. A man who looked like a grizzly bear was smiling at her while he stared at her breasts. *Just great.*

"What's a classy lady like you doing in a joint like this?"

"That's what I've been asking myself." She smiled back.

"My name's Rot, and this here is Beaver." He pointed to his friend, who was talking with Sherrie.

Sherrie was laughing her ass off about something, and Beaver took every sway as an excuse to put his thick arm around her waist and cop a feel. Sherrie was too wasted to notice, completely useless to help herself if things took a turn for the worse. *I can't let this guy grope her.* Again, Cara wondered why in the hell she didn't stay home. Sherrie was always talking her into doing something crazy. Ever since junior high, they'd shared some crazy adventures. Cara decided this night would be added to their list.

Rot kept leaning into Cara. He put his arm around her shoulder and yanked her toward him, crushing her breasts against his chest. She tried pulling away, but he held her tightly.

"Why don't you drink your drink? I ordered it for you."

"Thanks, but I've had enough. We've got to get going."

"Beaver and I will take you wherever you wanna go. We know a good place near here where we can have a fuckin' good time." He leaned his face into hers, trying to kiss her. She turned her head, a wet kiss catching her on the cheek.

"Not tonight, thanks," she said.

"Why the fuck not? I bet you have some real good pussy." He leaned in again. Cara tried pushing away, but his damn arm was like a rope around her. He leaned in closer as his hand moved down.

"I can fuck you good." Rot nibbled her ear.

"Back off. Now!" Cara yelled.

Taken aback for a moment, Rot stared at her. Leaning close to her face, he snarled, "Listen, bitch. You don't tell me shit. You're not being too nice, considering I bought you a drink."

"I didn't tell you to buy me anything. I told you to back off, and I meant it." She tried pushing him away.

"You heard the lady. Back the fuck off," Hawk growled.

Rot turned around. "Butt out. You may be VP of the Insurgents, but to me, you're nothing."

The tension in the bar was suffocating. Several people moved to the back of the room as the anger between Rot and Hawk escalated.

"I'm not asking you again. Leave the lady alone and get the fuck outta here." Hawk's eyes darkened dangerously.

Rot, sizing up Hawk's six-foot-three stature, sneered, "This bitch ain't worth shit. Fuck you, Hawk." Rot placed his hand on Cara's thigh and squeezed it. Outraged, Cara shoved it away.

"You fuckin' slut!" he yelled as he grabbed her arm.

The moment his hand reached her, Hawk jerked Rot away from Cara in a single movement.

"I said to fuckin' leave her alone."

"You sonofabitch!" Rot threw a punch. With an ease which caught Cara's breath, Hawk grabbed the biker's fist and bent Rot's wrist back until he yelled out in pain.

"Back off, asshole, or I'll break it."

Rot threw a vicious look at Hawk, but retreated. "You better watch your motherfuckin' ass, 'cause I'm not forgetting this shit."

Hawk sneered. "That better be a promise. Now, get the fuck outta here if you wanna keep breathing."

Rot yanked a befuddled Beaver off his bar stool and stormed out. Cara noticed the back of their leather jackets read *Deadly Demons* on the top and *Nomads* on the bottom. She shuddered. *I never want to bump into them again.*

"You okay?" a low, smooth voice asked.

She turned and looked into the deepest blue eyes she had ever seen. It took her breath away for a moment. "Yeah, thanks. Those guys were creeps."

He smiled and took a deep drink from his beer bottle. "Most of the guys in here are creeps."

"Are you?" The words tumbled out before she could stop them. Known to speak her mind, she chided herself for her lack of sense. Even though this biker was damn handsome, he dripped badass, and Cara didn't know him, or how he would react to her sharp tongue. She held her breath, her muscles tightening, but her facial expression remained defiant.

Hawk's eyes caught and held hers. "That's something you're gonna have to find out, babe."

His voice was like dark, melted chocolate, and the scent of beer, leather, and cloves emanated from him. The buttery softness of his black leather jacket rubbed against Cara's arms, and an uneasy desire to snuggle against it coursed through her, making her stomach somersault. Grabbing a cocktail napkin on the bar, she tore at it, willing herself to stop acting as if she were in junior high and meeting a boy for the first time. *What the hell is the matter with me?*

"What's your name?"

"Cara."

"I'm Hawk."

"That's unusual."

"So I've been told. Damn, woman, you're so outta place here. Did you stumble into this bar thinking it was a neighborhood pub?" He was talking in her ear, his warm breath tickling with each word. She almost felt his tongue on her earlobe.

"My friend likes the bartender. She talked me into coming with her."

"Remind me to buy your friend a drink to thank her." As he leaned into her, Hawk's hard dick pressed against her thigh, causing her heart to beat erratically. He was so close to her ear that his skin grazed against her jaw.

"Is this a biker bar?" *I can't believe I just asked that stupid question. I mean, duh, that's what it is. And I'm talking to a sexy biker.* Cara shifted in her seat, realizing how turned on she was, but also how angry she was at her body for acting out.

"What gave it away—the leather, or the motorcycles parked out front?"

"I know that sounded stupid, but I meant do only bikers hang here?"

"You a biker?" He traced her jaw with his finger—so gently, so seductively.

"You know what I mean."

"For the most part. The guys are bikers, and a lot of the women are here looking for guys to have a good time with. We're known to be good at partying… and other things."

Swallowing hard, Cara diverted her attention to her drink, moving the ice cubes around with her straw. Shivers pricked her skin as the softness of Hawk's t-shirt rubbed against her bare arms. She tried to avoid Hawk's closeness to her, his intense stare. This good-looking biker, who exuded danger and sex, unnerved her.

Someone had selected AC/DC's "Highway to Hell" on the jukebox. The hard rock beats filled the bar, and patrons began swaying and singing along to the song.

Hawk pulled Cara off the bar stool. "Let's dance."

He twirled her around and she broke free, a smile lighting up her face. Cara loved to dance. AC/DC was one of her favorite bands, and their hard-hitting rhythms made her sway and shake her hips and shoulders. Dancing released all the tension she had been feeling since she'd first entered the bar. Glancing at Hawk, his burning gaze made her move faster to the music; she wanted to avoid it and the pull he had on her. As she banged her head to each beat, her long hair flew around her.

At the end of the song, sweat glistened upon Cara's body and her black knit top clung to her large breasts. Gathering her hair on top of her head, she let the air cool her damp neck. After that dance, her body tingled with energy. It was what she needed to get rid of some of her pent-up tension. She was back in control. She liked being in control. She started to go back to her seat when Hawk grabbed her hand and pressed her into him. "Every Rose Has Its Thorn" was playing.

At the contact, Cara tensed all over again. Her mouth turned dry and a subtle shakiness invaded her limbs.

"I don't bite. Well, I do, but I promise I won't this time." Hawk dropped her hand, put both of his arms around her waist, and pulled her tightly into him. She tentatively circled her arms around his neck. Hawk cupped the back of her head and laid her cheek against him. She wasn't sure if she liked dancing so close to him, considering what she'd overheard him say to the bartender earlier. Deciding he was just engaging in "man talk," she thought she'd give him the benefit of the doubt. After all, he *did* come to her rescue, and so far, he had been behaving himself. Maybe she'd misjudged him, and maybe he wasn't such a jerk. Tentatively, she let herself breathe in his maleness.

Cara's head rose and fell with Hawk's breathing as he held her. Quivers ran up her spine as his hands moved up and down her back. It had been a long time since her body had reacted to a man's touch. Since her ex-fiancé had betrayed her a few weeks before their wedding, Cara had built a stone wall around her emotions where men were concerned. It had been four years since she had felt anything toward a man. But in this biker's arms, with her head against his beating heart, her body let her down. Her stomach was queasy, her nerves on edge, and a sweet sensation was forming between her legs. After all this time, why did her body choose *this* man and *this* place to try to break through the wall she'd erected?

Hawk was not the type of guy Cara was normally attracted to. She liked the preppy, debonair type, not tattooed, pierced men in leather. However, she was drawn to this biker. His incredible blue eyes and his rough edges pulled her in like a moth to a flame. His scent, cloves laced with motor oil, caressed her; warmness spread from her legs to her head. The earlier tension dissipated, and she found herself relaxing and losing herself in the music, in the moment. She looped her arms around his neck as she brought herself closer to his body.

Hawk held her, swaying from side to side. Bending down, he peppered kisses along her neck, taking her earlobe into his mouth and licking it while moving his teeth against its softness. She tried stifling her gasp; the last thing she wanted was for this stranger to know the effect he was having on her. She tilted her head back and looked into his eyes. A sheen of lust met her startled gaze. Once more, Hawk lowered his head and brought his mouth toward hers. Turning her head, Cara stiffened in his arms. He tried to kiss her again, but she resisted, murmuring her protests into his chest.

"What's wrong, baby? A mouth as luscious as yours needs to be kissed," he whispered in her ear.

His words shimmied down her neck and landed right in the pit of her fluttering stomach. Looking at him, she answered honestly, "I don't know you."

"Well, that's the point, isn't it? To get to know each other better? You're one hot babe, and you have the prettiest green eyes I've ever seen." He brushed his lips against her cheek. "Aren't you going to let me in?" His mouth was dangerously close.

Before Cara could respond, Hawk's mouth was on hers, gently sucking her lips. His tongue pushed against the seam, demanding it to open. She froze, her leg muscles tightened, and an overpowering urge to flee consumed her. Her clammy hands pushed against Hawk's chest in a desperate attempt to put some distance between them. Things were moving too fast. Dancing and holding each other was okay—safe—but kissing? No, that was dangerous.

Certain she would be nothing but a one-night stand, she couldn't risk being hurt. Even though her body was betraying her, her mind was acutely aware of the danger the sexy biker posed for her. Hawk was bad news, and she couldn't let herself falter. The earlier fluttering in her stomach turned to heaviness.

"What's going on, baby?" Hawk brought his lips to hers again.

"I don't want to. Please, I really don't." As Cara struggled, Hawk held her tighter.

"Come on, baby, I know you want this. I sure do." Running his nose against her jaw, his stubble scratched her face.

"I don't." Panic seized her and her heart raced, nearly exploding. Twisting away, she gasped, "Please, stop. I don't appreciate being mauled by you."

Anger shone in his eyes and he stiffened like a wooden board. It was as if she had thrown a bucket of ice water on him. "Baby, I don't *maul* women. It's usually the other way around."

"I only meant I don't like pushy guys. We're having a nice dance. Let's leave it at that, okay?"

"Whatever…." He put his arms around her waist again, but rigidity replaced the ease with which he'd held her before. This time, Hawk didn't place her head against his heart. She couldn't wait until the song was over so she could get away from this brooding man who made her body respond to his touch.

At last, the song ended and Cara quickly disengaged from Hawk. "Thanks, it was nice," she mumbled as she made her way toward her seat. Hawk gripped her arm and swung her into his hard chest. His mouth crushed hers. As she opened her mouth to object, his tongue slipped in, getting lost in her heat. Her body naturally leaned into his. *Crap! Why doesn't my body stop acting like this?* Willing herself to push him away, she broke free of him.

"You taste good, baby." Smiling, he licked his lips.

Before she could answer, Sherrie slammed into Cara. "Sorry, Car. I don't feel so good. I just puked. We gotta go."

Grateful for an excuse to get away from this mesmerizing man, Cara took Sherrie by the hand. "Sure, let's go." She glanced at Hawk.

"Do you need any help? How are you girls gonna get home?"

"I drove. We're good, thanks." Cara put her arm around her friend and walked toward the door. Sherrie leaned against her. Realizing it was impossible to help Sherrie *and* walk in four-inch heels, Cara glanced back at Hawk. Looking amused, a half-smile dancing on his lips, he came over and put his arm around Sherrie. Cara's jaw stiffened; she hated having to rely on him for help.

"Let me get your friend in your car."

With a pinched expression, she sighed. "Thanks."

Hawk, holding a not-so-steady Sherrie in his arms, followed Cara to her black Mercedes-Benz. He whistled. "Nice set of wheels. You got a sugar daddy?"

Ignoring his remarks, Cara said, "You can put Sherrie over here." She opened the passenger door.

When Sherrie was safely in the car, Cara started to open the driver's door, but Hawk tugged her around. She was shocked once again when

Hawk took her mouth and kissed her deeply. Tremors shook her body when the kiss ended, and he brought a handful of her hair to his lips, kissed it, then rubbed its silkiness against his cheek. He leaned into her, his hardness pressing against her stomach.

"I have to go. I don't want Sherrie to puke all over my car," Cara said with a laugh. She had to get away from him before she did something she'd regret.

"Can you come back? I can follow you and help you with your friend, and then we can get to know each other even better." He nuzzled into her hair.

"No, no, that won't work. I have to go."

"Fuck, baby, don't leave me wanting you. Let's have a little fun before you take off."

"I have to go. Thanks for helping me with Sherrie."

"If you have to go, then go." Hawk's jaw clenched.

"I *do* have to go."

Silence followed. Cara opened her car door, but she paused when Hawk gripped her arm, saying, "What's your number? Maybe we could hook up sometime."

Cara wanted to get far away from Hawk. Being with him was like riding on a runaway train. Not in the mood to argue, and certain that Hawk would not walk away empty-handed, she took out a tissue from her purse, scribbled a phone number, and put it in his hands. Closing her car door, Cara waved to him as she drove away.

THE RED TAIL lights disappeared into the night. Back in the bar once more, Hawk ordered another beer. A blonde with a tight t-shirt and denim Daisy Dukes came up to him. He recognized her as a hoodrat—the girls who came to the clubhouse to party with the brothers. He couldn't remember her name, but he remembered she liked it rough.

The bimbo placed her elbow on the bar. "Did you lose your girlfriend?"

"What the fuck?"

"I saw you and that stuck-up bitch. You were really into her. Where'd she go?"

"I don't know what you're talking about." Hawk yanked her toward him. Cara had given him a major hard-on, and he had to fuck some pussy real bad. "What's your name again?"

"Hawk, I can't believe you don't remember my name. It's Crystal." She pushed out her lower lip.

"Yeah, yeah. Let's go to the back room."

Crystal put her arms around him and tugged his face toward hers. She tried to kiss him, but he pushed back. "No kissing, just fucking."

"What the fuck? You sure were kissing Miss Bitch."

Hawk glared at her. "Listen, slut. If you wanna fuck, let's do it. If you don't, then fuckin' get away from me. I don't give a shit."

Hawk started to leave when Crystal grabbed his arm. "Let's go, handsome."

He walked with Crystal toward the back room, wishing she had long, chestnut hair, green eyes, and big, soft tits.

CHAPTER TWO

WALKING INTO THE Insurgents' clubhouse, it took Hawk a minute to adjust his eyes to the low light. The smell of whiskey, tobacco, pot, and pussy washed over him. He loved the feeling of belonging, which hit him every time he came back after being gone for a few days. He loved all his brothers—well, almost all of them. A few he could do without, but they were still family.

"Hey, Hawk, where you been?" Jax patted him on the back.

Jax was one of the younger members. He grew up with the club, since his dad was a die-hard brother. Hawk remembered when Jax was a gangly teen who hung out at the club, asking him a ton of questions about Afghanistan, women, and guns. He smiled to himself. Jax had come a long way since then. Being a patched member and the Sergeant-At-Arms, he didn't put up with bullshit. He was tough and never faltered, even when his dad was gunned down a few years before by a lone biker at Sturgis. Shit, Hawk couldn't even imagine how hard that must've been for Jax. The guy had been attached at the hip to his dad, especially after Jax's mother left him and his dad for another biker. *Why are women such bitches?* The title of Queen Bitch belonged to Hawk's mother.

"So, what have you been up to?" Jax invaded Hawk's thoughts.

"Not much, just working and customizing some bikes. How have things been around here?"

"The same."

Hawk looked around and saw several of the members in various stages of fucking. A few mamas and club whores were sucking some members' cocks, while a couple others were sucking dick while getting fucked at the same time. Yeah, everything was pretty much the same.

The Insurgents MC had different types of women: the old ladies, the mamas, the club whores, and the hoodrats. The old ladies were the women who held the club's respect; they belonged to the members who claimed them, and they proudly wore their man's property patch. The old ladies were envied by the mamas and the club whores.

The Insurgents had four old ladies. Banger's old lady, Grace, had been the matriarch before she died. Now Doris, Ruben's old lady, held the spot. Bernie was PJ's old lady and Marlena was Billy's, but she was usually pissed at him because he couldn't keep his dick in his pants around the club whores and mamas; and the newest was Sofia. She was twenty-three years old, quiet, and madly in love with Tigger. Tigger was doing a stint in state prison in Canyon City for beating a man nearly to death in a barroom fight. When the guy disrespected Sofia, Tigger charged into him like a bull and received a five-year sentence in the state pen. In eighteen months, he'd be up for parole and Sofia marked each day off on her calendar, holding her breath that Tigger's temper wouldn't screw things up.

Mamas belonged to the club at large, and they wore the patch "Property of Insurgents" on their jackets. Mamas were the sexual equivalent of a public well—they were available whenever a member wanted pussy. They belonged to every member and were expected to consent to the sexual desires of any member, or visiting member, at any time. Because they were club property, they were protected by the club, and they lived in the small rooms in the clubhouse's attic.

The Insurgents had three mamas, and they all wanted to be old ladies. Kristy desperately wanted to be Hawk's. Most of the women who came through the clubhouse wanted to hook up with one of the brothers and be a girlfriend or an old lady.

The club whores didn't live at the club, but hung around a lot, and were also available for any kind of sex whenever they were at the clubhouse. The whores didn't wear the patch and could be thrown out or banned from the club at any time, and they were also expected to give pussy whenever a brother or two wanted it. No arguments. Lola and Brandi were the newest whores in the club.

Hoodrats were the party girls who came for four or five parties and then moved on. They came to the clubhouse to fuck, drink, and do drugs, but if they were caught with anything other than weed, their asses would be tossed out and they'd be banned from coming to the clubhouse again. Most hoodrats loved the excitement of free sex, dangerous biker men, and the "anything goes" attitude.

There was never a shortage of women. They were drawn to the bikes, the chrome, and the lifestyle. It was like having a bunch of groupies. It was the life—pussy and cock-sucking any time a brother wanted it.

Kristy, a tall, striking woman with auburn hair and clear blue eyes, came over to Hawk. She put her arms around him and crushed her big tits into his chest. "Hi, honey. Haven't seen you around lately. I've missed you."

"Hi, Kristy. Been busy, that's all."

She whispered in his ear, "I've missed our good fucking. You've got the best cock for my pussy." She kissed him on his jaw line.

Hawk pushed her back gently. "Not today. I'm here to talk with the prez."

"Come on, Hawk, give the lady what she wants. We all have time for a bit of fuckin'." Jax laughed.

"Nah, I gotta talk with Banger. Another time, okay?"

Kristy pursed her lips into a pout and grabbed Hawk's face. "You promise?"

"Sure, why not?"

As he left, Hawk felt Jax and Kristy staring at him. He heard Jax whistle and say, "Shit, I never thought I'd see the day Hawk would turn down some prime pussy."

"Me neither. Now I'm hot and have no relief."

"I'll fix that. Come over here and let me fuck you good." Kristy laughed and wrapped her arms around Jax's neck.

Hawk turned back to see Kristy on her knees, pulling down Jax's pants. He shook his head. *When a bitch is horny, she's gotta get her pussy filled.*

Hawk opened Banger's office door. President of the MC, Banger was a good ten years older than Hawk's thirty-five, but he and Banger were as close as blood brothers. He respected and admired Banger. The dude had been through a lot with the death of his old lady, and raising his daughter, Kylie, all on his own. He deserved a lot of credit. It'd been hard on him watching his wife, Grace, succumb to ovarian cancer and still be there a hundred percent for the brothers. Shit, life sucked sometimes. Grace was the nicest old lady Hawk had ever known. Hell, she was the nicest woman he'd ever known, and she was six feet under, dying way too young and leaving a thirteen-year-old daughter motherless. He knew mean, nasty bitches who were going real strong. Life just didn't make sense sometimes.

"Hawk, good to see you. Takin' a break, or did you get hold of some great pussy?"

"Not that lucky yet. I met this hottie a few nights ago at Rusty's, and fuck, did she have a body that moved so right."

"Did you fuck her?"

"Nah, thought we were gonna, but her friend got drunk and kept puking her brains out. Kinda put an end to any pussy, you know?"

Banger laughed. "You're getting old. There was a time you would have fucked that bitch with her friend's puking as background music."

Hawk smiled. That night at Rusty's, he'd noticed Cara the minute he'd stepped into the bar. He was a tit man, all kinds of tits, but big tits always held a hot spot for him. And that sweet, sexy lady had his favorite kind. He could see his mouth kissing her breasts, his tongue circling her areola, then licking her nipples to stiffness. Fuck, he loved a soft, curvy woman with big breasts. He could get lost in them. If it was up to him, he'd have had his throbbing cock between those precious boobs before they even left the bar.

That night, Hawk caught her checking him out many times, and when he looked at her, she had acted embarrassed. He hadn't had a woman act shy when he stared in a long time. Not since Afghanistan, anyway, but that didn't count because most of the women cast their glances downward over there. He was used to the whores around the clubhouse who threw themselves at him. But he wasn't complaining, of course—a few of the mama sluts gave real good pussy and head, and it fucking kicked ass that he could have it whenever he wanted some. He just thought her embarrassment was cute. It was nice.

Shit, what the fuck was he thinking? He didn't do *nice*.

Hawk had wanted to fuck Cara real bad that night. Damn, her body shimmied every time she moved. He was getting a hard-on just thinking about her and remembering her soft, full lips. Those lips, wrapped around his cock, sucking him loud and wet…Yep, he definitely would've liked to have ridden that sweet one. He'd been thinking about her ever since Rusty's. She did something to him. *Aw, hell…*

"So, what's on your mind?" Banger asked, breaking Hawk's thoughts.

"I don't like the way the badges are focusing on us. Have you noticed it? I mean, they've been to my shop a few times looking for shit. I don't like it. Something doesn't feel right."

"Did they find anything?"

"Not a damn thing. I'm not stupid. I know my probation ends in two months. Maybe they just want me to screw up so they can throw my ass back in the slammer. The motherfuckin' pricks."

"It's not just you. They've hassled Tiny, Helm, Axe, and some others. Jax stopped them twice from coming in here and searching for drugs and guns. He called that lawyer we have on retainer, Anderson, and he came down and told the badges their warrants were full of shit. The next warrant they come with will be a good one, that I'll fuckin' guarantee."

"So, what the shit's goin' on?"

"I dunno, but I agree, they're trying to fuck with us. There's probably a crackdown on one-percenters 'cause of some political junk. They've done this shit every few years or so…motherfuckin' assholes."

"Maybe…it doesn't feel like that. It's like the MC is being targeted."

Banger slowly nodded. "We gotta address this at church next week. We need to be fuckin' altar boys until we get this shit straightened out."

"Okay, sounds good."

"I heard the mamas are gonna put some steaks on the grill. You stayin' for chow?"

"Yeah, I'll be around."

Hawk made his way back to the great room, the main place the members congregated to play some pool, watch football, shoot the shit, and drink. Couches around the perimeter, tables and chairs, bar stools, two pool tables, a jukebox, and a dartboard gave the room a casual feel. Hawk leaned against the wraparound bar. One of the prospects, Jerry, approached him.

"Get me a shot of Jack."

Jerry placed the shot glass down on the bar. Hawk took it and threw it back. With the whiskey's bite scorching his throat, he motioned Jerry for another.

He looked around the room as he swigged the second shot. He saw one of the old brothers, Rob, with one of the mamas. His wrinkled ass jiggled as he banged the whore. Hawk wondered if he'd be like Rob in thirty years: a wrinkled ass, no old lady, just club whores to fuck on worn-out sofas. He motioned Jerry for a third shot.

Yep, that'll do it. This was the one that gave him the buzz. Hawk pulled out a crumpled napkin and unfolded it, the one with Cara's number. He took out his phone and dialed it, wanting to see her again. He wanted to get to know her a whole lot better, especially her pussy and those tits. Damn, just thinking of her made his cock jerk. He was like a twelve-year old. *What is it about this one?*

"St. Clair's Hospital. May I help you?"

"Uh—sorry—I—uh—must have misdialed."

Hawk redialed more slowly the second time, making sure he punched all the right numbers.

"St. Clair's Hospital. May I help you?"

He narrowed his eyes into slits. He drew in his breath. "Sorry, wrong number."

"Sir, are you looking for someone in particular? Maybe I can help you."

"You already have." He slammed his phone on the counter. He picked up his shot glass and squeezed it, fury building inside of him. The glass shattered in his hand and drops of his blood dripped onto the counter. *Fuck!* Hawk would make her pay for this shit. No bitch made him look like a fool. Not. Ever.

CHAPTER THREE

"THEY FOUND ANOTHER body. I just heard it on the radio." Asher greeted Cara with the news as she came into the office.

"Crap, no. Where did they find it?"

"Some hikers found her in a shallow grave near Wolf Creek Pass. Can you imagine finding that on your hike?"

"Was it the same as the other ones?"

Asher nodded. "Yup. Blonde, young, stabbed, and probably raped."

Cara shivered. "What a sicko. There's no way this isn't a serial killer. This is, like, the seventh body that's been found in the last year: always blonde, young, with horrible things done to her. Why can't they find this psycho?"

"Yeah, he's a definite psycho. I worry about you."

Cara looked at her assistant and smiled. Asher had been with her when she first opened her law practice, about four years earlier, and was her first employee. Not only was he her legal assistant, but he acted as her receptionist and "track down witnesses and information" guy. Without him, the office wouldn't run as smoothly as it did.

"Haven't all the victims been blonde and very young? I think my brown hair is my shield, and even though I look good for twenty-eight, I don't look eighteen."

"I'm just saying, be careful. And you need to tell your friend Sherrie the same thing. She's crazy sometimes."

"I won't argue with you on that. She's crazy way too often."

Cara went into her office to prepare for her eleven o'clock appointment. Even though her workload was heavy, she had agreed to take on the referral because it came from a colleague who'd asked as a favor, since he had to have surgery and would be out of commission for a while. When she first finished law school, Les had been a great mentor to her, so when asked, she acquiesced to take the case.

Cara was tired, but she loved being on her own, and she found helping the underdog had its rewards. After all, wasn't that why she went to law school—to help people, to make sure justice was served for everyone and not just for the ones who could afford it? She knew her father was disappointed because she went into criminal defense instead of corporate law and didn't join his prestigious law firm, but she wanted to work with people, not companies and figures. She also wanted to make her legal mark on her own, without favors from her dad.

Sighing, she looked out the window. The Rocky Mountains, dotted with vibrant evergreens, never grew old. Cara wished she could stop a bit, breathe a little, and do something unpredictable. Her life had always been so well-manicured.

Coming from a good family burdened her with having to keep up appearances. Her actions had to be thought out; she couldn't bring shame and scandal to the family. Her cousin, Eric, who was like a brother to her, was a district court judge and was constantly reminding her that his position was an elected one. As such, the family name could never be tarnished.

It was so tiresome, so predictable. She longed to do something a bit wild, on the dangerous side. She had the appearance of being a goody two-shoes, and she was, for the most part. But a smoldering darkness lay deep inside her. It was that part of her that held dark, erotic fantasies she could never verbalize. Sometimes, the urge to break free and give in to her lust was all-encompassing, and Cara had to will her inner demon to stay hidden under the layers of her good-girl persona.

Meeting that biker at Rusty's the previous Saturday night threw her for a curve. Of course, he *was* hot and sexy, every part of him oozing machismo. Looking at him with his long, dark hair, blue eyes, tattoos, earrings, and leather jacket made her heart race.

The way she was attracted to the well-built biker scared the crap out of her. Cara had never reacted to a total stranger like that before. She'd convinced herself it was the alcohol, but the next day, and every day since, her skin tingled when she thought of him, when she remembered the way he kissed her, their close dance, and his arms around her.

Crap, I'm getting turned-on just thinking of him, and at work, of all places. What the hell is the matter with me?

The phone rang and Cara jumped out of her chair.

"Your eleven o'clock clients are here. They're early." Asher's lowered his voice to a whisper. "And they look badass scary."

Cara laughed. "Tell them to come in."

Heavy footsteps and jangling chains announced her clients' entrance into her office. Cara had her back to them as she rifled through a filing cabinet. "Have a seat, gentlemen. I'm just pulling a file." She swung around in her chair. Sitting in front of her were three leather-and-jean-clad men, all staring at her. The oldest leaned forward, saying, "I'm Banger. This here is Jax, and this is—"

Cara knew who he was before Banger said his name. Hawk's deep blue eyes bored into her, and his ebony black hair shined under the florescent lights.

"Hawk," Banger finished.

"Nice to meet all of you." She blushed when she glanced at Hawk. She couldn't believe *the sexy biker* was in her office. She hoped *he* wasn't the one who needed the legal help. *Crap, this is awkward.*

Hawk didn't say a word, his blue eyes fixed on her.

"So, what seems to be the problem? Les didn't give me too many details." She turned her attention to Banger.

"Well, I'll be honest here. We don't do business with bit—women. Les ain't able to help us 'cause he got some medical shit goin' on. He said you're fuckin' good, so we gotta go with you. But, you know, we don't have bitches—oh, excuse me, I mean women—who do this shit, you know?"

"Yeah," Jax whispered to Hawk. "We only have bitches for pussy." He elbowed Hawk. Both of them chuckled, Hawk's eyes never leaving her face.

Cara pretended she didn't hear. She looked each one of them in the eye. "You don't have to hire me. I won't be offended. I have a full caseload and agreed to meet with you as a favor to Mr. Anderson. I can recommend some excellent male attorneys in the area." She started flipping through her Rolodex.

"Hold on there, pretty one. We didn't say we didn't want you. It's just that we ain't used to relating to women in this way, you know?"

She looked at Jax, whose head bobbed in agreement. Hawk just sneered at her. *Why in the hell don't I just tell these chauvinistic assholes to get another attorney? You better appreciate what I'm doing for you, Les.*

"Just so no one's uncomfortable," she said.

"We ain't. It's just somethin' new, that's all." Banger smiled, the corners of his eyes crinkling.

"What's going on that brought you here?" Cara asked.

Banger pointed to Hawk. "Hawk here has had his shop searched a few times, and the fuckin' badges have come to the clubhouse and tried to pass some bullshit warrants, but Les took care of that."

"Why have they singled you out? Do you have a record?"

"He's on probation for assault," Banger answered for Hawk.

"Assault? What went down?"

"Just a barroom brawl. Nothing big," Banger said.

Turning her head, Cara caught Hawk's eyes. "Is that true? Nothing more than a few punches?"

Stone-faced, he nodded.

"Have they come to your home?" she continued.

Still staring at her, Hawk shook his head. Cara bit her lower lip. *Damn, he's good-looking.* His cut revealed geometric and swirled tribal armband tattoos over his muscular biceps. On his left forearm, he bore a tattoo of a fierce-looking hawk, its eyes piercing and intense. Framing the hawk's orange-yellow beak were sharp, black talons dripping blood. Its vividness was mesmerizing.

Patches covered his leather cut. There was a diamond-shaped one with the symbol "1%er" on the left side. Hawk's outstretched legs were tight in his blue jeans, showcasing his muscles. Cara licked her lips and forced herself to turn away. Instead, she focused her attention on Banger, questioning him about various incidents with the cops.

Out of the corner of her eye, she saw Hawk staring at her, a smirk on his face. *I bet he caught me checking him out.*

Turning toward Hawk, she said, "If the cops come over again, call me right away, okay?" He lifted his chin.

Banger got up, looking at Cara, and said, "You take care of us and we'll take care of you. You fuck us and, let's just say, we ain't the forgivin' type."

"I'll do my best with all of your cooperation." Staring Banger right in the eyes, she tried to prove she wasn't going to let any of these think-they're-badass bikers intimidate her. She could hold her own. "I need to know the truth at all times. No secrecy or game-playing. If so, I walk."

Hawk sneered. "Yeah, *truth* all the way, counselor."

Banger and Jax walked out. Hawk stayed back and said to Banger, "I'll catch up with you later."

Standing in front of her desk, Cara stiffened when she heard Hawk's words. The last thing she wanted was for him to loiter around her office. The minute he'd walked in, her body betrayed her. No, she did *not* want him to hang around.

"I have to prepare for my afternoon docket, so I can't chat, you know?" Turning around, she pretended to search for a file on her desk. With shaking hands, she tossed her hair over her shoulder.

Hawk came up behind Cara and slipped his arm around her waist, drawing her back into him. "You look sexy in your lawyer clothes, baby," he whispered in her ear. Though she tried to pull away, he held her tight. "Shit, babe, having a lawyer like you makes me want to commit crimes."

When he kissed her neck, her stomach flip-flopped and her skin buzzed. *Crap, one kiss from Hawk and my body does this.* She was so screwed.

"I saw you checking me out. Fuck, I can't believe you're a lawyer, *my* lawyer. This could be a lot of fun. Never had a lawyer between my sheets." As he brushed his face against her jaw, Hawk's stubble prickled her skin.

Cara squirmed out of his hold and pushed him back. Smiling, he raked his eyes over her body. "Do you moonlight at St. Clair's Hospital?"

Reddening, she looked down. "I'm sorry about that. Really, I am. It's just that I had too much to drink and it was a one-time thing, and I'm so busy with work. I'm sorry."

"Yeah, I bet you are." He stalked after her.

Cara tried to move behind her desk, but Hawk gripped her arms and pulled her toward him once again. Before she could react, he'd wrapped her hair around his hand and his warm lips were on hers. Urgent and probing, his tongue charged deeper into her mouth. When she moaned, his firm arms drew her closer as his free hand ran over her curves, pinching and cupping her ass cheek. Instead of shoving him away, Cara startled herself by leaning into him, a strong sense of comfort wrapping around her as she breathed in his smell.

Panting, she stood with her head on Hawk's shoulder, lost in the moment. As the minutes passed, unease and dismay replaced her feelings of desire and comfort, while a voice whispered warnings in her head, *This can't be happening!* She jerked away.

"What the fuck is wrong with you, baby?"

A pinkish flush crept across Cara's face while her stomach dropped. Clearing her throat, she said in a low voice, "This shouldn't be happening. I can't believe this."

"Don't play innocent with me, babe. I saw you checking me out during the meeting. What I can't believe is that you're leaving me horny as fuckin' hell." He grabbed his crotch, and Cara saw his dick straining against the zipper.

"Come here, babe, and put me out of my misery."

"Do you always talk this crudely?"

"Only when I'm turned on. Come here." Gripping her arms, Hawk guided her toward him.

Propelling him back, she said, "You have to leave. Now. I mean it. Go." Cara pointed to the door.

"What the fuck's your problem?" Hawk's eyes blazed with sudden anger. "You think you're too good for me? Were you slumming at Rusty's that night? Fuck that, I'm going to show you what your pussy has been waiting for. Once I fuck you, the assholes in suits you date will never satisfy you again."

Cara swallowed hard, lifted her chin, and met his gaze. "Don't bet on it. You're just a jerk in a leather jacket who thinks every woman wants him because he has a motorcycle. Move on to another woman; this one is not interested."

"Bullshit! You've never met anyone like me, and your wet pussy is telling you to shut off your brain, babe. The way you're licking your lips right now makes me want those sweet things wrapped around my cock, sucking the shit out of it. I want my dick so deep in your mouth that my balls will be part of your face. I'm hard just looking at your lips and tits."

She gaped. "How rude. I don't like you talking to me that way." Hawk's tone aroused, yet infuriated her. Hoping he didn't notice, she clenched her legs tighter together, trying to stem that sweet sensation fluttering around her sex. *Damn!*

"Your flushed face and squirming tell me I'm making you juicy. The way you were kissing and reacting to me tells me you like what I do just fine." The hairs on the back of Cara's neck stood up as his sensuous voice slid over her.

"I don't know what came over me. It shouldn't have happened. It was a mistake. Just go. Go!"

"Not until I get some of your pussy, baby. This is fucked up, and you know it. We're not in fuckin' high school. Get over here."

Hawk stepped toward Cara, but she ran over to the office door instead. Throwing it open, she yelled, "Asher, can you come over here? I want to go over a couple of cases with you before my next client comes in."

Hawk's face was a mask of rage. He looked as though he could kill her. Shaking, Cara's knees weakened as she grasped the doorway and said, "Can you come now, Asher. Please?"

"Sure thing, Cara. I'm just getting my notebook." Asher scooted his chair back and walked toward Cara and Hawk. Brusquely pushing past the legal assistant, Hawk kicked open the lobby door and slammed it behind him as he stormed out.

"Things didn't go so well?" Asher asked, wide-eyed. "That one's got a real temper on him. Watch yourself, Cara."

She let her breath go. "Things didn't go well, and I *do* have to watch myself around him." *My body deceives me every time I'm near him. He's not good for me.* "Now, let's go over the Remper case."

HAWK STOMPED OUT of the building, nostrils flaring. He punched the brick façade and blood oozed from the broken skin. "Fuck!" he yelled. The pain from his bleeding knuckles eased his fury a bit. He'd had it with this goddamned, cock-teasing woman—he hated women like that. She was such a stuck-up tight ass and thought she was too fucking good for him. Well, she sure liked his tongue in her mouth and his fingers on her ass, when she'd squirmed and moaned like a slut. He ground his teeth. *Fuck her!*

Swinging his leg over his Harley 1250cc, Hawk revved the engine. The bike's tires squealed as he shot out into the street. He needed to ride. Fast. That's what he loved about riding—it was freeing; just him, his bike and the wind. When he rode, nothing mattered, and it was his moment of peace—his glimpse of spirituality. Wanting to rid his mind of Cara—beautiful, sexy, and aggravating—he rode fast and hard.

OUTSIDE OF TOWN, as the sun dipped in the west, the man heard the roar of the engine. Tension spilled from his lanky frame as he licked his chapped lips; he didn't think the biker was going to show up. As the sound filled his brain, he breathed easier knowing he'd have his fix soon.

The gravel crunched under his feet as he went out to meet the biker.

"Why are you so late?" he demanded.

"I had bitch problems."

"Did you bring the girl?" He hated sounding desperate, especially in front of a dirty biker.

"Nope, I have a bitch who's giving me a run right now. I didn't have time to round someone up for you. It's too close, anyway. I mean to the last killing. You gotta ease up a bit."

Panic gripped him. "You know what our agreement is."

"Well, you're fuckin' sick. The agreement was sometimes, not all the time. We're doing shit for you all the time, and you're doing—"

"I'm risking everything!" he screamed.

"I'm here to tell you to fuckin' lay low for a while. Go to another county. The attention is on, and we don't want to be in the limelight. If you keep this shit up, you're gonna end up like your playthings. You fuckin' got that?" The gruff biker seized the lean killer by his shirt and shook him, then threw him on his ass. Spitting on the ground, the biker jumped back on his motorcycle.

Raising himself up, the trembling man wiped the dirt from his pressed pants. "When will you bring someone?" he whined.

"We'll let you know. Stay smart—being stupid gives you a one-way ticket to a painful death." Shaking his head, the leather-clad rider took off down the lone road.

The man listened to the sounds of nature, then heard a loud noise. Looking around, but seeing nothing except the woods, he gasped for air. The banging grew louder; it frayed his nerves. *Bang. Thump. Bang.* Sweat dripped from his hairline and he choked for breath. If only the noise would stop. Bending over at the waist, he clutched his chest and realized the noise was his pounding heart. He needed to satiate his hunger.

Gulping in deep breaths of air, he calmed his racing heart then walked to his car, turned on the engine, and drove in the direction of the neighboring town.

CHAPTER FOUR

MESMERIZED BY THE smiling redhead's picture on the front page of the *Pinewood Springs Tribune*, Cara read the caption—"Missing, 18 year-old Dana Squires." The girl was from Silverton, a neighboring town. Cara wondered if the girl's disappearance had any connection to the killings around Pinewood Springs. The girl in the picture wasn't blonde or petite, but it did seem odd. A cold chill ran up her spine. *What sick bastard would do this?*

Asher popped his head into her office. "I have a very irate biker on the phone cussing up a storm about the police."

"What's going on?"

"I don't know. Something about a search. All I can really understand is the word *fuck*." Asher rolled his eyes and shrugged.

"And that would be Hawk," Cara said. "Transfer the call to me, please." Nodding, Asher headed back to his desk.

A few seconds later, her phone rang. Grabbing the receiver, she cleared her throat then asked, "What's up, Hawk?"

"How did you know it was me? I didn't give your wimp-assed assistant my name."

"Your vocabulary gave you away. Stop calling Asher names. What's going on?"

"The fuckin' badges have searched my goddamned house. Fuck that!"

"Really? Did they have a warrant?"

"No, they don't need one. A term of my probation is a waiver of my Fourth."

"Why didn't you tell me you had a Fourth Amendment waiver when you were here last week? That's something I needed to know."

"I had other things on my mind, babe."

Cara blushed at the memory of his lips on hers.

"So, what the fuck am I supposed to do?" he said.

"Were you at the house?"

"No, Kylie was. She called me right after the motherfuckers left."

"Who's Kylie?" Cara regretted asking right after the question slipped out of her mouth.

"Why? Does it matter?"

"It can… she can object to the cops going into areas that aren't exclusively yours."

"She doesn't live with me."

"Oh… then… why was she—I mean, what time did the cops come to your house?"

"About ten in the morning. I was at my shop."

"Did they go there, too?"

"I don't know. I took off when Kylie called and told me what happened."

"Good move. Okay, come on over, and we can talk about what's going on."

"I'll be there in five minutes. I'm just outside your building."

Cara hung up the phone, reapplied her lipstick, and buzzed Asher. "Call the sheriff's office and see if they found anything at Hawk's house."

Decked in his leather jacket and tight blue jeans, Hawk stood in the doorway to her office. Taking off his sunglasses, he revealed his electric blue eyes surrounded by long, black lashes. He was an imposing figure of muscle and sex, and she wondered if she'd ever stop catching her breath when she looked at him.

"Sit down." She motioned to the brown, leather chair in front of her wood desk.

Taking the proffered seat, he stretched his powerful legs in front of him, licked his lips, and smirked. Her pulse raced. *Too sexy. Oh, so rough.*

"Hello, lawyer-lady."

"Hello, badass biker in trouble."

Hawk laughed. Spreading his fingers out, he leaned forward and said, "What can I do about these assholes who're making my life a pain in the ass?"

"Why do you have a Fourth waiver as a term of your probation?"

"I don't know. Les struck the plea. I always thought it was a shitty one."

"Your record says you pled to an assault. You told me the altercation was a routine bar fight. A Fourth waiver is a big deal, and it isn't ordered for just a few punches. You have agreed to let the cops search you and your property any time without a warrant. What the hell did you really do?"

"I never told you it was a few punches. I told you I beat the shit out of a guy who pissed me off."

"Did the guy end up in the hospital?"

"Yeah, counselor, I believe he did. What the fuck difference does it make now?" A scowl formed on Hawk's face and his eyes narrowed.

Damn, he's an impossible man. Cara had no idea what was going on inside of him, but she had a hunch he had some softness barricaded in there somewhere. Having a macho attitude clashed with her position of power, and she'd seen it all before—guys like this couldn't stand a woman calling the shots. Hawk was no different, and she suspected he hated to have her in control, but she *was* his attorney, after all. *How silly men can be.*

"Can you tell me why you beat the crap out of the guy?"

"He made advances toward Kylie."

There was that name again. Cara's stomach tightened.

"So, I told him to get the fuck away, he gave me shit, he took a swing at me, I sent him to the hospital for a rest, and I'm here explaining this shit to you."

"I just need to know everything so I can best represent you." Cara would rather give up her weekly manicures than ask him who Kylie was.

"You're the boss," Hawk said. *"For now."*

Ignoring him, she continued, "Okay, you have two months left on probation. It's obvious they're trying to find something to prove you violated it. If you get a violation, you'll be sent off to state prison for a stint. Have they done this crap the whole eighteen months you've been on probation?"

"Nah, they just started a few months ago. Not sure why. As Banger told you, they're trying to shut the MC down. They wanna put the Insurgents outta business. Don't have a fuckin' clue as to why."

"Did you have any guns or drugs at your house?"

"I can't have a gun. I'm on probation, remember?" He smiled.

"Drugs?"

"My house was clean. Not sure if sexy pics of my ladies count."

"The pictures won't matter to the police." Cara pressed her lips into a berry-stained slash. *His ladies? How many women does he have? Is Kylie his main girlfriend? Crap… why do I even care?*

Hawk's voice invaded her thoughts. "What should I do?"

"You can't go back to your house or to the clubhouse, since those are the first places they'll look for you. Right now, we don't know if they've found anything, so you have no legal obligation. If they found something, they'll get an arrest warrant. It's Friday, so if you get picked up, your butt is in jail all weekend. Bail won't be set for you until Monday at your bail hearing. Do you have anywhere to go?"

Hawk shrugged. His complacency was a common thread which weaved through a lot of Cara's clients. They never understood the seriousness of the situations at hand. And it got on her nerves—big-time.

"What about a motel?" she asked tersely.

"Are you gonna be with me?" He winked at her.

Twisting her mouth, she said, "I'll make sure you're settled. It would be best if you lay low all weekend. I'll try and find out what's going on and whether or not they found anything."

"What about me staying with you? They'd never look there, baby. We'd have some fun. I'd give you a real good time."

Cara licked her lips. "I'm sure you would. I can't have you stay with me. You're my client now, and I can't find myself in a compromising situation. I could be disbarred."

"You worry too much about all this shit, babe. Who's gonna tell on us? I don't play by citizens' rules. Fuck that shit."

"Well, I live in this so-called 'citizen' world. I've worked too hard to be where I am, and I'm not going to blow it."

"Come over here."

Shaking her head, Cara chewed her lower lip.

"I said come over here, woman," Hawk growled.

Cara kept biting her lip.

"Shit, you're the most infuriating woman I've ever known."

In two long strides, Hawk was next to Cara, grasping her arms, yanking her out of her chair, and crushing her against him. Putting both hands on his chest, she tried to break away from him.

"Settle down. Give me your lips."

When Cara tipped her head back and peered at his face, her breath hitched as Hawk's gaze dropped from her eyes to her shoulders, and then her breasts, assessing her. Slowly dragging his gaze to her mouth, he ran his calloused thumb under her bottom lip and smiled, inclining his head as he moved his mouth over hers, devouring its softness. A shiver of wanting ran through her, and her eager response to his mouth on hers shocked her. In response, Hawk's kisses grew more savage—he invaded her mouth with his tongue while his teeth grazed her lips. Fighting the desire that spread throughout her body, Cara twisted in his arms, but each movement made him hold her closer to him.

Her brain screamed, *Get away from him! What would your family think of you now?* But Hawk's kiss left her weak and confused. Her mind raced through a quick list of pros and cons, but her body lunged forward, lust tingling in her hands, her toes, and all her nerves. Silencing her mind, Cara grabbed a handful of Hawk's hair and leaned into him, her taut nipples rubbing against his chest. He grabbed her ass and kneaded it while trailing kisses down her neck.

Cara's legs clenched as a slow throbbing grabbed hold of her sex. Each stroke and kiss ignited a fire deep in her core. Her mind jumped back to chastising her body for its wanton behavior. Through muddied thoughts, Cara tried to focus and will her body to stop, but before she had time to think this through, Hawk slid his hand up her skirt. As he touched her panties and palmed her engorged folds through the thin fabric, he whispered, "You're wet, baby. Your pussy is screaming for me."

Cara's body exploded with the tenor of his husky voice. As he stroked her nub, Hawk breathed in her ear, "Fuck, babe, you're so ready."

Her mind whirled. Common sense told her she was on the brink of losing control, but her body was a traitor and craved his touch. Never before had any man had this effect on her, and it was awesome, even if it was wrong. Squirming under his delving fingers, she arched her back, thrusting her mound closer to him.

"You're greedy, aren't you, baby?" Flicking his thumb over her clit, he chuckled. "I bet you taste fuckin' sweet. Do you want more?"

Cara moaned.

Through the fabric of her panties, Hawk took her nub between two fingers, squeezing and pulling it. A bolt of pleasure ripped through her. She was so close.

And then he stopped. At first, she didn't realize what was going on and her mind raced, searching for answers. When she opened her eyes, Hawk stood by the door. Staring at him, her eyebrows knit together and sweat beads formed on her upper lip and under her arms. Her body was aching for release.

"What's going on?" she whimpered.

"Gotta find a motel, counselor."

"What?"

"Doesn't feel too good being left high and dry, does it, babe?" Hawk shot her a wry smile. "I hear there's a good motel next door to St. Claire's Hospital? Do you know it?"

"You vindictive bastard!" Realizing that he'd played her for a fool, Cara's face flushed and her skin crawled. A tinge of nausea made her clutch her throat.

"Another time?" He raised his eyebrows at her.

"Never!"

"We'll see." Smiling at her, he licked his fingers.

She wanted to slap that stupid smile off his face. And he had dimples. *Crap.*

Rocking back on his heels, he smirked. "By the way, is this one of those *compromising* situations you were lecturing me on earlier?"

Cara suppressed the urge to fling a law book at his smug face. She narrowed her eyes as he left her office, chuckling to himself. Standing in the doorway while fixing her hair, she stared at his back, her erect nipples visible through the fabric of her white shell camisole. Looking over his shoulder, Hawk winked at her as his gaze skimmed over her breasts. Then he swaggered out, closing the office door behind him.

"You okay?" Asher asked, taking in her disheveled hair and colorless lips.

"I guess. This client is such an asshole."

"What's up with his he-man attitude? It makes all us guys look bad."

Twirling a strand of her hair around her finger, Cara said, "Some men think they can grunt and bully their way through life."

"The sooner you get done with his case, the better. That guy takes badass to a whole new level, and the way he looks at you tells me he's got more than his constitutional rights on his mind."

Laughing, Cara replied, "They didn't teach *this* in law school."

Back in her office, she watched Hawk through the window as he jumped on his Harley. She held her breath when he glanced up at her, their eyes locking. Putting on his sunglasses, his face held that satisfied hardness that was becoming familiar to her. Even through the thick windows, she heard the Harley's engine purr.

Hawk simulated a kiss in her direction, and Cara stood transfixed as he made a U-turn and rode down Main Street until he disappeared.

CHAPTER FIVE

A S THE DAY wore on, Cara couldn't get her encounter with Hawk out of her mind. She couldn't believe she'd acted like such a slut. *How could I have let Hawk do those things to me? I hardly know him, and he's my client. Damn.*

She had broken so many rules on so many levels. For some reason, he brought out this irrational, horny beast in her. She grudgingly admitted he was hot, but it went deeper than that. It was like he stirred up buried emotions, dark fantasies.

Cara had always been a good girl: she did what her parents wanted, excelled in school, and she sure as hell didn't sleep around. She was the type of daughter all parents wanted. But like any hot-blooded woman, she had a raging fire deep in her soul, and she wanted to experiment, to give in to passion. It was downright exhausting being the "good girl" all the time.

Hawk was the first man who'd brought those deep-seated desires to the surface. The first time she saw him at the biker bar, he drew her in and stoked that fire inside her. It wasn't love at first sight—no, it was more like lust and restlessness crashing together. Since that night, the volcano within her had started to erupt.

Cara had never been with a man who was so blunt, demanding, and confident. Hawk was exciting and dangerous, and the perfect break for a controlled good girl. The problem was he was her client and was from the wrong side of the tracks. A complicated mess was in store for her if she continued to give in to her emotions. Her mother had drilled into her the importance of keeping up appearances ever since she was a child, and she would hate to disappoint her parents or tarnish the family name.

Just thinking about it made her stomach cramp. A distraction from her handsome client was necessary if she had any hope in jumping off this dark, dangerous ride.

The buzzer on her landline startled her. "What's up, Asher?"

"A Luke is on the line for you. Says it's personal."

"Okay, thanks. I'll take it."

"I'm taking my lunch now. Did you want me to pick you up anything to eat?"

"No, I'm meeting Sherrie for lunch. Thanks, though."

Cara pushed the flashing light on line one and said, "Hi, Luke."

"Hi, Cara, am I interrupting you?"

"No, you're not."

Luke Tanner was a junior associate in her father's law firm, nice-looking, in a male model kind of way. He had all the credentials: good law school, corporate lawyer, good family breeding—exactly the kind of guy Cara should've been going out with. He was always polite and considerate on their dates, but Cara didn't feel any excitement or danger with Luke, not like she did when she was around Hawk.

Parents loved Luke and Luke loved parents, especially rich fathers like Cara's dad. Luke had big plans for himself. He wanted to be partner by the time he turned thirty-eight (six more years), have a pretty, smart wife on his arm (Cara would do just fine), have a couple of kids (one of each sex would be great), and live in the Glenmore section of town in one of those mansions with a couple of servants to help out. Luke Tanner had big plans, and Cara Minelli was a key factor in them. What better way to advance his career than to marry the boss's pretty and curvy daughter?

Cara was bright, sexy, and a good girl. The way Luke saw it, her only flaw was that she was hell-bent on representing the dirt bags of the Earth. Not wanting to practice in her dad's law firm perplexed Luke—she could be partner in a year, with her connections. Why she wanted to be around those lowlifes she called clients was beyond Luke's comprehension, but he'd make sure that ended once she had his ring on her finger.

"What's going on?" she asked.

"Rescuing me from a very dull evening," he said.

This is the distraction I need. "Sounds intriguing," she replied.

"How about dinner and maybe dancing? I know it's last-minute, but I've been busy on a complex litigation case. I need a break, and I want to see you again."

"I don't have plans. Dinner and dancing sound great."

THIRTY MINUTES LATER, sitting at a table by the window in The French Bistro, Cara waved at Sherrie as she entered the restaurant. She hadn't seen Sherrie since they'd gone out two weeks before to the biker bar. The French Bistro was a newer, popular restaurant on trendy Spruce Street and was reminiscent of a neighborhood café on the Left Bank in Paris. Wrought-iron chairs around small, round tables adorned with lace tablecloths and flower-filled glass vases welcomed customers. Oil paintings depicting street scenes of Parisian life decorated the yellow walls, while the aroma of baked bread enveloped the eatery, tantalizing patrons as they entered.

After the waiter brought their food, Sherrie, munching on her paté and Swiss cheese sandwich, said, "What gives, Cara?"

"What do you mean?"

"You're hiding something from me. I know you, girl. 'Fess up. You're hiding something."

Pushing her salad plate aside, Cara chewed her lower lip and said, "Remember that biker guy I met at the bar a couple of weeks ago?"

"Yeah, how could I forget that cutie?"

"Well, he's now my client. I mean, he came into my office with some of his club guys, and I almost died when I saw him."

"Are you shittin' me? Your sexy biker is now your *client?*" Throwing her hands over her mouth, Sherrie laughed.

"Shh… not so loud," Cara said as she noticed a few people staring at them. "And no, I'm not shitting you. He's my new client, *and* it's *not* funny," she whispered.

"I can't fucking believe that. What are the odds?"

"First of all, he's not *my biker*. The case was Les', but he couldn't do it and asked me to take it as a favor. If I'd known *he* was the client, I never would've agreed."

"You have to admit, he's sexy, right?"

"Yeah, I'll admit he's sexy, but he's also arrogant and a smartass. I find him infuriating."

"I couldn't tell that by the way you were dancing with him." Sherrie raised her eyebrows.

"I had too much to drink. I was tipsy."

"Were you? You drove us home. Did you break your no-driving-if-tipsy rule?"

Sherrie knew her too well.

"Well?"

"Okay, so I knew what I was doing and I thought he was hot. So what?"

"So, nothing. It's just that I've never seen you do that in all the times we've been clubbing. That's all."

"I don't know, I guess I felt like letting loose. I had a long, stressful week, and I knew I wouldn't bump into anyone I knew in *that kind* of bar."

"You don't have to explain. I'm not judging you. Hell, I'd go for him. It looked like you guys had something going there. I remember that, even if I don't remember much more of that night. Talk about getting wasted." Sherrie giggled.

"He's not my type. He mostly makes me mad."

"Not mad, Cara, *hot*. Damn, it's been so long for you, you can't remember what it feels like. I mean, you've buried yourself in work for the last four years. I have to drag you out most weekends, and when we're at a bar, you send out don't-touch-me vibes big-time. That's what I'm saying—that Saturday, you were on fire. I don't care what you say.

This biker struck something in you."

"Okay, yeah, I feel drawn to him, but that's probably because he's so damn persistent and demanding. For reasons that probably would take years on a therapist's couch to figure out, I kinda find his arrogance a turn-on. Am I psycho, or what?"

Smiling, Sherrie said, "No, you're a woman who's been dry for too long. You need to go for it."

Cara sighed. "What am I going to do? I acted like such a slut with Hawk. I let him kiss me and do stuff in my office, and *he's my client*. It's like I know it's wrong, and he's bad news, but I kiss him anyway. My common sense has left me. Crap, I *am* psycho. I think a great-aunt of my dad's was. I've read that it can be hereditary."

"You're not psycho. You want to screw him. So do it."

Cara gasped. "I couldn't. We're too different. I mean, we come from such different worlds, and we don't know each other."

"I'm not telling you to marry him or even get into a relationship. Just screw the hell out of him and have fun. When's the last time you screwed anyone? Since you and Trevor broke up?"

Trevor and Cara had been engaged and planned to marry after law school, but she later discovered he was involved in extracurricular activities, like banging most of the first-year law students. She'd been devastated—she'd had such plans for their future—and had broken it off with him.

After that, she threw herself into passing the bar exam and setting up her practice. Four years later, she had a thriving law practice and Trevor was nothing more than a dull ache in her heart.

"So, when was it?" Sherrie's question pulled her back from her memories.

"I've been so busy. I—I don't know."

"The answer is you haven't screwed anyone since Trevor. Isn't it time to blow out the vigil candles you've lit for your hurt and betrayal?"

"You don't know how deceived I felt. I thought Trevor was my soulmate."

"He wasn't, and it's a good thing you found out *before* the wedding rather than *after*. That's a closed chapter, and it's time to start a new one. You need to let someone else into your life."

"I have. I'm going out with Luke."

Sherrie rolled her eyes and made a face. "Of course you are. He's safe because you don't have any feelings for him."

"Yes, I do," Cara protested.

"Like what?"

"He's nice and good-looking. We're both lawyers, so it's nice to talk to him about legal issues, and he's smart, ambitious, and a gentleman." Sherrie pretended to yawn. Shaking her head, Cara continued, "He'd never tell me that my pussy is wet and he wants to taste me. He respects me."

Sherrie leaned forward, her eyes bright. "Sexy Biker says those things to you? Damn, that's a turn-on."

"That's not the point, is it? Luke is future material and Hawk isn't. Hawk would probably be a great screw, and that's it."

"What's wrong with that? Luke is the guy who is the good-girl idea of what you should have, who your parents would approve of. Hawk is the badass biker who lives in your dark fantasies and would satisfy every urge in your body. What's wrong with having parent-friendly Luke in the limelight and hot fantasy-biker on the side?"

Cara giggled. "You're so bad, Sherrie. I know you'd do that. I can't."

"I'm sorry your hot biker didn't hit on me. I'd already be in bed with his sexy body." Sherrie licked her lips. "But he only had eyes for you. I saw it the minute he walked in the door that night."

Cara flushed, shivers playing up her spine and neck. Sherrie talking about Hawk wanting her made her happy.

"None of this matters anyway, because Hawk is my client."

"Hasn't seemed to stop him... or you."

Cara groaned. "I know, don't remind me. I feel bad about it. I'm so unprofessional."

"Who cares if you're screwing your client? Some arbitrary group of staunch men in a windowless office? Anyway, he won't be your client forever."

That's what I'm afraid of. Looking at her phone, Cara said, "I have to run. I have an evidentiary hearing in twenty minutes." She jumped up and threw thirty dollars on the table.

"Cara, this was supposed to be my treat."

"I know. You can get it the next time. Call me. I've gotta go."

SHERRIE WATCHED AS her best friend ran out the door, her heels clacking on the hardwood floor. The two had been through so much. They'd met when Sherrie's mother moved to Pinewood Springs after Sherrie's parents split up. Sherrie was in junior high, didn't know anyone at the school, and everyone had their clique; it was miserable. Cara befriended her, and they had been best friends ever since.

When they went out, Cara usually picked up the tab, and Sherrie appreciated it because she was always broke. Being a lead teacher at the Little Tykes Day Care Center didn't pay enough, but she loved the kids and the work.

Sherrie knew Cara was in deep with her sexy biker, and she didn't believe any of Cara's excuses or denials of her feelings for Hawk. She knew Cara, and Cara was scared shitless to open her heart to another man. Going out with Luke didn't pose any danger because he was so *not* Cara's type, and Sherrie knew he was just a safety net, even if Cara didn't know that yet. Sexy Biker was a different deal altogether. During their lunch conversation, and the way Cara brightened when Sherrie talked about Hawk's attraction to her, Sherrie detected that she had a primal pull toward him. Sherrie was rooting for Sexy Biker, because she knew her friend needed a real man to free her heart from the self-imposed prison she'd put herself in four years back. Sexy Biker would be the perfect liberator.

STAY IN A motel. Why the fuck would I do that? Even though it was early August, there was a chill in the air. Fall was going to come early this year. The crickets' symphony reverberated from the oak and maple trees as Hawk sped around the curves. Craving solitude, he took the back road to the clubhouse.

The wind whipping around him and the hum of his bike's powerful engine always made his troubles disappear. Out on the road, nothing mattered except for the asphalt and the ride. *Fuck, it's better than sex. Well, almost...* At least his Harley didn't talk back to him the way bitches did. Like Cara. She had a mouth on her. *Must be the lawyer in her, always ready to argue.* And she was so goddamn bossy. Who needed that shit? No, his love was a kick-ass, chrome powerhouse.

Hawk loved customizing his bike; it was his obsession. He and his bike were one—it was for the ride—it was *always* about the ride. The only ones who got it were bikers—true bikers—not those fucking weekend assholes who wore leather pretending they were bad. God, he hated them. Those jerks would come out with their buddies and ride around the mountain passes, acting tough, but they were just sniveling ass-wipes. They didn't know shit about the ride, the life, the brotherhood. He gritted and leaned low around the curve on Ghost's Pass, his shin inches from touching the road. This was freedom.

He came around the backside of the clubhouse. A thirty-foot, chain-link fence with barbed wire on the top surrounded it. The Insurgents had bought an old, three-story, red brick schoolhouse back in 1976. The founding president, Stinger Gaitlan, wanted a big enough place that could accommodate the growth of the club and the neighboring charters.

The clubhouse was twenty-five miles outside of Pinewood Springs. The front door bored the logo of the club—a flaming skull with two smoking pistols on each side—and the name "Insurgents" in large, red and yellow lettering.

There was a big parking lot in front of the fence, and evergreen, pine, and aspen trees surrounded the clubhouse. The Colorado River ran alongside the back of the club's property, and the river's swift, dangerous currents mirrored the craziness of the club's parties most weekends.

Hawk parked his Harley near the fence as he spied a couple of prospects cleaning out the trash cans from the previous night's party. Seeing a patched member, they scrambled out of the way so Hawk could pass. Prospects were vying to also become patched members and had to go through a probationary period to prove they were worthy to don the full colors on their cuts. Being a prospect meant doing whatever a member told them to, without any questions or arguments. They were responsible for the menial and grunt jobs around and outside of the clubhouse and were allowed to speak only when spoken to.

In the room behind the great one, there was a large kitchen where the old ladies would make the meals. Sometimes the whores would cook, as well, but mostly, they cleaned. Walking through the back door, Hawk saw Doris, Ruben's old lady, drying a large pot in the kitchen.

Doris had been Ruben's old lady for as long as Hawk had known them. They had a couple of kids and seemed to understand each other in a way he sometimes envied. Ruben had his pussy on the side, and Doris pitched in with club activities, but she mostly raised their two kids and lived her life away from the club. If Ruben's fucking around bothered her, she never showed it, and Hawk admired her for the respect she gave Ruben and the brothers. She knew her place. She knew the sluts Ruben sucked and fucked meant nothing more than pussy on a Friday night, and Ruben's heart and love belonged to her only. Doris was a good example of what an old lady should be—women could learn a lot from her.

"Hiya, Hawk. We missed you last night."

"Had some shit to do. Where's Ruben?"

"Snoring in one of the rooms upstairs. He got so fucking plastered last night." She smiled widely. "It was a helluva party."

"Banger around?"

"Yeah, he's in the great room."

Hawk nodded and walked toward the great room. Inside, he saw some of the brothers passed out on the floor, a few of them with naked women on top of them. A couple of his brothers were sitting wide-legged on the couch, beer in hand while two sluts, their tits jiggling as they moved their mouths and hands up and down, kneeled between their legs, sucking the shit out of their dicks.

Squinting, Hawk spotted Banger with his face buried in a whore's pussy, who sat on top of the bar, legs spread wide, playing with her tits as Banger ate her out. Hawk came over and slapped the president on the back. "Enjoying yourself?"

Banger pulled his mouth away and the slut pouted and scolded him. "I ain't finished yet, baby. I love the way you eat my pussy. I need to come for you and then suck your cock." She ran her purple talons down his back.

Banger pushed her away, saying, "Slut, get outta here. I got club business goin' now. Go on, get your ass outta here."

Crestfallen, she jumped off the bar and Banger slapped her ass. "Later, bitch. I'll finish ya later."

She walked over to another brother who was drinking a beer at a table and sat on his lap, her ass pressing against his cock. As she brought her mouth down on his, they kissed and groped each other. Hawk shook his head. "Who's that one? I haven't seen her before."

"Shit, I can't remember her name. She and a bunch of her friends came by last night to party. They were wild—gave the brothers a good time. This slut, she must've done all the brothers every which way. She's a damn good fuck. You should try her. She's eyeing you now."

Hawk looked over at the woman who was grinding her ass into Ronnie's cock. She winked at Hawk and blew him a kiss. He stared, stone-faced. "Nah, I think I'll pass. Not my type."

"When in the fuck did that matter?" Banger joked. "You've fucked two and three sluts at once, and it didn't look like you were all that choosy. Shit, it's good pussy."

Hawk shook his head; he didn't want any of the bitches there. Yeah, he was horny as hell, and it had been a while since he had some pussy, but the only one he wanted was Cara's. That woman was messing with his head, and it pissed him the hell off that he wanted her so much. He needed to just fuck the shit out of her and get it out of his system. After that, he could go back to his normal life: riding, working, drinking, and random pussy.

"The badges were here," Banger said after he shut his office door.

"Shit. I knew they'd show up here, the motherfuckers. What did they want?"

"Said they were looking for you. I told 'em I haven't seen you in days and they threw their chests out a bit, but a couple who are cool with us pulled the others back and they left. What the fuck's up with this shit? We've never had problems like this. In Denver, yeah, the fuckin' badges are a pain in the ass all the time, but here, we're on good terms with the sheriff and some of the deputies. Something's not right."

"Ya think? They're targeting me 'cause of that goddamned Fourth waiver. I should ring Les' neck for striking that deal. I was a fuckin' idiot to go along with it. Cara would never have given my Fourth away. We need to fire Les' ass for good and put Cara on retainer."

Looking at Hawk, Banger nodded. "I've been thinking the same thing. Les just wants his money. I don't think he gives a shit anymore, not like he used to. This woman lawyer, she knows her stuff, and she'll have our back. Let's see what she can do with this shit you're in. If she does good, we can put her on the payroll."

Hawk smiled. "That would be sweet."

"She'd be here to watch our legal asses, brother, not to fuck." Banger paused, looking Hawk straight in the eyes. "I know you want her pussy. I saw it when we went to her office, and I can see it every time you say her name. Ain't never seen you like this with any bitch. Don't know what she's got that the others don't, but with this one, you gotta remember, she's helping you. You don't wanna fuck this up 'cause your cock keeps jerkin'. We got plenty of hot club sluts, mamas, and hoodrats. Use their holes to drain your itch. Got it?"

As the vein in Hawk's neck pulsed, he fought the urge to slam Banger against the wall and tell him to fuck off. "I don't need your fuckin' advice on bitches and pussies."

Staring into Hawk's narrowed eyes, Banger said, "I can't have you go to the joint. Already have Tigger and Skeet doing time—don't need no more brothers in there. Don't distract your lawyer; let her do her thing."

"I'm not going anywhere, especially to the joint. I'll shoot the bastards before that happens."

"Just use your brain and not your cock in this situation. I'm not sure it's a good idea for you to be here. Did you talk to the lawyer?"

"Yeah, she said to stay in some shitty motel. I'm not doing that."

"She's right. The blue assholes will come back, and I don't want you to be around when they do."

"They're not gonna find me."

Banger sighed. "Okay. If they come back, go to the safe house."

"Just what I was thinking." Hawk walked toward the door.

"Where're you goin'?"

"I have a fuckin' ache that only a pussy can soothe."

Hawk walked out and down the hallway to one of the rooms. Cara was causing him all kinds of trouble, like making him almost punch the shit out of the prez. Just thinking about her had him horny and pissed. He needed to get laid in a bad way, and he wanted to fuck his lawyer, but she was keeping her legs closed. *Fuck that.* Tension racked his body. *Fuck!*

Scattered throughout the second and third floors of the compound were small and large rooms. They were for the brothers to crash, pass out, or screw in. The large rooms were for shooting pool, orgies, and pulling a train, if they got a bitch horny enough to want to screw all the brothers. It didn't happen often, but when it did, they all came to get in on the fun. The big-titted blonde Banger was licking pulled a train at the previous night's party—the slut was insatiable, and she was looking for more cock when Hawk came up to the third floor.

All of the officers had a permanent room on the third floor. As Hawk sauntered down the hallway, head down, he bumped into Jax leaving his room. Running his hand through his mussed-up hair, Jax rubbed the sleep out of his eyes.

"Waking up from your beauty sleep?" Hawk poked Jax in the ribs.

"Wild night. We had a group of new bitches who came to party, and shit, they could *party*." Jax smiled.

"Heard one of them pulled a train. Been a while since that's been done."

"Yup. It was wild. Where the hell were you? You've been missing a lot of good parties, brother."

"I got these badges on my ass, so I'm trying to fix it."

"Don't you have a lawyer who's supposed to do that?"

"Yeah, and she is. I just need to be around her, you know, to make sure all is cool."

"You're aiming for her pussy. We all know that. You tired of the common sluts? You want a high-class one?" Laughing, Jax patted Hawk on the shoulder.

A dark warning spread over his features. "She's helping me stay outta prison, that's all."

"Lighten up. Hell, if you weren't so puppy-love-shit over her, I'd get me some of her pussy."

Hawk's eyes glinted like shards of glass. Throwing his hands up in the air, Jax said, "Just messin' with you. No offense." He ambled down the hall.

Hawk froze, trying to regulate his breathing and rid his mind of the image of tackling and punching the shit out of Jax. Thinking of anyone but him having Cara's pussy made his blood boil, and just under the surface of his skin, a question poked at him: did someone have his cock in her? Not knowing if she was fucking some other guy drove him crazy, and he strained to dismiss the images of another man stroking Cara's soft skin, her silky hair, and her full lips.

Dammit! Hawk placed his fingers against his aching temples, hoping Cara would fade from his mind. *Shit.* Imagining her creamy-white skin, the way she smelled, and her soft lips on his made his cock strain against his jeans. *Fuck, she's hot.* He needed to get some soon.

"What're you doin', Hawk?" a sultry voice asked.

Turning around, he recognized the blonde who'd had her pussy in Banger's face. She wore shorts which showed her firm ass cheeks, and a low-cut tank top that exposed her ample breasts. Her blonde hair looked like it needed a dye job soon, but that didn't bother Hawk. Sliding up to him, she touched his arm. She licked her full lips and put a finger in her mouth, sucking it slowly, brown eyes sparkling.

"Looking for some fun? I'd love to show you a good time."

Hawk felt the pressure in his crotch. He'd had a hard-on ever since he remembered Cara's soft body against his. *She should be here with me, not this slut with the bad hair.*

Needles of anger pricked at his skin as recollections of Cara's haughty attitude and stubbornness invaded his mind. He hated the way she pretended she was so proper just because she grew up in the ritzy part of town and his beginnings were in an old, rusted trailer. Anger flushed his face. She didn't know shit—living in her rich, protected world. Who needed her bullshit? No, what he needed real bad was pussy. The uptight snob wasn't there, but this juicy blonde was, so he motioned with his head for her to follow him. The blonde squealed and grabbed his hand, but he pulled away.

"You don't like me touching you, darling?" she asked.

"If you wanna fuck, let's do it. I don't go in for the pretend-it-matters shit. Got it?"

"Whatever you say, honey."

In Hawk's room, the blonde stripped down to her neon pink thong before Hawk had his shirt off. "Anxious, are you?"

"For you. I've heard a lot about you. Some of the girls you fucked been talkin' around 'bout how you know how to please a woman. I seen you 'round town on that hot Harley you ride. You know you're handsome, don't you? I ain't met a good-lookin' guy who don't know it. I've had my eye on you for a while, Hawk."

"Do you wanna talk, or fuck?"

"I love doing both."

"I don't."

Hawk pulled the whore toward him. "My name's Lola," she whispered.

"So?"

He ran his hands over her body while one hand cupped her firm ass. As she dragged her purple nails up and down his back, he unzipped his pants, freeing his hard cock.

"Oh, honey, I like that," she cooed.

She rubbed herself against his body as she went down on her knees. Taking his dick into her mouth, she sucked it while rubbing his taut balls. With his cock practically down her throat, she bobbed her head up and down, stroking the length of him as her fingers played with her pussy.

Throwing his head back, Hawk moaned then pulled Lola up, pushing her onto the bed. With her legs spread wide, he could see that neon pink string shining between her swollen pussy lips. Hawk sucked her breasts and she pulled his hair, forcing his face up toward hers. When her lips sought his, he turned away—a rough fuck was what he wanted, not kissing. He massaged Lola's big tits, her peaks hardening, and he recalled how he loved the way Cara's erect nipples felt under the fabric against his chest.

"Ooh, honey, I love the way you squeeze my boobies. You're making me feel sooo good." Lola writhed.

He touched her clit with his finger; she was more than ready. He slipped two fingers into her hungry pussy, and, noticing she was too loose, he shoved in a couple more. Lola groaned and grabbed his cock, stroking it as he finger-fucked her, his thumb playing with her nub. Her body started jerking; she was ready to come. "Come inside me, honey. I want your big cock in me," she rasped.

Hawk leaned over and took a condom out of the nightstand. He ripped it open.

"No need for that, honey. I'm on the pill," she said.

He rolled it on. "Aren't you the one who pulled the train last night?"

he grunted.

"Ooh, that was a blast, but I'm clean. I like feeling it bare."

"Not with me."

Lola pulled Hawk toward her. He shoved his cock into her eager pussy and banged her hard. Flipping her around, he fucked her rough from behind while she wiggled her ass. As he exploded, he yelled out, "Cara!" then pulled out and collapsed next to Lola. She turned around and snuggled up to him, but he pushed her away. "You gotta go now."

She stared at him. "What did I do wrong?"

"Nothing, it was good. No reason to stick around."

She paused. "When're you gonna take me for a ride on your Harley?"

"Never. Don't let chicks ride on my bike."

"Ever?"

"That's right. Now, take it outta here."

"Who's Cara?"

Looking at her, Hawk shrugged.

"My name's Lola, prick." She zipped up her shorts and pulled her tank top over her boobs. Hawk had his back to her as she leaned over and kissed his cheek. "Another time?" she said sweetly.

She slammed his door as she left the room. The face he saw while fucking that slut was Cara's. *Damn.* The whore wanted him to kiss her, but he couldn't kiss anyone but Cara. Not anymore. Not since he'd tasted the sweetness of her mouth and felt the softness of her lips.

With a clenched jaw, he punched the mattress over and over while swearing. He *had* to reign in his emotions before he flipped out. After all, he'd just had some good pussy, but all he was left with was a headache. Yeah, his cock was satisfied, but he didn't feel full like he always did after a good fucking. Running his hand through his hair, he smoothed it back then tied it in a ponytail. He thought screwing this whore would ease his tension, but it didn't; he just wanted Cara more.

Shit, I just need to fuck her and get her out of my system for good.

Fuck...

CHAPTER SIX

A LIGHT BREEZE rustled through the trees in Cara's front yard as she sat on her porch, skimming a new cookbook. She loved to cook, and when her life got crazy with her heavy caseload, she often wished she would have opted for culinary school instead of law school. Sipping a glass of homemade lemonade, she basked in the peacefulness of the moment; she relished these isolated slices of quietude in her hectic life.

A loud ping from her phone broke the stillness. She opened the text.

Luke: *Last night was great. Had the best time ever. U?*

Cara: *Ya, was cool.*

Luke: *Later today? Do something?*

Cara: *Not 2nite. Working.*

Luke: *On a Sat?*

Cara: *I don't have regular paycheck. Work for myself.*

Luke: *U don't have to. U could have big pay and Sat off.*

Another ping. Cara opened the text.

Hawk: *Hey, babe.*

Cara: *Where r u?*

Hawk: *Miss me?*

Cara rolled her eyes as she pictured his smirking face.

Cara: *R u at motel?*

Another beep. *So much for a quiet moment.* Rubbing the back of her neck, she released a heavy sigh.

Luke: What u doing?

Cara: Client texting me 2.

Luke: This is your day off. Get rid of him.

Cara: Can't go out 2nite. Got 2 go. Bye.

She switched back to her conversation with Hawk.

Cara: R u at motel?

Hawk: Maybe.

Cara: Need to know.

Hawk: Want to visit me? Let's get together later.

Cara: This is serious.

Hawk: Am serious.

Cara: Not in mood 4 this. Come to office early Mon.

Hawk: Need to see u b4 then.

Cara: Can't. Come Mon. Going. Bye.

She threw her phone on the side table. It vibrated angrily against the glass tabletop. Cara shook her head; she was not going to answer. Hawk was so arrogant, and he annoyed the crap out of her. Why did she let him get under her skin? Many of her clients didn't listen to her advice—it went along with being a lawyer. She'd get pissed at them, but then she'd let it go and move on to the next case. Why couldn't she see Hawk as just another one of her cases?

His being sexy was a stumbling block, and there was no way women wouldn't drool over his chiseled features, sculpted body, and firm ass. But Cara felt something more with him, and she hated like hell to admit it. The whole situation would be easier if she just lusted after him, but behind those blue eyes, she perceived glimmers of vulnerability. She wanted to know him better, even though every sane thought in her brain screamed out against it.

Sipping her lemonade, she thought about how wonderful and sexy his lips felt against hers. Luke's kisses the night before were weak compared to Hawk's possessive ones. With his touch, his eyes, and his words, Hawk commanded submission. Cara sensed that it pissed him off having to take direction from her, and Cara understood this because she also needed to be in control, and she hated when men bossed her around. She was a strong woman and didn't need a sexy biker invading her life, but she had to admit, the idea of having someone else take control sometimes was enticing. Shouldering everything felt like a burden at times, and even though she longed to unload some of the weight, she was afraid to let go.

Her mind drifted back to Luke. Sherrie was right—Luke didn't do anything for her. Even though they had a pleasant evening and he was nice enough, he didn't light any sparks inside her. The steakhouse they went to was good, the conversation agreeable, and his goodnight kisses were sweet, but truth be told, she'd rather have stayed home with a good book. The night was, well... sort of dull, like walking through tepid water. It wasn't Luke's fault—he tried to show her a good time, and he was earnest in demonstrating to her why they would make the perfect couple. Hers, then? Maybe, but she knew one thing for sure—it was ninety-five percent Hawk's fault.

On her date, there were three of them: Cara, Luke, and Hawk. *Damn that man.* He'd entered her thoughts all night. Being with Hawk was like walking through a hurricane, and she wished he were the one holding her close under the stars at the nightclub. Instead of Luke's sloppy kisses, she had yearned for Hawk's demanding ones. Ever since the office "incident," her body craved Hawk's hands, and she couldn't stop replaying the feel of his lips on hers, his hands caressing her, his warm breath igniting her.

Damn. Damn. Damn.

Cara's cell beeped again. Ignoring it, she walked toward her vegetable garden to tackle the weeds. The afternoon clouds over the mountains were turning dark gray, signaling a thunderstorm may roll in. Along with the threatening clouds, a cool breeze chased away the heat from earlier in the day, making it a perfect time to work in the garden.

Putting in her earbuds, Cara knelt on the ground and pulled weeds. In the beginning of the summer, growing her own vegetables seemed like a good idea, but she wasn't so sure anymore. She liked the *idea* of getting her hands dirty and eating her own tomatoes, zucchini, and string beans, but bent over, fighting with the weeds, she wondered what had gotten into her. But she wasn't a quitter, so she pushed back her hair, knelt down, and pulled.

THREE HARLEYS ROARED up her driveway. Banger, Jax, and Hawk cut their engines. Looking at her modest 1920s bungalow, they exchanged surprised looks; they'd expected her to live in a mansion.

Hawk spotted Cara first as she bent over plants near the front porch, her ass cheeks dancing every time she pulled harder at the weeds. As his jeans became snugger each time her luscious globes swayed, he noticed the ink peeking out from under the waistband of her shorts. There, exposed on her lightly tanned skin, was the top of a tribal design with a hint of red; the rest of the design and colors lay hidden beneath her sexy shorts. *Fuck, that's hot.* Hawk never figured she'd be the type to go in for a tramp stamp, but it turned him on and made his cock strain against his jeans.

Behind him, he heard Jax mutter, "Sexy ass. Damn, she's a hottie."

Whipping around, Hawk grabbed Jax by the front of his t-shirt. "Don't ever fuckin' say something like that again. Don't even fuckin' look at her."

Jax, seeing daggers in Hawk's gaze, held up his hands, gesturing toward Cara. "She's all yours. Damn, never thought I'd see your head in your ass 'bout a bitch."

"Damn straight. She's all mine." Hawk ignored the pussy-whipped comment. What could he say? He *was* acting pussy-whipped.

Banger moved toward Hawk. "I don't have time for this shit from either of you. Don't you think you should let your lawyer know we're here?"

Hawk was behind Cara, and he wanted to fuck her right there, kneeling, with her delectable ass cheeks spread wide. He reached out and touched her lower back, tracing the tip of her tattoo with his finger. Jerking around, Cara's eyes widened while she pulled out her earbuds and tried to get up all at once. Extending his hand, Hawk helped her stand.

"You startled me," she gasped.

He winked at her as Banger and Jax stood by their parked bikes, looking her way. As she tugged at her shorts and crossed her arms over her chest, Hawk smirked and leaned in close, murmuring, "You got a nice ass."

Her cheeks burned red, and she moved away from him. "What are you guys doing here?"

"Banger wanted to talk to you about some things, and I wanted to see you. Jax had nothing better to do." He smiled, showing off his dimples. When he put his hand on her shoulder, she shivered, vibrating against his fingertips before she pulled away. Scratching her neck, she glanced sideways at him, watching as he flashed her a smug half-smile.

Moving toward the front porch, she waved at Banger and Jax. "I'll be out in a minute. Make yourselves comfortable."

SEVERAL MINUTES LATER, Cara came out with four glasses of lemonade. She had changed into a less-revealing sundress and blushed as she thought of the three of them ogling her while she was bent over. The three bikers gulped down their drinks. Banger wiped his mouth with the back of his hand. "What's goin' on with Hawk's case?"

After Cara filled him in, she turned to Hawk and said, "My sources at the sheriff's office told me that an arrest warrant is imminent."

"Fuck," Banger muttered. "I can't have Hawk do time."

"I'm not doing shit," Hawk growled.

"If a warrant goes out, you'll have to surrender yourself," Cara said.

Hawk stared at her. For the briefest moment, Cara saw a flicker of worry, but it passed as soon as it came. She reached out and placed her hand on top of his. "Don't worry; I'll get all this straightened out. I'm convinced this is a frame job. I haven't figured out why, but it is."

Hawk jerked away from her. "I don't go in for that pity shit, babe. Again, I'm not doing any time."

"If you don't surrender, it'll make things worse. If you listen to me and let me guide you, I can help. Don't be a macho tool on this, Hawk. If you do, you'll be screwed." Locking in on Banger, her eyes pleaded with him.

Clearing his throat, Banger barked, "Listen to your lawyer. I can't lose any more brothers to the asshole badges."

Looking at Hawk, Jax said, "If this was me instead of you, what would you tell me? Would you tell me to listen to her or be a dickhead and think I know better?"

Hawk narrowed his eyes, body rigid, hands clenched into fists. He looked at Cara, snarling, "Fuck, you're the boss." She smiled. "But only for this, babe. Remember that."

She wanted to slap his face but didn't think a lawyer should do that to her client, especially in front of witnesses. He was maddening, but at least he was going to follow her lead. That was a start.

"I'm not goin' to some shitty motel, though. I'll go to the safe house."

Banger and Jax nodded in agreement. Shrugging, Cara nodded along with them. She didn't care where he went as long as he stayed out of sight until she could figure out the warrant status. Since it was settled, unease crept around her as she sat on the porch with her three guests; she didn't entertain bikers. Maybe she should've offered them beer instead of her homemade lemonade? And Hawk wasn't making things any easier with his intense stare boring into her. She shifted in her wicker chair.

Jagged lines of lightning flashed against the darkening sky and thunder rumbled as the sky opened up, dropping torrents of rain and hail. The trees groaned as the wind bent their branches. Cara's dress swept up under a gust of cool wind, and, rushing to the screen door, she yelled, "Come on in."

Inside, a welcoming living room greeted them—hardwood floors and an open floor plan made the house seem modern in spite of its 1920s architectural designs. Post-modern and impressionist artwork adorned the pale yellow walls, and built-in bamboo bookcases held leather-bound books. The pillowy sofa and chairs by the fireplace lent an air of coziness to the room.

Cara gestured for the guys to sit down. Their blue jeans, leather boots, and patched cuts didn't blend in with her casual, yet chic décor, and she stifled a giggle—they looked so out of place.

Breaking the silence, Banger said, "What smells so good?"

"Yeah, it's like we're in an Italian restaurant, or something," Jax agreed.

Smiling, Cara nodded toward her gourmet kitchen. "I'm making meat sauce for tomorrow's dinner. My family usually has Sunday dinner together, and I'm having it here."

"If it tastes anything like it smells, that'll be one helluva dinner." Banger licked his lips.

"I've made a ton. Do you want to have dinner? I was going to make pasta and a salad. You're more than welcome to join me."

"If it didn't smell so good, I'd pass, but I gotta try that sauce. Spaghetti's always been my favorite. Do you have meatballs, too?" Banger was practically salivating.

"Meatballs, too. Let me grab you guys some beer and I'll start dinner." Cara handed the remote control to Jax. "You can watch TV while I get dinner going. I'll bring out some munchies. It'll take a while to boil the pasta."

Cara jumped up from the chair and shuffled into the kitchen. After pulling out three beers from the fridge, she turned around and crashed into a wall of muscled chest. Cedar, leather, and musk scents enveloped her while two of the beer bottles slipped from her hand. Hawk caught them before they shattered on the hardwood floor.

"I—I didn't expect you to be behind me."

Hawk took the third bottle from her, leaned in close, and whispered, "I love being behind you, babe. I love looking at your sweet ass." His breath was hot against her ear, making her stomach flutter.

All of a sudden, the room seemed hot and stuffy. He licked her earlobe then turned around, and headed back into the living room. Cara watched his tall, ripped figure. He was beautiful—breathtaking. He made her giddy and nervous at the same time. Why did she always revert to acting like a lovesick fourteen-year-old whenever he came into her space?

Shaking her head, Cara made a vow to work on not letting him get under her skin. After all, she was an independent *and* professional woman. If she could endure Professor Pratt's Property Law class and put up with Judge Reese's courtroom tantrums, she could handle Hawk, the sexy biker. Right?

As Cara prepared the garlic bread, she heard one of the breakfast stools scrape against the floor and whirled around, meeting Hawk's stare. She raised her eyebrows at him. "What are you staring at?"

He didn't answer, just continued staring. Deciding she was tired of his intimidation games, she ignored him and went over to the cupboard next to the breakfast island to grab a salad bowl. His eyes followed her every move, making her muscles twitch and her mouth go dry. Turning around, she closed her eyes and took a deep breath, then jumped when Hawk's arm encircled her waist, tugging her into him. His erection pressed against her lower back and he threaded his fingers through her hair, moving it to the side to kiss her neck gently.

Insides sizzling, she almost dropped the salad bowl her aunt had given her. His feathery kisses grew harder, more demanding, and her nerves burst into a thousand electric shocks as her red lace panties grew damp. Trembling under his mouth's assault, Hawk grasped her neck's tender flesh between his teeth and bit and sucked it hard. *Crap, he's trying to give me a hickey.* Panic seizing her, Cara twisted in a feeble attempt to pull her neck away. "Hawk, don't leave a mark on me. Don't do it!"

Laughing against her skin, he resumed sucking but Cara, using all her strength, squirmed out of his embrace, only to have him haul her back into him.

In a low, deep voice, he said, "I wanna see your tattoo. I never figured you'd go in for one, especially a low back stamp. I wanna see your ass with all the ink on it. Fuck, you're so hot. My cock wants in so badly, babe."

She leaned into him and rubbed her ass against him, and he moaned. Her panties were drenched.

"Teasing me, baby? Don't start somethin' you can't finish. I know if I put my fingers on your pussy, you'd be wet, right?"

Cara squeezed her eyes closed as she whimpered. *Crap... I can't believe I'm getting turned on by what he's saying.* Go figure; another surprise.

"Are those munchies comin'?" Banger's voice sliced through their desire.

While Hawk nuzzled her neck, it dawned on her that Banger and Jax had seen their kitchen sexcapade. Mortified about the two guys in the other room having a front row seat, she twisted away from Hawk, her face red. She glared daggers at Hawk, warning him not to come one step toward her, and then pointed her finger at the stool and mouthed, "Sit and stay seated!"

He sauntered over to the stool, sat down, and resumed his staring game.

Cara tossed her head at Hawk, then walked into the living room. She placed the platter of sliced salami, mozzarella, cherry peppers, and crispy breadsticks on the glass-top coffee table in front of Banger and Jax as they watched car racing on the television. Red streaks marked her cheeks as Jax grinned; she averted her gaze and hurried back to the kitchen.

Hawk stood up when she came into the kitchen. "Don't even think it," she hissed.

He sat back down, continuing to watch the way her curvy body moved as she cooked, and, out of the corner of her eye, she saw him fussing with his crotch. Turning to face him, she noticed he had a hard-on. His smoldering eyes told her that he wanted to relieve his dilemma, and she was his choice of the hour. Flashing him an in-your-dreams look, Cara went back to her cooking.

"What is this?" a voice from the living room boomed. "Who the hell are you, and what are you doing here?"

Hawk sprang to his feet and placed his hand on the knife hidden under his cut as Banger and Jax assumed poses. Cara, flustered, ran into the living room, and as Hawk tried to hold her back, she jerked away.

"Eric, what's the matter?" she asked, concern creasing her forehead.

A six-foot-tall man with a slim build looked in her direction. He had sandy brown hair and brown eyes, and his skin was pale with red blotches flecking his cheeks and chin. He had an umbrella in his hand. "What's going on?"

"Hold on, there. Who we are and what we're doing here is none of your fuckin' business." Jax stepped menacingly toward Eric.

Dismissing Jax with his hand, the man said, "I was speaking to Cara. What's going on here?"

Cara ran up to him and hugged him. "Nothing. I'm just making dinner, they're watching the race, and everything is good. Very good." She tried to sound perky but failed; she could never do perky very well.

"Who the fuck are you?" Hawk came behind Cara, grabbing her hand.

Before the whole room turned into a boxing match, Cara said, "I want you all to meet my cousin, Eric." Motioning to each of the bikers and slipping her hand out of Hawk's grip, she said, "This is Hawk, Banger, and Jax. Now, why don't you guys go back to watching TV, and Eric, you come with me into the kitchen so we can catch up."

Eric, taking calculated steps, followed Cara. Turning to Hawk, she said, "Can you give us some privacy?"

Glowering, Hawk swaggered to the living room. Cara exhaled after realizing she had been holding her breath. She didn't need any trouble, and Eric could be just that, especially since he had become more difficult than usual in the past several months. And the biker guys, well, attitude was written all over them.

"I didn't know you were coming over."

"That's obvious. What are these scumbags doing in your house?"

"I invited them to dinner, and they're fine, so be nice."

"How do you even know them? Do you know who they are?" The bikers glared at him from their places in the living room.

"Come on. Let's go out to the back porch." Cara walked out back, closing the door behind them. Looking at Eric, she said, "Stop being a pain in the ass. You're being rude."

"Good, I *want* to be rude to those scumbags. They're Insurgents— you know, *outlaw* bikers. Do you get what that means?"

"I'm a defense attorney, remember? One of the guys is my client and they came over to talk about his case. I asked them to stay for dinner. What's the big deal?"

"The big deal is that they're pieces of shit. They're involved in illegal activity like running guns, drugs, women, and children. Are these the kinds of people you want to eat dinner with?"

"You're kinda exaggerating, aren't you? I know they aren't choirboys, but trafficking? You've got the wrong MC."

"And that asshole Hawk is the worst." He looked at her, shaking his head. "I never thought I'd see the day that you'd have such scum in your home."

"I told you, one of them is my client. How do you know Hawk?"

"I know all of them. They're criminals. I'm a judge. I know what goes on in my county."

"You're overreacting, Eric. They're okay guys. Hawk is my client."

"Do you have all your lowlife clients over for dinner?"

"I didn't plan it, it just happened. It's pouring rain, and I didn't want them riding in it. There's no harm here."

Eric let out a long sigh, his mouth constantly twitching. He seemed weird—too hyper, too animated, and too angry. "What would your parents say?"

Cara swallowed. "They wouldn't like it, but I'm a big girl now. I'm not a cut-out figure of my parents."

"And the way he grabbed your hand. The nerve of that bastard. It was repulsive!"

"He didn't know who you were. He thought I was in danger."

Eric cracked his knuckles. "You know what really disgusted me was the way you looked at him. You're not falling for this trash, are you?"

Cara blushed. She hated that her eyes gave her away, and even though she didn't want to admit it, she did feel drawn to Hawk. The more she saw him, the more she wanted him, and being in his presence was intoxicating. She looked down. "No, I'm not falling for him."

"You better not be. You know that would ruin your family name, and your mom would probably have a heart attack."

"And you know you're over-the-top on this one. What's going on with you?"

"What do you mean?"

"I mean, you've been so moody and angry. You've changed from the fun cousin I hung around with in high school and college. What's up with you?"

"I have a lot of shit I have to deal with. Being a District Court judge isn't easy, and I've got my upcoming wedding. Nancy is making it into a huge deal. Now I have you hanging out with trash."

"I know it must be hard being the youngest judge on the bench, but it's something you wanted. You know that's all you talked about when you were in law school. As for Nancy, well, she's into appearances, so I'm not surprised that she's planning the socialite-studded wedding of the year. You wanted a rich girl, so you have to realize that she'll always suffer from Princess Syndrome."

"You don't. Your dad is wealthy, but you're not like Nancy or her friends. You're almost too open, like having these jerks over to your house. It makes me sick, Cara, it really does."

"That's just what I'm saying. If this were a few years ago, you'd have laughed your ass off at finding these macho men sitting on my cushy couches. I miss the old Eric."

Her cousin looked at her with shining eyes as tenderness softened the fury on his face. He opened his mouth like he was going to say something, but the softness disappeared and the hard fury returned. "I want you to tell them to go."

"What? Are you serious? I won't do that. You know, I've supported you through a ton of shit over the years, and I was with you even if I didn't agree with your decisions. You have no right to tell me to ask guests to leave *my* house. No way."

"So you're choosing scum over me, your family?"

"How did this turn into me choosing you or them? This is stupid bullshit, and you know it."

"I'm out of here." Eric turned around, went into the house, walked past the bikers, and slammed the front door. Cara ran after him, trying to catch him. Standing on her front porch, she watched Eric's car fade into the misty rain. *What just happened here? I can't believe we had a fight over three bikers in my house.*

Was Eric telling her the truth about the extent of the MC's criminal activity? Was that why the police were after Hawk? She couldn't believe that. He didn't strike her as someone who'd sell women and children, but how could she be sure? Maybe she believed what she wanted because of the budding feelings for Hawk.

"What the fuck's wrong with your asshole cousin?" Hawk's gravelly voice startled her.

She shrugged. "He's just stressed and over-protective."

"Stressed about what?"

"He's getting married in a few months, and he's only been a judge for a year. There's a lot of pressure with that. I don't know. He's just stressed."

"That fucker's a judge?"

"Hey, you're talking about my cousin. Yeah, he's a judge. Let's forget about all this."

"He's damn lucky I've got the hots for you, otherwise your cousin would be a bloody pulp on your nice floors. Insurgents don't tolerate disrespect from *anyone*. You better educate your cousin on that, 'cause next time, we won't be so patient."

Brute anger blazed in Hawk's eyes, and Cara didn't doubt his words for one minute. A strained silence veiled the room as the bikers' angry glances bored into Cara. Twirling her hair around her finger, her knees weak, she pointed toward the kitchen. "Dinner is ready."

EATING AROUND THE kitchen table, Banger raved about how good Cara's tomato sauce was and told her he wanted Cara to give his daughter, Kylie, the recipe so she could make it for him. *So that's who Kylie is, Banger's daughter. Does Hawk have something with her? I doubt it. Banger said she's still in high school, and I can't see Hawk banging the president's teenage daughter.*

"These are the best meatballs I've ever tasted," Banger said.

"It's my father's recipe. He loves to cook."

"Well, he taught you good." Banger took some more meatballs.

Jax and Hawk had three helpings, so she presumed they liked her food. Desire rippled through her body every time Hawk looked at her with smoldering eyes, and when he licked his lips, she could feel them on hers.

Cara packed four jars full of tomato sauce for the guys to take back to the clubhouse. She'd have to make another batch the following morning for her family dinner that evening. *Hopefully, Eric will cool down by tomorrow night, or dinner could be a disaster.* She didn't want to think about that right then, though. The bikers were leaving, and being a good hostess, she followed them out.

Swathed in cool night air, Cara wrapped her arms around herself as goosebumps covered her skin. The rain had stopped, and she inhaled the damp freshness which clung to the pine needles and saturated the ground. Hawk put his arm around her shoulders, lifted her chin with his hand, and kissed her hard—his tongue pushing its way into her mouth as she kissed him back. In her driveway, Banger and Jax's Harleys screamed to life.

Hawk jumped down her porch steps then swung his long leg over his Harley's seat before he roared his bike to life. As they pulled out of her driveway, he and his fellow bikers shattered the tranquility of the night. Hawk turned to look back at Cara and, as their eyes met, an electric current passed between them.

Cara stayed on her porch until she could no longer hear the rumble of his engine and the only sounds left were the crickets singing. Inside, in the hallway mirror, horror greeted Cara's reflection: a large, red mark on the left side of her neck.

Oh, my God, what a hell of a hickey. I haven't had one since high school. So much for my vow not to act like a teenager. Crap, what am I going to do about this?

CHAPTER SEVEN

SITTING WITH HIS jaw clenched, Hawk waited for Cara to come through the doors. The coolness of the wood chair under his ass contrasted with the raging fire building inside him. If he had to wait another minute, he would explode and bash all the windows in the small, sterile room. He'd beat the shit out of the fucking asshole deputy who thought he was something, and then he'd make each one of them pay for—

The door swung open, interrupting his thoughts. Standing in front of him, Cara wore a black pencil skirt and bolero jacket with a peek of lavender lace underneath it. She looked amazing. His eyes raked over her, and it took all his strength not to jump over the table, yank her to him, and kiss her.

"How are you doing? Are they treating you okay?" She smiled warmly.

"Get me the fuck outta this shithole or I'm gonna kick a lot of asses 'round here."

"I know this sucks, but I hope to get bail set for you. The hearing is this afternoon. Banger said the club could make the bail, even if it's set as high as a hundred thousand."

Hawk's eyes widened. "Why in the fuck would it be set that high? What're they sayin' here?"

"Sometimes judges set bail high if the defendant is on parole or probation. They say they found a half box of .22-caliber ammo on your kitchen table. Did you have the ammo?"

Cara jumped as Hawk slammed his fists on the table. "Those goddamn fuckers! I didn't have any ammo in my house. What, do you think

I'm stupid? Fuck this shit. Did they say they found a gun?"

Cara shook her head. "Calm down. I know this blows, but I had to ask. I'm sure it was a plant. The problem is, how am I going to prove it? I want you to know I'm working on it. If they can prove these rounds belong to you, then you're facing five years."

Hawk shook his head. "Fuck that!" He reached for her hands and looked deeply into her eyes. "When I find out what the fuck's goin' on, I'll kill every bastard who messed with me. This is bullshit."

He brought her palms up to his lips, licking and kissing them. Cara squirmed in her chair, cleared her throat, and pulled away from his grasp. "I have Asher calling the sheriff's office for the pre-raid photos. I want to see if the ammo was on the table before they started the search."

They sat there looking at each other, and Hawk thought he saw sadness in her eyes. He hoped she wasn't feeling sorry for him again; he'd survived four tours in Afghanistan and had seen his best friend blown up by a landmine, so a few days in this shithole didn't faze him at all. He was just pissed that he had to take the time out to deal with this trumped-up bullshit. Cara had no clue. No. Fucking. Clue. But she *did* look hot in her suit.

He folded his arms, tipped his chair back, and said in a low voice, "You look sexy playing lawyer. Do you have on those red lacy panties I saw you wearing when you were bent over your garden?"

She looked down, cheeks staining red, white teeth biting her lower lip. *She's so hot when she's all shy. Fuck, I want to spread her pretty ass cheeks and slam my cock right into her wet pussy.* He needed to fuck her rough and hard, to hear her scream as his dick hammered into her juiciness. He shifted in his chair, adjusting his now swollen cock. "Are you wearing the red panties?"

Twisting in her chair, she said, "I don't think my underwear should be on your mind right now, you know?"

"Right now, babe, that's the only thing on my mind. I hate all this, and having to be here is a load of shit and you know it. Your red panties and me thinking about ripping them off you is what's keeping me from kicking the shit outta one of these fuckin' badges."

"You *had* to surrender yourself. Like I told you, there was an arrest warrant issued for you over the weekend. I'll try and get you out of here today, but for now, I have to go. I'll see you in court in a couple of hours. It's going to be fine." She brushed his forearm.

"Who said it wasn't gonna be? I'm countin' on you, counselor."

Their eyes locked, and an understanding passed between them: she would take care of him in this arena. Shifting his gaze from her eyes to her ample breasts, Cara's cheeks crimsoned again as Hawk chuckled softly. He just couldn't figure her out—she was an aggressive attorney, but she acted all shy and shit with him. *Damn. Even in this shithole, she turns me on.*

"I'd think you'd have more pressing matters to think about other than my boobs," she said while standing up.

"When I stop looking at your tits, babe, then I'll know I'm up the river." His dimpled smile mocked her.

"I'd suggest you get your priorities straight. Stop undressing me every time we meet, and start working on your anger issues so you don't explode during the bail hearing."

"You like bossing men around, don't you? Does it turn you on, or something?"

"Unlike you, not everything turns me on. I just need you to focus on what's important so I can better defend you."

"Fuck, baby, you're enjoying this power trip. I'll give it to you, for now, but once this bullshit is over, I'm gonna fuck you like you were meant to be fucked."

"Yeah, right. Drop your tough attitude when you get in front of Judge Romero today. He won't be impressed any more than I am." She motioned to the deputy she was ready to leave. The door opened and she disappeared down the long hallway. The deputy then came for Hawk, dragging him down the opposite end of the hall toward the cellblock, where he belonged, according to the uniform.

Fucking badge.

Back in his cell, Hawk couldn't stop thinking of Cara. She had a mouth on her, and a feisty attitude, too. Her shyness threw him. He liked that she could give him shit yet still be timid when he checked her luscious body out. What blew him away was that he hadn't gotten her into bed, *yet*. He would; of that he was one hundred percent certain. She wasn't an easy touch, not at all, but he liked that about her—easy women bored him. This hot woman with an attitude piqued his interest, and he wanted to know more about her, as well as *see* a lot more of her.

Glancing at the hall clock, Hawk saw he had another two hours before he'd see her again. Sitting next to her in court, breathing in her vanilla-scented perfume and fantasizing about sucking her soft tits would almost make this bullshit worth it. As far as he was concerned, the time couldn't pass fast enough. He was banking on his sexy lawyer to get bail set for him; he was itching to return to his world.

WHEN HAWK ENTERED the clubhouse, all the brothers cheered and whistled as Banger stood at the end of the bar, grinning. *Shit, it's good to be home with the family.* He went to the bar and one of the prospects, Jerry, handed him a shot of whiskey. All the brothers came over to him, jabbing him in the ribs and clapping their hands on his shoulders.

"She done good," Banger said.

"Yeah. The prick DA was fuckin' pissed when the judge set bail." Hawk threw down his shot of Jack. The burning liquid was smooth as it went down his throat. "Thanks, brother, for getting the money together," he said to Banger in a low voice.

"No problem at all. You were a brother in need, and next time, it may be me or any of the other brothers. We're in this together and for the long haul."

The other men, fists in the air, cried out in unison, "Insurgents Forever, Forever Insurgents." Hawk downed another shot and slammed the glass on the bar. The hoots and whistles reverberated off the great room's walls.

"Go get some grub. The ol' ladies made some good pulled pork, and tell Doris and Bernie their men want them," Banger said.

Hawk, approaching the kitchen, overheard the old ladies as they talked.

"What's all the noise about?" Bernie, one of the old ladies, asked as she looked toward the great room.

"Hawk's back. He made bail and he's back where he belongs," Doris replied.

"They'll be partyin' hard, come Friday. PJ told me some other chapters are coming in from Wyoming. It's gonna be crazy." Bernie laughed.

"The other old ladies want to do a ladies' night. I'm havin' it at our house. We'll have pizza and shots. You down for that?"

"Count me in, Doris."

"Here's the hero," Doris said, smiling at Hawk as he came into the kitchen.

"I'm not a fuckin' hero," he grumbled.

"You got bail. How many brothers 'round here ever got bail?" Doris asked.

"I have a kick-ass lawyer. Ruben and PJ want you both in the great room." Hawk stuffed a pulled pork sandwich in his mouth. After eating institution food, the sandwich tasted like a gourmet meal.

When he was done, Hawk, bone-tired and achy from trying to sleep on a hard cot the previous night, climbed the stairs to his room, looking forward to lying down on his bed and shutting everything out. As he opened his door, a pervasive floral scent assaulted his nose. "Want company, honey?" a husky voice asked.

Turning around, he saw Lola standing behind him. Frowning and folding his arms across his chest, he shook his head. Leaning into him, Lola scratched his back with her fingernails. "Are you sure?"

"Go downstairs. There're a lot of brothers who would love your company. Not interested."

"I don't want none of them. I want you, Hawk. I love the way you fucked me. I've been thinkin' about it and been missin' you." She licked her red-tipped finger.

"I'm tired. Don't piss me off."

Seeing Hawk's menacing glare, Lola pulled away from him and retreated.

In his room, he put his jacket and cut on the chair. Lying down on his bed, he smiled as he remembered how aggressive Cara had been in court earlier that day, and how she had that DA pussy-whipped. The way she kept leaning forward, pressing her breasts together with her arms—that judge's eyes never left her tits. That fucking DA never had a chance against Cara, not with her beautiful face, her sexy cleavage, and her feisty attitude. Hawk was ready to fuck her right there on the floor, in front of the pimpled-faced DA, the lecherous judge, the prim court reporter, and those asshole bailiffs.

The way that black-robed jerk kept looking at her during the bail hearing drove Hawk crazy, and he started thinking all kinds of shit, like she and the judge were fucking, or they had a fling in the past. He hoped she hadn't fucked the judge because he didn't like the idea of other men seeing Cara's delectable tits, kissing her full lips, or stroking her wet pussy.

Rolling over on his side, Hawk punched his pillow, stretched his legs, and fought to be comfortable. Cara buzzed in his head, and he couldn't stop the thoughts. *I am totally fucked.* He thought about her all the time. Even during church he focused on her, wondering what she was doing. In all his life, he had never met a woman like her, or one who held his interest for so long—one he had yet to fuck. He wanted to be inside her, and he knew she wanted it, too. The fact that she held back pissed him off, yet also enticed the shit out of him.

Hawk unzipped his jeans to take the pressure off his erection, wishing Cara were there to suck his dick and play with his balls. Sleep eluding him, he sat up. He could open his door and have any of the club whores ease the tension in his hardness, but he didn't want any of them—he wanted Cara.

Fuck! What the hell was his problem? He'd always been a fuck-'em-

and-leave-'em kind of guy, and he viewed sluts as holes he screwed and nothing more. Since he loved pussy so much, any bitch would do, but since he met Cara, the only pussy he wanted was hers. Dammit to hell, he never felt such a pull with any other woman, and, yeah, it figured that he had a primal attraction to a wealthy, stuck-up chick who thought her shit didn't stink. What the hell was he doing? She was out of his league, but her kisses and moans told him she wanted him and he may have a chance. He figured they needed to fuck good and hard to rid the sexual tension that was between them. Yeah, that was all *he* needed: one night of banging his hot attorney, and he'd be back to normal.

Sighing, Hawk slipped off his pants and went into the bathroom to take a shower.

CHAPTER EIGHT

H ANNAH JACKSON TREMBLED as tears rolled down her sun-kissed cheeks, their wetness bringing some comfort to her dry lips. The man's back was to her, and she knew he was going to do horrible things to her. Already, he'd burned her with his cigarettes, the round, angry marks spotting her body. The pain had been excruciating, so she'd screamed. The louder she shrieked, the more he burned her, so she had bit her lips and tried to muffle her cries.

Hannah wished she hadn't decided to walk home after working at Della's Sandwich Shop. She should have waited for her brother to come pick her up, but Ricky, the guy she'd had a crush on since high school, said he'd come by, so she wanted to get home sooner to shower and change. Since she didn't want him to see her in her uniform, she didn't wait for her brother to pick her up, and then this guy drove up asking for directions. He had a map, and his overhead light was on. She couldn't see the map so well, and when he'd asked her to get in the car to show him where he was, she jumped in. She wasn't afraid of him at all—he had a nice face.

After showing him his destination, she reached to open the door when he stopped her. Before she reacted, he took out a gun, saying in a low, cruel voice, "Scream and your brains will be in your lap." Hannah looked at him, and his kind features had contorted into something evil. Shivers ran up the back of her neck, and as they drove away from her town, Hannah wondered if she'd ever see her parents again.

At that moment, Hannah's abductor moved toward her with a stun gun and two oversized dildos. Her eyes widened in fear as he knelt next to her prone form. Her arms were tied above her head and her legs fastened spread-eagle. He wiped away the tears on her cheeks and ran his fingers through her long, blonde hair.

"You're so beautiful," he said in a low, soft voice. Touching her, he placed a soft kiss on the base of her throat and she cringed. Sucking in his breath, his eyes misted with lust, he caressed her right breast then brought his mouth down over her burnt nipple, biting down hard. Hannah gasped from the pain.

When her torturer's smooth hand found her genitals, he rubbed his finger up and down, tugging at the light hair on her dry lips. Lifting his head, he stared into her watery blue eyes. With a cruel smile, he brought the stun gun up to her breast and zapped her. Unbearable pain ripped through her body, and she screamed. Laughing without humor, he zapped her again. Her delicate body convulsed, her mouth went dry, all her muscles tightened, and as she was reeling from the pain, the monster grasped one of the dildos and shoved it into her private parts. Searing pain shot straight through to her head as her hymen broke. As she cried out, he jammed the dildo in her even harder and deeper.

"I'm going to fuck every hole you have, slut!"

When he forced the dildo higher, Hannah realized she was going to die. She knew her last moments on Earth were going to be agonizing, and all the things she wanted to do—fall in love, finish college, have a family—would never happen. She was going to die on that dirty mat in a cold warehouse, and her damaged and bruised body would be the last image anyone would see. Terror's icy fingers seized her; she didn't want to die. The agony came in torrents, and she longed for the torture to stop. The pain numbed her brain, and darkness took over as Hannah slipped away.

"WHAT DO THEY mean, they lost the pre-raid photos?" Cara said.

"That's what they told me. I quote, 'The pre-raid photos have been misplaced,' end of quote," Asher answered.

"That's a crock of shit! Maybe these photos were 'misplaced' because they don't show any ammo on the table pre-raid? Dammit!"

"I know, boss. It sucks."

"It more than sucks. I need to get those pictures. Neither of us believes this bullshit story, right?"

Asher nodded. Cara threw her legal pad across her desk. All of her suspicions of a frame job were confirmed. This was bogus. She had to get a hold of those photos.

"I think I'll give Josh a call."

Asher raised his eyebrows. "Do you think you should start that up again?"

"Josh and I are friends. We haven't been romantic since before law school, like, seven years ago."

"He still carries a torch for you."

"Even better, because I need his help. Anyway, I'm hooking him up with Sherrie. She goes for guys in uniforms." Cara picked up the phone.

"I thought she liked the bartender at the biker bar."

"She's moved on. He was too busy gawking at all the girls. I've got to call her. Ugh, I'm too busy."

"With the biker boys."

Cara rolled her eyes. "Make yourself useful and follow-up on the DNA testing in the Osman case. He goes to preliminary hearing in three days."

Laughing, Asher left Cara's office to start his work. Cara smiled to herself, thinking how she'd lucked out with Asher as her legal assistant. He was a perfect match for her personality.

Cara dialed Josh's number. "Josh, hiya, this is Cara. It's been a while, but I have a huge favor to ask you."

HAWK, RUBBING HIS pulsing temples, cursed under his breath when he heard a knock on his bedroom door. Opening the door with a towel around his waist, he motioned for Banger to come in. The president entered the small room, sat on a cushioned chair by the window, and looked out at the hints of yellow dotting the mountains. "Fall's comin' early this year."

Hawk grunted. "I don't think you came here to take in the view. What's on your mind?"

"I thought I'd be interrupting a pussy session." Hawk stared, stone-faced, so Banger continued, "I guess I should be wonderin' why you ain't eatin' pussy right now. Shit, there're 'bout four whores downstairs who are dyin' to be ridin' your cock. What the fuck?"

"You came all the way up here to find out if I was fuckin' a slut? Why aren't you fuckin' one of them?"

"Already did."

"I'm tired, that's all."

"Is it? The lawyer bitch did a good job. I didn't think she could do it."

"Why not? She's smart and she knows her stuff. She's way better than that crook, Les."

"Why you callin' Les a crook? He got us the licenses for the dispensaries and we're making a shit load of money, legally." Banger laughed aloud. "Remember what a pain in the ass it was when the club was dealing in illegal drugs? The badges were always snooping around, especially in Denver when the brothers would do pick-ups or deliveries. Now, the club's making a ton of money by growing and selling weed. We live in a great state! Fuck, it's too sweet. We're pulling in millions, and it's all legal. No more dealing crack and smack. It's fuckin' ironic."

"Yeah, but Les wants a big piece of it. He's taking almost fifty percent," Hawk said.

"What? When did this happen? I gotta talk with him. No way are we paying him fifty percent. Fuck that greedy bastard!"

"Agreed. We should replace him with Cara. I know she wouldn't cheat us."

"How do you know she'd want to come in?"

"I can talk to her. Feel her out, you know?"

"Is this suggestion a hundred percent for the club, or you got personal reasons, too?"

Hawk narrowed his eyes. "What the fuck does that mean?"

"Don't get your ass in a hitch. As prez, I need to know. I've noticed that you've taken an interest in her."

"It's for the club. My personal life is my business."

"It is, but when it clouds your decisions, then it becomes *my* business. You have it bad for her. I ain't ever seen you like this before. Hell, we've known each other for over eleven years, and you never let a bitch get to you. I see it's different with this lawyer lady. Why don't you just claim her? You want in her pussy and she wants you in it, so do the grown-up thing and claim her. Make her your ol' lady, if you want."

"My reason isn't clouded by any bitch, okay? Again, this isn't your fuckin' business. I know you mean well, but stay the fuck outta my personal life. I don't want an old lady."

"Just sayin', brother. I know what it's like falling hard for a bitch. It grabs you. When I met Grace, shit, I knew I'd never look at another woman again. She was the best ol' lady a poor sonofabitch could have. I lost her too soon."

"Yeah, Grace was the best. You were lucky."

"Ain't that the truth. All I'm sayin' is that you should either claim the woman, or move on. Although, why you'd want a smart-mouthed woman like her is beside me. She also comes from a different background, so she's not used to the lifestyle. My Grace was born into it. This lawyer won't give you a smooth life."

"I don't like smooth. I'll figure it out."

"I'm just sayin', 'cause if she comes 'round here, she's open game if she ain't claimed. You know that."

"No one's gonna touch her. I'll make sure of that."

"Then claim her. No reason to have trouble over a bitch, right?"

Hawk's jaw tightened as he nodded. "Good talkin' to you, Banger."

He opened his door and stepped aside. Banger shook his head and walked out before Hawk slammed it behind him. It took all of his strength to stay steady while Banger butted his fucking nose into his business. Hawk almost punched his president's face in when he started his shit about Cara, and he seethed because he knew Banger was right—this woman was in his system. All his decisions revolved around her, and she was always in his head. He knew she was cautious because of their client relationship, but he didn't think he could wait until his case was done. Just thinking about her made his cock spring to life. *Fuck.*

YELLOW TAPE ROPED off the core area. The CSI tech arrived, blocking off an area larger than the core as deputies huddled, heads down, murmuring about the atrocious way the victim died. From their position, they could see the ligature marks around her small throat. The CSI began his systematic search for incriminating evidence, standing over the body of Hannah Jackson while performing a visual examination. He noted that she had been strangled. The cuts to her ankles and wrists indicated she had been tied up, as well as beaten and tortured, which he could tell from the other marks on her body. The blood between her thighs and at her anus pointed toward a strong possibility of rape and sodomy.

After hours of bagging evidence, combing the nearby woods, and sifting through the dirt for any clues, the battered and bruised body of Hannah Jackson was laid on the gurney. A white sheet covered her corpse. The ambulance doors closed. The lifeless form began its journey to the town morgue.

Hawk: *How r u doing?*

Cara: *Ok, too busy.*

Hawk: *Why haven't I heard from u? Been 3 days.*

Cara: *Nothing new. Trying to get photos. Will let u know if something new on your case.*

Hawk: *Don't care bout that. Let's get together to talk.*

Cara: Can't, busy with a murder case. Sorry. Will let u know re photos. Got to go. Bye.

Hawk: *Bye babe.*

Cara almost weakened by agreeing to meet Hawk and canceling her dinner date with Luke. She so wanted to see Hawk again; she missed him. For the last few days, she wondered if he was going to contact her, then his text came and her heart surged with joy. The previous night, when she was feeling lonely and empty, she made her decision: she would sleep with Hawk one time. She had a notion the sex would be mind-blowing, but one time was all she would give herself.

She decided to tell him the next time she had contact with him, but when she saw his text, she chickened out. After all, she rationalized, she *did* have an ethical obligation not to screw her client. But when her attorney-client relationship ended, she'd approach him and have one night of pure sex. Squaring her shoulders and inhaling deeply, she threw off the burden which had been weighing her down ever since she first locked eyes with Hawk.

The ringing phone broke through her thoughts.

"Hello?"

"Cara, it's Josh. I got something you're going to like."

Sitting straight in her chair, Cara said, "Don't tell me, you've got the photos?"

"Okay, I won't tell you," Josh teased.

"You do, right?"

"They'll be delivered to you tomorrow afternoon."

"Awesome! How can I thank you?"

"Don't tell anyone about this. And introduce me to your friend, Sherrie."

"It's a deal."

After chatting with Josh, Cara hung up the phone and yelled. Asher ran into her office. "What's wrong?"

"I got the pre-raid photos."

"Do you know if they have the ammo in them?"

"No, but I'll bet they don't. They weren't 'misplaced' for the hell of it."

Cara reached for her phone to tell Hawk the good news. She dialed his number then hung up, deciding to wait until she saw the photos before calling him. If the photos showed no .22-caliber ammo on his kitchen table before the raid, she'd go over to his clubhouse over the weekend and show them to him in person. The possibility of seeing him made her insides lurch.

Looking at the time, she jumped up from her desk. She was already late for her dinner date with Luke. They were meeting up at Big Rocky's Barbecue, the new restaurant by the lake, which boasted a menu of Colorado-grown beef and buffalo prepared Texas-style.

Grateful that she had brought a change of clothes, Cara slipped out of her tailored dress into a short, flounce black skirt with a spandex black and white striped top. A wide belt with a sprinkling of crystals gave the retro look an elegant flair.

After she touched up her hair and makeup, Cara glanced in the mirror; she looked nice, but a hint of dark circles under her eyes gave away her lack of sleep for the past two weeks. Her emotional life had been turned upside-down since she'd met Hawk at Rusty's six weeks before, and she wasn't used to chaos; her world had always been orderly and controlled. It was unsettling, and she had to admit a part of her loved the turmoil—it was exciting and new—but she promised herself she would get back to her old routine.

The good Cara was always reminding the want-to-break-free Cara that emotions had their time and place, and this thing with Hawk was neither the right time nor place; hell, he wasn't even the right person. Of course, the good Cara knew this and heard her family's voice in her head, but the break-free Cara longed for one sex session with the hot biker. She smiled at her reflection in the mirror, knowing the break-free Cara was going to win this one. *After all, one time won't hurt anyone, will it?*

CHAPTER NINE

T HE RESTAURANT WAS beautiful nestled among the evergreens on Aspen Lake, and the trees surrounding the water had tinges of burnt orange, a reminder that summer was winding down. The misty breeze off the lake was refreshing and cool, and the full moon cast a shimmering reflection while the swaying lanterns created dancing illuminations on the glassy water.

"The food was delicious. Thanks for bringing me here. I had a nice time," Cara said to Luke as they walked through the parking lot to his car.

"I'm glad to hear you say that. I had a great time, and being with you made it the best." As he smiled, his teeth shone in the moonlight.

Luke grasped her hand and squeezed it, then stepped closer to her, leaning his head down toward her lips. As he came in for a kiss, Cara turned her head and his moist lips landed on her cheek. He sighed. She knew he was disappointed, but she didn't want to kiss him. All she wanted was to enjoy a good dinner and conversation, and she didn't have those kinds of feelings toward him, especially since Hawk had come into her life.

Taking her face between his hands, Luke bent down and covered her mouth with his. Pulling back, he smiled. Cara smiled back; it was a nice kiss, but it wasn't anything like Hawk's demanding and urgent ones.

Stop doing that, Cara. Stop comparing everything to Hawk. Just stop thinking about him.

Luke kissed her again, this time longer and wetter, and she kissed him back. That made him more eager, and he drew her closer to him as he tried plunging his tongue deeper into her mouth. A rush of blood making her unsteady, Cara twisted her head sideways, causing his tongue to skim over her jaw while she pushed her hand against his chest.

"Get the fuck away from her!"

Luke dropped his arms from around Cara's waist and she jumped from his embrace. Turning around, Hawk's fiery gaze swung over her, and his lips pressed together in a thin line.

"Who are you?" Luke looked from Hawk to Cara, baffled.

"I'm the guy who's going to kick your pansy-ass." Hawk's voice was cold and lashing.

"Hawk, stop it." Cara glared at him.

"Thought you had to work, Cara. Is this your night job, going out with fuckin' pansies? Or is he a client? I know how you *like* your clients." He looked her up and down, and Cara saw desire in his eyes along with slivers of fury and… hurt?

"You know this guy?" Luke asked, wide-eyed.

"He's my client," she said icily.

"I don't know what your problem is, but Cara isn't on the clock right now. Call her tomorrow during her office hours." Luke waved his hand.

Hawk leaped forward and grabbed Luke by the collar. "Don't ever fuckin' wave your goddamn hand at me again, or I'll break it. You got that? You're with *my* woman, and you need to fuckin' leave."

Cara yanked at Hawk's arms. "Stop it, Hawk. This is insane." Tears laced her voice.

Hawk let go of Luke, shoving him away. He looked at Cara, his eyes softening, and whispered, "Let's go, babe."

Luke, smoothing down his shirt, opened the passenger door and said, "Come on, Cara. I'll take you to your car."

"Who do you think you are?" Cara snarled at Hawk. "What in the hell are you doing here? Are you following me, or what?"

"Following you? Don't flatter yourself. Insurgents own this restaurant. I came here with some of the brothers." He gestured toward the front of the building. Cara looked over and saw Banger, Jax, Ruben, and a few other guys she didn't recognize.

Looking at Luke, who was holding the car door open for her, and at Hawk, who was glaring at her, Cara wondered what the hell had happened. All she wanted was a good barbecue dinner, not all of this crap. *I should take a cab and leave both of these idiots here. That would teach them.*

She half-smiled at Hawk as she entered Luke's car. Looking smug, Luke slid into the driver's seat, rushing to close his door as Hawk moved toward the car. Under her breath, Cara said, "You better get going or I'm not going to be able to stop what may happen next."

Luke backed up the car. "I'm not afraid of that jerk." He flipped his finger at Hawk, and with his face a glowering mask of rage, Hawk lunged forward like a panther ready to kill his prey.

Luke squealed out of the parking lot, laughing.

"I wouldn't tease him," Cara said. "He's not the forgiving type, you know?"

"Asshole thinks he's cool and badass because he has a leather jacket and a motorcycle."

"He isn't trying to be cool or badass, or whatever; that's who he is, not an act. He's honest, not trying to fit into anything in our world. He lives by his own rules—his whole club does. And that's what makes him free."

"What the fuck are you talking about? Are you condoning his behavior tonight? What's going on between the two of you?" Luke demanded.

"I'm not saying that Hawk was right to come over and say all that crap. I'm pissed about it. I'm saying what you see is what you get. He doesn't kiss ass or wear leather to pretend to be bad, or whatever. I guess I'm saying he isn't shallow."

"And I am?"

"I didn't say that. Let's just drop it, okay?" Cara paused. "I did have a nice time tonight. Sorry about my big, scary client." She smiled at Luke and patted his hand.

"He has a thing for you. What did he mean by you're 'his woman'?"

"Biker talk, I guess. Who knows? *And* he doesn't have a thing for me."

"Yeah, he does, and you know it. Watch yourself, Cara. Don't do anything stupid. A guy like that is bad news all the way around." Luke squeezed Cara's hand and brought it up to his lips. "I don't want you to do anything stupid like falling for this asshole."

"I'm not falling for him. That's crazy."

"I saw the way he looked at you, but what hurt was the way *you* looked at him. I don't want to lose you, Cara." He ran his hand down her cheek.

Cara looked out the window; houses and trees were blurs against the nighttime backdrop. The street lights, like glowing orbs, seemed to float in the air as the car raced down the road. *It's more like you don't want to lose your chance of being partner at my dad's law firm. Or could it be that you want to get your hands on my dad's money? I don't buy this poor-me-I-love-you act for one minute.*

"I care very much about you, Cara. You know that, right?"

Nodding, she continued watching the town streak past her, thinking back on the restaurant incident. Hawk was so mad it scared her. If she hadn't stopped him, Luke would be riding in an ambulance on the way to the hospital, and Hawk's ass would be in jail. Goosebumps pebbled her skin; Hawk's intensity intrigued and frightened her. She wished Hawk would reach out to her as a confidant. Listening was one of her strong suits, and so many of her clients confided their darkest secrets to her. *I doubt that he trusts anyone. He has such a shield around him.*

Cara wondered if she'd ever get to meet Hawk, the man, or would she only know Hawk, the sexy biker?

As Luke's car disappeared down the street, Hawk slammed his fist against a customer's car and kicked the tire while holding back the urge to destroy the Lexus. He couldn't believe he'd seen her with that pansy asshole. *Damn her! What the fuck was she doing playing kissy-face in the*

parking lot with that fuck?

Of course, she *would* be with Mr. Three-Piece Asshole. Hawk knew he was right—she thought he was beneath her. Oh, he was fine to grope in the confines of her office, behind closed doors, but in public—no way. She wouldn't be seen with him because he wasn't some high-bred fuck like the pansy-ass. *Fuck her.* Why was he even bothering with her?

And she *left* with that ass. That was the worst of it. She left *him* standing there while she drove off with the wimp-ass suit. She was probably going to have a polite fuck, and Hawk would bet the asshole's polo shirt wouldn't be wrinkled afterwards.

His temples throbbed and his chest tightened. *She better not fuck that asshole.* Once Hawk got her where she needed to be, he'd give her a good spanking for pissing him off and dissing him like that. But thinking about her firm, rounded ass, red with his handprint, was giving him a hard-on in the parking lot. *Yep, she's in my fuckin' blood.* He slammed his fist harder on the Lexus' hood.

"Let's go, man. Ain't no bitch worth this shit," Banger said.

"And it's not good for business to ruin the customers' cars while they're eatin'," Jax joked.

But Hawk wasn't in a joking mood. He wanted to get drunk. Maybe he'd even fuck one of the club whores and show that stuck-up Cara he didn't need her pussy—there was plenty of it around.

"Let's go get some shots at the clubhouse," Hawk said.

"Now you're talkin'," Banger agreed.

AT THE CLUBHOUSE, Hawk sat at the bar, downing shot after shot as he tried to force the image of Cara's long legs wrapped around that pansy-ass's waist out of his mind. Jerry leaned over the bar and said, "Hawk, there's one hot slut checking you out."

Hawk looked over in the direction Jerry was pointing, and for a split-second, he thought Cara was standing there. His heart raced and blood rushed to his temples as he stared at her. She was near the pool table, and her long, chestnut-colored hair shone under the colored lights.

She wore a short skirt and a revealing top, her big tits falling out. One of the members, Billy, had his hand up her skirt, rubbing her pussy, and the way the slut squirmed and rotated her hips, Hawk knew Billy had his fingers inside her. As Billy's hand moved faster, she parted her lips, clenching and moaning while staring straight at Hawk. *Damn, that's fuckin' hot.*

Facing the bar again, Hawk slammed his shot glass on the counter and Jerry filled it up. He loved the way whiskey warmed his core, which was the problem with Cara—she was his shot of whiskey. *Ah, fuck.*

As he staggered toward the staircase, the chestnut-haired bitch came up to him, putting her arms around him and kissing him deeply. She tasted like beer with lime. Looking at her through his unfocused eyes, Hawk kissed her back, playing with her tongue and squeezing her big tits. Melding herself into him, she rubbed his bulging cock. He closed his bloodshot eyes; in his mind, he was kissing Cara, stroking her tits, rubbing her wet mound.

"Cara, baby, I can't wait to fuck you. I've been waitin' too long for you," he slurred.

"My name's Jessica, sweetie."

"What?" Hawk's eyes opened, realizing this woman wasn't his babe. "You're not Cara."

"I can be whoever you want me to be." She pressed her lips to his again.

Hawk pried her off him. "Wrong girl. My mistake."

He zigzagged toward the stairway and ascended to his room. Not bothering to take off his clothes, Hawk threw off his boots and flopped on his bed, and with images of wet pussies, big tits, and Cara's beautiful green eyes dancing through his head, he fell asleep.

WHEN CARA CAME into the office the next morning, a petite, thirty-something woman sat in one of the leather chairs in the reception area. She had shoulder-length blonde hair and pale blue eyes, and Cara racked her brain, trying to remember if she had set an appointment she had forgotten to put in her calendar. Glancing at the woman, she went over to Asher's desk.

"Did I screw up?" she asked, tilting her chin at the seated woman.

"No, when I came in at 8:30 she was waiting in the hall. She insists on seeing you."

"You mean she's been here for two hours? What does she want?"

"She won't say, just that she wants to meet with you. I think she's Russian, or something—she's got a heavy accent."

"Give me five minutes to settle then send her in."

The woman stood in the door frame. Looking up, Cara waved her into her office while saying, "Come on in and have a seat."

The lady sat in the chair as her hands played with her purse straps. Looking down, she licked her lips then cleared her throat.

"Would you like some water?" Cara asked.

The woman nodded and Cara buzzed Asher, asking him to bring in a bottle of water. After the woman took a drink, Cara said, "What can I do for you?"

"You been given me by people," the woman said.

"Someone recommended me to you?" Cara clarified.

A sad smile passed over her lips. "Yes, sorry, my English no good."

"It's fine. What's the trouble? Have you had some problems with the police?"

The woman's eyes bulged. "Police? No. My sister have problem."

"Okay, first, what's your name?"

"My name Tetyana Kravchenko. You call me Teti."

"So, Teti, what's the problem with your sister?"

"I no hear from her. She call me more than two months gone, and I no hear from her again. She tell me she have big problems."

"What kind of problems?"

"I no know. She say she come here to work with modeling, but she say no good. She has scared to talk, so we talk too fast. She say bad men with motorcycle have her. I no understand all, but I know she has trouble."

"Motorcycles? Was she here in Pinewood Springs?"

"I no know, but she come here from our village in Slovakia to do model. Our parents pay lot of money to send her. When she get here, she say not good. She say trouble and bad men."

After speaking with the woman for almost an hour, Cara gathered that Teti's sister had been lured to the United States with the promise of a modeling contract, only to find herself the victim of sex trafficking. She was brought either to Pinewood Springs or one of the nearby towns, and it appeared a biker club was somehow involved. Eric's warning that the Insurgents were involved in trafficking women haunted her, but she refused to believe Hawk would be a part of a club that would do anything so despicable.

"Teti, I'm a lawyer. I'm not an investigator. I can give you the names of some good private investigators who can help you find out what happened to your sister."

"I want you help me."

"I can't. I'm not the police."

Placing her hands over her face, her shoulders rising and falling with each sob, Teti's tears ran down her wrinkled cheeks. Cara's heart went out to her, understanding her pain—Cara would be rabid, if any harm ever came to her loved ones. The worst part was Teti not hearing from her sister again. Cara had seen the fear and despair so often in the anguished eyes of family members, whose loved ones just disappeared.

Cara said, "I'll make some phone calls and see what I can do."

"Thank you, thank you. I know you good when I see you kind eyes," Teti said, her voice hitching.

Dropping her voice, Cara said, "I'll make a phone call to the sheriff's department. They found an unidentified woman a couple of months ago in this county. I'm not saying it's your sister, but you need to be sure."

Terror filled Teti's eyes. Her purse straps were all knotted and twisted around her wrists, and she shook her head. "Can you come with me? Please," she whispered.

Cara moved her head in agreement; she would accompany Teti on the gruesome task of possibly identifying the seventh victim of a sadistic madman. She hoped for Teti's sake that Jane Doe #7 would not be her sister.

Late that afternoon, as the sun blazed over the jagged mountain tops, Teti squeezed Cara's hand as the deputy sheriff brought in the photographs of Jane Doe #7. Teti held them in her sweaty palms as she flipped through the ten photos. A low, guttural whimper emitted from her, starting deep in her throat. She threw the photographs down on the table and tears rolled down her cheeks as a shrill scream burst from her mouth. Teti pulled her hair, her body trembled like a leaf in the wind. Teti's wails were the only sound in the small room. Cara put her arms around her, knowing nothing would be enough to lessen the horror of it all. Silently, the deputy sheriff gathered the photographs, making notations on them. Jane Doe #7 had become Nadyia Kravchenko, eighteen years old.

CHAPTER TEN

SINCE FRIDAY, BROTHERS from the Insurgents chapters in Wyoming and Nebraska had been arriving, and the clubhouse party was in full-swing. All of the upstairs rooms and the guest houses out back were full, and about seventy Harleys lined the lot behind the compound, the sun's rays glinting off the chrome on the customized bikes.

The clubhouse came to life on Friday and Saturday nights, and getting fucked, drunk, and stoned were favorite pastimes for most of the members. Even though the Insurgents didn't allow any hardcore drug use, whenever a big gathering like this occurred, crystal and crank flowed freely. The home members turned a blind eye to it, but home club members were not allowed to do anything but weed.

There were always women at the big parties. Women loved bikers and their bikes, and the Insurgents had their own groupies just like rock stars.

The Insurgents never had a shortage of women. Chicks were drawn to the bikers' badass attitudes and rebel lifestyle. Horny women who wanted sex any way it came found the MC an exciting outlet for their fantasies, and bored, restless women who wanted to take a walk on the wild side were drawn to the macho men like magnets. There were those who got a rush from being with a feared outlaw biker, and others who loved the freedom from responsibility. There were also the women who confused sex with affection when the strong arms of an Insurgents member held them.

Every weekend, a throng of girls lined up in front of the club's gate, an excited glow emanating from them. They waited in too-high heels and barely there outfits for a couple of hours just to spend one night of wild abandon with the Insurgents.

"Fuck, haven't seen this many brothers in a long time. It's good to be together," Banger said to Ruben.

"Yeah, I haven't been to a crazy party in a while. I'm glad Doris was cool with this tonight. You know these old ladies—sometimes they're okay with all this, and other times, they're screamin' and madder than hell if you go." He laughed.

"I know what you mean, man. When my Grace was here, she'd monitor my club parties. She was my woman, my property, but shit, she had me wrapped around her little finger. She was the best. I miss her."

Ruben nodded. "She was a good woman. Doris can be a pain in the ass, but I don't know what I'd do without her."

"Tomorrow night will get wilder. I see a fresh pussy I'd like to try. You comin'?" Banger asked.

"Nope, I'm just lookin' for now. Go have fun."

Banger walked over to a voluptuous woman who was busting out of her strapless spandex dress. Banger liked a woman with some flesh on her; he wasn't into the bag-of-bones bitches who came to the club. His Grace had been a big, beautiful woman. He put his arm around the hoodrat and whispered in her ear, making her throw her head back in laughter while her hand stroked his growing cock.

WHEN HAWK ENTERED the great room, it was nearly midnight, and the smell of alcohol, tobacco, and weed hit him in the face. The room was smoky and dimly-lit, and all around him, brothers and bitches were fucking and sucking. The smell of sex enveloped him. He chatted with several brothers from Wyoming and Nebraska, guys he hadn't seen in a long time. The camaraderie was good, comfortable and familiar. This was his life, his family. It was where he belonged: a shot of Jack, Moonshine Bandits' "For the Outlawz" rockin' through the speakers, his brothers all around him. This was the life he loved.

There were a lot of hot, new women that night. A big party like that always brought out a shitload of women. It never ceased to amaze Hawk how easy it was to get one, and how these bitches threw themselves at him. He could have any woman he wanted without a problem, except for Cara, and it pissed him off because he knew she wanted him. He saw it in her flushed face when he was near her and felt it when she quivered under his touch, but it was the dark ache that burned in her eyes which convinced him that she desired him.

Yet she resisted. Hawk sensed that she struggled with some do-what-is-expected bullshit, but her body, and the way it responded to him, told him that she needed him just as fucking much as he needed her. *Fuck, I bet she's a wildcat in bed.*

As he looked around the room, emptiness grabbed hold of Hawk, and he wished Cara were with him. No, he wished Cara were hanging with him at his house; he wanted to take her out to dinner or a movie and spend time with her. *Fuck, what am I thinking? I fuck, but I don't date. This woman makes me want to break all my rules.*

Hawk threw back his shot, waved to Jerry behind the bar, and left the clubhouse. He revved up his Harley, speeding away into the darkness.

SITTING ON HER porch with a cup of coffee in her hand, Cara savored the peacefulness that Saturday mornings brought. As she did every morning, she thought of Hawk. She wondered if he had screwed one of the women who hung out at biker clubs the night before. She wasn't too sure what went on during the parties, but she had heard stories, and that made her worry.

Hawk was a woman magnet, and every time she was with him, she noticed women checking out his broad chest and firm ass. At his last court hearing, the court clerk and the bailiff both kept staring at his ass every time he bent over, and even in his orange jumpsuit, he looked hot. Watching the two ladies rake their eyes over his fine body, he'd flashed them a smile, dimples and all. He was such a flirt. Of course, the women melted, giggling and smiling at him. It was damn annoying.

Cara was sure the women who hung out at the club were more than willing to please Hawk any time he wanted it. *He probably screwed several of them last night.* The reality was the guy was horny, and all he ever wanted to do was kiss her or talk about fucking her. Whenever she tried to have a serious talk with him, his mind was always on her pussy, and he was so demanding. Most guys who acted like that were full of bullshit, but she knew that wasn't the case with him.

She hoped he hadn't slept with anyone, but she knew she was being ridiculous. After all, they weren't dating, or anything. Still, she didn't want to think of him with other women. She heard bikers were notorious for screwing around and not thinking twice about it, and she bet that Hawk had a past littered with satisfied women. On the flipside, Cara had only had two lovers: an awkward, quick bang in the backseat of her high school boyfriend's Mustang after her graduation party, and Trevor, the guy she thought was her soulmate.

Hawk had probably broken many hearts over the years, and even though the women who hung out at the clubs knew the score, they must fall for some of the guys. Although, she couldn't imagine any woman melting his heart since Hawk was so closed off. She perceived that he was interested in her, but she wasn't stupid enough to think she would ever matter to him beyond a good lay.

Her phone rang, and she hoped it was Hawk calling to apologize for his atrocious behavior the other night in the restaurant's parking lot. She looked down at the screen and saw it was Luke. She thought about letting it ring through, but figured that would be rude.

"Hi, Cara, how's it going?" Luke's cheerful voice grated her nerves, and she wasn't sure why.

"Fine. Just hanging on the porch, enjoying this beautiful weather."

"Do you have plans for Labor Day?"

"Going to my parents'. The family always has a big cookout. You know, tons of relatives and that sort of thing."

"Sounds fun. I'm not doing anything. I usually go water rafting, but this year I'm not up for it."

Grasping that Luke was hinting for an invite, she changed the subject. "My dad told me you handled the negotiations on the Cooper Mine Investments' case real well. Good for you." Cara imagined Luke's chest puffing out.

"Thanks, I worked real hard on it. I'm glad your dad noticed my efforts. What are you doing tonight?"

"I have plans, remember? I told you, I'm going out with Sherrie."

"I don't know what you see in her. You're both so different."

"You don't even know her, and she's my best friend. Don't even think of talking trash about her, Luke."

He sighed. "Are you going to ask me to go with you to the Boys Hope charity event in a couple of Saturdays?"

"Uh—yeah, okay. You want to go?"

"I'd love to. Your dad bought a table, right?"

Cara rolled her eyes; Luke's ass-kissing was too transparent. "Uh-huh."

"Great, we'll have a good time."

"Yeah, right. I gotta go now. Let's connect next week, okay?"

"You don't want to see me on Labor Day?" he whined.

"Won't work. It's a family thing, you know. We'll talk soon. Bye."

Cara hung up the phone, wishing she would have let his call go to voicemail. Hawk was right; Luke *was* a pansy-ass. Cara laughed. She should've been furious at Hawk for the way he acted in the restaurant's parking lot, but she wasn't, and his possessiveness and confidence turned her on. It had taken all her strength not to fling her arms around his neck and kiss him that night. *Why can't I get him out of my mind? It's driving me crazy. And why in the hell doesn't he call me?*

Standing up to get another cup of coffee, Cara's spotted the manila envelope on the table. Realizing that the pre-raid photographs were in there, she opened it up. A wide smile broke over her face as she scanned the pictures. She screamed out, "Yes!" while picking up her phone to call Asher.

When he answered, she blurted out, "There isn't an ammo box on the table in the pre-raid photographs! I've *got* this."

"Way to go, Cara. That's awesome news. Badass Biker will be happy, if that word can ever be used to describe him. Does he ever get rid of his scowl?"

Cara chuckled. "Yeah, he does, and he *will* be pleased. I think I'll go over to the clubhouse tonight after dinner and tell him."

"Why don't you call him?"

"He deserves to get this news in person. I'm filing a motion to dismiss on Tuesday and requesting a hearing. This is great."

"Do you think it's wise to go alone to a biker clubhouse on a Saturday night? I think you should pass and go tomorrow. Sunday is probably tamer."

"I'm not worried. I know Hawk and a few of the guys. I'll just be there for a few minutes. It'll be cool."

"I'm not so sure. You want me to come with you?"

"Don't be silly. You're going to Aspen tonight. Have a good time and don't worry about me."

"Okay, be careful."

"Sure. Have fun, and I'll see you on Tuesday."

Realizing she had a ton of things to do before she met Sherrie for dinner, Cara made herself go into the house. She couldn't wait to see Hawk, and this was the perfect excuse for her to seek him out. Disappointed that he hadn't contacted her, she could still tell him the good news about the recent discovery of what the pre-raid photos contained and see him without losing any pride. This worked out in her favor all the way around. She was going to see Hawk, and a delicious shudder heated her body.

CHAPTER ELEVEN

"WHERE THE HELL is this damn place?" Cara muttered. She must have gone up and down Highway 295 several times, and she had yet to see the clubhouse. It didn't help that it was pitch-black out, either. The clubhouse was twenty-five miles out of town and she figured it would be inconspicuous, but this was ridiculous. She could call Hawk, but she wanted to surprise him, which meant finding this on her own.

After the fifth time driving south on the highway, she spotted five motorcycles ahead of her and had a hunch they were going to the Insurgents' clubhouse. She followed them, and sure enough, they turned left down a small dirt road she never would've found. After following them for about two miles, Cara's brows knit and a quiver rippled in her stomach. Asher might have been right about the foolishness of her idea.

Just as she was ready to turn around, a three-story, brick building set back among the trees with a tall, chain-link fence surrounding it came into view. The Harleys she followed turned into the enormous parking lot, and she veered her sports car into the area, parking to the far-left side. As she switched off her ignition, her doubts intensified. *Maybe this wasn't such a good idea.* Looking over at the gate, she saw a group of men wearing leather jackets with the Insurgents MC patch on the back, and with bottom rockers stating "Nebraska," "Wyoming," and "Colorado." The men were sitting on their Harleys, drinking beers and laughing as they talked.

After taking in a few deep breaths, Cara opened the car door and walked toward the gate. Noticing her, the bikers yelled, "Hey, sweetness, come over here and give us some of that tasty pussy." Their hoots and whistles were deafening, but Cara ignored them, opened the gate, and headed toward the clubhouse door, hoping to see someone familiar. As she walked through the opening, a large hand grabbed her waist and pulled her back outside. Rancid breath burned her nostrils as one of the bikers leaned in close and sneered, "Where the fuck are ya goin', whore? Ya got brothers out here who need your pussy."

"What a hot piece of ass," said one of the bikers who wore the bottom rocker "Wyoming."

Cara swiveled away from the big guy, her blood pumping and her heart beating wildly as the horror stories about gang rapes with outlaw bikers flooded her mind. *This was very stupid, Cara.* Thoughts of kneeing the big goon right in his swollen balls came to her, but she decided that wouldn't be a smart thing to do considering the men outnumbered her twenty to one.

"I'm not part of the club. I'm a lawyer representing one of your brothers. I've come to give him some papers," she explained.

"Fuck, we got ourselves a lawyer whore. Shit, we're movin' up, brothers," a young, handsome biker said.

"We need you to help us, too, sweet butt," someone yelled.

Realizing she was fair game like all the other women at the clubhouse, Cara tried to run back to her car, but the group started up their bikes. Twenty engines rumbled like exploding bombs. The Harleys' headlights blinded her and she squinted, placing her hand in front of her face to block out the beams. The men formed a tight circle with their bikes around her. Looking like a deer caught in the headlights, Cara blinked rapidly, a cold sweat covering her body. Images of what-could-be flashed through her mind as her adrenaline spiked and her leg muscles tightened, readying to run. Moving her head sideways, Cara looked for a way to break free, but the bikers closed in tighter, hollering and hooting, pushing her back to the center. She had no way out.

AS HE DROVE up the road leading to the clubhouse, Hawk spotted the circle of bikes and a petrified woman dodging them. He hated shit like that. Fucking willing women was fine, but tormenting a woman like this was bullshit, and he had to stop it before it got out of hand. He wasn't used to this shit because his club ran clean: no rapes, no beating women, no torturing. The shit unfolding in front of him enraged him, and he stepped on the gas.

As he approached the circle, his posture stiffened and he did a double-take. *What the fuck? Cara?* He saw her dressed in her tight-as-hell jeans and skimpy lace top, trying to break through, only to have a bike inch closer to her, her outstretched arms trying to keep them away. Terror filled her eyes, and as he watched her bottom lip tremble, his nostrils flared, his ears pounded, and he saw red.

Putting on his high beams, he headed straight for the circle. When they saw him coming, the bikers stopped, their engines humming. Noticing the VP patch he wore, they made way for him to ride into the ring. Blinded by the bright lights, Cara looked down at the ground as Hawk stopped his bike in front of her, glaring at each of the men. Putting her hand down, she glanced frantically around her until her eyes landed on Hawk. With clenched jaw, he stared at her.

"Get on," he ordered, his thumb pointing behind him. Jumping on the bike, she put her arms around his waist as he peeled off, leaving a cloud of dust.

As Hawk drove fast through the canyon, the cold wind bit at their cheeks while Cara's arms wrapped tighter around his waist, her legs hugging the bike and part of his thighs. Her wind-whipped hair stung against his face, feeling like hundreds of pin pricks. Leaning her head on his shoulder lessened her hair's assault, but her breasts pressed against his back. As Hawk looked over his shoulder at her, their eyes locked. Eventually, he averted his gaze back to the road.

Having Cara on the back of his bike felt good, and her arms squeezing his waist and her tits crushing against him made his cock jump. Her vanilla-spiced perfume wafted around him. Her tight grip told him she was scared, but her body melding into his was fucking hot. He chuckled when his bike hit a bump and her hand slipped down past his waist, jerking away when it touched his raging hard-on. Having Cara plastered to him while riding was a new experience, considering she was the first woman he'd ever had on his bike. And he liked the feel of her; he could ride like this for hours.

Veering off the main road, he pulled into a small alcove hidden among the trees. The river's rush echoed in the distance and an owl hooted, angry at having been disturbed. Cutting the engine, Hawk swung off his seat, watching Cara with a bemused smile as she fell back against the bike on wobbly legs. In one stride, Hawk was next to her, pulling her toward him and pressing his lips on hers. He fisted her soft hair and tugged her head back, allowing him deeper access into her mouth. She moaned and snaked her arms around him as she kissed him back with urgency.

As she nibbled on his lower lip, Cara used her fingernail to play with his ear. Groaning, Hawk embraced her, rubbing against her as she shivered and clasped her legs together. Her desire-filled eyes urged Hawk to tug her closer, and as he did so, her hardened nipples brushed against his chest. When her tongue pulled in and out of his mouth while she ground her pussy against one of his legs, his eyes widened, his breath caught, and a flush of lust throbbed in his body. He'd bet everything he had that she was dripping, and for several seconds, he held his leg stiff while she moved up and down, gasping.

"Be careful, babe. Shit like that is gonna get you fucked," he rasped.

"I guess I better be careful. I saw how bikers can be," she murmured while nipping his neck.

Remembering her frightened look, Hawk held her at arm's length, scowling at her. "What in the fuck were you doin' at the clubhouse?"

"I came by to show you the pre-raid photos and give you some paperwork."

"Why didn't you call me? I could've come by your place. What you did tonight was stupid."

"Oh, excuse me. I didn't realize I couldn't go to your clubhouse without the risk of being raped. I guess I forgot to read the latest edition of *How to Avoid Biker Attacks.*" She tossed her head.

"You're damned lucky I came by. Fuck, thinking about what could have happened to you pisses me off!" Hawk slammed his fist into a tree trunk.

"I'm sorry," Cara said in a low voice. She brought his scraped hand to her lips and kissed his bruised knuckles. She leaned into him, whispering, "Can you forgive me?"

Hawk breathed out. "I'm not angry at you. I hated seeing you like that 'cause I know what could've happened. Promise me you won't do anything like that again. If you wanna come over then let me know. I want you to come. I want you to see my world, but tonight was not the night. We've got several out-of-state chapters staying with us. It's been crazy as hell these last two days."

"Have you been crazy with them?"

"What do you mean?"

"I mean with the drinking and the, you know, the women."

Oh, yeah, that's what I want to hear. She's jealous. "I had too much to drink last night."

"And too many women?" she asked in a small voice.

"Nah, I got plenty of offers, but the woman I wanted wasn't there."

"A girlfriend?"

"Not exactly, but she's someone I'm interested in."

"Oh."

"She's got a smart-ass mouth on her and can be a pain in the ass, but I like her a lot."

"Does she like you?"

"I think so. I know she wants to fuck me." Hawk, bending in close to Cara, grazed her earlobe. "Do you like me, Cara?" he whispered.

Flushing, Cara said, "I don't know you."

"Oh, you know me, babe, and that's why you're fuckin' afraid."

Cara jerked away. "I'm not afraid."

"Baby, I make your heart race and your tits ache, and I bet if I put my hand down your tight-as-hell jeans, your pussy would be drenched."

"Is everything about sex with you? Can we just have a normal conversation for once?"

"Babe, you're the one who was dry-humping me a few minutes ago, and I loved it. Sex is normal for us, but what isn't is you running away and hiding behind that fuckin' pansy-ass you were with the other night. Why do you keep fightin' me? You know you wanna fuck me, and I'm dying to fuck you, so what's the problem here?"

"Where did you get off, coming up to me the other night and ruining my date?"

"Date, my ass. I was saving you from that wimp. A sexy woman like you is wasting time with someone like that. He's lucky I didn't bash his face in."

"I didn't appreciate your intrusion."

"I didn't appreciate your insult by goin' out with that fuckin' suit."

"You aren't a part of my life. You're my client. You have your own life, and so do I."

"Do you believe the shit you say? If I wasn't part of your life, babe, you wouldn't have come out to see me. The photos are a lame excuse, and you could've called me, but you wanted to see me, baby. You wanted to make sure I wasn't fuckin' any whores tonight, and you caring turns me on like you can't imagine. Be honest with yourself."

"This is going nowhere. I see I made a mistake in wanting to share my excitement about the photos with you. I can get your case dismissed, if you care to know that. It seems all you have on your mind is pussy."

"Watch your mouth, baby, 'cause you're making me hard." Hawk winked at her.

"Ugh, you're impossible." Cara walked to the Harley. "It's late. I have to get home."

"You're gonna give in to your fear?"

"I told you, I'm not afraid. I'm tired. Please take me back to my car."

Silently, Hawk and Cara rode back to the clubhouse, and he walked her to her car. "Drive safely," he said, giving her a peck on the lips.

"We have to get together and talk about some things before the next court hearing. I have to know some stuff about your background."

"Like what?"

"Personal stuff. Nothing big. I need to prepare an argument for court."

"I don't know why the court needs to know all that shit."

"I'm the boss in this arena, remember?" He frowned, and she placed her hand on his arm. "It'll be fine."

Shaking her hand off, he said gruffly, "I know that."

"Are you happy about the photos?"

"Yeah, knew it was a crock of shit. I'm glad you can prove it."

"I'll call you to set up a meeting for next week so we can talk. No kissing. No touching. Just talking, okay?"

Hawk grit his teeth. "You're the boss."

He watched Cara exit the parking lot then jumped on his bike to make sure she got back to Pinewood Springs all right. Seeing her in the circle, knowing what could have happened to her, made him realize that Cara was special to him. She was the first woman he ever cared for in his life.

He had to make her his.

Chapter Twelve

CARA HUNG UP the phone. Her head was spinning. She had just spoken to Josh at the sheriff's office, and he confirmed that motorcycle tracks were visible near the area where they found several of the murdered women's bodies. The sheriff's department had concluded there were enough similarities between the murders to indicate they were searching for a serial killer.

Convinced some of the dead women were victims of trafficking, she called her friend, Jim Lambert, an agent with the Colorado Bureau of Investigations. She and Jim had become fast friends when they met at a training seminar in Denver a couple of years prior, and whenever she was in Denver, she met up with him for a drink.

"You got yourself in the middle of a maelstrom, Cara. You're dealing with some dangerous and sick people," Jim said.

"Do you think a biker club is involved with all this?" she asked.

"My department has been investigating sex trafficking for the last two years, and yep, outlaw bikers are involved in it. I can't tell you too much, you know, since it's still an active investigation. No offense, okay?"

"None taken. I understand. Can you tell me if the Insurgents are involved in this?"

"The Insurgents? I'd be surprised. They have a stronghold in the Summit County area, but it's been their territory for years. They're not into this kind of stuff, but with outlaws, you never know. It seems the Insurgents have been waning away from the illegal stuff. Their monetary interests are in strip bars, ink shops, restaurants, and dispensaries. We know the Insurgents have a few medicinal and recreational dispensaries, and they also grow the stuff."

"I can't believe the state gave them a grow and dispense license."

"They used a straw man. You know him. It's your old mentor, Les Anderson."

"Les is the guy who helped with the dispensaries? I didn't know he was in that deep with the Insurgents."

"Believe me, he gets a percentage. He's not doing it for friendship. Everything is about money."

"I think bikers are involved with the murders of the young women who have disappeared in my county for the last year," Cara said.

"Really? I don't know about that."

"One of the murdered women has been identified by her sister. The murder victim was smuggled to the US and her sister talked to me about it. She said bikers were involved, and I'm wondering about the Insurgents."

"If it's any biker gang, it's the Deadly Demons. They've been a pain in the ass to law enforcement for a long time. They do all kinds of shit, and they're brutal. It sounds like something they could do."

Cara took a second, trying to recall where she'd heard that name before. "Is the MC in Colorado?"

"Their main club is in New Mexico, but there are a few Nomads hanging around your area, and some charters in southern Colorado. The Nomads aren't in your county because if they were, there'd be a gang war for sure between them and the Insurgents, but they have some Nomads scattered near Summit County. You know, I'd like to talk to the victim's sister. I have two women here who are scared shitless, but willing to testify about their trafficking ordeal, and they also said bikers were involved. They're in protective custody right now."

"For some reason, some deputies in the sheriff's office here are trying to pin crap on the Insurgents, and that's how I first got involved. One of the guys is my client, Hawk." She loved saying his name.

"Cara, you're getting in close and that's dangerous, so leave this to the professionals. These guys don't play nice. If they catch a whiff that you're playing amateur sleuth, they'll come after you hardcore. I'm telling you this as a CBI agent and as a friend. You need to back way off."

Goosebumps pricked her skin at Jim's warning. She knew he was right. Playing Nancy Drew with the big guns wasn't the best of ideas, and this wasn't a script or novel she could write the ending for. She'd call her cousin, Eric, and tell him what was going on, and since he was a judge, he'd know what to do. *Hopefully.*

After making plans to have drinks with Eric later in the evening, she called Hawk. Ever since the scary-as-hell night at the clubhouse, she hadn't spoken with him, and she missed hearing his voice. Annoyed when he didn't pick up, Cara left him a message asking him to come to her office the following day so they could talk about his case. She needed to know something of his past so she could offer a sympathetic twist in her argument to the judge. Since the judge wouldn't be excited to let an outlaw biker off scot-free, it was her job to paint a positive picture of Hawk's contributions to society, like the charity runs he and his club did throughout the year.

Playing with fire was safer than digging into what was behind Hawk's scowls and stony exterior. However, from some of his actions, she gleaned that Hawk wasn't all hardness: wisps of hurt in his eyes when he saw her with Luke, genuine concern the night he rescued her from those drunken animals at the clubhouse, tenderness when he kissed her. She longed to peel back the layers of his rough exterior, no matter how pissed off he got.

Beep. Her phone startled her. Looking down, she read the text message.

Hawk: *Tomorrow is good. What time? Where?*
Cara: *Meet at Latte and Such at 2. K?*
Hawk: *K*

That was it, nothing more. *What's his problem?* Maybe he was mad at her for the other night when she came on to him like a total slut, then freaked out and ran home. Massaging her pounding temples with her fingertips, Cara wondered how her life had become so complicated in such a short time, and how Hawk always managed to invade her thoughts and body. She pondered whether she'd ever break free of him, and the big question, the one she avoided, was whether or not she *wanted* to.

HAWK COULDN'T GET Cara out of his mind. He had never felt like this with any other woman. He'd even let her ride on his bike, a fact that didn't go unnoticed by his brothers, and they gave him plenty of shit about it. Jax and Billy kept riding his ass about being pussy-whipped because he was acting all glum and dreamy-eyed.

Shit, dreamy-eyed. I don't even know what the fuck that means. If it meant having images of Cara always in his mind's eye, then yeah, he was dreamy-eyed.

Hawk couldn't blame the guys for giving him hell about the way he'd been acting lately. He couldn't stand the way he was acting, either, so he needed to straighten out and distance himself; after all, his case would be over soon. He was the man, and she was the woman who, at the moment, was playing boss and liking it too much, for his taste. What she needed was a good spanking. But he didn't want to go there. His brothers would have a heyday with his hard-on and no slut in the room.

What he needed to do was go back to his fuck-'em-and-leave-'em life, and she needed to go back to her princess tower. He could have ten women right that second, easy. Once his case was over, he would fuck her hard and rough, then move on to casual fucking.

He'd make certain of that.

"WHY ARE YOU involved in this? Aren't you supposed to be defending people *after* the investigation is over?" Eric asked Cara while they sat at the Regency Hotel bar.

"I got pulled into it, that's all. I know people are trying to frame Hawk in the sheriff's office. I think whoever is doing it is being paid by this other biker club, Deadly Demons."

"Whoa, Cara, you're disintegrating before my eyes. What's all this talk of Deadly Demons and bikers? Leave them all behind. I'm sure you have other cases, am I right?"

"An injustice is being done here. Don't you see it?"

"So what? They're all scumbags, whether they call themselves Insurgents or Deadly Demons. Who cares? Stay out of it, Cara. Anyway, you don't know if anything you're saying is true."

"I checked the judicial background of the Deadly Demons Nomads, and they haven't had one conviction in the last three years. Don't you find that suspicious? Something is wrong here. I know it."

"Are you saying the whole judicial system is protecting lowlife bikers? You sound like one of those people who think everything is a conspiracy. Move on, Cara."

"I can't."

"You must, or you're going to place yourself and maybe your family in danger. You don't want to drag your parents into harm's way, do you? You have no idea what these outlaws are capable of."

Cara slowly nodded.

"Now, let's forget this dirty biker world and talk about something else," he suggested as he brought his drink to his lips.

As the two cousins talked, a man in the shadows watched them. The glow of his cigarette reflected in his fierce eyes.

CHAPTER THIRTEEN

HAWK WATCHED HER come through the coffee house doors, and she was beautiful. Her hair hung down her back, her eyes gleamed, and she wore a tight pencil skirt with a fitted sweater top, her high-heeled shoes completing the sexy look he loved. He moved around in his chair, trying to get comfortable as his dick stirred.

"Sorry I'm late," she said breathlessly.

He smiled. "You gonna win this for me?"

"You bet. Those photos are gold."

"You look hot when you're excited. Is this how you'll look with my cock in your pussy?"

"Why do you say those things, especially in a public place?"

"You know you like my dirty mouth. You'd love it on your slippery slit right now if you had the guts to go in the back and let me."

"You see, that kind of talk won't get your case dismissed. We agreed to talk about your case."

"Fair enough, but am I allowed to fantasize about fuckin' you while you legalese me?"

"I can't stop you from thinking, if that's what you mean."

"Good. You want to know about me? I'll tell you in one sentence. My life and my family began when I walked into the Insurgents' clubhouse. End of story."

"You're not getting off that easily, Hawk." She smiled.

He loved hearing her say his name. *Fuck, I'm pathetic.*

"Let's talk a while, okay?" she said. Hawk nodded, urging her to continue. "I know you're the Insurgents' VP. Do you do anything besides MC stuff?"

"I do all the computer-related stuff for the club. I also own a bike repair shop. I repair and customize motorcycles, mostly Harleys, and I own a dispensary, but that's just between you and me."

"I wouldn't have pegged you for a geek," she teased. "Where did you pick up the computer stuff?"

"I studied all that at UCLA, and even received my degree in computer science."

"You went to college?"

"Don't sound so incredulous. We aren't all stupid and ignorant."

"No, I mean, I just didn't take you for a university-type of guy. I mean, it's cool."

"Babe, don't patronize me. I went on the G.I. bill."

"You were in the Marines, right? I saw it in the case documents when I ran a background check on you."

"Reconnaissance, Afghanistan."

"Tough. How many tours did you do?"

"Four."

"Wow… Wasn't it awful?" she asked softly.

"It was fuckin' brutal, but you do what you need to do and make sure your ass is still alive after you do it."

"Are you all right? I'm sure you saw a lot of horror during your tours. Is there something you want to talk about? I'm a good listener."

"I'm fine. It was a goddamn job, I fuckin' dealt with it, and all that shit is in the past. It's over. End of story."

"How did you end up with the Insurgents?"

Hawk took a deep breath and paused for a long while. His eyes had a distant look in them, like he was reaching back to the recesses of his mind and conjuring up long-forgotten memories. He said, "When I was in Afghanistan, I had my troops. We fuckin' had each other. We were brothers, doin' everything together: eating, sleeping, scouting, fighting, and killing. Shit, we even pissed side by side. We fuckin' had each other's back; there was nothing like it. We were like a family in Hell. I always knew I had my brothers beside me, and when we lost one, we all mourned. It fuckin' hit us hard, and it sucked."

Cara looked at him intently.

He cleared his throat. "Anyway, when I got back I was, like… lost."

"You didn't have your family?"

He snorted. "What family? You think I was raised in a two-story house with a fuckin' white picket fence?" He shook his head. "No, baby, I was born in a broken-down trailer near Truckee, California, to a teenage mom and a sonofabitch dad. The only thing my dad knew how to do was use his fists and belts on me and my mom. She fuckin' escaped the asshole by bailing out one day. She left me alone with him. After he broke a couple of my ribs, the authorities bounced me from one relative to another until there were none left. Foster care was the next step with another fuckin' bastard who liked the belt, so I split.

"I was thirteen and lived on the streets. This charity lady, Maddie, found me and saved me. I ended up stayin' with a friend and his mom for a couple of years before I joined up when I was seventeen. His mom pretended I was her son and signed for me." Hawk's eyes reflected the pain of a lost childhood.

"I'm so sorry. I didn't know the details," Cara whispered.

He shrugged. "I didn't give a shit. Hell, I should thank my fuckin' ol' man for making me tough."

"I'm sure it still hurts."

"Don't try to fuckin' analyze me, babe. Shit happens in life. You take it and go with it. I never had a family until I joined the Marines, and when I got out I had no one. In college, I didn't fit in with the preppy university students." He paused, looking out the window at the majestic Rocky Mountains. From the corner of his eye, he saw Cara looking at him, her eyes clouded with tenderness. He fought the urge to reach out and caress her cheek and place her head on his chest. All these feelings were messing with him, and he didn't want any part of it; he didn't have time to care about this woman. She waited for him to continue, her eyes never leaving his face.

Breaking the silence, Hawk said, "I was in a bar one night, and I had a bit of a goddamn meltdown. 'Freebird' was playing on the jukebox and I kept thinking about Rick, my best buddy, who was blown up by a landmine." He took a gulp of his coffee. "This old dude came up to me. He was wearing a worn leather jacket full of patches, and he put his arm around me. Just like that. I still can't believe I didn't fuckin' smash his face in, but it felt okay, you know? The old man leaned into me and said, 'Shit, kid, I know what's goin' on with you. I was in 'Nam and lost all but two in my platoon. Comin' back after the fuckin' shit we all go through isn't the same, man. That's why you need a brotherhood. We're family.'

"That night, I went with him to the Insurgents' clubhouse. I've been with the club ever since. I decided to go to Colorado and patch in with the national club, the one I'm with now. They're the best damn family I've ever had. We're blood brothers, and we have each other's backs, always. It's the best decision I ever made."

Hawk finished his coffee, his eyes dark and brooding. He was back, and the ghosts of his past retreated to the dark corners of his mind. Cara stroked his forearm. "I'm so sorry you had to go through all this."

Hawk heard the tears in her voice. He looked at her; her green eyes glistened. *Shit, I didn't mean to make her cry.* He could handle smart-ass, know-it-all Cara, or angry Cara, but he couldn't handle crying Cara.

He jerked his arm away from her touch as if his skin were on fire and, pushing back from the table, he hissed, "I don't need your pity, babe."

"I'm not giving you any pity," she said, "just friendship."

"I don't need your friendship, either. I have enough friends. I don't need any more."

"What's the matter with you?"

"Nothing. Not a goddamn thing. You wanted to know my life history, now you got it. I didn't tell it to you to get a reaction outta you. I told you because you needed it to impress some black-robed asshole. I hope I didn't disappoint you." Hawk got up from the table and threw twenty dollars on it.

"All I did was offer you kindness."

Hawk, bending down, spat in her ear, "I don't fuckin' want your kindness, your pity, or your friendship. I want your pussy. If you're ready to let my cock in, we're good. If not, then fuck off, counselor."

Cara leapt from her chair, slammed her head into Hawk's chin, and pushed him back with all her strength. Grabbing the edge of the table, he fought to maintain his balance.

"You arrogant prick! You talk about *me* being afraid? Look at yourself. You're so damn scared to let anyone in that you've made your life nothing but a big escape: booze to numb the pain, women to forget, anger to mask what you're feeling."

Hawk clapped his hands. "Congratulations, Dr. Freud! You've solved everything in three sentences. Now you can feel good and go back to your pampered life in your high tower to protect that precious pussy of yours."

"You're a total asshole!"

"I call it the way it is, baby." He smiled and winked at her.

The loud crack across his face stunned him, and Cara looked surprised, as well, even though she was the one who'd slapped him. He brought his hand up to his face's left side. *Fuck, that hurt.*

Cara, recovering from the shock, calmly said, "Fuck you." All eyes were on her as she turned on her high heels, opened the door, and left the coffee house.

Hawk stood there in disbelief. He rubbed his face. *Damn, she has a strong swing.* A smile crept around his lips. *Fuck, my woman is fiery.* His cock was ready to explode. He knew he was getting to her, but the problem was she was getting to him, too. *I spilled my guts to her. What the fuck was up with that?* He never told anyone all that shit, not even Banger. Rubbing his face again, he thought about how she'd pay for slapping him. Her sweet ass had a lot of spankings coming.

He swaggered out of the coffee house, hopped on his Harley, and sped down the street, his cheek still stinging. Breathing in the fresh mountain air, he rode toward the clubhouse.

Chapter Fourteen

IT WAS SATURDAY night and Cara hadn't spoken to Hawk since Wednesday. She still couldn't believe she'd smacked him across the face. In fact, she had never hit anyone in her life, but there was something about Hawk which caused her to act irrationally. The man infuriated her *and* turned her on at the same time, which was a bit unnerving, to say the least. When Trevor had cheated on her and broke her heart, she had been crushed and disappointed, but she'd never felt the urge to physically attack him.

Hawk brought out the best and the worst in her, and he turned her life into an out-of-control roller coaster. She couldn't wait until she finished his case. She never felt such a strong draw to anyone before, and it seemed surreal to her at times. Reminding herself that they belonged to different worlds had become her new norm: his universe was dangerous, rough, and demanded raw emotion while hers was safe, refined, and expected gentle feelings. Surviving in each other's worlds didn't seem possible.

Cara looked at her phone and saw it was five o'clock. *Crap, I have to meet Sherrie in thirty minutes.* As she put the last touches of gloss on her berry-stained lips, the doorbell rang. Before opening the door, she peered through the peephole and saw Hawk standing on her porch.

What in the hell is he doing here? Her pulse started racing, her stomach queasy. She opened the door and he stood in front of her with papers in his hand. The late-afternoon sun made his hair shine like spilled black ink. He wore his cut, and a tight sleeveless t-shirt which revealed sculpted biceps with armband tribal tattoos. When he moved his arm, his fierce-looking hawk tattoo came to life, and Cara stared at it in fascination.

"I brought the papers by like you wanted," he said.

"Oh, okay, thank you. You didn't have to come over. You could've dropped them off at the office."

"I was in the neighborhood. Doesn't your proper upbringing tell you to invite me in?"

She smiled. "I would, but I'm going out. I'm leaving right now."

His jaw clenched and his eyes hardened. "Like that?"

"Like what?"

"You're going out dressed like *that*?" His eyes ran up and down her body encased in a form-fitting black dress. He shook his head. "You're *not* going out like that."

Her eyes bulged. "What? Where do you get off telling me what I can wear?"

"No woman of mine is going to let another man see her sexy body."

"Well, that's easy. I'm not *your* woman, so none of your business."

She grabbed her purse, closed the front door, and pushed him out of her way. As she marched past him, his powerful arm yanked her into a wall of muscle. He grabbed a fistful of hair, jerked her head back, and crushed her lips with his; his kiss punishing and angry as he sucked and nipped her lips. Twisting, Cara sought to break free, but his arms, like vises, held her in place, making her a victim to his sensuous lips and plunging tongue.

Again, her body betrayed her and she leaned in to him, her tongue dancing with his as her legs shook and her thighs clenched together. As a delicious shudder heated her body, her heart hammered, her pulse leapt with excitement, and dampness coated her panties. *Damn him. Damn this body. I have to get out of here.*

With a strong wrench, Cara freed herself and looked at him, panting. Hawk smirked at her. She smoothed her hair down but he tugged her to him again, kissing her hard. "You're not my woman *yet*, babe."

"I. Will. Never. Be. Your. Woman."

He brushed her cheek with his thumb. "We'll see about that. How wet is your pussy, babe?"

"How dare you!"

"Next time, don't wear your fuck-me dress and heels." He swaggered past her, swatted her ass, and laughed. "Be good tonight, babe."

Incensed, she barreled past him to her car, climbed behind the wheel, and slammed the door. Stepping on the gas and peeling out of the driveway, she narrowly missed him. He jumped out of the way as she sped off without a backward glance.

"WHY DON'T YOU just screw him and get it out of your system?" Sherrie asked.

Cara took a sip of her vodka martini. "I don't know why I let him get to me. He's so different from anyone I've ever known."

"He gets to you because he drips sex. You know he wants to fuck you, and that's a huge turn-on. He's gorgeous. I'd have already feasted on his sexy bod."

"Okay, I *do* think he's sexy and incredibly good-looking, but he's so demanding and infuriating. I don't think sleeping with him would be a good idea. Yeah, it'd relieve my itch, but what could come of it?"

"A hot, memorable affair. I'd go for it."

"I don't know…"

"This kind of stuff doesn't happen every day. I think you'll be sorry if you walk away from this cutie. An affair is great: sex all the time, no strings attached, wonderful memories. When you're all settled in your mansion on the hill with your high-powered attorney husband and two kids, you can think of your sexy biker love affair when your humdrum life becomes too much."

"You make a good argument." Cara smiled. An affair with Hawk—could she do it without getting emotionally involved? She doubted it. "I wish I were more like you, but I'm sort of old-fashioned. I like a relationship. An affair isn't my style."

Sherrie grinned. "I keep trying to convert you. I was hoping you'd take the plunge."

"I feel like getting drunk and dancing the night away," Cara said while she waved over the waiter. She was going to let loose and have a good time, for once.

"THAT WAS FUCKING sloppy, bringing me a woman who has family in town. You told me none of these whores have anyone who would miss them. What the fuck?" the man screamed.

"Look, asshole, the bitch told us she was the only one in her family in the US. We don't do background checks on the sluts," the leather-clad man hissed.

"It complicates everything." The man paced back and forth on the gravel.

"And killin' those other two bitches who *are* from the area doesn't? You're losing it, man, and when we think someone is a liability, we get rid of them, got it?" The biker ground out his cigarette with his steel-toed boot.

"You tell us *we're* sloppy. Shit, you're the one leaving all these bitch-es strewn between three counties. You shoulda let us take care of the bodies like I told you. *You're* the fuck-up." The other biker leaned so close into the man's narrow face, the killer could smell beer on the biker's breath.

"It doesn't solve anything to start blaming each other," the man said, calming down. "We have to be careful, more so than ever. We have to go to a remote county."

"You have to stop leaving bodies around, asshole. If you want to do your sick shit, okay, but get rid of the sluts permanently. I thought you were supposed to be smart. Fuck, you went to all them schools and shit. You're nothing but a dumb fuck. Stop doing your shit on local bitches that got families. Got it?" The tall biker shoved him backwards.

"Okay, okay. The important thing is that we stick together. There's too much at stake, if we get caught."

"That fuckin' bitch lawyer sticking her pretty nose where it don't fuckin' belong is causing all kinds of problems," the biker seethed.

"Yes, that *is* a problem. Since she's not an investigator, I don't think we have too much to worry about, though."

"She has her nose where it don't belong. I'll take care of her. It'll be a real pleasure to fuck her before I cut her throat."

"No, no, I'll deal with her. She comes from an influential family, and we don't want them getting involved."

"I don't give a shit. When we get rid of a body, no one ever finds it. We don't leave bodies around like you. No one will ever find her."

"Let me try and deal with this. If it gets too messy, then you can do what needs to be done with her."

"We'll be watching you, *sir*." The biker laughed.

The man's shoulders slumped. His breathing was irregular. Things were closing in on him, and everything was spiraling out of control. He didn't know what to do. All he could think about was having a pretty, young, trembling whore tied spread-eagle and begging for her life. His cock pressed against his slacks at the thought. He hated the way the two bikers were staring at his dick and laughing at him and wished he could kill the dirty bastards and walk away from all this, but he knew he couldn't. After all, he depended on them to feed his craving—a hunger which overpowered him and made him do horrible things. The dirty bastards looked at him with disgust, and if these outlaws were appalled and disgusted with his actions, then what hope did he ever have for redemption?

"Getting hungry?" They both laughed.

Head down, cock engorged, he nodded.

"We have a fresh one, just came over from some crazy-ass eastern European country, and she's hot and young. I know your taste. You can have her, but we need free access to bring the rest of the trucks through. We got your word you'll fix that?"

His heart raced as he imagined his sweet little slut. "Yes, yes, I'll take care of that. When do I get to see her?"

"When the trucks have made it through this county."

"That soon? Good."

His blood pumped, and he was on top of the world again.

A very fine place to be.

CHAPTER FIFTEEN

"**A**LL THE EXHIBITS are marked, right?" Cara asked Asher. "Check."

"The witness, who can identify the photos and establish a chain of custody, is going to be in court for sure, right? I talked to him yesterday, but you double-checked it again last night, correct?"

"Calm down, Cara. Yeah, everything's confirmed and reconfirmed. I can't believe you're so nervous. I've never seen you like this." Asher smiled at his boss's flushed face.

"I know, you're right," Cara groaned. "I'm nervous that what *should* happen, like getting this case dismissed, *won't* happen. I know we have some dirty cops. I hope the courts aren't contaminated, as well."

"You don't suspect the whole judicial system, do you?" Asher teased Cara, his eyes twinkling.

"I know, I sound like a paranoid nut, but you have to admit some major criminal stuff has been slipping by, and someone in a position of power is making it possible." Asher rolled his eyes, and Cara shook her head. "I'm just saying, you know? Something weird is going on, and I don't think it's all cop-related."

"Go. You're going to be late."

As she rushed out, she yelled over her shoulder, "Wish me luck!"

"Good luck, Cara. Show them they can't mess with you."

Cara disappeared down the hallway.

HAWK, LEANING OVER and talking to the giggling court clerk, saw Cara enter the courtroom from the corner of his eye. He purposely kept flashing his dimpled smile as he inched closer toward the clerk to hear what she was saying.

"Hey, Casanova, can you come over here?" Cara pointed at the table furthest away from the jury box.

"I've been summoned," Hawk said to the clerk, making her laugh. He sauntered over to the table.

"Hi, babe," he said.

"Sorry to break up your cozy klatch, but we have a few things to go over before the hearing starts."

As Cara talked, Hawk checked her out. He saw her mouth twitch and her tone was stern; she was irked. Satisfaction coursed through his body. He'd played up his conversation with the clerk just to piss Cara off, and it worked.

As the deputy district attorney came into the courtroom, Hawk noticed he ran his eyes over Cara's amazing rack, and that pissed *him* off. Hawk wished he could take him in an alley and punch the shit out of his round, chubby face.

Hawk focused back on Cara—specifically, her tight black skirt and purple satin top. He loved the way she wore clothes. He didn't know how she did it, but she revealed more *in* clothes than all the women at the club did in their skimpy outfits. He could look at her all day, and the fact that she was doing and saying all this lawyer shit blew his mind. Her sass and confidence gave her a sexy softness, and he wanted to fuck her on the table in front of everyone with her law books around her. She blew his mind.

"Did you hear what I said, Hawk?"

"No."

"You need to pay attention because I may need you to be a witness if the court wants additional information. I can't have you zone out on me, understood?"

"You don't need to patronize me, babe. I know what's up." He reached out and touched her hand. She jerked it away from him.

"Are you crazy? Don't do that again. I don't need this case compromised because you can't keep your hands to yourself," she gritted.

Hawk glared at her. He should grab her and kiss her hard enough to show her and every other damned ass in the courtroom that he didn't give a shit about their rules. That was the trouble with citizens—they were so caught up in what people thought or said, making their insecurities their chains. He hated spending so much time in the citizens' world. *Fuck.*

The judge took the bench, and the Motion to Dismiss hearing began. Cara fought hard on Hawk's behalf. She produced the pre-raid photographs and authenticated them with a deputy sheriff who testified he'd received the photos from the lead investigator the morning of the search, and he'd marked and placed them in the evidence box. The deputy stated his surprise when the photos went missing. He swore he had no idea who took them out of the evidence box, but the photos Cara showed him in court were the same ones he'd handled that morning.

The deputy district attorney tried to punch holes in the deputy sheriff's testimony, but the witness was firm and unyielding.

After an hour of testimony, both sides rested. Cara made a compelling argument to the judge that the prosecution had no proof the .22-caliber ammo box belonged to Hawk.

"Your Honor, the only proof in this case is that my client, Mr. Benally, is the victim of a setup. From the pre-raid photos, we can see that the ammo box was not on the table, and yet, the ammo box magically appeared after the photos were taken. There were no guns, not even a .22 revolver, found on the premises. My client was not even in his home when the 'search' was conducted. This whole case reeks, and it would be a miscarriage of justice to allow it to proceed."

Hawk wanted to stand up, applaud her, then kiss her soft lips. She was so passionate in her arguments and had so much fire; he wanted to fuck her so bad. *Damn!*

The judge, looking at the prosecutor, asked, "Is that all that was found in the house? Is it true no guns were in the home?"

"Yes, Your Honor."

"The photos here don't show the ammo box on the table. Can you explain that?"

"No, Your Honor, I can't."

"Ms. Minelli, is your client in a biker gang?"

"No, Your Honor. My client is a member of a motorcycle club. The club is not a gang," Cara explained.

The prosecutor interjected, "Club, gang, what's the difference? The point is that he is vice president of the Insurgents—an outlaw biker gang."

The judge looked over at Hawk, who stared back expressionless.

"Your Honor, Mr. Benally wasn't arrested because he is vice president of the Insurgents. The prosecutor is setting up smokescreens. He doesn't have anything. The search was a violation of my client's rights, and the case needs to be dismissed. Mr. Benally has not had any trouble with the law since he's been on probation. He has done a ton of community service hours, he is a veteran who served his country bravely, he went to college, and he has made something of his life, even though his background has been fraught with family violence. The fact that this case has even made it this far is a travesty. What the prosecutor *should* be doing is finding out why the ammo box was planted and why the pre-raid photos went missing. My client is clean. He runs legitimate businesses and has organized numerous charity bike runs for the community."

Shit, she's good with words. She makes me sound like a poster boy for Citizen of the Year. Hawk smiled to himself. She was fighting for him. He figured she fought hard for all her clients, but he was hoping that her extra fervor was strictly for him. *Fuck, she's making me horny.*

After thirty minutes of legal banter, the judge dismissed the case against Hawk, and he chastised the prosecutor for pursuing the case in light of the pre-raid photos. Cara beamed, and Hawk was glad the legal bullshit was over because he wanted to properly thank Cara for her hard work. The chubby-faced prosecutor was perturbed. The court clerk smiled at Hawk as her eyes lingered on his mouth; she had no idea the only thing on his mind was fucking his attorney.

"Thanks, counselor," Hawk whispered into her ear, his warm breath tickling her neck.

She turned her head toward him, so close their noses touched. "You're welcome." Hawk saw her shiver slightly.

"Let me carry your books for you," he offered.

"I've got it. Let's go back to the office to wrap your case up," she said with an air of professionalism. "I have to give you back some of your documents and have you sign the release." Her tone indicated that would end their relationship.

Hawk, searching her face, saw a tinge of regret in her eyes. *Why can't she give in to what she's feeling? Why is she fighting this so hard? I know she wants to be in my arms. There's no way I'm letting her off that easy.*

"Lead the way, babe," Hawk said.

WHEN HAWK AND Cara arrived at her office, Asher had already left for lunch. Hawk followed her into her office and closed the door. Cara, her back to Hawk, put her file and books on her desk. Like a panther, he approached her slowly, putting his arms around her waist as he nuzzled her neck. "Thanks again, counselor, for all your hard work."

Cara turned her face toward his. "You're welcome again," she whispered. She looked into his smoldering gaze, and her face flushed. She squirmed, but his arms tightened.

"Is this wise, Hawk?"

"I don't know, and I don't care," he said as he lavished kisses on her neck.

"I don't think it is. We better stop."

"Counselor, you're in charge in the courtroom, but I'm in charge here. You know you want this. Fuck, we've both needed this for too long."

Crushing her closer to him, Hawk's rigid bulge rubbed against her lower back as he brought his hands up to her breasts. He had been dreaming of playing with her tits from the first time he'd seen her at Rusty's. "Take your jacket off," he commanded.

In Cara's eyes, he saw desire and surrender as she did as told, revealing a lacy purple bra and the goosebumps carpeting her skin. Hawk whistled under his breath as his fingers traced over the fabric, her tits were sexy covered in all that lace. He turned her toward him and kissed each breast, then licked her generous cleavage, making her arch her back. Her hard nipples strained against the satin top.

Unclasping her bra's front hook, Hawk freed Cara's breasts and inhaled sharply. "Fuck, your tits are beautiful."

Cara's cheeks reddened. Hawk brought her face toward his and kissed her deeply. As he kissed her, his forefinger grazed over her nipples. Circling her areolas with his fingers, he continued kissing her. Each time he came close to her nipples, his fingers would miss them, and by the way Cara thrust her tits toward him, he knew she was aching for him to touch and suck them. Wanting to tease her a while longer, he kept kissing and sucking her breasts, always just missing her nipples. As he licked her tits, she shivered against his tongue, and he was certain if he touched her panties, they would be wet.

As his right finger continued to circle her areolas, Hawk moved his left hand down over her hips, cupping one of her full ass cheeks. She whimpered while she moved her hands down to his trapped cock and began to unzip his pants, but moving her hand away, he said, "Not yet, baby. I don't want to come yet."

Hawk flicked Cara's erect nipples back and forth with the tip of his finger, and she bucked under his touch as a throaty moan escaped her. Hawk, pinching her right nipple, captured her other one between his teeth. He sucked and bit while she squeezed her thighs together. Cupping her breasts in his hands, Hawk tugged at her nipples as he brought his knee up against Cara's swollen pussy. As she ground her mound into his knee, he felt her lower body tighten with each rub, lick, and bite. Throwing her head back, she panted and moaned, "Oh, yes, that's good!"

Seeing her contort and writhe against him excited Hawk. He'd guessed she was a passionate woman, but he hadn't even begun to touch her and she was exploding. As he hugged her, her panting subsided and her breathing returned to normal. Hawk's enormous bulge pressed against her stomach, and Cara raised her head up at him and smiled. Unbuttoning his shirt, she marveled at his well-built, tattooed chest. When she spotted the gold nipple ring shining under the florescent lights, surprise registered on her face before she looped the ring around her fingernail, tugging it. Hawk moaned. When she kissed his chest, flicked her tongue over his nipples, and tugged on the piercing with her teeth, Hawk twisted in her arms, bent to her head, and whispered against her hair, "Fuck, babe, that feels good."

Her plum-tipped fingernail traced down his chest, over his stomach, landing on the waistband of his jeans. She cupped his hardness, stroking it through the denim material as Hawk breathed in through his clenched teeth. When she pulled his zipper down further, he whirled her around, his mouth close to her ear, demanding, "Tits and stomach on the desk." His right leg between her legs, he nudged her forward, bending her over with her boobs and stomach flat on her desk and her ass up.

Hawk leaned over her, taking her arms and spreading them out. He kissed her neck and whispered in her ear, "I'm gonna fuck your sweet pussy, baby. I've wanted to do this since I first saw you. Do you want me to fuck your pussy?"

Cara's legs were shaky, her mound dripping wet. She grunted.

"Babe, I can't hear you. Do you want me to fuck your pussy with my cock?"

"Uh-huh," she breathed.

"Counselor, it's a yes or no question. Do you want me to fuck you?"

"Yes!" she yelled out. "Stop the talking and start the fucking."

"Fuck, babe, you've got a mouth. For that, I've got to spank that sweet ass of yours."

"What? Did you say *spank?*"

"That's right, babe. I can't wait to spank your pretty little ass." He saw her thighs quiver.

Hawk moved in close behind her, unzipping and pulling her skirt down as she lifted one leg and then the other so he could toss it aside. He stood back and took her in, unable to believe how gorgeous she was. Cara's tits were smashed against the desk, her sexy round ass pointing up, and her sweet sex glistening. Her thigh-highs, purple panties, and high-heeled black pumps were the only things she had on. He almost shot his load just looking at her.

Ripping off her panties, Hawk ordered, "Spread your legs." Cara opened them more and Hawk placed his leg between hers, stretching them even wider and fully exposing her pussy. She looked over her shoulder at Hawk, her gaze burning with desire.

He traced her lower back tattoo with his finger. Ever since he'd seen a hint of it, he'd been fantasizing about it. A curly-Q tribal tattoo, it was done in black ink with red and yellow flowers and butterflies intertwined around the design. He leaned over and kissed it. "Hot ink job, babe." Cara's skin quivered as Hawk traced her tattoo, pinched her ass, and brushed her strip of pubic hair.

As he stroked Cara's pussy with his finger, he said hoarsely, "Fuck, babe, you're so wet for me." When he squeezed her swollen lips and her hardened nub, Cara's ass wiggled and her thighs tried to clench together, but Hawk held them apart. While he fondled and pinched her ass cheeks, he kept stroking her pussy, even as he knelt down and placed his lips on her ass. "Your ass was made for spanking."

He massaged the cheek, kissed it, nipped it, and then *smack*. Cara's ass jumped off the desk, her body tightening with the stinging pain. But as Hawk licked and kissed the red area, he felt her relax under his touch, the pain subsiding into pleasure as she moaned. Each time he slapped her sweet, round ass, Cara's mound became wetter, his fingers soon dripping from her juices. His luscious babe loved to have her butt spanked. The red marks he made on her ass made his cock throb and pulse in dark desire. As he caressed her ass, he separated her swollen lips and slowly put his index finger into her wet depths. "Fuck, you're so tight. Does it feel good, babe?"

Cara nodded.

"I want to hear you say it. Tell me how it feels to have my finger fucking your pussy."

"It feels so good."

"I bet it does, babe. Can your tight pussy take more?" He shoved two more fingers inside, her muscles instantly clutching them. Moaning, she pushed her mound toward him, her ass jiggling with each thrust of his hand. As he licked her wet lips, her nub hardened under his expert tongue. Hawk lapped up her wetness, and the fast movements of his fingers as he shoved them in and out of her heat made her push her ass up higher. Her short breaths, hoarse moans, and tightening muscles told Hawk she was ready to erupt at any moment.

Pulling away from her, and with Cara looking over her shoulder, Hawk tore open a condom wrapper, took out his cock, and sheathed it. Lying across her back, he pushed her face onto the desk and spread her legs even wider. He ran his long cock over her moist pussy and teased her clit, rubbing it in circular motions with his length. Cara let out a guttural moan.

Hawk pressed his cock at the base of her opening and edged it in as her insides gripped his thickness. He groaned with the pleasure of his dick fitting so snugly inside her, the tightness squeezing him like a vise. Grasping her hips with his hands and holding her ass and pussy in place, he thrust into her. Blood pumping into his brain, Hawk's heart beat faster and faster as he pushed harder and deeper into her. Her moans and writhing on the desk egged him on, and he plunged all the way in— her back arching, her breasts leaving the desk to swing with each thrust of his cock.

Hawk grabbed one of her tits, tweaking its nipple as he moved in and out of her, his balls slapping against her. He pressed his chest against her back, and he kissed her shoulders then trailed his mouth to her neck, kissing and sucking it while he moved in and out of her slippery pussy. Bringing his hand to her mound, he played with her sensitive nub while thrusting into her harder.

Sweat formed on Cara's neck and back, and tight muscle spasms grabbed his cock as her pussy exploded, her body trembling under him as she gasped for air. She screamed.

Cara's spasms clutched his engorged cock, and Hawk couldn't hold it back any longer. He threw his head back, his ass and legs stiffening, and grabbed Cara's butt as his cock released his hot seed, spurt after spurt. "Fuck, Cara," he growled.

At the sound of his voice, Cara looked back at Hawk, his teeth clasped down on his bottom lip. He stared at her, both of them feeling the intensity of the moment before she looked away, Hawk pulled out of her and exhaled.

Returning to normal, Cara covered her chest and sex with her hands; she was naked but for her thigh-highs and heels. Avoiding Hawk's eyes, she looked around for her clothes. Hawk, zipping up his jeans, watched her self-consciousness. They'd just had awesome sex, yet she was acting like she wasn't comfortable with him.

"Can I help you with anything?" he asked.

"No, you've done quite enough," she said.

"Is this what you want?" He handed over her clothes.

Cara took them and nodded. "Turn around."

"Are you serious, babe? We just had a fantastic fuck session, and you want me to turn around? I've already seen your tits and pussy, not to mention your luscious ass. So no, I'm not turning around."

Glaring at him, she turned her back and slipped her clothes back on. As she smoothed down her hair and sat behind her desk, she glanced at Hawk and said, "I have a full afternoon. I have to work."

"That's cool. I've gotta go to the clubhouse. I know Banger and the others will want to know how it turned out. He's been texting me for the last hour. When can we get together again?"

Cara stared coolly at him. "Never. This was a one-time deal. I'll admit that we've been lusting after each other for a while. We acted on it, and now it's done. I have to get back to my old life."

Hawk stared at her in disbelief. "What the fuck are you talking about? You make up all these stupid rules for yourself. Are you allowed to only fuck once?"

"It won't work between us. Now, I have to prepare for my afternoon hearing."

"Are you saying the fuckin' wasn't good? 'Cause you sure acted like it was great."

Crimson colored Cara's cheeks. "No, I'm not saying that. It *was* good... very good, in fact. I'm saying that this can't go anywhere. You get it; you're the fuck-em-and-leave-em guy, remember? What's the big deal?"

Hawk narrowed his eyes and his jaw twitched. "Yeah, no big deal, babe. You were a great fuck, now on to the next slut."

She winced and her eyes glistened. Grabbing his jacket, he walked out of her office without a backward glance. Hawk knew he'd gone too far with that slut comment, but she pissed him off. They had shared something that afternoon, or at least, he thought they had. After all this time, she ended up being another bitch who wanted to fuck a biker for the excitement. He figured she was different, and he thought they had forged something between them other than lust. *Fuck, I was way off-base on this one.* The worst part was that since he'd tasted her pussy and felt his cock inside her, he couldn't walk away. She was in his blood, and to him, she was his woman.

He could never let her go.

CARA WATCHED HAWK leave, tears wetting her cheeks. She felt cheap and played. She couldn't believe he'd said that to her. His words were like daggers in her heart, but she didn't expect anything more from him. Although, it was for the best, and her common sense told her this. She had hoped he cared about her a little, but in the end, it was like she'd feared it would be—just another fuck for the badass biker. Cara's worst fears were realized, and she cursed herself for giving in to her desire. It would have been better never to have tasted him, to have felt his touch on her skin. She didn't want to be another slut he fucked, but after what he'd said, she never wanted to see him again. Hawk was exactly what she thought he was—an asshole—and she was well rid of him.

CHAPTER SIXTEEN

"YOU FUCKED HIM?" Sherrie shouted into the phone.

"Yeah," Cara groaned.

"How was it?"

"Awesome."

Sherrie squealed, "I *knew* your sexy biker wouldn't disappoint you. I'm so jealous."

"He was amazing. He was rough and sexy, but also gentle. I've never had an experience like it before. You were right about taking the moment, and I'm glad I did. Now, I can move on and get back on track."

"What are you talking about? You're going to see him again, right?"

"No, it's time for me to move on. It was great, but now I have to concentrate on my work and Luke."

"Cara, what is the matter with you? You have a great guy who's totally into you and gives you mind-blowing sex, and you want to *end* it? You want to fart around with Luke, who gets hard every time he sees your dad and thinks about his money? You're way off on this one."

"Luke isn't that bad." Cara giggled. "Anyway, Hawk and I have been lusting after each other since we met at Rusty's, and now I'm just another babe he's screwed. I know you want to make more out of this, but there isn't anything there. It was lust, and now we move on."

"I don't know if we're talking about the same guy, but he doesn't see you as another notch on his belt. He has feelings for you. Can't you see that?"

"That isn't what *he* said," Cara whispered.

"What do you mean?"

"He told me I was just one more slut he'd fucked," Cara said, her voice breaking.

"And you *believed* him? What did you tell him *before* he said that? Did you say the crap you just told me about this being the only time, and it's just lust and all that?"

"Maybe I said *something* like that."

"*That's* why he said that shit! He was pissed, and you hurt his feelings. He probably didn't mean it."

"He shouldn't have said it, and he *did* mean it. I need to move on."

"Cara, don't close yourself to deep feelings. Explore this thing with Hawk."

"There's nothing to explore."

"I know you too well, Cara. I'm your best friend. I just knew that if you ever got together with Sexy Biker, you'd sabotage any hope of a relationship with him. You have to get back on track with life. You gotta let a man into your life in a deep and trusting way."

"I have. I'm going to the charity ball with Luke next Saturday. Hawk is out of my system, and I'm moving on."

"Of course, you'll go with Luke. He's not a threat because you don't have any deep feelings for him."

"I'm glad you can read my mind and know all my feelings."

"I just wish you would throw caution to the wind for once in your life. Just let yourself *feel* instead of always *analyzing* how to live your life."

"Hawk was a one-time thing. It's over. Gotta go. Later, Sherrie."

Cara hung up the phone. Patting her forehead, she tried to wipe Hawk's image from her mind, which wasn't an easy task because the sex had been so mind-blowing, and remembering the things Hawk had done to awaken her body made her stomach lurch and her cheeks burn. Nothing in her lovemaking with Trevor even compared to what she had shared with Hawk. She almost lost her mind when his warm tongue licked her pussy; no man had ever done that to her. Trevor had been a selfish lover. He'd wanted her to suck him, but he'd never go down on her.

She had to stop thinking of Hawk and how deliciously wicked their sexual encounter had been. He exceeded her expectations, she'd give him that, but it was time to get back on track with her life. A thriving practice took a lot of time and energy, so she wouldn't have time for him—not that he wanted to be with her, as he'd made very clear. Anyway, Hawk didn't have a place in her life, and she didn't plan on being his favorite slut to fuck whenever he wanted; no, his touches, his kisses, his cock inside of her had to be pushed back to the corners of her mind. Life was about beginnings and endings, and this thing with Hawk had reached its end. Luke would be her focus, and her life would return to normal. It just had to.

"I GOTTA CALL that lawyer of yours and see if she wants to join the payroll. She did a damn good job," Banger said.

"We don't need any bitches on the payroll. Les is just fine. He does what he's told, and he doesn't argue all the time. He's the perfect lawyer for the club," Hawk answered as he reached for his beer.

"What changed your mind? A few weeks ago, you were all for her taking Les' place. Did she tell you to go to Hell?" Banger laughed.

"It's better to leave women out of the business aspect of the club. Women are for fuckin', and that's about it."

"Whatever, we'll take it up at church next week. You goin' on the run?"

"When?"

"A few brothers are leavin' in a couple of days. I'm thinkin' of goin', but I don't want to leave Kylie alone. She's had some lovesick fuck hangin' 'round the house too much. I think I'll have to set him straight."

"Kylie's a good girl. She knows what's up."

"I don't want no boys 'round her. She's too young."

A few weeks before, Kylie had turned eighteen and was in her senior year at George Washington High School.

"She's not that young anymore. Next spring, she'll be outta high school," Hawk said.

As Banger cleared his throat, he glared at Hawk. "She's too young to think about getting serious with any boy. This isn't open for discussion."

Smiling, Hawk threw his hands up in defeat, knowing that when it came to Kylie, no one could tell Banger anything. Sometimes, Hawk felt sorry for the constraints Banger put around Kylie's life, and when she'd come over to his place to use his computers, she did a lot of complaining about her dad. Hawk could understand some of her issues, but he told her all the time how lucky she was to have a dad who cared about her. She'd had a great mother, too; Grace doted on Kylie, and when she died, Banger did a damn good job playing Mom and Dad, even though it had been tough. Just recently, Kylie shared her desire to leave, and she swore Hawk to secrecy. Although, she didn't have to worry about him telling Banger her plans; he knew the president would go ballistic because Banger never wanted her to leave his safe haven.

"I would like for Kylie to learn how to cook better. I loved the spaghetti sauce that lawyer made. Shit, she knows how to cook. You think you could arrange to have her teach Kylie how to make tomato sauce?"

"My case is over, and I don't think I'll be seeing her again. No reason to, you know?"

Pushing his stool away from the bar, Banger stood up, patted Hawk on the back, and smiled. "Like I said—when you talk to her, see if she can help Kylie with some cooking."

Grunting, Hawk swiveled back around, laying his elbows on the bar. Staring at the beer bottle in his hand, images of Cara bent over her desk, pussy and ass ready, flitted in his mind. He needed to see her again. Fucking her was better than he had imagined, and he was sure he had just melted the tip of the iceberg. Pretending their fucking didn't mean anything was a crock of shit, and she knew it. As he stroked her pussy, he felt her body shake from desire, and when they held each other's gazes, an intimate connection passed between them, something he'd never experienced before with a woman. There was no way he was going to stay away from her, but he'd give her some time. Before long, she'd be yearning for his lips on her tits and his cock in her pussy.

He could wait. She was worth it.

WHEN CARA GOT to the office, Asher met her at the door and whispered, "Very mean-looking badass in your office."

Cara's heart leapt; Hawk had come to see her. As her insides quivered, a huge smile broke out over her face.

Noticing her expression, Asher jumped to rein her in. "No, it's not Hawk. It's another biker, and he doesn't look friendly."

Curious, Cara walked into her office and saw a lanky man sitting on one of her leather chairs. Dressed in blue jeans, black boots, and a leather cut with a 1% patch, his uneven brown hair fell around his shoulders in layers. As he blew a smoke ring in her direction, his dull brown eyes raked over her body.

"This is a non-smoking building," she said.

"Good to know," he said as he continued to blow smoke in her direction.

Ignoring him, Cara asked, "May I help you?"

"Not really. I've come here to help you."

Staring at him, she raised her eyebrows.

"I hear that lovely nose of yours keeps getting into places where it doesn't belong."

"Who are you? I have a ton of work and a client coming in soon, so what do you want?"

"I'm Viper, president of the Deadly Demons Nomads." He extended his hand to Cara. Not taking it, she went behind her desk and sat in her chair.

"And why are you here? Do you have a problem?"

"I do. I have a pesky amateur who is playing cop and making all sorts of unnecessary noise. My brothers tell me to slice her throat, but I'm not an animal, you know, *sweetheart?*" His words shimmied up and down her spine. Telling him to get the fuck out of her office didn't seem like the best approach at the moment, though.

"Again, what do you want from me?" Her voice sounded much stronger than she felt. As Viper opened his cut, her eyes took in the hunting knife he carried in a sheath around his waist.

"I need some advice on how to handle a meddling bitch."

"Are you threatening me?"

"No, I'm seeking your counsel."

"I handle criminals, not barbarians, so you've come to the wrong law office. Sorry." She turned toward her file cabinet and took out a thick file. "I'm very busy, so I'll have to ask you to leave."

Viper's eyes narrowed into slits of steel, his jaw pulsed, and his hands formed into fists. On his feet and coming toward her, every nerve in her body went into high-alert as her heart banged against her chest. When he stood next to her desk, his crooked teeth bared, she willed her body not to shake and her voice not to tremble.

"If you'd like me to recommend anyone to help you, I could," she said sweetly.

Grabbing her arm, he jerked her up and shook her like a rag doll. "Listen, bitch, this is a one-time deal. Next time, while I enjoy every inch of your slut-ass body, you'll be begging me to kill you. My form of enjoyment is pain, and I'm an expert at inflicting it, got it?" Viper squeezed her upper arm, but she refused to flinch. He was so close she could smell the tobacco on his breath.

Staring at him, Cara grasped the edge of her desk, her knuckles whitening. "You don't scare me," she lied.

"I'm not trying to scare you, bitch. You're too pretty not to stay pretty." Viper ran his index finger along her jaw then pulled her into him and twisted her nipple. Gasping in pain, Cara tried to shove his hand away, but he pulled her hair, making tears roll down her face from the corners of her eyes. Slamming his mouth on hers, he forced his tongue into her mouth despite her resistance. As she twisted her head sideways, he bit down hard on her bottom lip and drew blood, then pinched her nipples again and hissed, "That's a fuckin' preview of what I plan on doing to you. Remember that, *sweetheart*."

Viper threw her against her chair, and Cara lost her balance and fell. Crying out when he kicked her hard on her thigh with his steel-toed boot, he ground his cigarette butt next to her on the carpet. "Just so you know, I fuckin' love the smell of burning flesh. Play it smart, bitch."

Viper stormed out, shoving Asher aside as he came running into Cara's office. He looked horrified when he saw Cara on the floor with blood dripping down her chin, a nasty red mark on her thigh. "Are you all right?" He went over to help her up.

Cara was fuming as she took the Kleenex Asher offered her and wiped her mouth. He'd bit her pretty damn hard. "What a fucking asshole!" She rubbed her swelling thigh.

"Why did he come here? Do you know him? Does this have something to do with your biker client?"

"He came here to threaten me to back off on finding the answers to the recent killings. I've never seen him before, and he's from another club Hawk has nothing to do with."

"Cara, you know I've never questioned anything you've done in the office, even though we've had some questionable people come through these doors, but I have to tell you to stop dealing with these bikers. They are dangerous, and they don't fool around. He could've killed you!"

"No, killing me would've been too messy. I now know I'm on the right path, and that the Deadly Demons Nomads are involved, but they're not doing the killings. They're working with or for someone who is."

"Why would they do that?"

"I can guarantee they're getting something for their efforts. That slime bag wouldn't do anything for free."

"You have to promise me that you're going to stop right now. This isn't make-believe. This guy and his gang are serious. He *will* kill you."

"I have no doubts about that. Don't worry; I don't intend to be a martyr. I'll call Jim at CBI and tell him about my not-so-friendly encounter with this Viper jerk."

"You should tell your biker about this. He'll make sure you don't get hurt."

Cara laughed dryly. "Hawk? He doesn't give a shit. His case is over, and he's history."

"He's *not* history. I've seen the way he acts around you and looks at you. I'll bet he's not ready to throw in the towel. You need to tell him what happened. You need his help."

Cara wanted to call Hawk. Even though she made light of the encounter with Viper in front of Asher, she was damned scared—she didn't want to draw attention from a ruthless group like the Nomads. She remembered those creeps who'd bought drinks for her and Sherrie at Rusty's were wearing the Deadly Demons Nomads rocker on the back of their leather jackets, and they were gross.

Tired to the bone, she yearned to go home, curl up on the couch, and forget about bikers, especially Hawk. If she were to tell him about Viper, he'd laugh at her and tell her it wasn't his problem. Why would he care? He didn't have any feelings for her. She was nothing more than a good fuck. No doubt, the brothers at the club cheered and whistled when he'd told them he'd fucked his lawyer. *I'm sure it made for good biker conversation.*

She'd opened her heart to Hawk, and what a big, foolish mistake that had been. What could she say? He didn't have a clue how to love a woman or have a real relationship, and even though she knew he was hardened, she stupidly let him get to her. She'd slipped up big-time. He didn't give a shit about her, so no, she wouldn't call him. Why should she? If he cared even an iota about her, he'd call her, but she bet she'd never hear from him again. *So be it.*

"Asher, after this next appointment, I'm going home. I've decided I'm done with all this biker crap. I'll let Jim know what happened."

"Good. I worry about you. I really think you should tell Hawk about this," Asher said.

"No worries. I'm done with all of it. The old Cara is back."

Staring at the phone, she sighed, picked it up, and dialed. After the third ring, she said, "Hi, Luke, this is Cara. Are you free for dinner tomorrow night? … You are? Great."

CHAPTER SEVENTEEN

THE CHARITY EVENT was at the Palace Hotel. Built during the Silver Rush of 1893, the Palace was one of the oldest hotels in Colorado. Dignitaries and presidents had graced the lobby and hallways, and the hotel still held its charm, its glitz, and its opulence. It was the place where actors, musicians, politicians, and plain old rich folks flocked to during the thriving ski season or the bluegrass festival held every August. During off-season, the rich gentlemen and their much younger mistresses rented rooms to indulge in a bit of pleasure.

No matter how many times Cara came to this grand hotel, the atrium, with its stunning, Victorian stained glass and four-story crystal chandelier, impressed her. Passionate about history, the Palace Hotel, in its splendor, epitomized her love for the Victorian era.

Smiling at her, Luke slipped his arm around her waist. Handsome in his dark blue Armani suit, with his short, wavy brown hair, clean-shaven face, and his killer Neiman Marcus tie, Luke was the type of guy she should stick with. For the few weeks she had been pulled into Hawk's seductive web, she had put Luke on the back burner, but since that was behind her, Cara had decided to give him a fighting chance. As far as boyfriends went, he checked off all the boxes, and her parents had been thrusting Luke in her face for the last two years.

"Hey, beautiful. Sorry I'm late." He leaned in to kiss her, and she turned her head. His lips brushed her cheek and his jaw tightened. *Crap, why did I do that?* She had kissed Luke before, like the other night when they made out at Rocky Mountain Lake. Noticing his pursed lips and deep frown, Cara didn't blame him for being perturbed with her. She wanted to embrace him wholeheartedly, but something was missing.

Even when they were at the lake groping and kissing each other, she hadn't felt anything spectacular, not like she had when Hawk kissed her.

Dammit. I need to stop thinking about him! Feeling guilty, she was aware she dated Luke in hopes that he'd make her forget about Hawk. She had to exorcize the biker from her mind and body, but it wasn't working too well.

While scanning the lobby, Luke asked, "Is your dad here yet?"

"No. He'll be here soon. We're sitting at my parents' table."

"That's fantastic." He looked like he'd won the lottery—he was *so* kissing her dad's ass.

Rolling her eyes, Cara feared it was going to be a very long night. Although she'd decided to give whatever she had with Luke a try, she longed to be alone—after all, she was busy with her career, and her clients took up so much of her time. She enjoyed hanging with her friends, working, and being on her own, but the nighttime was the hard part. When she was alone, Hawk invaded her thoughts and her body tingled in remembrance of their coupling.

Before Hawk collided with her world, she didn't care about having a man in her life, or having a man even touch her. But then he'd busted in, all six feet, three inches of sex, excitement, and badass, and he turned her world upside-down by placing her on a slippery slope of want and need. Closing her eyes, Cara repeated her mantra, *I'm with Luke, not Hawk. I'm with Luke. I loved Hawk's lips on mine and the way his hands and tongue caressed me. I loved the way… Dammit! I'm with Luke. I'm with Luke. I'm with—*

"Shouldn't we go into the ballroom?" Luke interrupted her. "What's the charity again?"

"It's Boys Hope. They help at-risk kids stay off the streets and get into loving homes. They started in California and spread throughout several states. It's something I believe in, which is why I volunteered to be on the board."

"I wish you would have talked to me about it before you signed up. You know, you're a very impetuous person."

"What does that mean? And why would I talk to you about signing up for anything?"

"I meant that I hoped we were growing closer together and would discuss things with each other that could impact our careers."

Cara looked quizzically at Luke. He continued, "You should have volunteered for something that had to do with the Historical Museum of Pinewood Springs. You like history, and it's more appropriate. It looks better to be involved with those kinds of people, you know what I mean?"

"Charity is charity. I believe everyone deserves a chance at a better life. I'm grateful I had the opportunities I did, so why not try and help bring hope and chances to others?"

"You're getting mad at me. I'm just saying that you have to grow up a little and drop the champion-for-the-underdog mentality. It's time you understood that your dad wants you to be at his firm working with civilized people. The thought of you being in the same room with sweaty, over-sexed criminals is, well… Don't take this the wrong way, but it's repulsive." He grimaced.

Cara glared at him. "I won't take it the *wrong way*. What's *wrong* here is me being with *you*." She turned to leave.

He clasped her arm. "Please, let's not ruin the night. Your parents are here."

Cara sighed. "Yeah, let's not let my dad know you've insulted and fucking pissed off his daughter."

Luke's eyes widened. "I never thought I'd hear that word come out of your mouth, especially at a nice event like this."

"Been hanging out with too many of my clients." Cara smirked. She turned and walked toward her parents with Luke at her heels. *He is such a kiss-ass.*

All the influential people from Pinewood Springs, and some of the surrounding towns, filled the ballroom. At two hundred and fifty dollars a person, the event was a success.

Cara's parents embraced their daughter. "You look lovely," her mother said. Cara's fuchsia, strapless cocktail dress complemented her gold-streaked hair and green eyes. The crystal beading gave the dress a subtle sheen. Cara looked both elegant and seductive, a combination that was not lost on Luke as he put his arm around her shoulders and pulled her to him. Her mother beamed at the gesture while her father waved to one of the district court judges. Annoyed, Cara's shoulders slumped.

"Hello, Luke," Cara's father extended his hand toward him.

"Hello, sir. How are you, sir? Nice event, isn't it, sir?" Luke gushed as he shook Mr. Minelli's hand. Making a face, Cara caught her father's eye, and his look acknowledged that there was nothing worse than a kiss-ass. As they both laughed, Luke, still clueless, joined in, making the duo laugh even harder.

The chiming bells signaled it was time to enter the ballroom and take their seats. At the table were Cara's parents, she and Luke, and two other couples, the Hughes and the Fitzgeralds, who were old friends of the family. Cara admired the shimmering gold candles in their crystal holders and the red and yellow roses decorating elongated silver containers. Each table setting had a bud vase with a cluster of miniature roses, glittering gold napkin holders, and brilliant, gold-toned chargers. Cara marveled at how the whole room glittered, and it reminded her of a ball from one of her childhood storybooks. *Now if I had my Prince Charming next to me, all would be good.* She smiled to herself.

"Cara, how's your practice going?" Mr. Hughes asked her.

"Interesting, as always."

"Any good cases?"

"Well, I just finished a case with a biker who was my client."

"Is it finally over?" Luke asked.

"That's what I said. A lot of people think of the Insurgents as this scary biker club, but they can be quite nice." *Except for Hawk, who is an asshole, but is oh-so-hot.*

"I can't believe you." Luke was not smiling.

"If I were choosy about my clients, I'd have none." She laughed.

"Everyone deserves the right to be represented. They know a good attorney when they see one. They're lucky Cara took their case on," Cara's dad said, beaming.

"Oh, of course, I know. They *are* lucky because Cara is the smartest and best lawyer I know. Every one of her clients should appreciate her. I know I do. I think—"

"Enough already, Luke. We get it—I'm wonderful." She and her dad exchanged smiles.

As she talked with her parents and the other people at her table, Cara felt someone staring at her. She glanced around and saw nothing out of the ordinary, but she couldn't shake the feeling that someone was focusing on her. Swiveling around, Cara looked behind her and there *he* was, standing in the back of the room near the brass and cherry wood doors. Her heart skipped a few beats. *What is Hawk doing here?* Her mind couldn't process Hawk being *there,* of all places.

Hawk's eyes bored into her and she smiled weakly, nodding to him. He didn't react, his blue eyes darkening as he continued staring. *Why does he always play these badass games? Why doesn't he come over here and say something, or if he doesn't want to talk to me, then fine. Why in the hell is he just standing back there staring at me? And why is he here?*

"What's up, darling?" Luke whispered in her ear as his arm wrapped around her shoulder. "What are you looking at?"

As Luke pulled her to him, Cara thought she could hear Hawk's feral growl as she saw his eyes turn to steel. Flustered, she moved away from Luke. "It's nothing. I was looking for a friend of mine." She turned around again and Hawk was gone. Had he been there? Did she imagine it? The whole thing was too weird.

During dinner, Annabel Logan, the chairwoman of the charity event, clinked her wine glass while she stood at the podium on a makeshift stage. It took many clinks to get the crowd quieted before she began her speech by thanking all the sponsors and people who made the event possible. Cara tuned her out while she scanned the room. No sign of Hawk. Was he stalking her or trying to scare her? Maybe she'd imagined him. Was she going crazy?

Her thoughts were cut off when she heard his name over the microphone in Annabel's hand. "…a warm welcome to Hawk Benally."

Cara's head whipped forward as she watched Hawk's imposing figure fill the stage. The microphone looked small in his large hand, and throughout the room, women gasped and gawked at the tall, muscular man at the podium. His physique commanded attention and respect, with his leather cut—the diamond 1% patch prominent—a gray shirt, blue jeans, and his leather biker boots. His hair, pulled in a ponytail, glistened under the bright stage lights while his blue eyes shone, his biceps flexing whenever he moved. Hawk was gorgeous.

A twinge throbbed between Cara's legs; she so wanted him right then. How she wished Hawk's arm, instead of Luke's, was around her. The room grew smaller as she saw him right then and there, of all places. The room spun around her, her body thrilling at the sight of him. She needed him like an addict needed a fix.

As his eyes fixed on Cara, Hawk addressed the crowd. Several eyes turned toward her, and she blushed and squirmed in her chair.

"Isn't he the asshole who accosted me in the parking lot?" Luke whispered.

"Yeah, he was a client of mine."

"What in the fuck is he doing here? And why does he keep looking at you?"

"Not sure why he's here. He's probably glad to see a familiar face."

"He doesn't look like the type who would be intimidated by a crowd, or *anything*. He's that outlaw biker, right? This is the reason you should give up working with your lowlife clients and come to your dad's firm."

"Don't start with that 'work in my dad's law firm' spiel again. And stop talking in my ear. I'm trying to hear what he's saying."

"Are you going to tell me—" Luke boomed.

"Shh," the people at and around their table said.

Leaning close to her ear, Luke whispered, "I can't believe you're interested in this *outlaw*. What's your problem, anyway?"

"I'm not *interested* in him. I'm just curious as to why he's here at the podium," Cara said, her eyes bright and fixed on Hawk's.

"You know, your cousin Eric thinks this asshole is bad news, too. He said this biker's club may be involved with the killings that have been going on for the last year."

"I don't give a damn what Eric or you think of Hawk. His club is *not* involved with the killings. I don't want to talk about this. I'm trying to listen," she said.

"How could you even look at him like you are with me next to you? He's a lowlife, and I'm a successful attorney and a great catch. What the fuck is your problem?" he hissed.

Ignoring him, Cara watched Hawk as he gripped the podium. *I know what those hands can do to my body.* Her skin prickled as she remembered their lovemaking—dull, throbbing spasms pulsed deep in her core while she replayed Hawk's tongue and fingers stroking every part of her. Shifting in her chair, her need for him at that moment was great. If only Luke knew what she was thinking. She smiled wickedly.

"I'm glad to be here tonight, and it's because of this great charity that I'm able to address all of you. I am a product of Boys Hope. I found myself on the streets when I was thirteen years old, eating out of trashcans, sleeping in doorways, fighting off the creeps who prey on young, homeless kids. Before that, I bounced from relative to relative, and then to some foster homes. I'd had enough, so I took off. If it hadn't been for Maddie Rendon, who actually gave a shit about me, I'd have wasted away on the streets. I'd be in prison instead of in front of all of you.

"Boys Hope gave me a safe place. It set me straight, got me back in school, and eventually living with a friend of mine and his family. Maddie Rendon stood by me during my journey from homelessness to home. She was the best.

"This is a good charity, so support it. My MC helps by doing charity runs. Our next run is scheduled two weeks from this Saturday. Come out to Cooper's Peak to give your support." As Hawk paused and looked at all the faces in the room, he cleared his throat. "Seriously, I'd have been fucked but for this organization." He turned toward Annabel, handing her the microphone.

A huge round of applause filled the ballroom, and people were getting on their feet. Cara sat speechless in her chair. She had no idea Hawk would ever open a part of him to a room full of strangers, but he did it for Boys Hope. *He* does *have a soft spot, just like I suspected.* Hearing him share the hardship of his childhood brought tears to her eyes. Her heart broke when she thought of the thirteen-year-old Hawk sleeping on the streets at night, scrounging to find something to eat, trying to survive when he should have been in school and playing sports. No wonder he was so damn hard. No wonder he didn't trust anyone.

Hawk left the stage and people, mostly women, reached out to him, trying to hug him or shake his hand. It was like they needed to touch him, feel his muscled arms, and have a piece of him.

Out of the corner of her eye, Cara saw Hawk walking over to her table. Not wanting to engage in conversation with him, she pretended to be absorbed in the table's discussion as she sipped her wine.

"You were marvelous," one of the patrons gushed.

"Your story was so inspiring," another woman squealed while checking out his crotch.

Nodding at them, Hawk gave a tight smile. Gripping Cara's arm, he leaned down, his hot breath scorching her ear as he whispered, "We gotta talk."

Gulping the rest of her wine, she stood up, pushing her chair back. "Excuse me, I'll be right back."

"Where are you going?" Luke asked. "I'm coming with you."

Hawk threw him a menacing look and Luke sat back down, watching Hawk take his date through the crowd.

Hawk dragged Cara through the throng of people, and she barely kept up with him in her high heels. He didn't stop until they entered a small room down the hall from the ballroom.

"What is your prob—"

Hawk silenced her as he sucked her lips, licked her teeth, and swirled his tongue inside her welcoming mouth. Drawing her close to him until she melded into his strong chest, his cock grew hard against her. "Fuck, you smell good," he rasped as her vanilla and baby powder scent wrapped around him.

As Cara circled her arms around his neck and tangled her fingers in his ebony hair, he groaned and ground against her. Feathery brushstrokes from his fingers made her quiver as he moved his mouth down to her neck, kissing it while he licked the sensitive skin below her ear. Cara squirmed and clenched her thighs together, her panties' dampness cold against her heated sex as a spasm went to her core. *Crap, I'm going to come right here with him kissing me.* Her brain told her how ridiculous that was but her body betrayed her, gagging her common sense.

I can't believe I'm ready to screw him with my parents and Luke right next door. Have I lost my mind?

The door opened, a waiter turned on the lights, and Cara thought she was going to die. She pushed Hawk back and straightened her dress as Hawk's eyes raked boldly over her body. "I like the dress, babe. You look hot. Are your panties all lacy and shit?" he asked, licking his lips.

The waiter stood in the doorway, watching them until Hawk turned to him and growled, "Get the fuck outta here if you want to work another day."

The young man turned around and ran out. Hawk threw his head back and laughed.

"Do you enjoy intimidating people?" Cara snapped.

"Do you enjoy my tongue fucking your pussy?"

"Is everything about sex with you?"

Looking perplexed, he answered, "Yeah."

"Oh, you're impossible. I have to get back." Cara tried to pass by him, but he pinned her against the wall.

"Why are you with the dumbfuck in the suit?"

"You mean Luke? He's my escort."

"He's the same ass-wipe who almost shit his pants in the restaurant parking lot. Is he your boyfriend?" he growled.

Stammering, she replied, "I… uh… I don't know."

"It's a yes or no question, babe." His voice was harsh, impatient.

"No, it's not. It's complicated. I mean, we go out. I guess he's my sometimes-boyfriend."

"What the fuck is that? Have you given your pussy to him?"

"That isn't any of your business. Why would you ask me something like that?"

"Cause I need to know. I can't stand the thought of that fucking suit putting his weak dick in you."

"You're such an asshole."

"No argument there. Again, did you fuck him?"

"I have to go. Let me pass."

"Not until you tell me if you fucked that pansy-ass suit."

"No, okay. Satisfied?"

Hawk leaned in and nuzzled his face in her neck as he licked her earlobe and breathed into her ear. "Good. Don't even think of fucking him."

He was so arrogant. Cara should have been outraged at his nerve, but she wasn't. She found his possessiveness, his warm breath, and his hardness against her very seductive. Had she lost all sense? She was even using the word *fuck* more. Hawk was bad news, and she had to get him out of her life fast before she lost herself.

"How can you even be with that weak-ass after being with me?"

"You're pretty full of yourself, aren't you?"

"You bet. You know no man has ever fucked you like I did. You keep hangin' out with pansy-asses who don't have a clue what it means to be a man. How can you go out with him after our fuckin'?"

"Why haven't you called me? You think being a man is about shoving your dick into a woman? I got news for you—it isn't."

"You loved every second of my cock in your wet pussy. Your moans and screams told me I was doing something right. Don't act like you get fucked like that every day, babe."

"You don't get it, do you? Yeah, it was good. I told you that. We lusted after each other, you scratched my itch and I scratched yours, but that doesn't make you Man of the Year."

"What do you want from me, baby? I fucked you and you pushed me away. If you think I'm the type of guy who runs after a woman, you're dead wrong."

"I don't know why I even bother with you." Her eyes flashed.

"I do—you want me in your life. I'm cool with that. You're the one pushing me away. You think you're too good for me."

"Maybe I am. I mean, you don't fit into my world. And you know I'm right," she muttered. She regretted her words the moment she said them, watching his eyes flare with anger and his hands curl into fists. "Look, you and I had a business relationship. We got way too personal. I'm to blame, too. You stay out of my life, and I'll stay out of yours."

"That's fine by me. Like I told you, you were one of the better fucks I've had. Bitches come and go. I have a few sluts waiting for me at the clubhouse just dying to get my cock in their pussies."

"Do you really feel this way?" Cara whispered, searching his face.

Stone-faced, his voice dripped ice. "Damn straight."

She winced at his words. "I guess that's it, then."

"Guess so."

She walked toward the door, and he shouted, "Remember, no fucking the suit, got it? If you want him to keep walking upright, don't fuck the wimp-ass."

Confused, she looked back at him. "Why do you care? Are you threatening me? Are you *really* doing that?"

"Nah, not threatening, just saying."

Exasperated, Cara yelled, "Get out of my life!"

Storming out, she ran to the ladies room, her head down and tears rolling down her cheeks. *He's such an asshole. How did I ever let him touch me? Fuck him!* In the mirror, she touched her swollen lips with her fingertips, noticing Hawk's cologne still lingered on her skin. Wiping herself with a damp cloth, Cara washed off his scent and fixed her face before going back to her table.

"DID THAT LOWLIFE do anything to you?" Luke asked.

"No, we just talked, that's all," Cara said.

They sat in Luke's car outside Cara's house. She was tired, and her head hurt from the evening's events.

"Are you going to ask me to come in?" Luke said, putting his arm around her.

Shaking his arm off, she replied, "Not tonight. I'm very tired."

"If I was that badass biker, you'd let me in, wouldn't you?"

"No, I wouldn't. I'm tired and want to go inside, *alone*. Thanks, Luke. I had a nice time tonight."

"Will I see you tomorrow?"

"I don't know. Call me. Goodnight." She leaned in and gave him a quick kiss on his cheek. Before he could react, she was out of the car and on her porch, opening the front door. She waved at Luke and closed the door.

Cara breathed a sigh of relief when she heard Luke's car leave; she wanted to be alone. Replaying her encounter with Hawk in her mind, his mean but truthful words echoed over and over. His harshness hurt her.

After she washed off her makeup, hung up her clothes, and slid under her comforter, she cried herself to sleep.

PISSED, LUKE SPED out of Cara's driveway. The night hadn't ended the way he'd wanted. The plan was to fuck Cara after the event so he could cement their connection, believing a nice girl like Cara would take the fucking to mean more than it did. He was mad at that outlaw biker for ruining his plans. Luke gathered Cara was smitten by the biker, and he also suspected the dirt bag said or did something to her to cause her to shut down, because when she came back to the table she was different, sullen and sad.

Luke was a little surprised the biker was interested in Cara since he had his pick of sexy, nasty women who loved hanging around bad boys. He wondered why the outlaw biker would be interested in a goody-two shoes like Cara. Luke had a hard-on just thinking of the nasty women who hung around biker clubs.

Looking at his watch, he noticed it was a little past midnight. He could still go to his main strip club, Dream House, see his favorite dancer, Missy, and if he tipped her well enough, he may score a blowjob from her. Forgetting about Cara, Luke raced toward downtown.

HAWK AND JAX watched the new dancer grind and shimmy around the pole at Dream House. As the girl spread her legs wide and blew a kiss at Hawk, Jax poked him in the ribs, laughing. Obviously, she didn't know Hawk was one of her bosses. The Insurgents owned the strip club, and Hawk, who handled the books, came by to check out the crowd, since earnings had fallen off in the past several months. Looking around, the club was packed, and Hawk's stomach tightened as his suspicions of someone skimming off the top were confirmed.

Stealing from a club owned by an outlaw MC was not a smart move. Hawk hoped like hell Emma wasn't the thief, because he liked her and didn't want to hurt her. Emma had been a club whore for several years until she hooked up with Danny. She didn't wear his patch, but she had been with him for a long time. After she and Danny got together, the Insurgents promoted her to manager of the strip bar. She was in charge of all the women and handled the money. When Hawk came in a few days before to go over the books, he'd noticed someone had dummied them up, and he seethed. He'd find out who was cheating the club, and there'd be hell to pay.

"This bitch is hot, don't you think? She's a great addition to the line-up," Jax said.

Hawk looked at the woman gyrating on the pole. "Yeah, she's good with her moves."

"Are you going to initiate her into the club?"

"No, I'm not here for that."

"Then I have free rein?"

"Yeah, go for it."

Hawk noticed the way the stripper was eyeing him, and he knew all he had to do was wink at her and she'd have her full lips around his cock. He should fuck her; it'd serve Cara right if he fucked this bitch. He couldn't believe Cara admitted he wasn't good enough for her. Her words had cut him like a knife. *I knew she just wanted a fuck and nothing more. She's so stuck-up. She thinks that fucking suit is the better match for her. She doesn't know shit about herself. She's a smoldering fire who needs a man to ignite her, and pansy-ass doesn't have a clue how to handle such a woman.*

"Hey, Missy, come give me a dance," Jax said to a pretty brunette dancer.

"Hi, Jax." She smiled as she looked across the room.

"How've you been?"

"Okay. Can I catch you the next time? I have a customer waiting. You know, I need the big tip he gives me. Rent's due, and I'm short this month."

"He can wait. I'll give you a bigger tip," Jax said as he stared at her tits.

Hawk said, "Go on to your customer."

Missy threw Hawk a relieved look. "Thanks. See you around, Jax." She walked across the room to a corner table.

"What the fuck did you do that for?" Jax sniped.

"This is a business, not a whorehouse. If you wanna fuck one of the dancers, then do it after hours, not on the Insurgents' clock, got it?"

Jax mumbled something under his breath. Standing up, Hawk said, "I'm gonna find Emma to talk to her about the books. Don't bother the dancers while they're working."

As Hawk walked toward the office, he passed the table Missy sat at with her customer. He jerked his head back when he saw Luke give Missy money for a lap dance. *Fuckin' suit is her big-tipper. What the fuck is he doing here?* Hawk realized that if pansy-ass was there with his tongue hanging out for Missy, then Cara must have sent him packing. All of a sudden, the darkness that had been hanging over him since his encounter with Cara lifted.

Entering the office, he looked back at Missy. Her pussy was inches from Luke's face, and he had his hand in his pants, rubbing his dick. Hawk turned away in disgust. *There's no way Cara wants that fuckin' suit. She's too proud to admit she wants me. I'll give her some space, but I'm not letting her outta my life. No fuckin' way.*

Hawk closed the office door.

CHAPTER EIGHTEEN

LOOKING AT HER ransacked office in disbelief, Cara asked, "What happened?"

"I don't know. I just got here," Asher said.

Glancing around the room, Cara noticed files strewn over the floor in the reception area and in her office. "Someone broke in. Have the computers and printers been stolen?"

"No, nothing expensive is missing," Asher said.

"It seems like whoever did this was looking for something, but what? What do I have that anyone wants? What a mess," Cara said.

"Maybe it's a warning."

"You think? That asshole already came by and 'warned' me. Why would he trash my office?"

"Probably to see if you had any files on the case. He's also a fucking psycho, so I don't think he needs a reason to do stuff to you."

Cara picked up some of the papers. "We might as well get this mess cleaned up. It's going to take us hours to get the documents in the right files. Damn, like I need this crap. The last few days have been totally shitty."

"You didn't have a good weekend? How was the charity ball?" Asher asked while sorting through the papers.

"It was a disaster. Hawk was one of the speakers there. I couldn't believe it. Boys Hope helped him out when he was a teenager on the streets. He never mentioned to me who helped him out."

"How did Luke like his competition?" Asher asked with a twinkle in his eye.

"It was a fiasco."

"I hope you chose Hawk."

"You, too? Are you and Sherrie conspiring against me? What's wrong with Luke?"

"If I have to tell you, then you're more clueless than I thought. So, Sherrie thinks you belong with Hawk?"

"Her libido is always in overdrive, so yeah, she would pick Hawk. He's got the whole physical package, you know?"

"You're the only one who can decide who is best for you." Pausing, Asher put his arms on Cara's shoulders, looked at her intently, and said in a low voice, "You need to call Hawk and tell him what's going on with these Deadly Devils."

"Deadly Demons."

"The operative word here is *Deadly*. Your biker guy knows this world, and you don't. You need to let him in on this. This isn't small stuff, Cara."

"I know, but I'm out of the whole thing. I'm done with it. Once Viper sees that I'm finished with anything biker, he'll get bored and move on. The last thing I'd do is call Hawk."

"I hope you know what you're doing." Kneeling, Asher scooped up pages of documents.

"I do." The truth was she was in over her head, and she had some vicious outlaw biker fixated on her. Her instinct told her to lay low for a while. "I may take a few days off next week."

"You should do it now," Asher said.

"I can't. I have the Morrison trial starting tomorrow, remember?"

"With all this outlaw biker junk, who can remember anything?"

"Let's get through this week. I know this will all pass."

They worked most of the day putting all the files back together, and by the end of the afternoon, Cara was exhausted.

There was a chill in the late October air as Cara walked to her car. Wisps of smoke curled around the town like ghostly fingers while streams of it drifted from the chimneys of the houses dotting the hills around the town center. The thick scent of hickory permeated the town, and the streetlights lining Main Street cast eerie reflections in the dark, misty night.

As Cara approached her car, footsteps echoed behind her. She paused. The footsteps paused. She took a few steps. The footsteps took a few steps. As the hair lifted on the nape of her neck and arms, iciness weaved throughout her body, making her muscles tighten and her nerves jump. Stopping in the parking lot with a few steps to go until she reached her car, she froze while her heart pounded and her pulse raced. Behind her, a shuffled step scraped the asphalt. She sucked in her breath as she willed herself to move, but she couldn't. Small sparks reflected on the mist-coated pavement, then the sliver of a flickering flame danced against the wind. Lighter fluid invaded her nose, and she swore she felt the heat from the narrow flame. Cold sweat poured down her back as she swallowed hard, heaving her body forward in an unexpected burst of energy.

Clicking on her car's keyless entry and remote-start buttons at the same moment, her door unlocked and her engine sprang to life. With stinging eyes and pumping adrenaline, she leapt to her car door and flung it open. From the corner of her eye, she saw a shadowy figure stretching out a thin arm toward her. Yelling, she threw herself into the driver's seat, but before she could close the door, a strong hand yanked her hair and pulled her backward. With a force she didn't know she possessed, she shoved the hand away from her, slammed the car door, and floored the gas pedal.

As her car surged forward, a macabre scream bounced off her car windows, and a deep, creepy voice screamed, "Bitch!" Rubbing her aching scalp, she glanced in her rear view mirror and observed the silhouette of a tall man holding a cigarette in his hand, its tip glowing in the night. Shuddering and her teeth chattering, she exited the parking lot.

Driving around for a long time, she debated whether she should go home since she lived alone and had no doubt Viper knew her address. Not wanting to involve her parents, she dialed Eric's phone number.

"Hey, Eric, it's me."

"What's wrong?" he asked.

"Nothing. Why?"

"Come on, Cara, I can hear it in your voice. Something's wrong."

"Can I come over?"

"Sure, you don't need to ask."

Fifteen minutes later, Cara found herself curled up on Eric's couch in front of a spitting fire, sipping hot tea. Eric stared at her.

"Are you going to tell me what this is all about?" he asked.

Cara told Eric about her ransacked office and her scare earlier that night.

"Are you sure whoever was following you was part of this biker gang? I mean, you *do* have a lot of shady people for clients. Maybe it was one of them?"

"I don't think so. I know it was Viper. The way he grabbed my hair and his damn fingernail cutting me, it felt like the time he did that crap to me at the office. The guy following me was also tall and lanky, like Viper, and he had a cigarette. No, I'm sure it was that asshole." Cara shuddered as she thought of what could have happened if she hadn't made it to her car.

"I told you to drop all this fucking shit."

"I did. I'm not involved with any of it anymore. I just looked into it because the sister of one of the murder victims came and pleaded for me to help her find out what happened to her sister. I've moved on, really."

"Good. I'm sure this biker guy, what's his name, will lose interest in you," Eric reassured her.

"I don't know. I kind of doubt it. I don't know what to do. Asher told me I should tell Hawk."

"Fuck no! Why the hell would you go to *him*? You're done with his case, so move on. He's not of our class. He's scum."

"He's *not* scum. He's intelligent, and I'm pretty sure he'd know how to handle this thing with Viper. How did you know I was done with his case?"

"You told me."

"No, I *didn't* tell you. I'm positive I didn't tell you."

"Then I must have heard it from the other judges. You know, we *do* talk about each other's cases. Anyway, what difference does it make? The point is, you've got yourself mixed up with a bunch of trash, and the sooner you stay away from all of them the better you'll be. You should be concentrating on Luke. He's a real nice guy."

Cara rolled her eyes. "He doesn't do anything for me. I know you, my mom, and many others think Luke is the catch of the century, but he isn't. He isn't *that* nice, and he has ulterior motives, like making partner in my dad's law firm and placing his greedy hands on my dad's money. Ha, like *that's* going to happen."

Eric shook his head. "Okay, so Luke isn't for you. Find another guy in your class then, but don't degrade yourself by running into the arms of that fucking outlaw."

Cara opened her mouth, ready to argue, but she remembered Hawk's hurtful words. He told her more than once she was just another slut to him, and what they shared was just a good fuck. So why was she defending him to Eric? *He hurt me, and he hasn't even called to apologize or see how I am. Crap, why can't I stop thinking about him?*

At the charity ball, Cara perceived hints of hurt reflected in Hawk's eyes when she told him he wasn't in her league. Of course, she didn't mean it, but she was confused and angry at him because he'd made her fall for him while he used her and didn't give a damn about her. When he tossed her aside, she acted like she didn't care, but his rejection pained her more than she thought possible.

"Cara, are you zoning out on me?"

Eric's voice brought Cara back into the conversation. "Sorry, Eric, I guess I did tune you out. I'm tired, and it's been a long day." She yawned.

Eric smiled. "Take the guest room. Promise me one more thing, okay? No more bikers and no more investigation. Got it?"

Cara nodded. "Okay, but I would like to check the Nomads' conviction rates in this county."

"Cara, you stop it! Now. You're going to get yourself killed!"

Surprised, Cara said, "Lighten up, I was only kidding. I'm too busy at work for all this. I told you, I've moved on."

"Make sure you have. I know the Deadly Demons Nomads aren't too nice to people they want to get rid of. Now, go to bed. Tomorrow will be better, I'm sure."

Cara padded up the stairs and went into the guest room. After slipping out of her clothes, she laid her head on the down pillow, and in a matter of seconds, she was fast asleep.

A shadowy figure, obscured by gnarled-branched trees thick with autumn's colored leaves, stood outside Eric's house smoking a cigarette. When he saw the guest bedroom's light go out, he smiled. "Sleep well, slut. Real soon now, you're going to be a guest in *my* house, and I'm gonna fuck you in all your holes before I get rid of you." Then he stubbed out his cigarette with his steel-toed, black leather boot.

FOR THE NEXT several days, Cara was a bundle of nerves. She stopped coming in early to work, making sure Asher was there before she was, and she no longer stayed late, leaving when most of the people in the building did. Installing a burglar alarm at her house, deadbolts on all her doors, and extra locks on all her windows and sliding glass doors made her feel more secure.

"What's going on with you, Cara?" Asher asked.

"I'm just a bit rattled, you know, with the break-in and all."

"Has something happened besides the break-in here?"

"Don't freak out on me, okay? Someone has been following me. I think it's Viper. He almost got me a few days ago in the parking lot, but he ended up with a handful of my hair. Since then, I have a creepy feeling he's watching me. I can't prove it, but I know he is. I know he's trying to intimidate and scare me. Crap, it's working."

"This is insane, Cara. You have to go to the police," Asher said.

"You know they can't do anything. I can't prove it's him. I *know* it's him, but how can I prove it? I'm hoping he'll get tired of this and go away."

"Seriously? I don't think guys like him just 'go away.' I'm afraid he's going to escalate things, and I can't even imagine what he'll do."

"Me, too," Cara whispered.

"You need to tell Hawk. This goes beyond pride and playing games with him. You're in some serious trouble here, and you need to call him."

"No, I don't want him around. I'll call the police, I promise."

Cocking his head while he raised his eyebrows, Asher said, "You better do something, Cara, sooner rather than later."

"I will. I'm so beat and it's Friday. I think I'll take off now and go home. I need to think."

"Do you want me to spend the night with you?"

Cara, touched by his offer, patted his forearm. "Thanks. That means the world to me, but I can't pull you into my mess. I'll be fine. If I feel freaked, I'll go to Eric's again."

"You're taking next week off, right?"

"Yeah. I almost changed my mind, but after the week I've had, I need it. I may go to Denver and stay at my parents' condo. I need to get away from all this."

"Be safe and call in so I know you're fine," Asher said.

"I will, promise."

THE ENTIRE TIME she drove home, Cara kept her eyes glued to her rear view mirror. Looking around her front yard, she scoured the trees and bushes to make sure no one lurked anywhere. Once inside her house, she turned on her burglar alarm, double-locked the door, and checked all the windows.

Changing out of her work clothes into black jeans and a fitted berry t-shirt, she went into the living room and snuggled on her floral damask couch while leafing through one of the many cooking and travel magazines she had yet to read. She jumped when the doorbell rang, dropping her magazines. *Who the hell is at my door? I'm not expecting anyone.*

Panic seized her as loud pounding made her door rattle. Leaping to her feet, she tiptoed to the door and looked out the peephole. No one was there. Her body tingled in fear. More pounding, but that time she spied an arm encased in leather banging on the door. *Dammit! Will this nightmare never end?* Convinced Viper was outside, her body went into panic-mode: small, panting breaths, black spots in front of her eyes, the room spinning. *Don't pass out, Cara. That's not going to help.* Sweat beads formed along her hairline and the back of her neck as she stood frozen, not knowing what to do.

Bam, bam, bam! The door groaned under the assault. Daring herself to look out of the peephole again, she gasped. Standing in front of her door, making all the racket, was Hawk, and he looked madder than hell.

Relief flooded over her, and Cara unlocked the door and flung it open.

"What the hell are you doing here?" she hollered.

CHAPTER NINETEEN

"WHY THE FUCK didn't you tell me Viper came to your office?" he demanded.

Cara cursed Asher's big mouth under her breath. "I didn't think I had to report everything to you. This doesn't concern you, Hawk."

"The fuck it doesn't! That asshole comes to see my woman, and you don't think it concerns me? What the fuck's the matter with you?" Hawk glared at her. Cara had never seen him so enraged before, and she looked down for an escape.

"What the fuck do you have with him?"

"What do I *have* with *him*? Nothing. Do you think I'd *have* anything with that jerk?"

"He didn't come in for the hell of it. What the fuck's going on?" Hawk inhaled as he clenched his hands.

"Nothing's going on. This doesn't concern you, and you need to butt out."

Drawing her into his arms, he wrapped them around her waist and pressed her head against his heaving chest. "Of course this concerns me, babe. Everything *about* you concerns me. Whether you want to admit it now or later is up to you, but we are together. I have your back. Now, tell me what the fuck's going on."

They stood, silent as Hawk's breathing returned to normal. Cara relaxed in his embrace, enjoying how good it felt to have his arms protectively around her. Ever since Viper came to her office, she had been on pins and needles. Hawk holding her, his chest cradling her head, and his scent of motor oil and musk comforted her. A steady, calm pulse and heartbeat replaced the rapid hammering she had felt for the previous couple of weeks. Dealing with Viper and the fear of the unknown had been draining, but in Hawk's arms, peacefulness covered her like a blanket. She was ready to share the burden with him, ready to let go of her stubborn pride and let him in to help and protect her.

Grasping her chin, Hawk tilted her face toward his then bent down and softly kissed her lips. Cara gasped and wrapped her arms around his neck as she thrust her tongue into his mouth and pressed closer into him. For a moment, time stood still and all seemed right. They just stood there, the late-afternoon sun streaming in from the picture window, sharing an intimate moment.

Hawk pulled back and looked into Cara's eyes. "Tell me what's going on, babe."

She sighed as images of Viper hurting her pierced the magic of the moment. "Viper came to warn me to back off. I guess I was asking too many questions about a murder victim."

"What murder victim?"

Cara went on to explain how Nadyia's sister came to see her and prompted Cara to look into the rash of murdered women in Summit and Gilpin counties. She told him the CBI and local investigators believed a biker club was involved.

Hawk shook his head in disbelief. "Why didn't you tell me any of this?"

"I wasn't sure which biker club was involved. I didn't know who to trust."

"What? You think *I* could do this shit? *Really?* You know Banger, Jax, and some of the other brothers. How could you think any of us could be involved in hurting those women?"

"I didn't know any of you, at that point. After I came to know you and the Insurgents, I didn't think it involved you."

"Didn't involve me? How can you say that? You don't understand that you've caught the attention of a dangerous group of fuckers. Viper and the others are a Nomad charter of the Deadly Demons, and they don't play nice at all." Pausing, he said, "Even though they *are* all about violence and pain, I doubt they murdered those women."

"Why do you say that?"

"Because if they did, their bodies would've never be found. Believe me, none of us leaves evidence."

"How do you know that with such certainty? Have you ever…"

With an edge to his voice, Hawk replied, "Club business stays with the club. I know because I'm in a biker club. All bikers will tell you that. Anyway, that's not the point, is it?"

Cara shook her head. "The CBI is looking at the Deadly Demons for trafficking women. One of the murdered victims was smuggled, and I think she was being held by the Deadly Demons, the Nomad group."

"The Nomads have been trafficking for a couple of years now. They've been able to do it through this county and others. They're greasing the hands of the badges and some higher-up officials, no doubt."

Cara nodded. "I think that, as well. I also think the phony search at your house was a set-up to divert attention to the Insurgents and create suspicion."

"Yeah, that's what I think. This fuckin' sicko who's raping and torturing these girls is somehow able to let the illegal shit the Nomad Demons do pass without notice, as long as he's fed a steady supply of vulnerable girls."

"And I know some cops are involved, because one person couldn't do this alone."

"So, you've decided to play private eye? Do you know how stupid that is?"

"Yeah, I realize that now. I'm done with it, anyway. I called my friend at CBI and told him about Viper. I've moved on."

"The problem with that, babe, is Viper has targeted you. Believe me, he hasn't moved on." After a long pause, Hawk asked in a low voice, "Did he touch you?"

"Viper? No," she lied.

"Tell me the truth, Cara. Did he touch you?"

"I said no."

"I know this fucker, and I know you. Don't lie to me. I need you to trust me. Did he touch you?"

Wringing her hands, she whispered, "Yes."

Hawk slammed his fist on her coffee table. "That fuckin' asshole is dead! What did he do to you? Tell me. Now."

"He—he forced me to kiss him, and he bit my lip." Her voice trembled.

"Go on."

"It's over and done, I'm okay, and that's what's important," she said.

"Go on," he demanded.

She winced with the memories. "He pinched my nipples, threw me down, and kicked me in the leg." She exhaled, not realizing she had been holding her breath until then.

"Fuck that! I'll stomp on his balls. I'll kill his ass!" He looked at Cara, whose face was a mask of terror. His features softened as he reached out to her. "Come here, baby. I'm not mad at you. The thought of that fucker touching you enrages me. It also makes me worry for you. I know those assholes, and they won't stop. If anything ever happened to you, I'd lose it." He held her, stroking her hair and kissing the top of her head.

"I'm sorry. I wanted to tell you, but you told me you didn't care, so I didn't want to bother you." She sniffled into Hawk's chest, making him hold her tighter.

In a low voice, Hawk said, "I didn't mean what I said in your office or at the Boys Hope fundraiser. I was mad at you for acting like we just finished a fuckin' business conference after we spent some incredible time together. You're never a bother to me, and I want you in my life. I've missed you."

Cara looked up at Hawk, and he lowered his mouth and kissed the tears off her face. When his lips brushed hers, she tasted the saltiness before she kissed him back, pulling him into her. "I didn't think you felt that way about me."

"Yeah, babe. I feel that way about you big-time."

Excitement built inside Cara like bubbles in a glass of champagne, and her body stirred from her toes to her head. She couldn't believe she had been so stubborn and unyielding, never giving Hawk a chance. Cara had it in her mind that he just wanted sex and nothing more from a woman, not understanding he was protecting himself from being hurt the same way as she was.

"That's good, because I feel that way about you, too. I didn't mean what I said about you not being in my league. You hurt me, so I wanted to hurt you back. I've been missing you, too."

"Is that the truth?" he asked, looking deeply into her eyes.

Squeezing him tighter around his waist, Cara nodded.

"I guess I misjudged you. I didn't think you could see me beyond a fuck 'cause we were from different backgrounds," Hawk said.

"I see you as a person and not a list of credentials I have to check off. You do something to me no man ever has. I feel connected to you."

He tightened his arms around her. "More than you do with that pansy-ass suit?"

"Luke? I don't feel connected to him. I don't feel *anything* for him. You're the one who occupies my thoughts and dreams." Brushing her tongue over his lips, she kissed him. He groaned, tugging her closer.

Clearing his voice, Hawk said, "You're not safe here, babe. You must know that."

"I installed a burglar alarm and extra locks on the windows and doors."

"You can't think that's gonna keep the Nomads out. You gotta lay low for a few days or more, just until I can get a handle on this."

"Should I go to my parents'?"

"Not if you don't want to drag them into this chaos. You've got yourself into some dangerous shit. Sherrie isn't a good option, either. There's no sense in bringing her into this. You'll come to my place for tonight. I'll talk to Banger and the brothers tomorrow, and we'll go from there."

"Luckily, I took some time off next week. Let me grab a few things and we can go."

ORANGE AND PURPLE brushstrokes painted the sky over the mountaintops as Hawk pulled up to his house. His arms circled Cara's waist as he helped her off his Harley, and she smiled. "I loved the ride."

"Did you?"

"Yeah, the first time I rode on your bike it was scary, but exhilarating at the same time. It was fast. This time, I knew what to expect, so I just went with it. It was awesome." Cara's cheeks were red from the cold, and her long hair was tangled and messy.

"You're definitely my type of woman," Hawk chuckled.

When Cara entered Hawk's house, she was surprised how neat it was. The décor was western with southwestern undertones. The first floor was all dark hardwood floors, and a large stone fireplace was the focal point in the living room. A sectional couch in a Navajo pattern sat in front of the stone hearth, while sand and oil paintings depicting life on the range adorned the walls.

Hawk put down her overnight bag and went over to the fireplace, fussing around for several minutes until licks of yellow, red and blue jumped around wooden logs. He closed the fire screen and motioned for her to have a seat on the couch.

"Nice place. I love what you did with the furnishings. Did you have help with that?"

"No, I did it by myself."

"I'm impressed. If you ever want to do something else, interior decorating could be an option."

"Yeah, like that will ever happen."

"How long have you lived here?"

"I bought this place about four years ago. I stayed at the compound for around seven years. Don't get me wrong, I'm good with my brothers, but I felt an itch. I wanted to have something of my own, my own space, you know?

"I do. I like having my own place, too. Do you have some of the guys from your club over here?"

"Yeah, we have barbecues. It's cool."

"Do you have wild parties here, too?"

"What is it with you? Do you think I party all the time and fuck anyone with tits?"

"Yep, pretty much," Cara joked.

Grabbing her, Hawk threw her down on the couch, turned her over, and swatted her ass. "You need a good spanking for that one." He smacked her ass again lightly as he tickled her sides.

Cara was laughing so hard she was afraid she would pee her pants. She yelled, "I give up, stop!"

Hawk turned her onto her back and loomed above her. Staring into her green eyes, his lips sought hers. In response, Cara wrapped her arms around his neck, brought him closer to her, and kissed him. Propping himself on his elbow, he outlined her face with his finger, saying, "Except for Kylie, who's like my niece, you're the only woman who's been over here."

"Really? Why?"

"I never wanted to share this with any woman. You're also the first woman who's been on the back of my bike, so you see what you've done to me?"

Cara didn't know what to say. Hawk could have any woman he wanted, but he chose her to share his private world with. As her heart exploded, Cara pulled his head toward her, kissing him all over his face.

"You're so beautiful, Cara," he murmured.

Her insides flipped when he said her name.

"Do you want to change or something? You still have your jacket on," he said.

"I *would* like to freshen up. Where can I put my stuff?"

"Follow me."

She followed Hawk up the stairs to a huge master bedroom replete with fireplace, sitting area, and a large balcony. She walked out onto the balcony and marveled at the forest of Aspen trees and the gurgling creek running through Hawk's backyard. A deer, drinking in the creek, looked up at her.

"It's gorgeous out here. I could sit here for hours and watch the view. I can see why you love it."

He stood behind her, rubbing her shoulders. "The view is what sold me." He ran his hands down her back and hips, resting them on her ass. He cupped each cheek, breathing in her ear, "I've been missing your ass, babe."

Leaning back into him, his hardness pushed against her as her pussy clenched. They stood there for a while, him massaging her ass cheeks, her pressing into him, each of them watching the beauty of the sun as it sunk behind the snow-capped mountain peaks.

"Brrr, it's cold. Let's go inside," Cara said.

Hawk pulled her inside and showed her where she could hang her clothes. Then he emptied a dresser drawer for her to put her things in.

"I'll let you get settled." He kissed her. "Do you need anything?"

"Some towels. I'd like to take a warm shower."

Hawk came back with a couple of plush bath towels. He kissed her again then left the room.

Cara went into the spacious bathroom, and her bare feet thanked Hawk for installing heated floors. The shower was enormous and had more knobs and buttons than the cockpit of a jet. She didn't have a clue what to do. She also didn't feel like reading a manual to figure out how to start the damn thing.

She stepped into the shower and turned the larger knob, and a stream of warm water cascaded over her. Messing with a few more, jet sprays embraced her body. One of the sprays hit her in just the right spot, and the pulsating stream vibrated against her already-aroused pussy. *Shit, that feels good.* Making a mental note to install similar heads for her shower at home, she let the warm water play with her pussy as she cupped her breasts and fondled her nipples.

Cara, busy stroking her mound, jumped when she heard Hawk's hoarse voice. "Seeing you touch yourself is fuckin' hot." Kissing the back of her neck, he ran his hands down her body.

Cara spun around—she hadn't heard Hawk enter the shower. He stood in front of her, a sculpture of male eroticism. His muscular legs, chiseled chest, broad shoulders, and rigid cock took her breath away. *He should be bottled and sold as a female aphrodisiac.* Looking at him standing there in all of his glory, with his long, black hair loose around his shoulders and water drops trickling down his body, made Cara's pussy go crazy. She licked the water from his shoulders, biting him roughly then gently. Then she switched to his nipples and pulled his nipple ring roughly with her teeth while he moaned and shifted his weight. His cock grew larger, if that was possible.

Yearning for his cock in her mouth, Cara curled her fingers around his thick dick, pushing her hand up and down as she licked the smooth head. With a tightened grip, she ran her hand along his hard shaft as she looked up and saw Hawk's head thrown back, his chest moving rapidly.

He tugged her to him, kissing her deep and hot as his tongue thrust in and out of her mouth with urgency. She yanked her mouth away then moved in and kissed him again. They repeated their battle, but when she tried to retreat again, he said, "Not this time, baby. You're driving me fuckin' crazy with your teasing." Holding her face between his hands, his thumb stroking her bottom lip, he buried his tongue in her mouth, pushing it so deep Cara felt it tickle her throat.

When he let her breathe, she drew back and licked his lips then trailed her mouth to his earlobe, flicking his earrings with her tongue as he groaned. She said, "I want to suck you."

He crushed her with his arm. "Babe, I want to fuck your sweet pussy with my cock."

Lowering his lips to her nipples, he sucked loudly, and each time he pulled her hard nipples, she gasped as bolts of desire zigzagged through her body. Arching her back, she pushed her heated mound against Hawk's cock. Kneading her tits, Hawk grazed his teeth over her nipples while his tongue teased the tips. Burning ache consumed her wetness, and seeking relief, she placed her fingers on her swollen pussy lips and rubbed them. Taking her hand away, Hawk said, "That's all for me, baby."

"Touch me down there."

"Where?"

"Down there."

"Tell me what you want, babe. Spell it out for me in my language."

"Touch my pussy. It needs your touch. It needs release."

"All in good time, babe."

As he lavished kisses and bites on Cara's red, hard nipples, spasms of ecstasy coursed through her body and centered on her tense, wet heat. She was ready to come, and his expert tongue on her tits almost brought her to orgasm. As her heart pounded an erratic rhythm, her sex was on fire. Placing her hands on top of Hawk's head, she guided him downward as she held her breath in anticipation of his tongue on her clit.

He laughed. "Can't wait anymore, baby? Okay then, let me lick your tasty pussy."

Biting her lower lip, her body tensed as his dirty mouth's promises turned her on. *Fuck, he is so much man.* As he played with her tits then moved his mouth downward on her flesh, Cara squirmed and writhed.

Hawk dropped to his knees. Cara looked down at his corded back and saw a large tattoo which resembled the Insurgents' logo. As she scrutinized the tattoo, his mouth nearing her pussy distracted her. As she leaned against the tile wall, Hawk spread her legs and rubbed her swollen lips with his finger, causing Cara's sex to clench. Rubbing his finger up and down the side of her mound, he grazed her hard nub with his thumb. As she bent over, he pushed her legs farther apart and placed one on the shower bench while he put his mouth on her sweetness. His firm tongue stroked her clit while he eased two fingers inside her tight pussy, pushing them high inside her. He crooked his fingers and slid them over a rough, ridged area deep in her. He touched it, arousing her G-spot with static strokes while his tongue laved her hardened clit.

Cara's pussy felt different as slow waves of spasms began on the outside of it, but deep inside her, Hawk's fingers were making her pussy feel engorged and tight. The core of pleasure inside her was deep and intense, and as the spasms from her clit peaked, sensations from Hawk's fingers on her G-spot ignited an explosion like she had never experienced. She let out a blood-curdling yell. Her fingernails dug into Hawk's back as she thrashed against the wall, her knees weakened, and she slipped down to the shower floor. Seeking his lips, she kissed him passionately as her body reeled from the intensity of her orgasm.

Watching Hawk, she panted. "That was mind-blowing. What the hell did you do?"

Smiling seductively, he held her against him. Pushing him back on his ass, she rubbed her body against his, and her tender mound felt his stiff cock.

He got up and sat on the shower bench. "Come over here," he commanded.

Cara obliged, kneeling before him. She licked the head of his cock, tasting his briny pre-come, then she stroked his shaft as she licked her lips. Catching Hawk's eye, she moved her hand up and down his cock, and while she slowly grazed her mouth against his dick, her eyes locked with his. Cara tightly gripped Hawk's length at the base, and while she skimmed the tip of her tongue around the hard ridge under his head, Hawk closed his eyes and moaned.

Cara sucked the head while she licked his cock, like she was enjoying her favorite popsicle. Hawk's thighs tightened as she steadily tasted his dick. Opening her mouth wider, she took in more of his cock until she had his full length between her lips, moving up and down gently at first then faster and harder. Like a vise, she clamped tighter around his shaft as her fingernails dug into his hips. She looked into his smoldering eyes and stopped to give him a devilish grin. He grabbed her hair, yanking it hard before he guided her mouth back to his rigid cock.

Cara sucked tightly on his dick, and Hawk's groans of pleasure told her she was stroking all the right spots. Withdrawing his hardness from her mouth, she gently glided her teeth along his shaft, trailing it with her tongue. Lightly scratching his swollen balls with her nails, she delicately took one into her mouth, rolling it around and licking it with her tongue. Hawk moaned, shifted his position, and pulled her hair harder. As she lavished feathery kisses on his other ball, she moved her hand up and down his cock.

"Fuck, babe, you're killing me. My cock feels good in your mouth, and what you're doing to my balls... fuck, just fuck," he rasped.

Cara held his balls in her hand as she put his cock back in her mouth. She bobbed up and down, her sucking and groaning reverberating in the shower. Hawk placed his hands on her shoulders. "I want to fuck you. I want my cock in your tight pussy."

Hawk stood up, jumped out of the shower, rifled through one of his bathroom drawers, and came back with a condom. After he slipped it on, he drew Cara into him for a feverish kiss. Then Hawk swung her around and had her bend over the shower bench.

"I can't wait to get my cock in your hot pussy, babe. You ready for me?"

"Yes, I'm dying to feel you inside me."

Hawk rubbed his cock between Cara's ass cheeks while he massaged her pussy with his hand, her ass wiggling as his dick played between her rounded globes. He slid his hardness down to her heat, coating it with her wetness before easing it into her tightness. Thrusting slowly at first, he picked up his pace as she squealed in delight.

"Faster. I want it hard and fast," she said.

"I'll fuck you rough, baby, rougher than you've ever had it. I love fuckin' your pussy."

Hawk slammed into her over and over, his cock slippery from her wetness, his balls slapping against her thighs. Cara ground her ass into Hawk's cock each time it came in; her tits bounced, her ass wiggled, and her pussy was on fire. From Hawk's thickness in her and his grunts, she knew he was ready to explode. The heat in her rose steadily, and the contractions started slow and built to a peak as wave after wave of bliss sent her over the edge again and again. "Hawk!"

"Fuck. You're squeezing the shit outta my cock as you come. Fuck, baby." Throwing his head forward, he kissed the back of her neck, cupping her breast as his legs tightened and he exploded in her. With each thrust, he grunted as he expended the last of his come inside her. Withdrawing, he pulled her into his arms, and they held each other while the warm water bathed them.

For the first time, Cara felt complete with a man, and she adored this badass with the piercings and tattoos. She loved the way he looked in his leather and denim, the way he walked, and the way he rode his Harley. Denying her feelings for too long, she let her reason get the best of her, but the truth was she couldn't get enough of him. She decided to let herself go on this wild passionate ride. Protected in his powerful embrace, for the first time since Viper came to her office, she knew everything would be all right.

CHAPTER TWENTY

THE NEXT MORNING, Cara woke up to the tantalizing aroma of fresh coffee and sizzling bacon. When she reached out beside her, Hawk's place was empty. She snuggled deeper under the down comforter, but her stomach growled. Reluctantly, she left the comfort of the bed and went to wash up before going downstairs.

Cara watched Hawk as he stood by the stove, turning the bacon in an iron skillet. He had on gray sweat pants and was bare from the waist up. In the sunlight, Cara saw the large back tattoo of the Insurgents' emblem—an ink replica of the patch he wore on the back of his leather jacket. She remembered reading that a member's back piece represented his undying loyalty to the club. It also told other biker clubs that a member had been in the motorcycle club for ten years or more. On the back of his right arm, she noticed the initials "IFFI" (Insurgents Forever, Forever Insurgents) in Germanic script. His back and arm muscles rippled with each movement he made. *He is magnificent.*

She padded over to him and looped her arms around his waist, kissing his upper shoulder. "Morning," she breathed into his back.

Hawk turned his head toward her, smiling as he kissed the top of her head, saying, "You smell wonderful."

"You, too," she said, breathing in his fresh-soap scent. Standing on her tiptoes, she kissed him on his lips.

He kissed her back while his tongue demanded possession of her mouth, and she gladly parted her lips. Swinging around, he crushed her against him as he kissed her while she grabbed his ass with her hands, digging her fingernails into his firm flesh.

"Fuck, I can't keep my hands off you," he growled. He cupped her tits and brought his mouth down her neck, kissing, biting, and sucking urgently.

"No, Hawk, not there. I can't have it showing on my neck. I can't go to court like that."

"I want every man to see my mark so they know they better fuckin' stay away from you."

"Please, Hawk. I'll have to wear scarves for a week. I hate wearing anything around my neck," she murmured as her body tingled.

"Too late, babe. You're wearing my mark."

"You should do it where no one but me can see."

"I can do that," he said as he tugged her t-shirt up over her breasts. Bringing his mouth down over her tits, he sucked as she swayed and moaned. As he marked her tits, he pinched her nipples between his fingers. "Fuck, your tits are so soft. I love the way they feel in my hands."

Cara's panties were completely wet and she drew Hawk closer to her, making his hard cock press into her stomach as she moved her body sideways then up and down. Hawk breathed in through his clenched teeth. "Take your pants off," he ordered.

Cara shrugged out of her black yoga pants and bikini panties before he picked her up and placed her on the counter. She shivered as her bare ass touched the granite countertop. Hawk stood in front of her, and she wrapped her long legs around his tapered waist as he licked her nipples with his tongue while he rubbed her pussy up and down his cock. Touching her sensitive nub, he rolled it between his fingers. She pulled out his hair tie and ran her fingers through his long, silky hair.

When his fingers went into her pussy, she cried out while he pushed her back so she was resting on her elbows, giving him greater access to her throbbing mound. Goosebumps pebbled her skin as his soft tongue traced her body down past her ribcage, her stomach, and ultimately to her engorged pussy. He licked her slick lips, cooling some of the heat. Her mound clenched wildly as he licked, nipped, and squeezed it, then his tongue entered her tightness and fucked her as he rubbed her hard nub.

"Hawk, it feels so good," Cara said as the tightness turned into blasts of relief over and over again as her pussy exploded. Then, in the midst of this explosion, Hawk's hard cock slammed into her. Her pussy encased his throbbing dick like a glove, and he grunted as he thrust in and out of her while she scratched his back with her nails, drawing him closer to her.

"Fuck, I can't get enough of your pussy. It's perfect for my cock. Fuck," he grunted between pants.

She screamed out at the same time he yelled, "Cara!" They both climaxed, melding into each other as one.

"Fuck! This is one of the most intense fuckings I've ever had," Hawk panted.

Cara, reeling from multiple orgasms, stroked Hawk's hair. "You know how to please me." *I'm hopelessly hooked.* Realizing they hadn't used a condom, Cara's stomach lurched. She knew she was clean, and she had started on the pill a few weeks before, just in case. Covering her mouth with her hand, she said, "Oh, shit."

As if reading her mind, Hawk said, "I know, babe, we did this one bare. I just wanted to fuck you so bad that I didn't think."

"I'm on the pill, and I'm clean. You?"

"I'm clean, but I'm not on the pill," he joked.

She slapped his shoulder, laughing.

"Damn, the bacon is burnt to a crisp. I forgot about it," Hawk said as he ran over to the stove to turn it off.

"I thought it was our lovemaking that was causing all the smoke." She winked.

Staring at her for a few seconds, he cleared his throat and said, "Yeah, our *fuckin'* is damn hot."

He opened all the doors to air out the room before the smoke alarm went off, placed another frying pan on the burner, then looked at her with a dimpled smile, saying, "Let's try this again."

While they ate their bacon and eggs, Hawk talked Cara into staying with him for the next week until he got things under control.

"You should be okay here. No one knows you're here, right?"

"Only my cousin Eric and Asher. I didn't tell Sherrie because I don't want her to be involved."

"I told you not to tell anyone."

"Eric is cool, and so is Asher. I trust them."

"In a situation like this, you can't trust anyone. You shouldn't have told them where you were. Even if you trust them, you've opened them up to danger."

"You're right, I didn't think."

"You gotta come with me to the clubhouse. You'll be safe there."

"What if I don't want to go? My only experience with your club-house was that night with all those guys. I don't want to go."

"That was different. You were alone. The members thought you were a hoodrat—a woman open for sex with any brother, any time. It'll be different now 'cause you're with me. You have to remember to stay with me at all times, especially during a party. You can't wander around by yourself. You got that?"

"It's ridiculous that I can't be safe if I go to the bathroom by myself. What kind of club do you belong to?"

"It's just the way it is, babe. Don't fuckin' argue with me about this. You need to stick by me, if you want to be safe. You're not claimed and you're not wearing my patch, so you need to be smart and stick to me, got it?"

"What do you mean by claimed and the patch thing?"

"When a woman is claimed and wears the brother's patch, she be-longs to him. All Insurgents members and other biker clubs respect the woman 'cause they know she belongs to a patched member."

"'Belongs'? What does the patch say?"

"It says 'Property of' and the member's name."

"'Property'? You look at the woman as your *property?*" she asked, her voice rising.

"It's not what you think. You citizens don't get it. It's like the woman belongs to the member and the member belongs to the woman. It's a respect thing. It's like wearing a ring or a letterman's sweater. In our world, the women wear the patch."

Cara shook her head. "I don't know, it sounds sexist to me."

"Would you wear a ring if a guy gave it to you as something serious?"

"Yeah, I would."

"It's the same thing, but instead of a ring, the woman gets the patch. It means respect and love, you know?"

"I guess."

"Anyway, you gotta stick with me because you don't have a patch. A sexy woman like you can get into all kinds of trouble if you wander off without me. Tonight, the chapters in other parts of Colorado are coming for a party, so it'll be wild. You *have* to stay with me, no fuckin' arguments." Hawk's eyebrows knit together as he looked at Cara.

With pursed lips, she nodded.

"Let's go back to your place so you can pack some things. You can drive and I'll follow you. I know you know where the clubhouse is."

She was scared to go to the clubhouse, but she was also curious as hell to see what went on behind those brick walls. She would heed Hawk's words and stick to him at all times. A touch of what those guys were capable of was enough to know she didn't want to end up on the floor of the clubhouse servicing a bunch of rough, drunk bikers. She shuddered. Five months back, she never would have dreamt that she'd be hanging out at the Insurgents' clubhouse with a sexy, rough biker as her lover. *Life is strange.*

"IT COULD BE a real problem having her here while she's not claimed. Besides, we got members coming from several chapters, and they don't know who the hell she is," Banger said as the other members nodded in agreement.

"She'll be with me at all times, and I'll make sure of that. Believe me, everyone's going to know Cara's with me tonight," Hawk countered.

"I don't want trouble over pussy. Shit, these bitches ain't worth it," Banger stated.

"Why don't you just patch the bitch and be done with it?" Ruben asked.

"Youse been thinkin' with your cock for the last few months. It'd be better to claim her as your ol' lady so youse can get back to being a full member again," Billy snorted.

Hawk glared at Billy. "Fuck off."

"Billy's speaking the truth," Axe said. The other members around the board table nodded.

"Fuck all of you," Hawk snarled.

"Gotta admit that you haven't been 'round here much, and when you do come, you stay for a short time and take off. Your mind's on your cock up her pussy too much. That's shit, and you know it. I gotta have you focused," Banger said.

Hawk knew they were right. Ever since he'd first seen Cara at Rusty's, he couldn't get her out of his mind—her warm eyes, vanilla-scented hair, soft tits, and sweet pussy mixed him up too much. Thinking if he fucked her hard a time or two, he'd get her out of his system, but he realized he just wanted her more. He was surprised at the way Cara made him feel, and deep-down stirrings of feelings he thought had died decades ago gnawed at him. *Fuck.* He didn't know what the hell was the matter with him; all he knew was Cara made him feel good, and he wanted to spend time with her.

The brothers were right in that he was negligent with the club; he did the minimum since all of his thoughts were on Cara, which was lame as shit. He'd be the first one knocking a member for being bitch-whipped if the brother behaved like he had been acting. But what could he say? He'd never felt like this with any woman he fucked, and he had fucked a ton of bitches.

All eyes were on Hawk, who cleared his throat and said, "I know I've been fuckin' with Cara for a while now. I'm not going to say I didn't have club business at the forefront, but I *have* been preoccupied."

Banger, satisfied that Hawk owned up to his indiscretion, said, "Your bitch is your responsibility. If someone messes with her, it's on you. I don't want no shit over a bitch, but she is *your* bitch, and no brother in this membership will bother her. You better damn well make your intentions clear with the charter members tonight. Now, let's move on to the Deadly Demons Nomads. What the fuck are we gonna do about those pieces of shit?"

"I'm going to kill Viper for touching my woman. No one does that shit without a payback," Hawk seethed.

"Do we want to start a war over a bitch?" asked Axe.

Hawk had to hold himself steady, because he wanted to leap out of his chair, pounce on Axe, and beat the shit out of him for being so stupid and disrespectful.

"It's not just about Hawk's woman—it's also about us. There's evidence these motherfuckers were framing us for all kinds of shit, including the murders of those women. That can't fuckin' be ignored," Jax said, pounding the table with his fists.

"They also sent in a woman to Dream House. She was one of the strippers, but she was stealing from us and giving the money to the Nomads. I found out she's one of the motherfucker's old lady," Hawk said.

"I made sure she'd never steal again, the fuckin' whore. Those assholes have crossed the line!" Jax fumed.

The members murmured their agreement. Banger said, "Those motherfuckers messed with us—game on. We'll stomp their fuckin' brains out, no hesitation, not a fuckin' blink of an eye. We *will* fuck them up. Let's bring it to all the members tomorrow evening. We'll call an emergency church. If everyone agrees, then we're gonna take care of business."

"Yeah, we'll show those assholes not to fuck with Insurgents," Jax cried out.

The rest of the members were chanting, "Insurgents forever! Forever

Insurgents!"

Hawk's chest swelled with pride. This was his family, and they'd do anything for each other. They were Insurgents three hundred sixty-five days a year, twenty-four hours a day, seven days a week. They didn't let anyone fuck with them, and they always had each other's back. He'd make sure to tell Viper he'd fucked around with the wrong club as he stomped on the fucker's balls.

CHAPTER TWENTY-ONE

THE MOTORCYCLES STARTED arriving around three o'clock that afternoon. The old ladies were busy in the kitchen making mountains of baby back ribs, boiled corn, coleslaw, and mashed potatoes, knowing the members would be hungry after riding from various parts of the state. The chapters came from Cortez, Niwot, Fruita, Erie, and Silverton. There was a buzz of excitement in the air, and the brothers were ready to get crazy.

Cara watched out the window in Hawk's room as the members began turning into the compound in droves. The leather-clad men were black ink streaks on their Harleys, and in the afternoon sun, the motorcycles' chrome shone like the gleam of a sword. The engines' rumble made the window vibrate. Cara had never seen anything like it.

Hawk came into the room and walked toward Cara. Putting his arms around her, he drew her against him, nuzzled her ear, and said, "Are you feeling the fever in the air?"

"Yeah, I am. I've never seen this many motorcycles, or men in leather, in my life."

"Wait 'til you go to a rally, like Sturgis. It's fuckin' awesome." He licked her earlobe.

"Are women invited to the party? I don't see any women, only men on their Harleys."

"Old ladies don't come to these parties. They're making the food, but they'll leave after everything is prepared. The women who come to these parties are lookin' for a good time: booze, fucking, drugs. That's the way the brothers like it."

"Is that what you like?"

"I did. I'm not gonna lie to you, baby, I loved goin' to club parties. I fucked and drank hard for years. I don't drink as much as I used to, and I don't want to fuck anyone but you." He kissed her neck. "Why would I go lookin' for pussy when I've got the sweetest one of all?"

Cara smiled, but she couldn't help but wonder if any of the women Hawk had been with would be at the party that night. Of course, she wanted to ask him, but she didn't want to sound like a jealous shrew. She knew he had a past, and she knew the reputation of bikers, so she couldn't be surprised he had been with so many women. Even knowing all that, she still felt a stab of jealousy. How could she compete with these crazy, wild women who threw caution to the wind and embraced life with abandonment? Were they better at pleasing Hawk than she was? *I'm being dumb. Hawk is with me. He could be with any of these women tonight, but he's with me. I have to quit obsessing about his past sexual life.*

"What are you thinkin' about?" he asked as he squeezed her.

"That I'm hungry."

He laughed. "Food will be ready at six o'clock. I'll come up and get you."

"Are you leaving me?"

"Babe, I'm the vice president, and I have to greet the out-of-towners. Why don't you chill, and I'll be back in a couple of hours, okay?" He turned her head and kissed her deeply, tasting of whiskey.

"Go on, do your duties. I'm going to take a shower and get ready," she said.

He kissed her again. Before closing the door, he warned her, "Make sure to lock it. I have a key, so don't open it to anyone."

She blew him a kiss, and he was gone.

Cara locked the door and went back to the window. Most of the guys were inside the clubhouse, but a few groups of men stood around talking and drinking. She noticed a few women come toward the gates. The women were scantily dressed in very short shorts and skirts, their ass cheeks noticeable, and way-too-tight tops—or even no tops, just stickers over their nipples. Cara swallowed hard; she was going to stand out like a sore thumb. These were the women Hawk screwed. *He must like women who dress like that. I wonder why he came after me?* She stared out the window, transfixed, as more and more women came to the compound. *I've got to stop doing this. This is crazy.*

She made herself leave the window and take a shower, wondering what Hawk was doing while she was alone up there. Figuring a lot of the women downstairs would make a beeline for him, would he fuck one of them? He could do it, and she'd never know. Didn't these bikers think it was okay to fuck if they felt like it? For that matter, didn't *most* men think that?

Trevor's infidelity assaulted her thoughts. *Stop it, Cara, Hawk isn't Trevor. You have to start trusting a man sometime.*

Finished with her shower, she went back to the window and watched the party unfold as she towel-dried her hair.

"BORN TO RAISE Hell" by Motörhead vibrated the overhead speakers as more members came into the clubhouse. Many brothers hadn't seen each other since the previous year's Sturgis rally. They milled around with beers in hand, or engaged in some serious conversation about engines and chrome; motorcycle talk was number one, more important than booze or women.

The regular club whores, Lola and Brandi, walked around the throng of men, giving them a sneak peek of their assets. Lola hated to compete with the hoodrats who came to party on the weekends; to her, the hoodrats were cop-outs—they weren't committed to the biker-club life at all. She was available to the members all the time and was part of the club's fabric, seeing herself as a necessary spoke in the club's wheel that kept turning, and it pissed her off that the weekend sluts came to the club acting like they owned it. Just the week before, Lola had to show one of the bitches who was boss. The brothers loved watching Lola and the slut punch it out, but for Lola, it was a matter of protecting her turf.

There was no way in hell she was going to let one of those weekend whores act like they were in charge. She kicked the skinny slut's ass good, and she noticed the brothers treated her with a bit more respect for holding her own.

Lola scanned the room for Hawk; she wanted to fuck him for sure during the party. In the last few months, she hadn't seen him around and she missed his presence, having a soft spot for him ever since he'd fucked her. Spotting him near the bar, she walked over to him and drew close to his ear, whispering in a sultry voice, "Hiya, handsome. It's been a while since I've seen you 'round here."

Looking sideways, Hawk's eyes rested on her highly made-up face. Pressing into his side, she squeezed his bicep and rubbed her boobs, hanging out of her skimpy neon green top, against his tattooed arm.

Frowning, Hawk jerked his arm away and said, "I've been busy."

"Are you ready to have some fun tonight, darling?"

"It's good to see members I haven't seen for a while."

"What about you 'n me goin' someplace to fuck?"

"Not gonna happen, but there are plenty of brothers who'd love to fuck your pussy."

"The one I want tonight is you. I've reserved myself for you only."

"I'm not available," Hawk stated, turning his back on her.

Lola blinked several times then said, "What do you mean, 'not available'?"

"Not that it's any of your fuckin' business, but I'm with a woman now. Conversation over. Move on."

"What woman? You got yourself an old lady?" Surprise and disappointment laced her voice.

"I said, move on." Waving his arm, Hawk yelled out to a heavy, bearded man who had an arm around a slut and a bottle of whiskey in his hand. "Bones, when the fuck did you get here?"

The bearded man made his way to Hawk, embraced him, and said, "It's been too long, brother. I knew you were here when I saw your fuckin' shit-kickin' Harley. You customized the hell outta it."

"Fuck, yeah." With Hawk's arm around Bones, he said, "Let me get you a beer." The two men walked toward the bar, arms clasped around each other's shoulder.

Lola stared dumbfounded at Hawk's retreating figure. *Hawk got himself an old lady? What the fuck?* Lola knew a few of the men had old ladies and some of them had girlfriends, but it didn't stop them from fucking her, Brandi, or the mamas. Shit, she'd have to find out more about this skank who had a hold of Hawk's cock.

A tall member from Cortez came over to Lola, pulled her into him, and said, "I need some fuckin', whore." Putting her arms around him, she kissed him on the lips and yanked him toward the hallway to secure one of the small rooms. She would fuck him, but she knew she'd be wishing it was Hawk's cock inside her.

CARA HEARD THE lock turn before Hawk came into the room. His gaze roamed over her body, and she noticed desire building in his eyes as she stood in the middle of the room wearing a short, black flounce skirt, a black and red striped crop top, and short, black boots with silver buckles and studs.

Hawk whistled between his teeth. "You look tempting. Get over here."

A flush crept across her cheeks as she took a few steps toward Hawk. Impatient, he stretched his arms and grabbed her, dragging her into him. He skimmed his hands over her curvy body then reached under her skirt and touched her bare ass cheek.

"You're killing me, babe. I gotta kiss that sweet ass of yours." Spinning her around, Hawk plopped Cara face down on the bed then lifted up her skirt, revealing two firmly shaped globes separated by her thong's black string. As he leaned over her, a sharp zip rang in her ears as he opened his jeans. Reaching backward to clutch his cock, Hawk grasped her arms, raised them over her head, and held them in place.

"Don't move your arms, got that?" he commanded.

"Yes," she breathed.

Twisting her head over her shoulder, she saw Hawk hold his stiff cock in his hands then rub his pre-come over her firm, white buttocks while he slid his hardness up and down her crack. Squirming under his touch, she reached backward to touch him.

"I'm not going to tell you again. Keep your arms over your head."

"I want to touch you," she protested.

"You're not fuckin' listening to me. Hands. Over. Your. Head."

As he bent down and kissed her ass cheeks, his panting filled her ears. Not being able to stand it, her arm stretched behind her as she searched for his hardness while his mouth kissed, licked and bit her round globes. When her fingers brushed against his dick, her grasping hand squeezed his shaft, but before she enjoyed the feel of him, Hawk gripped her wrists and secured her arms over her head.

"You don't take directions too well, do you? I'm going to have to teach you a lesson."

Before Cara could answer, Hawk lightly spanked one of her ass cheeks. Cara gasped. He slapped her again, that time a little harder, making her moan while she clenched her ass. As he smacked her even harder, he pressed against her and, with his hot breath on her neck, he said, "Do you like that, baby?" She whimpered. "I'm asking if you like it."

"Yes, I do," she panted.

"Your ass is so fuckin' sweet, babe." Hawk planted another slap on her ass; her butt cheeks were red from his hands. Licking her ass, his tongue cooled the stings from the spanking while Cara arched her back to push her butt closer to Hawk's demanding mouth. He chuckled under his breath. "You're a hungry one, aren't you, baby?" She pushed her ass further into his face.

"I bet if I take my finger and stroke your pussy, it would be sopping. Am I right, babe?" he asked between licks and kisses on her ass.

She moaned her answer.

Hawk ran his fingers between her engorged lips. "Yep, that's what I thought, soaking and aching for my touch." He roughly squeezed her heat while Cara squealed in delight. As she was on her knees, she lifted her ass higher and spread her legs wider, causing her drenched mound to hang down, her arms still above her head. Taking his index finger, Hawk flicked her clit over and over, and it felt fucking awesome: the gravity pulled her clit downward and Hawk's teasing ignited her. Pressure built up in her core and heightened her arousal. *Damn, I want him slamming into my pussy.*

"Fuck me, Hawk. Push inside me."

"Fuck, you're impatient. I want to taste your luscious pussy before I jam my cock into it."

Flipping on his back, Hawk scooted under Cara's dripping slit, and with his hands on her hips, eased her down until her sex was right above his mouth. Replacing his finger with his erect tongue, he stroked her nub. Cara threw her head back, her guttural moans filled the room. As he licked her pussy, he entered her with his finger and twirled it around inside her tight heat. Pulling out, he took his saturated digit and rubbed it around her anus. With slow, gentle movements, his finger entered her ass while his other fingers dove into her pussy.

Pleasure darted to every nerve in her body as Hawk fucked her ass with one hand and her pussy with another while his tongue swirled on her clit, making her pleasure rise to a fevered pitch. Her first spasm sucked his fingers deep inside her, and she cried out as one ripple after another rolled from her hot pussy, to her stomach, and to her brain. As her insides clasped around his finger, he withdrew it, then, standing behind her, he entered her with his cock, her tightness covering him like a sheath.

"You're mine, babe. Your pussy is mine, and only *my* cock will fuck you. It's all mine," Hawk rasped as he banged her hard.

Careful not to put too much pressure on her sensitive clit, Hawk gently massaged her. As his cock stiffened, he grunted and released his seed inside her. Cara's pussy spiked again as the warmth from his come dripped down her thighs.

Lying on top of her, his breathing labored, Hawk kissed her damp neck and whispered against her skin. "Fuck, babe that was awesome."

She sighed. *Fuck, yeah.*

As he rolled off her, he drew her into his arms, and they cuddled while listening to each other's breathing. Tenderness shone in Hawk's eyes when Cara looked up at him and met his gaze.

"I'm happy," she said.

Kissing her forehead, Hawk stroked her cheek as she nuzzled closer, happy to be back with him.

THE BLUE SKY disappeared into black velvet as the harvest moon illuminated the small, quiet room. For the past hour, Hawk had cradled Cara in his arms, but then a loud growl punctured the serenity. Hawk laughed. "You want to get somethin' to eat, babe?"

Nodding, Cara said, "I'm starving. I haven't eaten since this morning. Let me freshen up. I'll just be a sec."

As she brushed her hair, Hawk watched her. "What're you thinking about?" she asked.

"The way your hair feels on my body. It's like silk." He stood up and put on his jeans. After combing out his hair, he pulled it back into a ponytail then slipped on his tight black t-shirt and cut. Finished with the final touches of her makeup, Cara smiled at Hawk. "Ready?"

"You're beautiful, and you look classy. The bitches around here look all painted-up, but you look natural. You do something to me, babe," he said, affection warming his eyes.

As his words embraced her, Cara's cheeks flushed and shivers coursed through her body.

"Before we go down, I gotta tell you what to expect. This isn't the type of party you're used to. You'll see people fucking right in the open, and as the night goes on, the members and the sluts get drunker and all kinds of shit happens: two whores fucking a guy, two guys fucking a slut, a slut fucking five or six brothers, group sex, even pulling a train, although that doesn't happen very often anymore."

"What's pulling a train?"

"A slut fucks all the brothers, any way they like it, one right after another."

"Oh, that sounds bad."

"It's what the slut wants and it's her choice. We don't do the gang-rape shit that some clubs do. Every sex act is voluntary, you know?"

"If that's true, then why are you worried about me wandering off by myself?"

"Because the brothers will think you wanna fuck. When a slut's here, she's sayin' she's here to fuck whoever wants to fuck her. That's what she wants and why she came here tonight. You're here 'cause you're with me—it's different. Got it?"

"I wish you'd stop calling the women 'sluts.' They're women."

"Baby, you don't get our world. Women like you are women, old ladies are women, the ones who come here and fuck whoever are sluts. They even call themselves sluts and whores. Now, are you sure you want to go to the party? I can bring the food up to you if you'd rather stay in the room. It's up to you."

"No, I'll go. I'll just hang onto you."

"Damn straight. Don't let go of me. I don't want to fight one of my brothers tonight."

"Fight someone? Why would you do that?"

"If someone touches you or says something disrespectful, I'll punch his fuckin' face in. I won't let anyone talk shit to my woman. Sticking with me, kissing me, and holding me shows everyone you're my woman. Are you good to go?"

"Yeah."

As they stepped in the hallway, a cacophony of noise enveloped them: laughter, squeals, moans, punching hard rock music. Cara held Hawk's hand as they descended the stairs to the insanity below.

CHAPTER TWENTY-TWO

H AWK LED CARA through a crowd of people as they made their way to the yard to get some food. The smell of tobacco and weed hung heavy in the air, and the dense smoke made it difficult for Cara to see in front of her. Hawk guided her to the long buffet table where heaps of baby back ribs filled aluminum tins. Cara licked her lips while the ribs' hickory scent teased her stomach. She was ravenous.

After filling their plates, she and Hawk found a spot at one of the many long wooden tables set up outside. Biting into the succulent ribs, Cara savored the robust barbecue sauce and finished her half-rack of ribs in no time. As she came back to the table with her second helping of food, several of the members at the table slid their eyes over her. Slipping in next to Hawk, she ignored them. A couple of the members stared at her breasts, making Hawk stiffen beside her. Cara didn't want any problems so she wiped her mouth, pulled off some meat from one of her barbecued ribs, turned to Hawk, and said, "Open up, honey."

When he opened his mouth, she put the meat along with her finger into his mouth. Closing his mouth over the digit, he licked the sauce off before she moved her finger in and out of his mouth. Leaning in close to him, she replaced her finger with her lips and kissed him deeply in front of the brothers. Hawk pulled her closer, kissed her, and patted her thigh. After seeing the exchange between Hawk and Cara, the members averted their glances away from her. Cara smiled. *Mission accomplished.*

While they were eating, Jax came over. "Good to see you guys. I didn't think you were coming. How do you like our party, Cara?"

"The food is good. The jury is still out on the party. I'll let you know later."

"Fair enough."

"Jax, can you stay here with Cara while I go and get some drinks?" Hawk asked.

"Sure."

Hawk came back with a bottle of vodka, a bottle of tonic, a glass of limes, and a twelve-pack of Coors. Jax caught the beer Hawk threw his way, and while Jax and Hawk talked, Cara surveyed the scene around her. Some men staggered around the yard with their arms around women, who had very little on, while other men laughed, talked, and smoked in groups. Several drunk women swayed to the music of AC/DC as it rocked the club, and in the darker corners of the yard, women gave blowjobs to the members. *Hawk was right. I've never been to a party like this. It makes the frat parties I went to during college seem tame.*

Bending down, Hawk pulled Cara up and pressed her close to him. He lowered his head, then kissed her, plunging his tongue halfway down her throat as he groped her ass. Startled, she pushed back. "What the fuck? Why are you pulling away from me?" he demanded, his eyes flashing.

"I didn't mean to. You took me by surprise, that's all," she said.

"Fuck, woman, I don't want you pulling away from me. I want to fuckin' kiss you, so kiss me now."

Pissed at his brusqueness, Cara stiffened, then kissed him while looking behind his shoulder at a group of members who watched them and a peroxide blonde who glared at her. The blonde had one of her tits out of her top while a member played with it. *This is surreal.*

Hawk hugged her tightly as several of the brothers cheered and clapped. *This must be some barbarian rite of passage in the biker world.* Deciding to humor Hawk because this seemed to be important to him in front of his club, she squeezed him back, but she hoped, for his sake, he didn't take it too far and unleash her anger.

"How are ya doin', little lady?" Banger said to Cara.

Cara smiled warmly at Banger. She liked this weathered biker who had a good heart. "Not too bad. How goes it with you?"

"Fuck, I'm still here, ain't I?" He and Cara laughed.

"The food was very good, especially the ribs."

"The old ladies made the grub. Speaking of that, I don't know if Hawk mentioned it, but I'd like you to teach Kylie how to make your spaghetti sauce and give her some basic tips on cooking. Shit, that girl don't know nothin' when it comes to the kitchen."

"Hawk did mention it, and I'd be pleased to help her out. Maybe she can come by sometime this coming week? I'll be hanging here for a few days."

"I'll tell Hawk when, and he can set it up with you," Banger replied. He jerked his head as a twenty-something woman walked by dressed in a tie-dye thong, bikini top and cowboy boots. Banger's blue eyes lit up like a blowtorch as he licked his lips.

Hawk slapped the president on his back. "Go for it, if you think you got the stamina."

"I'll show you what kind of stamina your fuckin' prez has." Banger took off after the young woman.

Cara watched as Banger came behind the woman and grabbed her by the ass. Squealing in delight, she spun around and crushed Banger's head between her tits. Cara, feeling like a voyeur, turned away.

"I have to go to the bathroom," she said to Hawk. "Where do I go?"

"Follow me." He held her hand and led her through the labyrinth of men and women.

On the way to the bathroom, a wall of people stopped them in the hallway. A couple of guys came up to Hawk and high-fived him.

"Been a long time, brother," one of the members said to Hawk.

"Rollo, I missed you at Sturgis this year," Hawk replied as he patted the portly man on his back.

As Hawk and the two members talked, Cara noticed there were a bunch of guys crowding a doorway to one of the rooms off the hallway. Curious to see what they were looking at, Cara squeezed herself through the crowd. Looking into the room, a naked woman kneeled on a low table and faced the door. One guy fucked her pussy, another one banged her ass, and a third guy thrust in her mouth while two more guys yanked and sucked her tits. Swaying from side to side, the woman moaned while several onlookers rubbed their cocks. The man who fucked her mouth groaned, pulled out his cock, and squirted his come over the woman's face before he hauled off and punched her in the nose, making blood spurt onto her face, chest, and the table.

Recoiling in horror, Cara shrieked, "Stop that! What the hell are you doing to her?"

Silence descended over the room as the woman looked at Cara with bulging eyes. Dozens of hungry on-lookers feasted their eyes on Cara, and, feeling exposed, she began to back out of the room. However, she was stopped as hands slipped under her clothes and groped her tits and ass. Someone's finger poked at her pussy, but she twisted and clamped her thighs together while looking around wildly for a way to escape. Panic seized her, and she craned her neck to find Hawk outside in the hall, but a sea of men with lust-filled eyes filled her field of vision.

"Come on, whore, start fuckin'," one of the men slurred.

The others jeered and shoved her further into the room. "Hawk!" she screamed.

Too many hands touched her and forced her to the ground. She closed her eyes and fought the bile rising in her throat.

"Get the fuck away from her!" Hawk bellowed.

The members jumped back from Cara, and in one swoop, Hawk lifted her from the floor. "She's my woman. Who the fuck wants to fight me on this?" His eyes, savage with rage, scanned the room.

The men mumbled, "Sorry, brother, we didn't know. We never would've touched your woman. We didn't mean any disrespect."

One young member sniped, "What the fuck was she doing in here anyways? What were we supposed to think? Why the hell don't you control your bitch?"

Hawk's swift fist landed on the young member's jaw and knocked him flat on the floor. Staring at the men, Hawk said, "Does anyone else want to ask me any fuckin' questions?" The room was quiet. "Didn't think so. You're all on notice. This is my woman, so leave her the fuck alone." He put his arm around Cara's shivering shoulders and walked out of the room. Cara looked back and saw the woman on the table, her legs spread open, a bearded man licking her pussy, and her nose still bleeding. Cara buried her head in Hawk's shoulder.

Dragging Cara to the barn next to the yard, Hawk's glowering eyes stared at her. "I told you to stay with me!"

She took a step back from him. "I was with you, but you were talking with those guys, and I was curious to see what everyone was watching in the room."

Rubbing his hands over his face, he said, "You don't need to know what's goin' on unless you want to be part of it. I explained how this shit is around here. You're fuckin' lucky I found you. I didn't know where the fuck you disappeared to. Your ass would've been raped if I hadn't come. Fuck, Cara. Fuck!" He slammed his fist into the barn's door. "You got to *listen* to me, woman!"

"Sorry. I screwed up," she said in a low voice.

"Fuck yeah, you did."

"I said I was sorry."

Cara stepped over to him, put her arms around his waist, then kissed his chest and laid her head against his shoulder. He trembled from anger, and she held him until his breathing calmed down and his anger abated.

"What were they doing to that girl in there? It was horrible," she said.

"I don't know. I wasn't looking at her when I came in the room."

"She had all these guys on her, like they were feeding off her, and this guy came all over her face then punched her in the nose. It was awful," her voice cracked.

Rubbing her back, Hawk said, "Babe, I told you it gets wild at the parties. Anything goes here, and the sluts are in tune with that. They know the score before they get here. They choose to come here. Do things get out of hand? Yeah, they sometimes do, but the sluts know all that going in.”

“Why did he hit her like that?”

“It’s called Strawberry Cheesecake, and it means a guy comes over a woman’s face then follows it with a hard punch in her nose to draw blood.”

“That’s supposed to be pleasurable?”

“Babe, this has nothing to do with us. I’m with you, and I don’t get it, but who knows what gets people off, right? The point is she was into it. It’s their business. Okay?” Hawk tilted Cara’s face up, and he lowered his mouth over hers. “You okay?”

“I guess. The whole thing was disturbing.”

“I know, baby. It’s a lot to handle. Stay with me, and don’t separate again, got it?”

She nodded. The image of blood streaming down the naked woman’s face burned in her mind.

“Let’s go have a drink,” Hawk said.

With his arm around her shoulders, they walked back to the yard where a huge bonfire crackled, its yellow flames leaping toward the twinkling chips in the sky. Finding a place by the fence, Hawk spread out his jacket for Cara to sit on. As she sat on the ground, he pulled her between his legs, and she leaned her back into his chest. While taking a deep drink from his beer bottle, he handed her another vodka tonic. “Bat out of Hell” by Meatloaf belted out of the speakers which surrounded the yard.

Men and women threw bottles, chairs, blankets, and most anything they found into the bonfire. At that point in the night, most of the people were drunk or close to it, and all around Cara, people fucked. Never having seen so many people screw each other in public, she was amazed how freely they dropped their pants and hiked up their skirts to screw wherever they were.

Sipping her drink, Cara wondered if Hawk liked to fuck in public. After all, this was his club, and earlier in the evening he admitted he loved to party. As she took in the party antics, someone watched her.

Glancing to Cara's right, the bleached-blonde woman stared at Cara with daggers in her eyes while a member banged her hard. *Is she one of the women he's been with?* Fearing the answer, Cara erased the question from her mind and ignored the woman's dirty looks.

Hawk, stroking her hair, brushed it behind her ears then leaned in and kissed her neck while his fingers massaged her shoulders. His breathing deepened, and against the small of her back, his hardness pressed into her. While he licked and kissed the nape of her neck, he brought his hand down and cupped one of her tits.

A few feet from them, a woman groaned as a man sucked her nipples and another slammed his cock into her pussy. Peeking at the threesome having sex made Cara's panties damp, and a red tint colored her cheeks as a sweet throb pulsed in her sex. *What the hell?* The live sex show aroused her and compulsion forced her to become a voyeur. Shame mixed with stimulation as she shifted her weight from side to side.

"Are you getting turned on watching them?" Hawk breathed into her ear.

Cara held her legs together and pinkish splotches scattered across her face at his words. How had he guessed? Was her arousal that transparent?

"My cock wants in, Cara," he rasped as he tweaked her nipple through her top's fabric.

Cara stiffened. Did he want to screw her in public? It was one thing to watch *others* do it, but for *her* to do it? She wasn't crazy about that. *No, not at all.*

His finger came up from behind her ass, and he stroked her wet pussy. Biting her lip hard, she stifled her moan.

"You're wet again, babe. Fuck, you're insatiable." He chuckled under his breath. "That works out great for me, because I can't get enough of you." He swiveled his hips, moving his stiff cock against her back. "See how hard you make me?"

Tilting her head up, he kissed her while his finger played with her mound, but Cara clamped her legs together as she twisted her hips.

"Come on, baby. Open your legs more so I can get into your hot pussy."

Resisting, Cara said, "I don't feel comfortable. You know, doing it in public and all."

"No one's looking, Cara. Everyone's too busy fucking to give a shit about what we're doing. I'm fuckin' horny for you."

"Some of the people are looking. I see them."

"You worry too much about that kind of shit. This is about you and me wanting each other. Come on, babe, I need you," he coaxed.

Cara's heart thumped and her pulse raced. Maybe it would be exciting. Hawk wanted to bang her, and he didn't seem bothered by the fact that there were about forty people out in the yard. She *did* want to please him, but in public? Her stomach was a tight ball, and she had the urge to run away. In the golden reflection of the bonfire, and in the shadowy darkness of the yard's outskirts, everyone was fucking and no one cared who was looking, but Cara didn't want the pleasure she and Hawk shared to be on display. It just wasn't her style, and if he cared anything for her, he'd understand. *Call me a prude, but this isn't my scene.*

"Come on, babe, open up." Hawk's hands tugged at her closed legs.

"Hawk, I'm sorry, but this isn't for me. I know you're cool with this, but I'm not. I don't mind kissing and stuff, but screwing you in front of a bunch of people just isn't my thing."

Hawk was quiet.

"I know this is the way things are done in your world, but you have to respect my world, too. I don't feel comfortable with all this. I hope you understand," she said.

Hawk still didn't say anything. He withdrew his finger, wrapped his arms around her, and ran his fingers through her hair.

"Are you mad?" Cara said.

"No, I'm not mad. I don't want you to do anything you feel uncomfortable with. It's cool."

"I like our intimate moments to be for us only. It makes it special that way, you know?"

"You don't have to explain, babe. I get it." Hawk kissed her head.

Turning around, she cupped his chin in her hand, licked his lips, and kissed him possessively.

"Down deep, you're a real sweetheart," she murmured.

Holding her close, they sat on the ground, arms wrapped around each other, and watched the sparks of the bonfire spit and sputter. Well after the flames died to smoldering embers, they held each other.

LATER THAT NIGHT, in his room, Hawk held Cara as she slept, allowing an intimacy he had never felt with any woman grab hold of him. It amazed him that he could enjoy holding a woman without fucking her. Remembering their fucking, his cock twitched. *My wildcat is too fuckin' hot. When I'm deep in her pussy, it's like nothing in life matters except for her. Fuck, I need her in my life.*

Earlier that day, Cara told him she was happy, and he wanted to tell her he was happy, too, but he couldn't. Fearing that his revelation would give her the upper hand, he didn't say anything. *Shit, what the fuck is wrong with me? Cara is the best thing that's happened to me besides the Insurgents. Why can't I tell her how she makes me feel?*

Trusting a woman was not in his makeup—in the end, they always fucked the man over. Even though what he had with Cara was good, it was almost *too* good, and dread permeated his mind at the thought of losing it. Fear she'd take off like his bitch mom gnawed at him. He couldn't be sure Cara would stick around for the good *and* the bad, and although the barriers around his heart weakened, he wasn't ready to give Cara all of it.

Shit, I'm fucked-up.

CHAPTER TWENTY-THREE

THE EARLY MORNING frost crunched under the detectives' feet as the sun attempted to cut through the clouds' grayness. The small group of men viewed the lifeless body of a young, blonde woman on the mountainside next to Platte Creek. Her body had all the earmarks of the Mountainside Strangler, a name coined by the Pinewood Springs Tribune.

"Fuck, the sick bastard did a number on her," Earl McCue, lead detective, hissed through his teeth.

The men stood over the body and imagined the horrific way this young woman spent her last hours. The detectives were quiet; a few thought of their own daughters, safe at home in warm beds, while others thought of stringing up the sadistic fucker responsible for such havoc.

"He stepped up his game on this one," observed Earl.

Young Jane Doe #8 had the same bruises, cuts, cigarette burns, and ligature marks around her neck as her predecessors. However, the killer added a new twist to his mayhem: he sliced off her nipples and slashed open her vagina.

In canvassing the area, the investigators located motorcycle tracks again, as well as car tracks. Earl had no doubt an outlaw biker gang was messed up with this. He didn't think they did the murders, but their involvement was clear. Except for Hannah and Dana, all the other women the fucking monster tortured and killed were petite and blonde. They had also been Jane Does until Nadyia Kravchenko; the sheriff's department received a big break when her sister identified her.

The two local women didn't fit the pattern, but the way they were tortured and killed was the same as with the other victims. *Fuck, we have to stop this sick bastard before he kills another.* Earl rubbed his face, and the pressure to catch the serial killer possessed him. He lived and breathed this case, the images of murder victims invading his dreams. Knowing he'd never rest until he cracked it, Detective McCue shuffled around the area to look for more clues.

The morning wore on as the evidence was collected and bagged. Finally, the team of investigators, grim-faced and silent, treaded back to their vehicles as the body of Jane Doe #8, bagged and on a gurney, trailed behind.

HAWK WOKE CARA up as he rummaged through the small dresser drawers. Glancing at her, he saw her rubbing her eyes as she yawned. "What time is it?"

He came over and kissed her forehead. "Sorry, babe, I didn't mean to wake you. It's eight o'clock."

"Damn, it's too early to get up on a Sunday morning. Come back to bed." She patted the empty space beside her.

Hawk stared at her hand. "Don't tempt me. I gotta go. I'll be back later."

"Where are you going?"

"Club business."

"You're not going to tell me?"

"Club business, babe. You know I can't tell you."

"Are you going alone?"

"No, Jax, Axe, and Chas are going, too." He came over, gave her a tight hug, kissed her, and pinched her exposed nipple. "You make it hard for me to leave," he said, winking at her.

He kissed her pouting lips, then was gone.

Hawk and the others mounted their Harleys, but before he took off, he glanced up at the window. Cara watched him, standing at the window with a blanket draped over her naked body. It took all his strength to keep himself from running back to his room to fuck her.

Tearing himself away from her gaze, he hit the open road. They had a mission to accomplish: scope out the Deadly Demons Nomads. The vote from the members was unanimous; they'd teach the fuckers the Insurgents did not tolerate any one fucking with them. Hawk chomped at the bit with anticipation, knowing he'd enjoy every punch to Viper's face.

No one touched his woman.

GOING BACK TO bed, Cara tried to sleep, but Hawk had only been gone fifteen minutes and she already missed him. Feeling claustrophobic, she wished she could meet up with Sherrie, but knew she couldn't. Since she'd arrived at the clubhouse, Hawk had given her strict orders not to leave the compound until he told her it was okay. Saying she was antsy was an understatement.

It wasn't so bad when Hawk was around, but Cara's confinement made her climb the walls. Anxious about her clients and the piles of work on her desk, she had to get back to work the following week, whether this thing with Viper was resolved or not. If she remained incognito, she might as well shut down her practice, and she wasn't going to do that.

After a long shower, she turned on her laptop. When she typed in "Pinewood Springs," the headline of the Tribune read, "Mountainside Strangler Strikes Again." As Cara read the article, nausea assaulted her. *Why can't they catch this sadist?*

Something wasn't right. Cara grabbed her phone and sent a quick email to her buddy, Josh. Playing a hunch, she had to know if she was on the right track. Of course, Hawk would be livid if he knew she was still playing sleuth, but this was *her* club business.

After a couple of hours online, Cara's stomach rumbled. She hadn't eaten anything since early last night, so she padded to the kitchen to scrounge up some food.

When she came into the room, Brandi and Kristy sat at a table, drinking coffee. They looked like they had partied too much the night before—Brandi had her head in her hand while Kristy stared at the wall in front of her.

Cara opened the refrigerator and found eggs, green peppers, cheddar cheese, and leftover potatoes and made a quick meal. Sitting at the table across from the two women, she ate her breakfast burrito.

As Cara finished her food, Lola strode into the kitchen and glared at Cara. "What the fuck are *you* doin' here?"

"Excuse me?" Cara asked as she shuffled back a step.

"You heard me."

"What's your problem? I don't even know you. Back off."

Brandi and Kristy, sensing drama, perked up.

"My problem, skank, is that you think you're better than us just 'cause you've got Hawk's cock in your pussy."

"I don't think that's any of your business."

"The fuck it ain't. You can't come here, acting like you own the place, fuckin' Hawk like you're his woman. You ain't shit, bitch."

"I'm not going to stand here arguing with you. You're jealous of my relationship with Hawk. That's your problem, not mine."

"You fuckin' slut. You think 'cause you got yourself a high-class pussy that you're woman enough for Hawk? You ain't, bitch!"

Cara turned away from Lola.

"Don't you turn your back on me, slut! Let me tell you something: Hawk's been in my pussy; he ain't a one-woman man. He'll get tired of your girlie-ass cunt, and he'll be comin' to me when he craves a real woman's pussy. Got that, slut?"

Banger, Ruben, and Billy stood in the doorway and watched as Lola, red-faced from anger, yelled at Cara as she turned toward the door.

Lurching, Lola grabbed Cara's shoulders and dragged her forward while Lola screamed, "I told you not to fuckin' turn your back on me, bitch!" Shaking her, Lola drew her face close to Cara's and hollered, "Get the fuck outta here! You don't fit in!"

Watching in amusement, Brandi encouraged Lola, "You tell her, girlfriend. This thinking-I'm-better-than-you skank needs to be taught a lesson. Fuck, her weak pussy will never keep Hawk satisfied."

Kristy laughed.

Lola hissed, "Bitch, none of us are gonna give up Hawk's cock in our pussies, especially to a whore like you." Lola pushed Cara hard. She fell against one of the tables as all the women laughed.

With her hand raised, Lola rushed toward Cara, but before she struck her, Cara lifted her right hand and *whack!* The force of Cara's slap threw Lola off-balance as she stumbled backward, landing on her round ass. The right side of her face bored Cara's red handprint, and her tender flesh swelled.

Shocked, Brandi and Kristy stared at Cara. Lola, holding her face in her hands, glanced at Banger as he and the brothers cracked up. With twinkling blue eyes, he said, "You got what you had comin' to you, slut."

Brandi brought an ice pack over to Lola, who put it on her swelling face as she threw dirty looks at Cara. Cara, mortified she'd succumbed to a brawl with a woman Hawk banged, scurried out of the kitchen, up the stairs, and locked herself in Hawk's room.

Cara replayed the scenario again in her mind. How could Hawk have slept with that horrible, vulgar woman? How many times had he been with her? As hard as she tried, Cara couldn't stop the images of Lola and Hawk together in the bed she shared with him. *What if Lola's right? Will Hawk get tired of me and go back to her?* Cara couldn't bear it if he betrayed her. Having allowed herself to become too wrapped up with Hawk, she couldn't turn back. She had guarded her heart for so long, but since she had given it to him, he'd probably hurt her more than any other man ever had.

How stupid could she be to think Hawk would *ever* be satisfied with just one woman, let alone one like her who wasn't experienced or adventuresome? Even though he said he was cool, she knew he was disappointed because she wouldn't screw him in public the night before. Her stomach roiled and she laughed dryly. She'd never satisfy him or be enough for him. Loneliness surrounded her like a shroud, and she just wanted to go back to her house.

Pressing her throbbing temples, Cara tried to dispel images of the last few days with Hawk. At that moment, she wanted to run far away from him, the Insurgents, the Deadly Demons, and the women who serviced all the men anytime, anywhere.

Cara sat by the window and stared at the pine trees clustered around the clubhouse grounds, their frost-covered needles sparkling like diamonds. The dying leaves of the almost-bare trees around the compound swirled in the icy wind. As the sun hid behind the gray clouds, the dreary weather complemented her mood. Her body craved Hawk's protective arms, yet her common sense told her to run away. A knot of desire and fear consumed her.

In order to quell the mounting inner stress, she decided to give Hawk the benefit of the doubt and speak with him when he came back. Curling up in the recliner, Cara covered herself with one of Hawk's jackets, his sandalwood scent filling her nostrils. Bringing the garment around her chin, she burrowed deeper into the chair, apprehension seizing her as she wondered if the club business Hawk was taking care of was dangerous.

HAWK, JAX, AXE, and Chas stayed in the brush and watched the Nomads' clubhouse. It was an old three-story farmhouse with a barn and a whole lot of barbed wire around the structures. Parked to the left of the barn was a large truck.

Hawk surveyed the area to see the layout of the clubhouse and to get an idea of how many Nomads were in there. The Nomads had owned a clubhouse for several years, and even though they were independent, they still answered to the national president of the Deadly Demons. The Insurgents never had trouble with the Nomads because when they moved into the county next to Insurgents territory, Hawk and Banger told them, in no uncertain terms, that if they didn't want trouble, they had to stay low and out of Insurgents' fucking business.

For many years, the Insurgents and the Deadly Demons used to be rival clubs, and club wars were the norm. After years of killing each other and having brothers on both sides locked up, the two clubs called a truce. They both recognized that neither side was winning, but they were all losing, so for the past five years, the Deadly Demons did their thing and the Insurgents did theirs. As long as the Deadly Demons respected the Insurgents and their territory, the Insurgents had no reason to mess with them.

The Nomads seemed like they respected the truce between their mother club and the Insurgents, but they didn't—they'd overstepped the line, and some retribution was necessary. The Nomads not only trafficked women and meth through Insurgents territory, they had also placed a thief at Dream House, had the fucking badges focused on the Insurgents, and their asshole president, Viper, had messed with Cara. Whether the national president, Reaper, condoned the betrayal was unclear, but what *was* clear was that the assholes needed to be set straight.

Viper came out of the clubhouse and walked toward the truck, and it took all of Hawk's resolve not to shoot him on the spot. Seeing Viper's hands, he pictured them on Cara's body, and he grunted angrily. Jax, hearing Hawk's short breaths, whispered, "Easy, now, you got time for all that. We're here to scout."

"I know. I just can't wait to stomp on that fucker's balls," Hawk hissed.

Viper opened the back of the truck, and two Nomads jumped into the back. "Out, get the fuck out. Now. Come on sluts, out!"

Fifteen young, terrified ladies jumped out the back of the truck. Viper touched each woman as they passed him, grabbing their tits, asses, and pussies. The women recoiled from his touch, and a pretty blonde girl with ice blue eyes sobbed. Viper pulled her from the group. "Put this one in the basement in the Dungeon Room," he said to one of the members. As she twisted in Viper's grip, he backhanded her, then dragged her to the cellar door.

A brunette dressed in leather shorts and a tight top stood shivering in the late-morning air. Viper pulled her to him and squeezed her tits. Yelping, the woman struggled to break free of him, and a cruel smile played on Viper's lips. "You're a fighter. I like that. We're gonna have some fun before I send you to Phoenix." Viper shoved her into a side door, saying, "Take her to my room."

For half an hour, the women were checked in, groped, slapped, and shoved through various doors. Each time one of the Nomads abused a woman, the Insurgents clenched their jaws. They would've liked nothing better than to take out those motherfuckers and free the women, but the Nomads overpowered them in numbers—there were twelve members including Viper. Hawk didn't want to jeopardize their lives, but he hated to see the women mistreated. Although, he knew after the women left the clubhouse, a dire fate faced them as they'd be smuggled to various massage parlors and brothels across state lines.

"You two stay here to see when the women leave. These assholes won't risk keeping them here overnight. My guess is they'll move them out soon. Jax, give Banger a call with the details. I'll send some more brothers. Once the women are out, riddle the club." Several assault weapons and grenades accompanied the group on their scouting mission. "Blow it to fuckin' Hell," he said.

"Can't wait," Jax said while Chas nodded. Everyone's adrenaline pumped.

"We'll get a few members to intercept the truck and let the women go. This trafficking is pussy bullshit. I knew the Nomads were nothin' but bitches," Hawk sneered. "Keep Viper alive until I get back. That fucker is mine."

Hawk rolled his Harley down a ways so as not to create suspicion among the Nomads. Then he jumped on and hauled ass to Pinewood Springs.

When Hawk entered the clubhouse, Banger greeted him and said, "The grapevine is tellin' me these bastards are acting alone. If we don't stomp them out, the national Deadly Demons' president has word out to the New Mexico clubs to take them out. Seems they neglected to tell Reaper they had a sex-trafficking side business that brings in hundreds of thousands of dollars, and they forgot to tell him 'bout the meth they've been cooking. Looks like these fuckers don't wanna share, and Reaper ain't too pleased."

"Good, then when we blow them to Hell, the Demons aren't gonna shed any tears, right?" Hawk asked.

"Hardly. They'll be grateful to us for doin' their dirty work and keepin' them under the radar."

"Can't wait to kick some Nomad ass." Hawk clenched his fists.

Hawk turned to go upstairs to see Cara when Banger said, "You've got quite a woman."

"What do you mean?"

"Lola was givin' her a hard time this morning. She was in Cara's face, and I thought your woman was gonna wilt, but fuck, she walloped the shit outta the bitch. The slut is still in the kitchen holding an ice pack. Her face is swelled up like a melon. Shocked the hell outta all of us."

"Cara decked her?"

"Yep. Fuck, I was impressed. She's got a fire in her."

"I know." Hawk smiled.

In the kitchen, Hawk found Lola who held an ice pack on the right side of her face. She averted her gaze as he stood in front of her with blazing eyes. "You ever bother my woman again, I'll throw your fuckin' ass outta this club, got it?"

"Yeah," Lola mumbled.

"You're damn lucky she isn't wearing my patch, 'cause your ass would be hitting the asphalt right about now. Don't you ever fuckin' disrespect my woman again, bitch." Hawk stormed out of the kitchen and ran up the stairs.

When he came into his room, Cara sat at the computer.

"Hey, slugger," he said, winking.

Cara groaned, "You heard? I didn't mean to hurt her."

"You got a strong swing, babe. I know," Hawk reminded her, rubbing the side of his face.

"She was awful. She gave me shit, pushed me, and raised her hand like she was going to hit me."

"You don't have to explain, babe. I know the score. You defended yourself. I'm proud of you."

"I *do* have to explain, because this isn't like me. I don't go around hitting people. I've never hit anyone except for her."

"And me, remember?"

"Yeah, but you deserved it," she joked.

"Probably, and so did she. Don't concern yourself over it. She won't bother you again. I told her to back off or her ass is outta here."

"You told her that?"

"Of course. Do you think I'm going to let a slut disrespect my woman? Fuck no," he said, pulling her into him.

Cara wrapped her arms around his waist, and warmth spread over her as she realized Hawk was willing to throw Lola out of the club for her sake.

"What did she say to you?" he asked.

"She said you two have been together, and you were not a one-woman man. She said you'd get tired of me and go back to her and other women. Did you have something with her?"

Hawk tilted her face up toward his and looked into her eyes. "I didn't have *something* with her—we fucked, and that was it. I've been with a ton of women, but they were there to give me pleasure. I've been honest with you about my past. You gotta go beyond this."

"I'm trying, but it's hard. I've trusted men before, and I've been hurt. It seems men promise you what you want to hear, but they don't deliver in the long run." She broke away from his stare.

"I'm not other men. I'm not that fuckin' jerk who broke your heart in law school. I don't do bullshit. If I wanna fuck other women, I'll tell you. I don't believe in doin' shit behind your back."

"Do you want to be with other women?"

"I wanna be with you."

"Am I enough for you? I mean, you're used to so many types of women with a lot of experience, and I'm scared I won't be enough."

"Cara, look at me," Hawk said, as he lifted her chin up. "I don't wanna be with any other woman but you. All those other women were for fucking, and you're more than that. Do you wanna know something? You're the only woman who has ever spent the night with me. After I fucked, I'd throw the slut's ass outta my bed unless she was dead-drunk, and then I'd throw her ass out when she woke up. You mean something to me." He kissed her deeply. "You have to trust me," he murmured against her lips.

"I want to. I really do." She kissed him back.

A knock on the door interrupted their intimate moment. Hawk opened it, and Banger motioned for him to come out. Stepping out in the hallway, Hawk closed the door behind him.

"Jax called. Looks like the fuckers aren't movin' the women 'til tomorrow. I told him we're sending ten brothers down early morning, and I need you to go with them," Banger said.

"Okay. What time do we leave?"

"One thirty."

Hawk nodded, his jaw tight. He went back into his room.

"What's going on?" Cara asked.

"Club business. I feel like a steak. Do you want to go out to dinner?"

"Are you asking me on a date?"

"No, I'm not. I'm asking if you want to get a steak." *What the hell is she talking about? I never fuckin' date.*

"Sorry to inform you, but that's called a date."

"No, it isn't. Do you want to go, or not?"

"Are you asking anyone else to go with us?"

"No."

"Are you paying?"

"Yeah. What kind of question is that?"

"You're asking me to a restaurant, right?"

"Yeah. What's with the cross-examination, counselor?"

"It's a date. You're asking me on a date," Cara said smugly, her green eyes sparkling.

He looked hard at her. *She's an impossible woman.* "Okay, it's a date. Do you fuckin' want to go, or not?"

"Yes, I'd love to go," she replied, smiling.

"You're too much, woman. All this bullshit for a steak. Shit."

Cara giggled.

THE BUCKHORN STEAKHOUSE served the best steak in the county, and although it was expensive, it was well worth the price for its melt-in-your-mouth dishes. Linen tablecloths and napkins, rich burgundy leather booths, cherry hardwood floors, lavish Karastan rugs, and two wood-burning fireplaces created an elegant ambiance. After a cold ride on the motorcycle, Cara and Hawk welcomed the warmth of the crackling fire as they entered the restaurant.

Asking for a window seat, the hostess escorted them to a table replete with a shimmering candle encased in crystal. The breathtaking view included the snow-capped peaks of the majestic Rocky Mountains, which signaled winter was right around the corner.

After ordering a beer on draft for him and a vodka martini for Cara, Hawk brought her hand to his mouth and brushed it over his lips then licked and kissed it as he held her gaze. His blue eyes revealed a level of tenderness she had not seen before, and her heart skipped a few beats. Was that love in his eyes? Holding her breath, she bit her lower lip as she averted her eyes to two women seated at the table across from them. The women, in their early twenties, ogled Hawk. *They're practically drooling.* Hawk, oblivious to everyone but her, caressed Cara's cheek with his palm. She blushed.

"Why are you acting shy, babe?"

"I don't know. I guess the vibes you're giving me are different, that's all."

"I'm glad to be with you."

"On our date?"

"Yeah, *on our date.*"

She stroked his hand. "Me, too."

Her filet mignon with roasted asparagus spears in a balsamic sherry glaze was excellent; there wasn't a morsel left on her plate. His Porterhouse steak was enough for a family of four, but he managed to eat every bit of it including the sautéed mushrooms in red wine and the blue cheese scalloped potatoes.

As Cara was drinking her after-dinner liqueur, she noticed Hawk's gaze focused at the bar. "What are you looking at?"

"Nothing."

He glanced over a few more times. "Hawk, are you checking out a woman at the bar?"

"No."

"Who are you looking at?" Twisting around, she expected to see a knockout with big boobs on a barstool.

"Babe, I'm looking at that pansy-ass you went out with. He's got his tongue halfway down one of my dancers' throat."

"Luke?"

"Yeah, that fuckin' suit."

Looking toward the bar, Luke's mouth covered the woman's who sat on the barstool next to his. He looked like one of those creatures from a cheesy 1950s sci-fi movie. When she was a kid, she and her dad used to watch reruns of the campy movies, and she loved to sit in the dark, eat popcorn her dad had made, and watch the alien monsters devour their victims. Yeah, Luke looked like the Creature—the one with the vacuum mouth who sucked salt from its victims.

God, Luke is such a jerk. Cara hadn't spoken to him since the charity ball, and didn't even care that he had his tongue down the stripper's mouth and his hand up her skirt. *He's such an asshole.*

"I told you he was a pansy-ass," Hawk said.

"You were right. I was never interested in him, anyway."

"You're too hot, babe. You need a man to stoke the fire in you," he said, his voice husky.

On their way out, Hawk guided Cara past Luke. Hawk said, "How are you, Missy?"

Missy pushed Luke away, startled to see Hawk. "Fine, thanks."

"Who's your friend?" he asked.

Luke, recognizing Hawk, scowled.

"What's your name again, darlin'?" she asked Luke.

"He knows who I am," Luke said, ignoring Hawk.

"Oh, yeah, it's pansy-ass." Hawk's eyes dared Luke to start something with him.

Luke and Missy stared awkwardly at Hawk.

"I'm not working tonight, and—"

"What you do on your own time is your business," Hawk told Missy.

As she stepped from behind Hawk, Cara said, "Hiya, Luke."

Luke's face dropped when he saw Cara, and he darted his gaze from her to Hawk. "What are you doing here *with him?*" he asked.

"On a date, same as you." She grinned.

Hawk put his arm around Cara's shoulders and drew her close to him. When he kissed her head, Luke's face turned so red, he looked like he would explode.

"Do your parents know you're out with *him?*" Luke asked in disgust.

"My parents quit monitoring my dates when I got out of high school."

"What about Eric? I bet *he* doesn't know. Maybe I need to call him."

"Go ahead. I think you should." She leaned close to Luke's ear and whispered, "I think my dad would love to know one of his associates made an ass of himself while he tongued a stripper at The Buckhorn. You know, very good for the firm's public image." She tossed her hair and circled her arm tighter around Hawk's waist.

Luke's face turned ashen. "You wouldn't, would you?"

Staring at him, she said, "Yes, I would. Nice seeing you, Luke."

Hawk walked away from the couple, his arm around Cara. He stopped at the exit, drew her into his hard chest and gave her a full-tongue kiss. From the corner of her eye, Cara observed the shock in Luke's face as his eyes glued to them. Within earshot, Cara eavesdropped on Luke and Missy's conversation.

"What's wrong, darlin'?" Missy asked. "Do you know that lady?"

"Yeah, I *know* that lady." Anger glowed in his eyes as he slammed his fist on the bar. "I can't believe I lost her to a fucking lowlife biker. I'm pissed for blowing this. Fuck that bitch!"

"Am I missin' something here, or are you havin' this conversation with yourself?" she asked as she ran her hand up and down his thigh.

"Forget it, it's not important. I was gearing up to win the lottery. I'll just have to go hunting again, that's all. Now, why don't you help me forget that frigid bitch?" he said as Missy snickered while moving her hand closer to his crotch.

Shaking her head, Cara breathed a sigh of relief that she'd followed her instincts with that asshole.

As they left the restaurant, Hawk held Cara close to him. Luke's eyes boring into him satisfied him. *That fucker never had a chance with my wildcat. He could never satisfy her the way I do. She's well rid of that asshole.*

Hawk, breathing in the frosty air, started up his Harley. Cara's warm arms wrapped around his waist and her head rested on his shoulder. The night was perfect: he had his woman with him to enjoy a great meal, he made pansy-ass feel like the pussy he was, he was going to give Cara the best fucking she'd ever had, and then he was going to stomp some Nomad asses. *Yeah, a great night all around.*

CHAPTER TWENTY-FOUR

B EFORE CARA CLOSED Hawk's door, he kissed the base of her throat and squeezed her tits. She kicked the door shut and wrapped her arms around Hawk's neck, and as she kissed him her tongue pushed against his teeth, urging his mouth to let her in. Opening his mouth, her tongue delved inside, and he moaned as she twisted his hair in her fingers and drew his lips even closer to hers until there was no space between them.

"Fuck, baby. You want it bad, don't you?" he breathed against her lips.

"Yeah, I need you," she said seductively.

Hawk pushed her toward his bed, and she swiveled around and shoved him on it instead. Landing with a soft thud, surprise etched on his face. Cara pulled away from his grasp and, as she threw him a sultry look, she slowly unzipped her leather jacket and tossed it on the chair. Rubbing her fingertips up and down the sides of her body, she languidly unbuttoned her blouse, revealing more skin with each opened button before she touched her neck and collarbone. Transfixed, Hawk readjusted his crotch to release some of the pressure from his raging hard-on.

With her blouse open, Cara brought her fingertips to her waist, eventually touching around her crotch, her red fingernails glistening under the lamplight. Lowering the zipper on her pants, she exposed black lace panties, and Hawk breathed in sharply. Their eyes locked, smoldering with desire before a devilish smile swept across her lips. She ever-so-slowly shimmied out of her pants and kicked them to the side then turned around and dropped her blouse on the floor. Her black lace bra looked like velvet against her creamy skin. Arching her back, she tousled her hair while she held Hawk's gaze. Unhurriedly, she unclasped her bra hooks one at a time, drawing out the anticipation. Hawk's breathing grew erratic and he unzipped his jeans, releasing his cock.

"You're killing me. You're teasing the shit outta me. Come here. I want to fuck your hot pussy," he said hoarsely.

With her back to him, Cara lowered one bra strap then the other while she peered over her shoulder. The lust in Hawk's eyes combined with his erect cock made her wet. She released her bra, letting it fall to the floor. As she bent over, she rolled her ass in circles, her firm cheeks aching to be kissed. Hawk whistled under his breath.

"Fuck, Cara, I'm going to explode. Get your sexy ass over here."

Shaking her head, Cara swayed her ass around.

"I said get your ass over here, woman."

Giggling, she spun around, her hands covering her ample bosom.

"You're asking for a spanking, woman," Hawk growled.

"Promise?" She licked her lips.

Cara uncovered her tits—her nipples cherry red and erect—then cupped her breasts and squeezed them slightly as her fingers trailed over her sides, stomach, and hips. Looping a finger under her panties' waistband, she pulled it down a hint, playing with the lace edge before she pulled her panties back up again.

"You're fuckin' killing me, Cara. I know your pussy is wet. Show me your sopping pussy."

Cara thrust her pelvis in and out, and taking her time to pull her panties down, she let them slide down her smooth legs then stepped out of them. As she stood naked in front of Hawk, he grabbed her and dragged her to him, and she landed on his chest. "Roll over," he demanded.

Cara, ignoring his order, pinned down his shoulders then kissed his lips before she brushed his mouth, jawline, and earlobes with her tongue. She pulled on his earrings and nipped his neck, causing him to moan under her.

As she caressed his chest and ran her tits against his nipples, he grunted. "Fuck."

She lowered her body so his stiff dick was in front of her mouth and opened his belt, tugging at his pants to lower them and licking her lips when she spotted his large, tempting cock. With the tip of her tongue, she stroked his shaft's head and made sure to run it on the underside. His breathing turned into pants while she took him in her mouth as far as she could. Holding her breath, she pushed him deeper into her mouth, and soon had all of him inside with his balls against her chin.

"That's the way I like it, babe. Fuckin' deepthroat me," he coaxed. His slippery cock slid in and out of her mouth, each thrust harder than the next. "Yeah, I love fucking your mouth," he groaned.

Cara withdrew his dick, wet from her tongue and his pre-come, from her mouth and stroked the tip with her hard nipple. With ragged breaths, he clasped and fondled her chest.

"I'm gonna fuck your beautiful tits," he said as he placed his hardness between her breasts and pushed them together, creating a warm, tight cavern for his cock. His shaft, lubricated by her mouth, thrust up and down while he pinched her nipples, making her cry out in pleasure.

"Hawk, I could have you touch my nipples all day," Cara murmured against his chest.

"I don't want to come yet, baby. I want to play with your pussy and make you come," he said through clenched teeth. He tried to roll her off him, but she said, "No way. I'm riding you tonight."

He watched as she mounted him, the tip of his cock in her pussy, her tits swaying above him. Grabbing one of her tits, Hawk put it in his mouth and sucked it; the pain mixed with pleasure made Cara want more. "I like when you manhandle my breasts," she said, arching her back.

"Fuck, you're on fire, babe. I don't know how much longer I can hold out."

As she slipped Hawk's dick into her drenched pussy, she swayed back and forth. She lifted and teased him back into her a little bit at a time. Hawk's shaft pushed in further as he craved the tightness.

While playing with her tits, Hawk circled her silky clit as Cara rode him hard, her ass slapping against his thighs. Whenever Hawk flicked his finger over her hardened bud, she contracted her pussy muscles over his pulsing cock, and he grunted as she encased it. Hawk's short breaths and taut muscles told his release, like hers, was imminent. His finger tweaking her clit tipped her over the edge of ecstasy, and she screamed at the same time Hawk emitted a low, feral growl. Her pussy's tremors practically sucked the seed out of his cock.

Cara, sweat pouring down her neck, lay spent on his chest with Hawk's drained dick still inside her. While his breathing came back to normal, he stroked her hair. "Fuck, you're more than hot tonight, babe."

"You make me hot, each and every time," she muttered into his chest.

"You liked being in charge, huh?" He laughed.

She buried her head in the crook of his arm and giggled.

"Now it's my turn to be the one calling the shots," he said huskily. He rolled her over on her back, kissed her lips, and sucked her bottom lip while he played with her tits. Squirming under his deft touch, Cara moaned into his mouth. *Damn, he knows how to touch me to set me on fire.*

Hawk lowered his mouth down the length of her body, taking special care to kiss, blow and nip her at the base of her throat, her tits, her sides, and her inner thighs. Brushing his mouth over her damp pussy, he made sure to take time to stroke her inner folds. His tongue found the spot that drove her wild and he placed his mouth on it, gently taking her sensitive bud between his lips. Cara thrashed and bucked as she climaxed again from his hot mouth and expert fingers.

As she peaked, he stuck his fingers inside her pussy, and when the spasms subsided, Hawk wiggled them. Then he flipped her over and placed her on her knees, where she spread her legs wide as her sex glistened.

"Fuck, your pussy is juicy. And your ass. Damn, I can't get enough of your hot little ass," Hawk rasped.

Cara wiggled her butt and he rubbed her ass cheeks then bent down to kiss them, her tattoo beckoning to his mouth. He kissed and sucked her cheeks while his fingers opened her lips, exposing her clit. She ground her butt into his mouth.

"Love this ass, babe." Hawk smacked her cheeks hard and she yelped, not expecting it to sting so much. As he spanked her again, her ass jumped and Cara, locking eyes with him, watched as his semi-hard cock grew stiffer with each slap. Even though Cara winced at the stings, they titillated her, and his fingers went deeper into her pussy while his lips and tongue soothed the slight pain. More aroused than she had ever been in her life, the tremors built once again. As Hawk ran a finger over her ass crack, she shivered while her ass tightened in anticipation.

"I'm gonna put a finger up your ass, and then I want my cock in it. You comfortable with that, babe?" he asked huskily.

"Will it hurt?"

"I'll go real slow. I'm not gonna hurt you, and you're gonna love the feel of my cock in your ass."

Cara's stomach fluttered. Even though backdoor sex had always been a dark fantasy of hers, Hawk was the only man she'd let touch her there.

"You wanna try it, babe?" His lips against her ass tickled, making goosebumps pebble her skin.

When she nodded, Hawk took his finger, smeared her own juices as lubricant, and then slowly inserted his finger in her sweet, puckered entrance. "Relax, babe. You gotta relax. Just let your body act on its own."

Cara let go as his finger pushed further down, noticing her ass felt full. As he wiggled his finger at her opening, jolts of ecstasy ripped through her pussy. Hawk reached over to the nightstand by the bed, opened a drawer, and took out a tube of lubricant. After he stroked the entry to her ass and his cock with it, he parted her ass cheeks and stroked her again.

"You have such a sweet pussy and a luscious ass that now, I'm not sure which one I want to fuck. So, babe, I'm going to fuck you in your ass and pussy at the same time. Is that what you want?" he pressed.

"Aren't you too big? I'm afraid it'll hurt," she said.

"It'll hurt at first because you got a virgin ass, but go with me. You want it?"

"Uh-huh."

"Tell me what you want me to do," he demanded.

"Make me feel good."

He smacked her ass cheek. "Tell me you want me to fuck your pussy and your ass."

"I want you to do that."

He smacked her ass cheek again.

"Beg me. Tell me you want my cock in your ass and my fingers in your pussy," he barked.

"I want you to fuck me in the ass and pussy. Right now, I want you to do it."

"Good girl."

Hawk put his knees between her legs and spread her wider, her pussy glossy from her juices. Placing his tongue on her clit, his warmth emitted quivers from her core, and he slurped her wetness and flicked her hard bud with the tip of his tongue. Moaning, she threw her head back while he reinserted his finger in her pussy and his thumb stroked her clit. As she nudged her mound down on his finger, she ground her ass against his cock.

"Can't wait for my cock to be in your ass, can you?" Slowly, he put his dick's head against her entrance. "Relax, babe. Breathe out and push down with your sweet ass," he guided her.

She did as instructed, and her opening took in the tip of his cock. Then he held her ass cheeks open and gently slid his cock inside. At first, Cara bucked at the burning sensation as it seared through her bottom to the pit of her stomach. As she cried out, Hawk kissed her neck and upper back. "It's okay, babe, just relax. You're doing great."

Hawk's fingers continued to move in and out of her pussy while his cock was halfway in her butt. He bent over, grabbed a breast, and tugged at her nipples. Volts of intense pleasure coursed throughout her body, and Cara gasped at the intensity. As he played with her tits and fucked her pussy, Hawk pushed his length into her ass and rocked back and forth, slowly at first, then increasing his speed. Instinctively, she pushed back into his hardness and took his rod deeper into her.

"Fuck, my cock loves being in your tight ass," he panted.

He moved in and out of her ass while her tits tingled and his fingers fucked her pussy. The building tension exploded into a series of frenzied spasms, which spread from her clit to her head, and from deep in her throat, she let out a primal scream.

Cara felt Hawk's balls tighten against her ass cheeks, and when he pulled out, his hot seed spurted over her rounded globes. He panted and grunted as the last of his essence spilled out. Dropping to his side, he cradled Cara to him, and with her back against his chest, he wrapped his arms around her waist.

"Fuck, babe, that was awesome," he said, caressing her neck.

She bent her head back and sought his lips. As she placed her hands over his, he held her close and they drifted to sleep.

THREE HOURS LATER, Hawk's phone alarm pierced the quiet in the room, and he sighed as he turned it off before it woke Cara up. Not moving, the only sound in the room was Cara as she breathed through her nose. As he watched her shadowed form, he brushed his fingers over her cheek then tenderly kissed her left temple. Rolling out of bed, he shuffled to the bathroom to take a quick shower.

The hum of several motorcycle engines woke Cara up, and Hawk's silhouette against the early morning darkness piqued her curiosity. Propping her head up on her elbow, she yawned. "What're you doing?"

Striding over to the side of the bed, Hawk leaned over Cara, stroked the side of her face, and said, "Go back to bed, babe. I gotta go. Club business."

Cara, wide awake after that, sat up in bed, switched on the small lamp, and held the sheet over her bare breasts. "At this hour? Where are you going?"

Hawk kissed her. "Club business," he said against her lips.

"When will you be back?"

"Don't know for sure." Hawk tightened a bandana tied to a large padlock and placed it in his back pocket. The padlock was a weapon of choice for many of the Insurgents; it acted like a blackjack and could knock the hell out of anyone.

"Is everything okay? You're not in danger, are you?" Her voice carried fear.

"Go back to sleep, baby. I'll see you later." When he hugged her close to him, her sheet fell down and her bare tits crushed against him, making his cock jerk. He kissed her then pulled away. On top of his desk, he picked up his kill-light—a large industrial flashlight, and one of his favorite weapons. All the brothers carried a kill-light since it was a legal weapon and the badges couldn't do shit if they found it on them.

Hawk locked with Cara, and he noticed her bottom lip quiver. He had to get out of there, because if she cried, he'd never be able to leave her.

Going over to her again, he pulled the sheet and blanket around her as he brushed her lips, noticing her chattering teeth vibrated against his mouth. His heart lurched when Cara's arms encircled his neck and tugged him closer to her. Prying her away, he whispered, "Gotta go, babe." Opening the door, he said over his shoulder, "Don't go anywhere. Stay at the clubhouse until I get back. No arguments. Got it?"

Nodding in agreement, she said in a shaky voice, "Be safe."

Locking the door behind him, Hawk entered the empty hallway and made his way to the parking lot. Outside, the icy air slammed him in the face while puffs of his breath created smoke rings. Looking at the other riders, he jerked his head toward the open road, and the rumble of eleven motorcycles shattered the quietness of the early morning as the riders disappeared into the darkness.

CHAPTER TWENTY-FIVE

A S HE RODE toward the Nomads' clubhouse, the freezing wind pelted Hawk's face. *I'll teach that motherfucker Viper to mess with my woman.* Since he first learned of it, he'd brooded about Cara's encounter with the jerk. He couldn't stand for *any* man to even look at his Cara, let alone a fucking asshole like Viper.

A slow smile spread across his face as Cara entered his mind. They were good together, and the way she writhed and moaned, confirmed she lusted for him as much as he did for her. And she had no problem showing him how much she enjoyed it. His sexy wildcat threatened his heart, and he had no clue if she felt something other than lust for him.

Earlier in the night, when she climbed on top of him and rode his cock, he decided she was more than his favorite fuck—he wanted Cara as a part of his life. Realization had slammed him in the face, and not having her in his life was not an option, but the biggest shock was he craved more than fucking with her. He wanted the whole damn package: conversations, laughing at stupid stuff, knowing she'd be in his room when he came back. As far back as he could remember, he'd never wanted to belong to any one woman—that shit was alien to him. In his life, he had belonged to two things: his troop and the Insurgents. He had never belonged to any woman.

After his mom left him in the hands of his monster dad, he swore off women except for fucking. But then he met Cara, and she did something to him no woman had ever been able to do—she made him care. His wildcat softened the edges of his hard, jagged heart and threatened to break the shell, stirring emotions deep in the caverns of his heart. In the beginning, he'd tried to stay away, but he couldn't. Cara had already claimed his cock and was going for his heart, and he never saw it coming—*him*, of all people. Figuring he'd be the last one who would ever fall for a woman, the brothers looked at him in amusement, but she had him on her hook. *Damn, look at Cara: her soft skin, her luscious body, her laugh, her sass. Fuck, I never stood a chance.*

The riders started their descent into the canyon which housed the Nomads' clubhouse, and all eyes were on Hawk as they waited for him to give the gesture to kill their motors and roll their Harleys. Stretching his arm, he signaled them to stop and cut their engines, which lent an eeriness to the night.

"Jax said four fucks drove the truck with the women. The brothers went to intercept them," Ruben said.

"Good. Are there any women in the house?" He wanted to punish the Nomads, but he didn't want innocent women hurt or killed.

"As far as we can tell, Viper keeps the women in the basement in separate rooms. There may be some in there," Ruben answered.

"No one upstairs except the motherfuckers?" Hawk wanted to be sure.

"Don't think so."

"I want to air condition the house, but I don't want anyone to be hurt except the fuckin' Nomads," Hawk said.

Air conditioning a rival's clubhouse meant riddling it with bullets. The Insurgents strove to keep peace, but if someone crossed the line or disrespected them, they had no problem showing their strength.

Hawk nodded at several of the brothers, who took out their AKs and semi-automatics—two of the brothers carried a few grenades in case things went out of control. Armed and ready, the group was on stealth-mode as they approached their target.

A series of pops shattered the still night. Lights flicked on, illuminating the clubhouse and members as they screamed, "What the fuck?" Windows cracked under the assault while wood panels groaned when bullets bore deep into them. Inside the clubhouse, pandemonium broke out, and Nomads ran every which way. Some pulled out their pistols and shot into the inky blackness, but it was obvious the Nomads didn't know what hit them.

Jax ran toward Hawk, who motioned Jax to come to the clearing to the right of the clubhouse where it was quieter. Jax said, "We intercepted the truck, and we're going to drive it back to Pinewood Springs. What are we gonna do with the women?"

"Banger doesn't want them anywhere near the clubhouse. Drop off the truck at the county line then text Doris. She'll make the call to the officials and they can sort all this out. We don't want too much involvement with them. You can take care of it, right?"

"Yeah, sure. I'll take Chas with me. We'll head out now," Jax said.

Hawk nodded, and Jax took off through the forest of evergreens.

When Hawk came back to the Nomads' clubhouse, the Insurgents were inside. Jumping up on the porch, his steel-capped boots crunched over the spent bullets. Inside, streaks of red were on the walls, and pools of blood stained the floors. Going to each downed Nomad, Hawk kicked them over, face-up, trying to find Viper. Not seeing him among the casualties, he went upstairs, weapon drawn, and kicked opened the closed doors. No one was there but a petite brunette chained to a bedpost; naked and crying, she bore the angry markings of a beating on her delicate skin. Staring through frightened, swollen eyes, she moved closer to the bedpost as if to make her body as small as possible. With each step Hawk took, the young woman flinched until she cried out when he bent down on his knees next to her.

"It's okay. I'm not here to hurt you."

As tears rolled down her face, she whimpered and winced when they fell onto her split lip.

Not finding a key to release the chains, Hawk located a bolt cutter under the bed, broke the chains, and freed the woman.

Hawk looked at her. *Fuck, she isn't more than eighteen years old. Fuck these assholes.* He extended his hand, and the young woman hesitantly placed her hand in his. Helping her to her knees, he gave her the bed sheet to cover her nakedness.

"What the fuck happened?' he asked.

She shook her head, saying, "No English, no good."

The woman is no help. "Who did this to you?" Hawk asked as he pointed to her bruises and bloody lip.

She hung her head down, her small shoulders shaking as sobs overtook her. "Vip do me."

"Viper?" Hawk clarified.

She nodded. Hawk gestured for her to sit on the bed and wait for him to come back. In the hallway, he saw Ruben. "Have you seen that asshole, Viper?"

Ruben peeked around Hawk's shoulder. "Who's the bitch? Is she Viper's whore?" he asked.

"More like his victim. She doesn't speak English. He did a number on her. I think she's one of the women who were smuggled, but I can't learn anything from her. Where *is* that motherfucker?"

"No Nomads are up here. The brothers found a couple of girls in the basement: one is a cute blonde all prettied up, and the other one is in a cage, naked and wearing a collar and a gag. What do we do with them?"

"We'll take them with us. We can't leave them here. Let's take them to one of the safe houses away from the clubhouse. The less they know, the less they can talk. It'd be too bad to have to dispose of them if they see too much, you know?"

"Okay, Hawk. I'll take care of it."

Before going downstairs, Hawk gave Ruben a towel and motioned him to hand it to the terrified woman for her bloody face.

Mayhem greeted Hawk as he approached the main floor. Six of the Nomads were on the premises, and they lay in puddles of blood. Looking at the grim scene, Hawk said, "Let's take care of this." The brothers went to work, making sure nothing would trace back to the Insurgents.

Opening a door off the kitchen, Hawk went downstairs to the basement. Entering a large room, he observed the two women Ruben told him about. The blonde was the same one he'd seen the morning before, and he recalled Viper singling her out. Looking closely at her, Hawk noticed she was young and petite, with small tits and blue eyes, and she looked familiar to him. Staring at her, he tried to place her, and her eyes shone with fear and contempt. Sitting on a concrete bench, dressed in a short, gold skirt with a crochet cream top which revealed her lacy gold bra, she looked like a young girl playing dress-up. It was like she decided to be a prostitute for Halloween, and her thick makeup lent a ghoulishness to her delicate features. Turning her eyes away from Hawk's stare, she focused her gaze on the ground.

Entering the room, Chas and PJ looked at the pretty blonde. "Are there any more women down here?" asked Chas.

"Not sure. I'm gonna check the other rooms. Have any of you seen that sniveling pussy, Viper?" Hawk darted his eyes down the dark basement's hallways.

Shaking his head, PJ said, "We haven't come across him. Maybe he's hiding in the woods like a pussy."

"Sounds like him. These motherfuckers must've had quite a trafficking business going. What a bunch of sick assholes," Chas said.

Nodding, Hawk walked down the hallway. Behind the basement room doors, the terror the women suffered made Hawk see red. Seething, he went through the rooms looking for Viper. Most of the rooms he entered resembled torture chambers, filled with whips, hooks, pussy lip stretchers, and wall-mounted ankle and wrist shackles. A few of the back rooms, under the stairs, resembled medieval dungeons, complete with steel puppy cages, punishment benches, suspension bars, and stockades. The smell of urine permeated the basement, and Hawk covered his nose with his hand. In all the rooms, dog bowls with water and food were on the floor, and dried blood speckled the walls.

Hawk left the basement in disgust; he was the last one to judge how people fucked, but it was about pleasure, not forcing women to do this shit. *It figures that asshole Viper has to rape women to get them to fuck his limp dick. Where the hell is that sonofabitch?*

Surveying the upstairs rooms, Hawk nodded in satisfaction while he gave the brothers the thumbs-up for clearing the room of all evidence. Looking at the women they found in the house, Hawk thought the club could find something for them to do in some of the MC businesses, and he figured they'd rather work at a dispensary or restaurant than be deported, but he'd let the women decide what they wanted to do.

As the brothers prepared to leave, Ruben came up to Hawk. "Word is Viper and two of his members are in Pinewood Springs."

"Why the fuck didn't any of you see him leave? Who the hell dropped the ball? Shit, let's get going. I want to find that fucker." Hawk's jaw tightened. Cara was in Pinewood Springs. He signaled the Insurgents to follow as he raced to his woman.

In the distance, the low wail of sirens echoed in the canyon before Hawk's phone rang.

"Fuckin' badges are comin'. Shit, there's a goddamn light show," Jax said.

"Get your asses outta there!" Hawk shouted. "Leave the truck and haul ass. Take the back roads, and we'll meet up with you at South Bend."

"What about the women?"

"The badges will find them and deal with them. Do any of them speak English?"

"Not that I could tell," said Jax.

"Good. Everything's been cleaned up, bodies gone, and nothing links us to any of this shit. Now get the hell out. We'll see you in about an hour."

Increasing the speed on his motorcycle, Hawk and his brothers rode toward Pinewood Springs.

STREAMING SUNLIGHT WOKE Cara up and she stretched out her arm, hoping to find Hawk's warm body. Nothing—he was still gone.

She sighed and worry creased her brow as images of him hurt and bleeding stabbed her mind. Fretting, she washed up and went downstairs for a hot cup of coffee, entering the kitchen she looked around; she didn't want a repeat performance with Lola or the other ladies. Thankfully, no one was in the kitchen.

After she poured a cup of coffee, Cara opened the refrigerator and searched for something to eat. A chair scraped against the concrete floor, and Cara whirled around; a young blonde woman greeted her with a big smile. She was a pretty girl with sparkling blue eyes that looked familiar. Walking over to Cara, hand extended, she said, "Hi, I'm Kylie. You must be Cara."

Smiling, Cara shook the young woman's hand. *Of course, this is Banger's daughter. I should have known that from her eyes.*

"How do you like it here?" Kylie asked as she took a bite of a chocolate iced doughnut.

"It takes some getting used to."

Kylie shrugged. "I suppose. This has always been my life, so I don't know anything different."

"For someone not used to the life, it can be a little overwhelming," Cara said.

Kylie eyed Cara as she chewed her doughnut. "Aren't you the one who's supposed to teach me how to cook spaghetti sauce and other things?"

Cara smiled. "Your dad mentioned it to me. If you're interested, it would be my pleasure."

"My dad sure loves your cooking. He's crazy for your spaghetti sauce. I've never heard him rave about anything so much. He wants me to learn how to make it."

"We can set up a time in the next few weeks," Cara said.

"How long are you staying here?" Kylie asked.

"I don't know, but I hope to go home soon."

Jerry walked in and grabbed a cup of coffee. He looked Kylie up and down and lingered on her rounded ass and curvy hips. Since Kylie had her back turned, she didn't notice Jerry checking her out, but his lustful sweeps over her body were not lost on Cara.

"Hi, Kylie. You're looking good," Jerry said.

Kylie spun around, her cheeks reddening. "Thanks."

"Does your dad know you're here?" he asked.

"Maybe," she replied.

"I bet he doesn't. You better go on home before he sees you."

"I don't care. It's boring at home. Anyway, I haven't seen you guys in a long time." She placed her waist-length hair behind her ears, jumped up on the counter, and crossed her long legs. Cara saw the lust in Jerry's eyes as he looked at Kylie's denim-clad legs while he shifted from one foot to another.

"Better watch yourself, or Banger's gonna beat your ass if he catches you staring at his daughter," Johnnie said under his breath.

Cara didn't notice Johnnie come into the kitchen because the exchange between Jerry and Kylie distracted her. Her stomach twisted when she heard Johnnie warning Jerry. Knowing Johnnie spoke the truth, she hoped Jerry heeded his words.

"He'd beat your ass even harder if he finds out you're *talking* to his daughter."

Jerry hurled Johnnie a steely glare while Kylie, twirling a strand of hair around her finger, said, "So what if she talks to me?"

In the short time Cara was at the clubhouse, she picked up on two rules: Prospects didn't talk until they were spoken to, and no one, patched or not, talked to Kylie unless Banger approved it. Kylie was off-limits to club members, and to men in general. The way Jerry acted toward Kylie was unacceptable, and if a member saw him, Jerry would receive a beatdown. Cara overheard him tell Johnnie that Kylie was the prettiest woman he had ever seen. Cara liked Jerry, but she knew Banger was overprotective of his daughter and had no tolerance for anyone who talked or flirted with her, especially a club member.

"What the fuck are you doin' here, Kylie?" Banger loomed in the doorway.

They all jumped at Banger's voice, and Johnnie busied himself by emptying the trashcans as Jerry, mug in hand, dashed out of the room.

Cara cringed when Banger threw Jerry the evil eye.

"Hi, Daddy," Kylie said. "Cara and I were arranging when I can start my cooking classes."

Banger's face softened. "Okay, that's good, but you know I don't like you hangin' 'round here unless I'm in the room with you."

"Oh, Dad, these guys are my extended family. They always have my back, you know that." Throwing her arms around his neck, she kissed him on the cheek.

In front of Cara's eyes, Banger melted, and the way his eyes shone with love for his daughter reminded Cara of her relationship with her own father. She padded out of the kitchen so father and daughter could share some time together.

As she started going upstairs, her phone beeped.

Sherrie: Where r you? Been trying to find you????

Cara: Sorry for disappearing, had to get away. Will be back in a few.

Sherrie: R u in Denver?

Cara: No, in woods resting. Needed the break. Don't have good reception here. Will call when I get back. K?

Sherrie: K, but know u aren't telling me whole story. :(

Cara: Will tell u everything when I get back. Promise. All is good. See u soon.

Cara hated to lie to Sherrie about what was going on and where she was, but she couldn't risk Sherrie's involvement.

As the pack of motorcycles roared into the compound's parking lot, the ground vibrated. Cara's heart leapt with joy as she let out a sigh of relief. *Hawk's home and he's okay.* Tingling with excitement, she ran to the great room as the front door opened and a group of members clad in blue jeans and leather walked through it. The minute Hawk came into the room, their eyes locked and she rushed up to him, flung her arms around his neck, and hugged him close to her. He dropped his head and crushed her mouth with his. Hawk's lips tasted of salt and grit, and he smelled like the wind and the earth. As he devoured her mouth in front of everyone in the room, a primal sexiness emanated from him, and not caring how many eyes were on them, she pressed into him and stroked his broad back. Hawk was back and that was all that mattered to her.

"Oh, Cara," he murmured, his nose running along her jaw down to her neck.

"Is everything okay?" she asked as she cradled his head against her shoulder.

"Yeah."

Opening her eyes, Cara saw a young, pretty blonde with heavy makeup behind Hawk. "Who's that?" she asked.

"Who, babe?"

"That girl behind you?"

Hawk swung around and saw the girl. "Fuck," he muttered under his breath. "What the fuck is she doing here? Can't anyone do anything right?" he yelled.

"Who is she?" Cara asked again.

"I don't know. We kinda found her. I don't think she speaks English."

Cara stared at her in disbelief. "Hawk," she whispered. "She looks like the women who've been murdered by the Mountainside Strangler. It's too creepy."

Hawk's eyes widened. "Yeah, she does. That's why she looked familiar to me. She's been made up to look like the next victim. I fuckin' knew the Nomads were involved in this sick shit."

"Where did you go this morning?" Cara questioned.

"Club business. Change the subject." His voice dripped ice.

Cara opened her mouth to protest but changed her mind as many pairs of eyes shot through her. "What's she doing here?"

"Fuck if I know," Hawk said, looking around to find Jax.

"I didn't want to go to some fuckin' safe house," the blonde snarled.

The room fell silent as all eyes were on the petite blonde.

"Why the fuck is everyone staring at me?"

Hawk cleared his voice. "You're American? Why the fuck didn't you tell us you spoke English?"

"Because you didn't fuckin' ask me."

"What were you doing with all those foreigners?" Jax asked as he approached her.

"Assholes picked me up. I was hitchin' a ride, so I jumped on one of the bikes and my hell began," she said matter-of-factly.

"Cara, go up to the room. We got club business here," Hawk said.

When she opened her mouth to object, Hawk sent her a look that told her to back off. She turned around and went up to Hawk's room.

CHAPTER TWENTY-SIX

O NCE CARA LEFT, Hawk glowered at the girl. "You should have fuckin' told us you were an American. Were there any other Americans in the group of women?"

"No, I was the only one. The dirtbags liked the ones who couldn't speak English."

"How long you been with the Nomads?" Hawk asked.

"'Bout a week."

"Why weren't you in the truck with the other women?"

"That asshole, Viper, said he saved me for something special. Some rich guy wanted me. He made me dress and put makeup on in a certain way 'cause he said the guy liked women who looked like that. He said he'd get a shitload of cash for me."

"What's your name?" Jax asked.

"Who the fuck cares?" Hawk shouted. Pissed that one of the brothers screwed up by bringing a witness to the clubhouse, Hawk pounded his fist against the concrete walls. The bitch knew about everything: the hit on the Nomads' clubhouse, the safe house, the Insurgents. She was a fucking loose end. *Fuck!*

"I care," Jax said.

"Cherri," she whispered.

"Well, Cherri, what are we gonna do with you?" Jax asked in a soft voice.

"I dunno."

"Let's fuck her and throw her whore ass out!" one of the brothers yelled. Some of the other brothers hooted and clapped in agreement.

"I don't care what you do," she muttered.

Glaring at the brothers, Hawk said, "Shut the fuck up! No one is touching her. Got it?" Turning to the young woman, he asked, "What kind of jobs have you done before?" He wanted to keep this one close to home in case she squealed.

She shrugged. "For a short time I danced in a strip bar. It was okay and the tips were good."

"How old are you?"

"Twenty-one."

"Do you want to dance at Dream House? It's the club's strip bar, and the money is good. If not, I can get you a job at one of the restaurants. Have you waited tables before?"

"Yeah, I've waitressed before. I'd rather be a dancer. It's a helluva lot easier and the money is way better. Dream House sounds okay."

"Then it's settled; you'll dance at Dream House. One of the women will get you settled, and tomorrow, you'll learn the ropes," Hawk said. Turning to the members he added, "Get Emma. She can go over everything and set this one straight."

Jax jumped out of his chair. "I'll get Emma. And I'll keep an eye on this one." He glanced at Cherri, who stood against the wall, her eyes fixed on the floor.

Hawk perceived the desire in Jax's eyes, and he guessed Jax wanted to fuck her. "She's your project now, Jax. Don't fuck it up."

Hawk turned toward the stairway; he was tired and craved Cara's warm body. He climbed the stairs to his room, and when he opened the door, Cara sat on the bed. Crossing the room in three strides, he leaned over and kissed her.

"Don't you think it's spooky she looked like one of the victims? I'll bet she was going to be delivered to the sicko who's been doing the killings. Damn, she was lucky you found her," Cara said.

Hawk had been thinking the same thing. If he hadn't hit the Nomads' clubhouse, she would have been the eleventh victim. *She owes the Insurgents. That's for damn sure.*

"Are you going to call the police?" Cara asked.

"What? Are you fuckin' nuts? We don't call the badges for anything. We take care of business ourselves, Cara. Leave it be." His tone was ominous, and her expression changed to one of complacency.

Glad Cara didn't push it, Hawk rubbed his hand over his face. Exhaustion took over, and Cara's cool hand soothed him as she stroked his cheek. "You look tired."

"I am, babe." He shrugged off his jacket, kicked off his boots, then lay down next to her. Nudging her close to him, his mouth sought hers as her scent consumed him. Fisting her hair in his hand, Hawk explored her mouth with his tongue. Cara moaned and drew him nearer to her, his cock straining against his zipper. As his hands traveled down to the waistband of her jeans, she caressed his leg with hers. Sliding his hand into her pants, his fingers sought her warm, wet pussy. He tickled her mound while she clenched her thighs and rolled her body in a figure eight. Each time she moved her sweet ass, her stomach rubbed his cock. *Fuck, she knows how to turn me on.*

His finger, buried deep in her wet folds, swept her to an intense, pulsing orgasm, and her whimpers blended with his pants. "It feels so good, Hawk. So good." She bowed at the waist and clamped her legs together as he held her beside him until the spasms subsided. As she burrowed her head into the crook of his arm, her moaning lessened. His cock, still hard, twitched as he ran his fingers through her hair; he loved to watch her while she came with intensity and abandonment. He loved the fire in his wildcat.

As Hawk massaged her mound with his knee, Cara tilted her head upward and cried out while his mouth caught her last sounds of pleasure, pushing his tongue into her mouth. Languidly, she massaged his balls through his pants, causing him to suck in his breath through his parted lips. Unzipping his jeans, she freed his cock and smeared the beads of pre-come over his silky head. Little by little, she removed his pants as he twitched underneath her, his chest rising and falling. Drawing away from him, she tugged at his t-shirt and pushed it upwards before he yanked it off over his head. He held his breath as she traced his tats with her tongue, nipping and kissing his chest and arms while his cock dug into her soft flesh.

"Fuck, Cara, what are you doing to me? You've cast some kind of shit over me. Fuck, fuck." Hawk exhaled and tangled his fingers in her hair.

Down, down, down she went with her lips, her tongue, and her nails as Hawk, propped back against the headboard, allowed himself to relax. He relished the fire she lit in his cock and balls. *I can't get enough of my wildcat.*

When her lips wrapped around the satiny head of his dick, he gasped. Then she brushed her tongue over the top of his cock, slow and steady, as he wrapped a fistful of her hair in his hand and guided her movements. Holding his shaft, she stroked it hard as she curled her tongue around the tip and twisted it in circles. "Fuck, you're killing me," Hawk said in a ragged breath.

Lifting her eyes, she met his smoldering gaze, caressing and sucking his cock as they stared at one another. "Mmmm, I love the way you taste."

"Fuck, babe, you look hot with my cock in your mouth. I want to fuck you hard."

"All in good time," she teased as she tickled his balls. His strong legs tensed as she pushed his legs apart and kneeled between them. Putting her left hand under his ass, she kneaded it roughly, scratching it with her long nails. Her tongue licked the length of his dick as he grew harder and thicker with each pass of her tongue, and he felt as though his skin would tear apart each time her wicked tongue stroked his shaft. He jerked as she gripped his hardness, putting it into her mouth, sucking it noisily while taking in more and more of him.

"Fuck that feels awesome. Fuck... fuck..." His cock throbbed as Cara sucked him mercilessly.

As Hawk's dick pulsed inside her mouth, she squeezed the base and sucked harder while her pace became frenzied. With his cock deep in her throat, Hawk's whole body stiffened. *Fuck! I've never had a blowjob like this.* Hawk closed his eyes and the mounting tension reached its limit, then burst in a stream of desire, and he jerked his head back, moaning, as his liquid trickled down Cara's throat. Digging his hands in her hair, her strands twisted around his fingers, she moaned and rotated her hips.

Opening her mouth, Cara licked away the wetness on his cock, and he yanked her up next to him. His mouth on hers, he tasted his salty tang on her lips. At that moment, he never felt so close to any one person as he did to Cara, and the intensity of her pull amazed him.

As Cara laid her head on his chest, he brushed her back with his fingertips while his racing heart slowed down. When a drop of water landed on his chest, he tilted Cara's face up and a pair of glistening eyes met his. *Why is she crying?*

"Are you okay? Did I hurt you or something?"

Nuzzling his chest, she muttered, "No, I'm fine."

"If you're fine, then why are you crying?"

"It was so intense. I'm just in a good place right now." She snuggled against him.

"Oh, okay." For as long as he lived, he'd never figure out women.

She wiped away her tears, kissed him, and said, "I've never shared anything this intense with any man. You make me feel things I've never felt before. It's good, honey. It's all good."

Hearing her call him *honey* pleased him, and he wanted to tell her she was his everything, but fear of rejection stopped him. Even though the magic of the moment shrouded her, she didn't tell him she wanted *him*, and he wasn't ready to open his heart all the way. Embracing her, their bodies meshed together as one, and they fell asleep as the first snowflakes of the season whirled outside their window in the frosty wind.

CHAPTER TWENTY-SEVEN

THE NEXT MORNING, snow blanketed the ground, and the late-morning sun strained to break through the clouds as thin shards of ice hung precariously on tree branches. Not wanting to leave the warmth of Hawk's bed, Cara pulled the covers over her head. Rolling to her side, she watched Hawk as he slept, the usual scowl gone from his face. Smiling, she brushed his cheek.

I adore you. I want to tell you I can't imagine my life without you, but I'm afraid you'll push me away. We have great sex together, but for me, it's so much more. Do you feel anything for me besides the physical pleasure we share? Cara yearned to bare her soul to him but, fearing rejection, she buried her feelings.

Her phone's beep interrupted her thoughts and, not wanting to wake Hawk up, she picked up her phone and changed the profile to "vibrate."

Josh: Found out something interesting. Can u get to a computer? I'll email u what I have.

Cara: Send it to me.

Josh: K Share this with CBI. Don't do anything alone. B careful!

Cara: I will. Thx will call u.

Glancing at Hawk's sleeping form as she crept out of bed, her stomach fluttered. He would be mad at her for asking Josh to give her information about the murders, but she had a hunch there was a conspiracy which would rock the whole county, if uncovered. Problem was she didn't know who was involved, or how to prove it. She hoped Josh gave her a credible lead, and if necessary, she'd enlist Eric's help; he was in thick with many of the court personnel, since he was a judge.

Of course, anything she found out, she'd turn over to her friend, Jim, and let CBI do the heavy stuff. Hawk wanted her to stay out of it, but she couldn't. Ever since Nadyia's sister came to see her, she couldn't let go of the killings, and Nadyia's lifeless eyes haunted her. Hawk didn't understand, and knowing he'd thwart her efforts, she decided not to tell him anything until later.

Sitting at the computer, she focused on the attachment Josh sent her as goosebumps covered her arms. She read the document several times hoping she missed or misunderstood something.

"What are you doing?" Hawk's voice broke her concentration.

Closing out the screen, she snapped down the cover of her laptop. "Nothing much, just checking e-mails. Sorry if I woke you up."

"You haven't told anyone you're here, right?"

"I haven't. Everyone thinks I went away for a few days to decompress."

Hawk narrowed his eyes, and she avoided his look.

"You sure? You're acting funny." He set his jaw and lowered his head, studying her face.

Swallowing hard, Cara said, "I'm sure, no one knows. Are you working today?"

A couple of minutes passed before Hawk answered. "Yeah, I'm going to check out my dispensary, then I have some club business to do. I'll be back later tonight. You look worried."

"Do I? I guess I'm nervous about all the work I have piling up with all the different cases."

"I want you to stay inside the clubhouse, got it? I know you're getting antsy, but for now, you have to listen to me on this. Viper is in Pinewood Springs."

Cara's eyes widened. "How do you know that?" The memory of Viper's thin lips on hers made her tremble.

"I just do. Stay put."

"Yeah, okay. I got it."

Going over to her, he hugged her and kissed the top of her forehead. "Be a good girl, okay? Stay here 'til I get back. Should be around eight or so."

Cara wrapped her arms around Hawk's waist and kissed his bare chest. "I'll be here when you get back."

A tinge of nausea rolled around in Cara's stomach as Hawk went into the bathroom. She hated deceiving him, but she had to meet with Eric, because the document Josh sent opened up new concerns and questions. Deciding to wait about an hour after Hawk left, she'd zip into town and meet up with Eric. Figuring she'd be back way before Hawk ever returned, he'd be none the wiser.

Her phone vibrated and she viewed the text message:

Eric: Where r u now? I thought u were out of town? What's going on?

Cara: Can't explain now. Need to meet u. Got info re killings. Can meet u in hr?

Eric: Can't. In court—trial. What about later?

Cara: Not too late. What about 6?

Eric: 6:45 is earliest I can do.

Crap, that won't give me much time before Hawk comes back. If he comes home early, I'm screwed. Maybe I should just wait for tomorrow. Who am I kidding? I can't stand waiting. I have to meet with Eric to figure out what's going on. She chewed her bottom lip while pondering the pros and cons of meeting Eric so late, finally deciding that she'd limit her meeting to thirty minutes, max.

Cara: K but let's meet closer to Ridge View. Downtown too far.

Eric: What about Prospect's Mine? Close to Ridge View.

Cara: K see u 6:45 at the mine. Later.

She put her phone down as Hawk came out of the bathroom, a blue towel snug around his waist, his hair hung loosely down his back. He winked at her as he took out a clean t-shirt and a pair of blue jeans. Watching him as he grabbed another towel and dried his hair, his biceps flexing with each movement, she ran her eyes up and down his body. *Damn, he's sexy in his towel and tats.*

Turning around, he caught her checking him out and chuckled. "Babe, you're gonna give me a hard-on looking at me like that. Fuck, my cock's already twitching."

She turned away, her cheeks bright at being caught.

"Don't have to turn away, baby. If you like what you see, feast your eyes on it, but be ready to fuck me."

Instead of responding, Cara opened her laptop and pulled up a game of Spider Solitaire. She couldn't make love to him right then. She was too anxious about meeting Eric and Hawk finding out. Although she hated to admit it, she wanted him to be on his way.

Hawk slipped his jeans on over his bulging cock, smoothed down his black t-shirt, put on his cut, and his boots, then grabbed his leather jacket. He came over to Cara and cupped her chin, dipped his head, and kissed her. Grasping one of her tits, he tweaked her nipple as she moaned and squirmed in the desk chair. "That's to hold you over until I get back," he said.

She hugged his waist. "Come home soon," she said. *But not before eight o'clock.*

Hawk left the room. When she heard his motorcycle's engine, she watched him from the window until he and his Harley were mere specks on the desolate road.

AS HE EXHALED, Viper's breath came out in puffs of smoke. *Where's the fuckin' whore?* He stood on her porch and tried to look through the closed shutters. He'd been waiting for the slut to come home since the night before, but she hadn't shown up yet. *No doubt fucking that piece of shit's balls off. What a fuckin' cunt.*

Lighting a cigarette, he inhaled the nicotine deeply. It calmed him.

He itched to fuck the big-titted slut, mark her soft flesh, and make her his own sex slave. She had become more than a nuisance to the Nomads with all her prying. He'd teach her a lesson, and he'd throw it in Hawk's face. That motherfucker needed his ass knocked down several rungs on his high-and-mighty ladder. Hawk was into this slut, and Viper didn't blame him; she was a hot one. She had a fire in her, and he'd felt it when he'd held her in her office as she'd fought him. He was going to love taming the bitch. Of course, when he tired of her, he'd slit her pretty throat.

Fuck, it's cold out here. Viper breathed into his ice-cold hands, trying to give them some warmth. The more he stood there waiting, the madder he got. The slut kept causing him trouble, and he couldn't wait to fuck every one of her holes. He planned to ram his cock so hard in each one that she would beg him to kill her. His cock strained against his jeans as he thought of the fun he'd have with Cara. *Fuckin' slut, she's gonna get everything she deserves.* He mashed his cigarette out on the pristine snow.

His phone vibrated, and as he looked at the text message, an evil sneer spread across his face. By the end of the night, he'd have the bitch fucked, trussed, and on the back of his bike. He'd show her how to behave, and if she gave him lip, well, he'd just have to punish her.

THE DAY DRAGGED on, and Cara was so nervous she practically jumped out of her skin. She noticed every place she went, Ruben followed and, convinced Hawk made him her bodyguard, she worked on devising a plan to ditch the biker. Knowing Hawk meant well didn't take away her indignation—sometimes he treated her like a child.

The heat from her ire rose from her neck to her forehead. She was a grown woman who could take care of herself. Cara knew he fancied himself her protector, but even though she liked the way he made her feel safe, sometimes he was too much. Whenever she was with Hawk and men looked at her, he'd throw them one of his menacing scowls, making them turn away. Of course they didn't want a confrontation with the tall, muscular man wearing his leather jacket with the Insurgents colors. She liked that; she felt protected and cared for. She enjoyed having someone other than herself taking care of things, and that surprised the hell out of her. That day, however, she wished Hawk would have left his he-man attitude in the bedroom, since she needed to get out of the compound without Ruben following her. *Damn.*

Kylie came into the kitchen and waved at Cara. Waving back, Cara approached the young woman, figuring it would pass the time if she taught Kylie how to make spaghetti sauce. Also, Kylie could be instrumental in her plan to ditch Ruben.

Kylie was a quick learner with a wry sense of humor, and Cara enjoyed the afternoon with her. At the end of her cooking lesson, Kylie had two large pots of simmering spaghetti sauce, one of which she would take home to her dad, and the other one she'd leave for the members' dinner. While the women cooked, the enticing aroma of garlic, onions, and basil brought the members into the kitchen, beckoning them to dip freshly baked Italian bread into the simmering sauce. The rave reviews pleased Cara, and she was glad her old family recipe found new people to appreciate it.

The sun set over the mountain peaks as the moon rose in the darkened eastern sky. Cara glanced at the clock in the kitchen and noticed it was six-fifteen. She had to get a move on, so she motioned Kylie over.

"What's up?" Kylie asked.

"I need to go out for a bit, but I don't want Ruben tagging me. Do you think you can distract him for about fifteen minutes or so?"

"Why would Ruben follow you?"

"Hawk isn't here, and he wanted to make sure I'm doing okay. You know how these men are."

"God, I love these guys. They're my family, but they can be so infuriating with their possessiveness," Kylie said, rolling her eyes.

"Tell me about it. I need a little time to myself, you know?"

"Oh, yeah, I get it. I'll distract Ruben for a bit."

"Thanks. I owe you one," Cara smiled at the girl and headed toward the stairs. As Ruben followed her, Cara said to Kylie, "I think I'll read in my room for a while. Let me know when dinner is ready."

Kylie came up to Ruben and asked, "Do you know if my dad's here?"

Cara pretended to climb the stairs, but the minute Ruben turned his head toward Kylie, she tiptoed down the hallway into the mud room. Looking over her shoulder to make sure no one was behind her, she opened the back door. The bitter cold slapped her in the face and she pulled her sweater tighter around her chest. Inside her car, she switched on the ignition and killed her headlights. She drove to the chain-link fence and jumped out to open it. Her fingers, numb from the cold, fumbled with the lock as she checked behind her shoulder.

"Where're you going?" a gruff voice asked.

She turned around and expected to see Ruben, but instead, she looked into Johnnie's eyes. "I'm running to do an errand of the female type," she said.

Embarrassed, he looked down, and said, "Do you need help with the lock?"

"Yes, please. My fingers are so cold I can't move them right."

He came over, and with his gloved hand, opened the lock. Relief flooded over her. She knew Ruben would climb the stairs to make sure she was in Hawk's room, and she had wasted precious time with the damn lock. Smiling at Johnnie, she said, "Thanks." She plopped in her car, turned on her headlights, and drove into the murky night.

CHAPTER TWENTY-EIGHT

ERIC LOOKED AT his watch. It was almost seven o'clock, and Cara still wasn't there. *Maybe something held her up.* He decided to give her five more minutes, then he'd leave. It was damn freezing in the shack near the abandoned mine. Thinking back to his high school years, he remembered coming to the mine with his buddies to drink beer, and sometimes they'd bring a few girls to make-out with. The girls were afraid the shack and mine were haunted. Those were the carefree days, when he didn't have much to worry about and his life was in order.

Those days seemed so long ago, and he was weary of everything. He didn't want to marry Nancy because she was a demanding bitch, but her father had a lot of money and political clout, so she was a necessary component in his plan to run for mayor. How he wished he could stop the tedious wheel his life was on.

Where is Cara? He needed to talk to her to find out what she thought was so urgent. Why couldn't she keep her nose out of this mess like he had asked her to? She'd always been a curious girl. Back when they were kids, she'd questioned everything, and whenever they'd watch police shows together, she'd tell him how she would've done things differently. He smiled to himself; he and Cara had been so close growing up. Over the last few years, they had drifted apart, and he knew it was more his fault than hers because he was the one who'd distanced himself. He felt vulnerable, like his world was closing in around him, and he didn't want Cara to see his weakness.

I'm so stressed. All Cara cares about is her lowlife, outlaw biker. The thought of her with Hawk revolted him. *How can Cara even think of going out with a man like Hawk? Why does she find him attractive, he's—*

Tires crunching on the snow in front of the mine interrupted Eric's thoughts. He peered out the doorway and saw Cara park her sports car.

"It's about time. You're late. I was ready to leave," Eric said when she entered the shack.

"Sorry, I didn't mean to be late. How are you? You look tired," she commented.

"Work is a pain in the ass, and Nancy is driving me nuts with all the wedding plans. I'll be glad when that's all over. You look great, rested and happy," he said, his eyes scanning her face.

She laughed. "A few days off works wonders."

"What's this emergency that made you drag us out in the freezing cold?"

She took a deep breath then opened her purse and removed several folded sheets of paper. Handing them to Eric, she said, "A friend of mine sent this to me. He works with law enforcement, so he's going to share this with the detectives."

"Share what?" Eric said, taking the papers from her. "What the hell is this?"

"Your court schedules, your sentencings, your convictions, and your mistrials."

Eric looked at her, puzzled. "Why are you giving this to me?"

"Why are you protecting the Deadly Demons Nomads? Look at your record—most of your mistrials had the Nomads as defendants. When they *have* been convicted, you gave them community service or deferred sentences. Eric, you haven't sent a Nomad to prison in the last two years, and yet, you're all over the Insurgents for crimes they haven't committed or ones that aren't a big deal. Why?"

"Is this what this goddamn rendezvous is all about? You want to protect your boyfriend's dirt bag gang?"

"No," she said in a soft voice. "I want to understand the disparity in justice, that's all."

"What are you trying to say? What are you accusing me of?" Eric's face turned red as he screamed at her.

"I'm not accusing you of anything. I'm trying to understand what your connection to the Deadly Demons Nomads is."

"We're his supplier, fuckin' cunt." Viper's icy snarl cooled down the tension between the cousins. Both Cara and Eric whirled around at the sound, Viper's narrow eyes shining like sleet in the darkness.

"What are you doing here?" Eric yelled.

Cara whispered, "You know this guy?"

Eric hung his head, mumbling something inaudible.

Viper smirked. "He knows me well, *sweetheart*. We've been doin' business for a while now, haven't we, Judge?"

Eric grimaced. "Leave her out of this."

"Out of what? Eric, tell me what the hell is going on."

"Go on, Judge. Tell her what the fuck's goin' on. And I'm not leavin' her outta shit. The whore wanted to be involved, and now she's *very* involved."

"Eric?" Cara stared at him.

Eric covered his face with his hands, then Cara watched as he removed them, a scowl replacing his concerned look. "You couldn't keep your goddamn nose out of this, could you, Cara? I begged you. I told you to back off. I fucking *warned* you to stay out of this, but you couldn't do it, could you? Now there's nothing I can do. Nothing."

"What are you talking about? Are these guys paying you big money? If you needed money, you could have come to me or my dad. I would've helped you. What possessed you to go to *them* of all people?"

"You think this is about *money*? This has *nothing* to do with *money*! If only it did, life would be a lot simpler." Eric turned away from her.

Cara moved toward him, but Viper put his foot out and tripped her. "Stay where you are, bitch."

"Why are you involved with these guys? Tell me now, Eric."

Shaking his head, Eric mouthed the words, "I can't."

Viper sneered, "Enough of this bullshit. You wanna know why the judge here came to *us*? He had a craving so bad, *sweetheart*, nothing could satisfy him except young, pretty things. He needed us to feed his hunger."

"That's enough, Viper!"

"You don't fuckin' tell me shit, sicko." In one long stride, Viper was in front of Eric, grabbing him by the neck and squeezing. Eric gasped for breath. "You got that, asshole?" Viper's eyes blazed as he pressed tighter around Eric's throat.

"Stop it! Leave him alone!" Cara rushed over and pounded on Viper's back. Viper released Eric only to backhand Cara. Falling backwards, she landed on the plank floor, her lip cut open and bleeding. She wiped her mouth and glared at Viper.

"You'll be punished for that, and I'm going to enjoy every second of taming you, slut."

Eric, bent over, wheezing as he tried to catch his breath. Viper shoved him against the wall. "You fuckin' said you'd take care of this slut, and you didn't. I'll do the job you weren't man enough to do." Facing Cara, Viper said, "Your asshole cousin isn't a man. He's nothin' but a perverted wimp, who gets off on playing with and cutting young pussies. He's not even man enough to get his own bitches. Yeah, that's right, *sweetheart*. Your upstanding cousin is the fuckin' Mountainside Strangler. How's that for a family tree?" He laughed without mirth.

"What?" Cara folded her arms over her trembling body as she darted her eyes from Eric to Viper. Eric cast his gaze to the floor, unable to look her in the eye.

She wailed, "This isn't true! Tell me this isn't true, Eric. Tell me he's making this up. Tell me it isn't true. Eric, tell me! Oh, please, tell me this isn't true." Her teeth chattered as sobs racked her body. "This can't be true. I know you, Eric, you're my blood. We grew up together. We went on double-dates. We shared secrets. We were so close. Why aren't you denying this? I don't believe it. I *won't* believe it. Oh, my God!" Holding her hands over her face, Cara crumpled to the ground as her sobs overtook her body.

Waiting for her wailing to subside, Eric finally spoke, his voice cracking. "I'm sorry, Cara. I am."

Cara, tears streaming down her face, searched his face to find answers. "How can this be happening?"

"I don't expect you to understand. I've always been two people, good and bad, but the bad won out. The Nomads bring women to me no one wants or will look for, and I help them get their trafficking trucks and meth through this county. I have a hunger I can't control. I know you don't understand that—no one does—but to me, it's real, and it's with me most of the time. It worked until you started nosing around. I told you to leave it alone. I told you." Eric buried his face in his hands again.

Cara looked fixedly at Eric. "You are not the Eric I know and love."

"Sorry to break up the family reunion, but we gotta take care of business," Viper snapped.

WHY THE FUCK isn't Cara picking up her phone? Hawk set his cell down for the second time, worry creasing his brow. He didn't want to think the worst, figuring she was in the shower or maybe she fell asleep. His gut told him something wasn't right, and his woman was in trouble, but before he called her again, one of the wholesalers came into the dispensary. Vowing to call her after he finished his business transaction, Hawk decided if she didn't pick up her phone, he'd haul ass back to the clubhouse.

TWO NOMADS WALKED into the shack. One went by Eric, and the other stood by the doorway. They looked somewhat familiar to Cara. She knew she had seen them before, but she couldn't place them.

Viper ogled Cara as he clucked his tongue. "I'm gonna have some fun biting those big tits, bitch. You've caused me all kinds of trouble. You fucked up my association with the good judge, you got the damn cops to look in places they never should've, and your fuckin' man did some serious damage at my clubhouse. I'm gonna show you how a good slut is supposed to behave. Hawk's been too soft on your ass and pussy. I plan on changing that." Viper strode over to her.

Cara, still reeling from Eric's revelation, didn't pay attention to what Viper said. *I should have listened to Hawk and waited for him to come home.* Devastated at learning about Eric, she still couldn't fathom the enormity of the situation.

She felt Viper's hands around her arms as he jerked her to her feet, and she stood in his grip like a rag doll. Grabbing her hair, he pulled it, forced her head back, and placed his thin lips on hers while his tongue coerced her mouth open. His serpent-like tongue darted in and out of her mouth as his hand clasped her nipple, pinching it viciously. As she cried out in pain, Viper twisted her nipple harder and jammed his knee into her pussy while his hardness rubbed against her belly. As a wave of nausea hit her, she shoved Viper away, bent over, and threw up.

"Leave her alone," Eric said.

"What are you gonna do if I don't?" Viper challenged, and Eric just hung his head. "I didn't think your wimp ass would come to her rescue." The other two Nomads laughed. The one closest to Eric punched him in the stomach, and he groaned as he sank to his knees.

Viper jerked Cara up by her hair once again. "Your break's over, bitch. Rinse with this." He shoved a bottle of beer in her hands. As Cara rinsed and spit out the beer, she knew she was in trouble. There was no doubt in her mind that Viper, and the other two thugs, would rape her. She didn't think they were going to kill her yet, but she was pretty sure she would be hoping they would.

Viper knocked the beer bottle out of her hand, clasped her face, and kissed her mouth hard. This time Cara didn't resist, and as the wound from her split lip opened, her blood flowed. Viper plunged his tongue deep into her mouth. *I could bite down hard and give the asshole some of his own medicine. It would be worth it for that moment, but I'm sure he'd make me pay for it. Oh, Hawk, I'm sorry.*

Viper slammed her down on her knees then unzipped his pants. Cara squirmed as she tried to turn her head away from him. "Keep your face still, slut, or I'll beat the shit outta you." He slapped her across the face; the blood from her nose was cool against her hot cheeks.

"After you're done with this bitch, I want a piece of her stuck-up ass. I've wanted her pussy ever since I'd seen her at Rusty's," the bearded man said. The other Nomad sniggered, nodding in agreement.

Through bleary eyes, Cara looked at the two men and remembered them as the jerks who came on to her and Sherrie at Rusty's after they bought them drinks. Never thinking she'd see them again, she gritted her teeth at the irony of the situation.

"You can have her when I'm done," Viper said to Rot.

Rot leered at Cara and while cupping his crotch, he licked his lips. As the bile rose in her throat, she gagged.

"Hey, boss, Prez is on the phone. He wants to speak to you," Beaver said, holding the phone in his hands.

Cursing under his breath, Viper kicked Cara's legs. "I'll be back soon, cunt, and when I come back, I'm gonna fuck your mouth so hard you won't be able to talk for a week." Rot and Beaver hooted, and Viper took the phone outside.

Beaver, by the doorway, asked Viper, "What does Reaper want?"

"Wants to know why the fuck we were holding out on him with the sex trafficking and meth sales. He's also madder than hell we've stirred up all this shit with the Insurgents." Viper glared at Cara. "If this cunt would've stayed outta this, none of this would've happened. Bitch is gonna pay!"

"What's Reaper gonna do?" Rot piped in.

"I don't give a fuck about Reaper," Viper spat. "I just want to fuck the slut, and knowing she's Hawk's whore is gonna make it sweeter." A cruel smile cracked his face as he lit a cigarette.

Chapter Twenty-Nine

"RUBEN, WHY IN the hell isn't Cara answering her phone? I've called her three times," Hawk said, worry in his voice.

"She went up to her room to read about an hour ago," Ruben told him.

"Are you talking about Cara?" Johnnie asked.

"What of it, Prospect?" Ruben said. "Prospects should speak when spoken to."

"She left to do an errand. I opened the gate for her."

"Are you sure?" Ruben said.

"Yep."

"What the fuck is going on over there? Did he say Cara left?" Hawk yelled.

"Chas, run upstairs to Hawk's room and see if Cara's there," Ruben said.

"Weren't you supposed to be watching her? What happened?" Hawk demanded.

"She said she wanted to read, and then Kylie came up to me and started talking. Shit, I was double-teamed by the women. Fuck. Sorry, Hawk. I can't believe I was so stupid."

Chas came back into the great room and shook his head. "She's not there."

"Fuck," Hawk muttered. "I'm on my way."

Hawk raced to his bike and hauled ass back to the clubhouse.

When he burst through the front doors, Ruben said, "Sorry, brother. I fucked up."

Hawk glared at him. He was madder than hell, but he knew Ruben felt like shit about Cara. He said, "I gotta get her. I'll need you, Jax, and Chas to come with me."

"Do you know where she is?"

"I figured she wouldn't listen to me, so I installed GPS on her phone. I can track her. It looks like she's over by Prospect's Mine. Let's go. My gut's telling me Viper's not far away."

They jumped on their Harleys and rode against the wind. *If anything happens to Cara, I'll never forgive myself. I'm gonna kill that fuckin' Viper. Fuck!* They rode fast and hard, and when they were one mile from the abandoned mine, Hawk motioned for them to cruise in. He didn't want his arrival announced.

"NOW, WHERE WERE we, bitch?" Viper snarled as he came in from outside. Cara cringed as he approached her. Grabbing a fistful of her hair, he dragged her in front of him. "Mouth open wide."

"Stop it, leave her alone," Eric said.

"Fuck! Will you shut that whiny motherfucker up?"

"Anything you say, Prez." Rot took out his hunting knife, and in one swift move, slit Eric's throat. He gurgled, then grew silent as his body landed with a thud on the cold, wood floor. Cara's screams bounced off the shack's walls.

Viper punched her in the face. "You'll be next, if you don't stop." Tugging her face to his crotch, he unzipped his pants and pried her mouth open. "Let's have some fun, whore."

CHAPTER THIRTY

HAWK CREPT TOWARD the illuminated shack like a panther stalking his prey. He moved silently, freezing every so often to avoid detection. Jax and Chas, hidden by the shrubs, sneaked on each side of the shack and positioned themselves by a window dirtied from age. Ruben stood watch in the distance in case other Nomads were in the area.

Beaver stood just outside the shack and watched his prez smack Cara's face. Shrouded in the darkness, Hawk seethed as he saw Beaver rub his dick while his eyes fixed on the scene unfolding in the shack. The more Cara cried and twisted away from Viper, the harder Viper yanked her head back. Beaver's hiss through his teeth when Viper cut Cara's t-shirt and bra down the middle enraged Hawk. Viper's coarse, smoker's voice filtered outside the shack. "You got great tits, *sweetheart*. I can't wait to squeeze and bite them. Open up, slut. You got some cock to suck. Damn, your tits feel good in my hands." Beaver rubbed himself harder and harder, and Hawk saw red.

Before he could jerk off again, Beaver was down on his stomach, a hand over his mouth and a wild beast on his back. He didn't have a chance to fight back, and in a matter of seconds, he was out cold. Hawk motioned Chas to drag the asshole's body away.

Hawk, looking through the small window to the right of the shack's door, saw Eric's motionless body in a pool of blood, Rot jerking off, and Viper in front of a kneeling Cara, who was bruised and bloody. He saw her lips quiver, her exposed breasts, and Viper stuffing his dick in her mouth. In a flash, all logic and reason dissipated, and Hawk became feral.

He rushed into the small room and sprang toward Viper. With his arms extended, Hawk grasped Viper's neck and shoulders, placed his hands around Viper's neck, and pressed tightly. Viper, startled by the attack, thrashed his arms before he regained his balance, looping his leg around one of Hawk's and kicking it out from under him. Hawk fell down and Rot, wielding a small hunting knife, threw his weight on top of him. Grabbing Rot's arms, Hawk fought to keep the knife away from him. As Hawk fended off Viper and Rot, Jax stormed in and dashed over to help his brother.

The loud pop deafened Cara's ears, and everything presented itself in slow motion: Hawk's fight, Jax's shocked look as blood oozed out of his lower stomach, Viper's .22 revolver pointed at Hawk's head, Chas frozen at the door. There was no doubt in her mind that Viper aimed to kill Hawk, and if Chas rushed toward Viper, Hawk and Jax would both be killed. Feeling like she was in a dream, placid-faced Cara picked up a splintered plank covered in cobwebs and dust, stood behind Viper, threw her arms back, and slammed the rotting plank on the back of Viper's skull. It sounded like wooden sticks breaking. Dropping the gun, Viper fell to his knees as dark-red streaks gushed down his neck. He toppled over onto the rough floor, and the dirt, like a sponge, sopped up his blood.

Rot turned to see what happened to Viper, and in the split-second he diverted his attention, Hawk had him on his back, punching the shit out of him. Chas ran over to Hawk and said, "We gotta get outta here. Jax's hurt bad."

Hawk ran over to Jax's side as his eyes rolled back in his head, blood oozing from his wound. "Don't die on me, brother. Don't fuckin' die on me." Hawk took off his shirt and pressed down hard on Jax's wound to try and stop the bleeding. His pleas to a fallen brother broke Cara's heart.

"Let's go. We've gotta get him help. Let's move!" Chas ran out of the shack and screamed for Ruben.

Cara stared wide-eyed at Hawk. "You can't move him. If you do, he'll die. You know this is insane."

Hawk, kneeling by Jax, extended his hand to Cara. She grasped it and he drew her close to him before he hugged her and feathered kisses on her beaten face. Holding her next to him, he whispered, "I can't let Jax die. You're right. If he doesn't get to a hospital, he'll die. Call 911."

"I already did."

When Ruben and Chas came back in, Hawk said, "Take off. No sense involving yourselves. I'll handle this. Badges and ambulance are on their way. Ride to freedom. Go. Now."

"We're standing with you, brother," they said. "We've got your back."

No matter how hard Hawk argued, Chas and Ruben were resolute in their decision.

Cara sat on the ground, transfixed. She hadn't seen Viper move since she cracked his skull. *What if I killed him? I can't deal with this. But, I had to stop him. I had to. He would've killed Hawk, but I can't believe I killed him. I can't believe any of this happened. How did my life get so fucked-up?*

Hawk, his eyes narrowed in hatred, walked over to Viper. As he stood over the crumpled man, he stomped his leather boot on Viper's balls with full force. "Never." *Stomp.* "Fuckin'." *Stomp. Stomp.* "Touch my woman." *Stomp.* Two kicks. "Motherfucker!" Two more kicks to the side and face. The wail of sirens drew near, and Cara moved away from Hawk and walked over to Eric's lifeless body. Kneeling, she put her head on his cold chest and shivered. She smoothed out his shirt with trembling fingers, her breathing labored. Squeezing her eyes shut as her shoulders shook, Hawk came over to rub her back and stroke her hair in silence.

Red and blue lights flashed through the grimy windows, and Ruben and Chas stood aside as the paramedics rushed in, kneeling beside Jax. Right away, they placed him on high-flow oxygen after they examined his airway then placed a pressure bandage on his wound to stop the bleeding. One of the men checked Jax's pulse and said, "Sir, can you hear me? Sir?" Jax's eyelids fluttered.

The men worked fast to get Jax on a long back board. They rolled him toward them, and one of the medics patted down his back to look for the bullet's exit wound, but found nothing. When they loaded him on a gurney and into the ambulance, Cara heard one of the paramedics ask, "Are you feeling any pain?" She looked at the opened door and saw Jax hooked up to two IVs. One of the paramedics came back into the shack. "I need someone who can answer some questions about the injured's alcohol or drug usage tonight and when he last ate. I also need to know if he's taking any medication or if he has any allergies. Who can help me with that?"

Giving Cara a hug, Hawk stood up and walked toward the ambulance. She watched the doors close, then the red flashing lights and wailing siren sped away.

A grip on her shoulder forced her to turn around. Josh gave Cara a faint smile and held her arm as he helped her to her feet. Her legs were wobbly, and she collapsed into his arms. Two police officers taped off the area around Eric's body as they processed the scene. Josh dragged her out of the way, the biting cold reviving her as Cara gulped in breaths of icy air.

"Eric did horrible things to those women, Josh. How could he? How could I not have known something was wrong?" she said in a flat voice.

"I know this is hard, Cara, but please don't blame yourself. Eric was a very disturbed man. Try to think of the Eric you knew, not the one he had become."

"I think I killed Viper. I know he would've killed Hawk if I hadn't stopped him. I think I killed a man." The gravity of her statement hit her full-force, and warm dampness streaked her face.

"Viper isn't dead. He's hurt, but he isn't dead."

Cara crossed her arms around her chest, took a deep breath, and geared herself up for a long night. She wanted to go home, take a warm shower, and shut off her memory. She looked at Josh and said, "Let's get this over with."

Inside the shack, she saw Chas and Ruben as detectives spoke to them, answering the investigators' questions in single syllables. They avoided her looks. One of the detectives walked over and told her he wanted to take her statement. Cara sighed before she recited what happened on one of the longest nights of her life.

CHAPTER THIRTY-ONE

I T SEEMED FITTING that Eric's funeral was on a gray, bleak morning. Dressed in black, the mourners looked like a flock of crows, their coats and veils whipping furiously in the bitter wind. They crowded before a mahogany casket, a white cloak draped over it. Cara's aunt, Eric's mother, sat on a canvas folding chair, sobbing, while Cara stood by her parents. Her father held her gloved hand and squeezed it as dampness glistened on her lashes.

Cara tossed a dozen roses on the grave, and their red petals looked like drops of blood against the snow. She patted Eric's coffin and whispered, "You're finally rid of your demons. I'm sorry I couldn't help you." Her voice cracked, and she cleared her throat then retreated with the other grievers. She noticed Nancy was not at the funeral, but she didn't blame her. Nancy knew Eric during his dark years, and she had been, understandably, appalled at the news that her fiancé was the Mountainside Strangler. Cara felt blessed she had many years of good memories with Eric, but she couldn't get the mutilated bodies out of her mind, and Nadyia's dead eyes haunted her sleep.

She saw Hawk by the tree, its gnarled branches a perfect backdrop for the gloominess of the day. His gaze held desire, tenderness, and sympathy. Nodding to him, she turned her head away. *I'm sorry, Hawk. I know I owe you an explanation, but I just can't deal with anything right now. I know I'm avoiding you by hiding out at my parents' house, but I can't be a part of your world anymore. Our worlds are too different. I miss you terribly, but it's for the best that we go our separate ways. I'm sorry, Hawk. So sorry.*

She slid over the hearse's cold, leather seats to make room for her family, looking out the window at the snow-covered graves. The mausoleums and statues lent an air of desolation to the scenery. As snow flurries swirled down from the sky, the limousine began its retreat from the cemetery. Cara stared at Hawk and their eyes locked for a heartbeat. As the limo passed, Hawk blew her a kiss.

THE CEMETERY HAD been empty for a long while as Hawk stared at the newly dug grave. During the burial, he stood in the back, watching Cara. Since that night, she had withdrawn from him. He respected that she needed time with her family to grieve the loss of her beloved cousin and to come to terms with the fact that Eric had bestowed so much sorrow on so many lives. Hawk decided early on he would give her space. He was hurt she didn't seek him out for comfort, but he knew she needed to be with her parents. Eight days had passed since Eric's murder.

I miss my sweet wildcat. My bed is empty without her warm body and ass pressed against my cock. I need to fuck her. I miss our conversations and bantering. I need her on the back of my bike. Fuck, I miss her bad. I need to talk to her so we can get back on track.

Reaching down, Hawk picked up one of the red rose petals Cara had strewn over Eric's grave. Rubbing it against his cheek, its softness felt like her caresses on his face. He knew she hurt, but he hurt as well, wishing like hell he could have been there to save Cara from all the pain and humiliation she'd endured in the shack that night. She relied on him to keep her safe and protected, and he'd fucking failed her. It was something he'd have to live with for the rest of his life. All he wanted was to hold her and tell her it would get better. He needed her in his life, and he had no intention of letting her go.

Placing the rose petal in his pocket, Hawk walked out of the cemetery, the snow crunching under his boots.

CHAPTER THIRTY-TWO

"CARA, YOU'RE GOING to have to join the living again," Sherrie said as she sat cross-legged on Cara's bed.

"I know," Cara muttered.

"It feels so weird sitting on your bed in your old bedroom like we used to do in high school when we'd spend all that time talking about guys."

Cara nodded. She didn't feel like talking, but Sherrie was right about having to get back out in the world.

"Speaking of guys, what's going on with Hawk?"

"Nothing. It's over."

"Over? Why? I thought he made you happy. You know, girl, you were happy when you and Hawk were an item."

Cara shrugged. "It's over. Things don't last forever."

Sherrie took one of Cara's hands, gripping it. "Cara, I know you're hurting about Eric. I loved him, too. We all had some crazy fun over the years, but the Eric you and I knew wasn't the dark Eric that took over his life."

"I just need some time, Sherrie. Leave it alone."

"I won't because I know you'll go deeper inside yourself, and for what? Hawk has been calling me several times a week asking about you. He said you won't answer his phone calls or texts, and you haven't been to the office. You at least owe him an explanation."

"I know," she whispered. "On another note, Jax is out of the hospital, and he's doing great. I went to see him a few times. Kylie keeps me informed."

Sherrie shook her head. "It's useless to talk to you. You're so damn stubborn. When you make up your mind, there's no changing it."

"Then don't try."

"I think you're making a big mistake. I hate to see you sabotage yourself. I care about you."

"I know you do, Sherrie, but if I'm making a mistake, it's *my* problem, okay?"

Sherrie leaned over and hugged her best friend. "I'm there for you, no matter what. It's okay, because when you're ready, you'll know."

I'LL NEVER UNDERSTAND women. When I think I got 'em figured out, they do shit like Cara's doing. I don't know what I did to her. I told her to keep her ass in the clubhouse that night. She didn't listen, and all kinds of shit happened. Damn, why didn't she stay at the clubhouse? She won't return my calls, won't even speak to me. What the fuck did I do to piss her off like that? I've given her space, but it's been a month, and I'm done with waiting for her to come around. I miss her too much. Fuck, that's why I never wanted any attachments, because you just get burned in the end.

Hawk thought about Cara all the time; he couldn't believe how she had taken over his thoughts, his heart, and his life. He couldn't imagine his life without her. When he saw her half-naked and trembling in front of Viper, his cock in her mouth, Hawk went ballistic. His one regret was that he didn't kill the motherfucker; however, his boot-stomping made Viper impotent, something that pleased Hawk to no end. If he ever saw that fucker again, he would kill him without any hesitation. Although, he figured he wouldn't be seeing Viper any time soon, since he was in federal prison awaiting trial on a slew of charges, among them sex-trafficking, first-degree murder, and aiding and abetting.

Hawk learned from CBI that Viper and the others wouldn't see the free world again. Hawk knew the Nomads would be lucky if they made it six months in prison. Through the outlaw grapevine, Hawk learned Reaper promised punishment for the Nomads for holding out on all that money and for double-crossing the other chapters. Viper would get what he deserved.

"You still sulking?" Banger asked as he slid on the bar stool next to Hawk.

Hawk glared at him, threw back a shot of whiskey, and then motioned for Jerry to bring him another. "Jerry's close to getting patched in. He'll make a good addition to the brotherhood."

"Yeah, he will. You know, you got a spitfire as your woman." Banger laughed. "Fuck, she cracked Viper's skull, almost killed him. She's got gumption."

"She's not my woman."

"The hell she ain't. No woman does that for a man without being his woman. Problem with you is you're acting like a pussy, sulking around here instead of claimin' her and makin' her your ol' lady."

"Butt out, old man."

"Get off your sulky ass and claim her pussy so we can get on with club business. Fuck, because of your pussy-whipped ass, I can't run the club. Get your shit straight." Banger downed his shot, clapped Hawk on his shoulder, and walked over to Brandi. Hawk watched as Banger grabbed her ass, and tugged her close then kissed her. Dragging her behind him, they went to one of the small rooms.

Banger's words echoed in Hawk's mind. He threw back his last shot, nodded to Jerry, and walked out of the clubhouse. He jumped on his bike and headed toward Pinewood Springs.

Cara owed him an explanation, and he was fucking going to get it.

HAWK STOOD ON the mansion's porch between two stone columns; he had never been to a house this big or ritzy. As he rang the bell, he hoped Cara would answer, but a slim, attractive woman in her early fifties opened the door instead. She greeted him with a look of utter disapproval. "May I help you?"

"I'm here to see Cara."

"Cara? She's not available. Is there something I can help you with?"

"I know she's here. I need to talk to her."

"Is this about the problem she's having with her car? I think my husband found a mechanic."

Knowing this bitch was his babe's mother kept him from being rude, but she had such a high-and-mighty air about her that he would have loved to have set her straight. Biting his tongue, Hawk just stared at her. She appeared to be flustered by him and his tattoos, her eyes glued to the hawk. It struck him as funny, since she didn't seem to be the type of person who would fluster easily.

As she closed the door, Hawk put his foot out to prevent it from shutting.

Surprise shone in her brown eyes. "I'm going to have to ask you to leave, sir. I know who you are—you're that hoodlum who's been sniffing around my daughter. Eric told me all about you and your gang."

"I don't belong to a gang, and I don't sniff around anyone, ma'am," he said.

"It's a slap in my face that my daughter would even entertain going out with you. And you standing here now, well, you don't even have the decency to be embarrassed about the situation," she said in a tight voice.

As anger flared in his eyes, he said, "I don't embarrass. Now, ma'am, will you please get Cara? I need to talk with her." He stood his ground, his foot still in the door.

"What's going on here, Cathy?" a man's voice boomed.

"Nothing I can't handle," his wife replied.

Vincent Minelli was a tall man in his mid-fifties. His thinning hair had specks of gray among the brown strands, and he had warm, green eyes and a winning smile. He came to his wife's side, hand on the small of her back, and asked, "What seems to be the problem?"

"There's no problem. I'm here to talk with Cara. We know each other," Hawk said.

"I've already told him Cara isn't available," Cathy said in a high voice.

"Nonsense, Cara's here." Vincent went to the bottom of the grand staircase and bellowed, "Cara, come down here."

"Vince, I don't think we should allow this." She wrung her hands. "This isn't something we want to encourage."

"What's up, Dad?" Cara said as she came down the stairs.

"Your friend is here to see you," her father explained.

"Cara, you don't have to—"

"Come on, Cathy, let Cara and her friend be alone." Turning to Hawk, he said, "What's your name, sir?"

"Hawk."

"Interesting."

Vincent led his wife out of the foyer and into the living room. Cathy kept looking over her shoulder, worried to leave her daughter alone with such a man.

Cara stood in front of Hawk. *Fuck, she looks beautiful. I can't let her go, no matter what she says. I can't let her go from my life.* Cara barely had any makeup on and wore black yoga pants with a white, long-sleeved t-shirt, her clothes molded to every curve of her body. *I want to pull her into my arms and kiss her soft lips. I want to crawl all over her. Easy, Hawk, slow down. Don't scare her. You gotta play it cool.* His cock pushed against his jeans. She was the only woman who gave him a hard-on just by looking at him.

"How have you been, Cara?" he asked softly.

"I'm better. Why did you come?" Her eyes were downcast.

"I want to know what's going on. You haven't returned any of my calls or texts. You haven't been at your house or office. It's like you disappeared from my life. Look at me and tell me what's going on."

She raised her eyes to him, bit her lower lip then mumbled, "Sorry, I didn't mean to leave you hanging. I thought you would've moved on by now." She shrugged, as if that explained everything.

"Moved on? From what? From us?" Hawk stomped his numbing feet "It's fuckin' freezing out here. Can I come in?"

Cara moved aside and let Hawk in. "Follow me."

Hawk followed her to a large room enclosed in glass windows on two sides. The other side had a fireplace with a log burning brightly, and overstuffed chairs and couches, along with floor-to-ceiling bookcases, made up the sun room. Hawk imagined Cara, as a child, sitting and reading her favorite books there. The room suited her, and her bungalow had a lot of the same coziness.

"Hawk, I can't do this anymore. I need normalcy in my life, not shoot-outs with rival clubs, wild parties, and all the other chaos that goes with your world."

Hawk paused before he spoke, choosing his words carefully. "Cara, I'm sorry about Eric. I'm sure this is hard for you, but don't blame me and the club for the stuff he did."

"I can't do it anymore, that's all," she whispered.

"That isn't *all*. Fuck, do you know what hell I've been through this last month? I didn't know what the shit was going on. Did you even care or think about me?" Hawk paced around the room.

"I shouldn't have done that to you. I *am* sorry."

"Sorry doesn't quite cut it, Cara. You ran out on me when things got tough. I was there for you. I *always* had your back, but you couldn't trust me enough. Fuck!"

"I needed time away from everything."

"I get that. I gave you space and time with your parents, but what about me? Why did you push me out?"

"Your world is too violent for me. I have enough crap in my practice. I don't want to have it during my time off."

"What did the Insurgents do? We got the fuckin' Nomads shut down, we got the women they smuggled to a safe environment, and we stopped that asshole, Viper."

Cara shuddered when she heard Viper's name. "I know. And I also know I was responsible for being there that night. You told me to stay at the clubhouse, and I didn't. It's just that everything is so muddled. I'm just so confused."

Hawk rubbed his hands over his face. "Confused about what? Dammit, talk to me!"

"About everything! About Eric, you and me, my life, all of it."

"Okay, I don't know why Eric did what he did, but you and I are separate from all that."

"I know you're just having a good time with me, but I guess now I realize I don't want that anymore."

"Is that what you think? After all we've had, how can you say that? You're the *only* woman I've let into my heart and my life. You don't even fuckin' know what you do to me. Babe, I think about you all the time. You're in my soul. I've never felt this way about another woman. I love you, Cara. I want you to always be in my life. I can't lose you." Hawk reached out, drew her in his arms, and held her close. Stiff at first, she relaxed as he stroked her back.

"I'm so twisted inside. I know Eric did horrible things to those women. He destroyed their lives and the lives of the ones who loved them. For God's sake, he threw the women out like pieces of garbage! I *hate* him for what he did, but I still *love* him. I don't know how to reconcile this, I just don't." Cara's voice cracked as a sob escaped from her.

Hawk held her trembling body closer to his and kissed the top of her forehead. "Babe, sometimes life fuckin' sucks. You can't figure out all the answers because sometimes there aren't any."

"I'm not strong enough for this."

"I am. Lean on me. I'll carry you through."

Cara looked up at Hawk, and his determined eyes held hers as he bent down and covered her mouth with his. She parted her lips, and he kissed her deeply as he conveyed courage and conviction to her. "I know I've been a fool and blamed myself for Eric's evilness and death. I punished myself by eliminating any happiness, and by denying you in my life."

"Shh… it's okay, babe. Everything is gonna be fine, and you've got me to help you through all this," he whispered as he caressed her hair.

Cara circled Hawk's neck and kissed him at the base of his throat. Burying his face in her hair, he breathed in her familiar vanilla scent. His cock ached to be back in her pussy, and he wanted to throw her down on the plush couch and fuck her until they were both covered in sweat, but it wasn't the right time—he'd have to take it slow. He muttered in her ear, "I've missed holding you, babe. I love you."

She met his mouth and murmured against his lips, "I love you, Hawk. I've loved you for a long time, but I was scared to let go. I'm not scared anymore."

He kissed her and his tongue swirled around her mouth. "Go get your things. We're going home," he said against her lips.

Cara hugged his waist before breaking away to pack her suitcase.

She met her mom in the hallway as Cara descended the stairs, suitcase in hand.

"Honey, what are you doing?"

"I'm going home, Mom. It's time."

As Hawk stood by the front door, Cathy's eyes narrowed and her lips turned downward. Hawk walked over to Cara, took her hand, and said, "Mrs. Minelli, I know you don't approve of me, but I love your daughter. She's going to be fine with me, I promise you that. I will take care of her."

"Cara, you can't be *serious*."

"Please don't make a scene, Mom. I know Hawk isn't what you envisioned for me, but he's perfect for me. It's my choice."

"What will people say? Cara, think of your family. We've just gone through one scandal and now this? I won't allow it."

Vincent, hearing the ruckus, came into the foyer. He glanced at the suitcase in Cara's hand and Hawk's arm around his daughter's shoulder.

Cathy yelled, "Don't just stand there, Vince, do something!"

Vincent extended his hand to Hawk, who shook it with a firm grip. "Be good to my daughter, or I'll break your goddamned neck."

Hawk smiled. He liked Cara's dad.

"Have you lost your mind, Vince? You've always been too permissive with Cara. Now look what she's doing. She's running off with a hoodlum."

Vincent hugged his daughter. Looking at Cathy, he said, "Yes, look at our daughter. She's happy for the first time in weeks. Maybe you're all right with your daughter being unhappy, but I'm not. Seeing her now so joyful is more than a father can ask for."

Cara kissed her dad's cheek while she hugged him close to her. "Thanks, Dad. You're the best."

Vincent wiped the moisture off his daughter's cheeks and cleared his voice. "You better get going; it's starting to snow. Call us when you get home."

Cara and Hawk stepped outside. Behind them, they heard her mother raising her voice to Cara's dad.

"I knew my mom would be pissed. I wish she could be happy for me."

"She'll come around, babe. It'll probably take a long time, but she'll eventually accept me."

Snowflakes danced around them as Hawk went to Cara's car and loaded her suitcase in the trunk. "I'll follow you."

"You don't have to. I'm fine."

"I'll follow you, woman."

"I'm fine, I told you. By the way, stop calling me *woman*. You sound like you're a caveman, or something. You know, things have definitely evolved since the caveman days, and women are equal to men. Did you—" Hawk's lips on Cara's interrupted her monologue.

Cupping her chin under his hand, he said, "It's good to have you back, babe."

CHAPTER THIRTY-THREE

O PENING HER FRONT door, Hawk said, "I'll spend weeknights here with you, and you'll spend weekends at my place."

"Do I get a say in that?"

"No."

Shaking her head, Cara kissed Hawk on the cheek. "Sounds good to me. I've missed you."

He drew her into his arms, crushed his mouth on hers, and ran his hands over her curves. As he caressed her tits, she stiffened. "What's the matter, baby?" he asked.

"I'm not ready for *that*. The whole thing with Viper, you know, I'm just not ready yet, Hawk. You'll have to be patient with me."

He hugged her. "Take your time, babe. I'll always be here for you." *Even though my cock wants your pussy in the worst way.* He wished he could have saved her the fear and humiliation that fucker put her through. *I'm just glad I got there before he raped you. I can't even think about that. If I do, I'll break something.*

Later that night, they settled on the couch, Cara hugging Hawk's knees, her head on his lap. He stroked her hair as they watched reruns of *The Twilight Zone.* They had discovered that they were both huge Rod Sterling fans, so when Cara found out *The Twilight Zone* marathon was on T.V., she knew Hawk would want to see it with her. It was fun to watch the show with each other.

As they watched the episode "Nightmare at 20,000 Feet," Cara laughed.

"What's so funny?"

"I remember watching this rerun when I was a kid. Eric, Sherrie, and

I were avid *Zone* fans, and we'd go through bowls of popcorn during a marathon. We loved this episode, and we'd always laugh when we saw the gremlin. Eric used to say it looked like a guy wearing a shag carpet. It was so cheesy it was funny, you know?"

"Damn, it *does* look like the actor's in a shag carpet." Hawk chuckled as he looked at her shimmering eyes. Leaning into her, he played with her hair. "Babe, don't let sadness creep in. You have a happy memory of your cousin, and that's good."

"Yeah, I know. I did have good times with him in the past. Tonight, you and I are making new memories. I love that." Cara snuggled into the crook of his arm while she embraced him.

Stroking her cheek with his thumb, he said, "I love you, babe."

"I love you, too."

When they went to bed later that night, Hawk cradled Cara in his arms as she fell asleep. He stared at the curve of her breasts as his cock throbbed, but he knew she needed time to wipe out the bad memories so she could begin to trust a man's touch again. Even though he was ready to explode, he'd wait for her to make the move. *Fuck, I love this woman. I never saw this happening in my life. She pulled me in the first time I saw her. Never saw this comin'.*

CARA AND HAWK woke up to two feet of fallen snow that sparkled like small pieces of glass under the sun.

"Are you going to your shop today?" Cara inquired.

"Yeah, I got some bikes I'm customizing. I'm behind schedule."

"I'd like to go. I want to see your bike shop. I want to see what you do."

"I didn't think that would interest a woman."

"You've seen me at my office. I want to see you at yours."

"We leave in twenty minutes."

Hawk's shop was full of motorcycle parts, accessories, and several Harley models, like the freewheeler, road glide, and ultra-low. He also carried a Harley-Davidson Dyna Low Rider *Vintage* Racer and a 1946 Knucklehead. Hawk had restored both of the vintage cycles. His biggest source of revenue in the shop came from customizing motorcycles.

Cara perused the shelves which contained chrome accessories, bars and grips, windshields, filters, and cam engines. There were shelves which held skeleton hand mirrors and chrome exhaust pipes, as well as various fender ornaments like skulls, zombies, eagles, American flags, and wild boars.

"Where did you learn to repair and customize bikes?" Cara asked.

"I've loved motorcycles ever since the next-door neighbor at the trailer park took me for my first ride. My dad was drunk, and my mom had already split. I was about ten years old when I took my first spin. The minute I felt the wind rushing all around me and the sense of freedom and openness, I was hooked. After that, I learned everything I could about bikes. The neighbor, I think his name was John, was a mechanic, and he customized the hell out of his Harley. He taught me how to work on them."

"It's good you had him around."

"Working on bikes with him that summer and riding on his Harley made the shit with my old man tolerable." Darkness crossed his brow as the cobwebs of the past cleared, making his childhood memories more vivid.

Hawk saw Cara start to move toward him then stop, like she was going to give him a pity hug but decided not to. He was glad she changed her mind because he couldn't stand that pity shit from anyone, even his woman. He didn't need any sympathy when he felt the pain of his past.

Cara stood to the side of him, her eyes downcast.

Hawk cleared his throat. "You like the shop?"

"I love it. I can see your mark everywhere."

Hearing the phone ring in the back office, Hawk went to answer it. Looking through the office's window, he saw one of his regular customers, Ross, come into the shop. He heard Ross whistle as he raked his eyes over Cara's body, lingering on her big tits. A deep heat filled Hawk's chest, his temples pounding as he saw Ross ogling his woman. *Fuck that!* Seeing that Cara tugged on her red sweater, trying to make it less form-fitting, Hawk felt her discomfort. Ross flashed her a big smile.

"It's good to see a pretty woman in here for a change," Hawk heard him say.

"I don't work here," Cara said.

"Just visiting?" Ross came over to her, his eyes still fixed on her chest.

Hawk saw Cara's chest moving in and out as a light sheen coated her forehead and upper lip. She darted her eyes from side to side, shifting her weight from one foot to another. To Hawk, she looked like a caged animal trying to get free.

"I gotta call you back, I got an emergency here," he said to the customer on the phone. Hanging up, he rushed out of the office, saying, "Ross, I'm not quite done with your bike."

Upon hearing his voice, Hawk saw the panicked look in Cara's eyes disappear. She took a deep breath and her shoulders slumped. She threw him a relieved and grateful look as she wiped the beads of sweat from her forehead.

Standing there, Hawk's blood rose as he saw how Ross stared at his woman. His fists clenched—turning his knuckles white—as slivers of anger flashed in his eyes.

"You have a pretty visitor here," Ross said, leaning toward Cara.

Putting his arm around Cara's shoulders, Hawk stared daggers at Ross. He leaned in and kissed Cara gently on her lips.

Ross said, "I get it. I'm supposed to back off."

"Fuck yeah, she's my woman."

"I don't want any problems, man. You're a lucky guy. Give me a call when you've finished with my motorcycle."

After Ross left, Cara put her head on Hawk's shoulder. "I freaked out when he checked me out. All I could see was Viper's thin lips, greasy hair, and cruel smile flashing in front of me. I was petrified. I started having a panic attack, and I couldn't breathe. Am I ever going to get over this and be whole again?" She sniffled against his chest.

Holding her, Hawk said, "I'm so sorry, babe. I wasn't there to protect and keep you safe. You'll be okay, I promise. It's just gonna take time, babe." *I should have killed the bastard when I had the chance.*

CHAPTER THIRTY-FOUR

ARA NEVER GREW tired of watching the deer drink from the creek which ran behind Hawk's house. Snow frosted the evergreen and pine trees, which lined his property. It was frigid. Hawk called her from the shop and told her to get the grill fired because he bought two steaks for dinner. He was a grilling man no matter what; he'd stand outside in ten degrees below zero temperatures, grilling steaks, red peppers, and corn. Cara, amused, stayed curled up on his couch in front of a blazing fire and sipped a glass of red wine. It could be a blizzard and Hawk would be outside grilling up steaks. Cara loved him for that.

She leaned over the balcony to throw some carrots down for the rabbits. She didn't hear Hawk come out onto the deck before feeling his arms as he hugged her waist. "You smell good." He breathed in her powdery fresh scent. "Did you get the grill fired up?"

"Ready to go. I got us a horror movie to watch, and I'll make popcorn later."

He shook his head. "You're obsessed with horror movies, but I don't mind. I like the way you hang on to me during the movie. Babe, you *do* know you spend most of the movie with your face in my chest, right?"

Cara swatted his arm. "I do not."

A big smile spread across his face. "Yeah, you do, but I'm not complaining. Fuck, that's one of the things I love about you."

Giving him a hug, she said, "Get grilling, I'm starving."

After dinner and the movie, Cara poured herself another glass of wine and gave Hawk another beer. As she sat down beside him, her back into his chest, he twisted her hair around his fingers and said, "I have something for you."

"You got me a present?"

Reaching down, he pulled a box from underneath the couch and handed it to her. "Open it."

Cara opened the box, and folded inside was a black leather vest. The leather was butter-soft and felt good against her fingers. She turned the vest around and on the back, it read, "Property of Hawk, Insurgents MC." She stared at it.

"Cara, I love you. I want you to be my old lady."

She paused. "I know this is a big deal in your world. Is this like being engaged?"

"Yeah, sorta. To me, it's more. I'm asking you to share your life with me, and to become a full partner in my world."

"The *property* thing is a bit unnerving," she said.

"It means you belong to me and I belong to you. It tells everyone you're my woman and to back the fuck off. It gives you respect, and it gives me pride."

"I will be your old lady, but there are a few conditions."

"Do you ever just agree with something? You love to negotiate." Hawk rolled his eyes and smiled. "Okay, go on and tell me your conditions."

"You know you'd be bored if I were always agreeable." Cara stared at him. "I *am* proud to wear this vest and be your old lady. I *am* willing to be a part of your world, but you have to be a part of mine, too. I can't abandon my world. I won't give up being a lawyer—I've worked too hard for that. You want me to understand and be in your world, but you have to understand and be in mine, too."

"Being my old lady doesn't mean you can't be a lawyer. You'll have to do more club stuff, but I'm cool with doing non-club stuff with you. I refuse to do pansy-ass stuff, but a charity event or hanging at your folks once in a while is okay."

Holding the vest close to her, she said, "I'm honored to be your old lady."

Hawk yanked her into his arms, kissing her deep and sweet. "You'll make a kick-ass old lady," he breathed into her ear. "Let's go into the bedroom. I want to see you wearing my property patch and nothing else."

It had been over six weeks since they'd made love, and Cara wanted him badly. She could see the desire in his eyes, as well, reflecting her own. Grateful he'd been so patient with her, she decided it had been long enough. *I need to trust his touch. I need to throw away the images Viper planted in my mind. I love Hawk, and I want to make love to him.* Cara placed her hands on each side of Hawk's face and kissed him all over, her feathery pecks making his cock twinge. "Let's go, Hawk." She stood up, took his hand, and led him to the bedroom.

Hawk stood over Cara as she lay in his bed. The leather vest covered some of her tits, and her pussy looked sweet with a close-cropped strip of light brown hair. They gazed into each other's desire-filled eyes. "Damn, I can never get enough of you. I want to make sweet love to you, Cara." He leaned over and kissed her ready lips. She felt his cock jerk as she rubbed his crotch with her hands. He tore off his t-shirt revealing a new tattoo on his chest—"Cara" in bold black letters with red rosebuds and green vines curling around the letters.

Touching it, she said, "For me?"

"All for you, babe. You're mine forever. Love you." He kissed her and her body arched toward his chest, his nipple ring rubbing against her tits. The leather vest she wore felt cool on her skin, and she pulled Hawk closer to her body as she wrapped her legs around his waist, pushing his hardness against her soft skin. She moved her pelvis backwards and forward, and Hawk groaned. He pulled open her vest and covered her tits with tongue-filled kisses. Grazing her nipples with his teeth, he urged them to erection. Cara squirmed under his soft touch as he left her nipples and ran his tongue down her tits to her ribs, and her stomach.

Hawk parted Cara's legs, his tongue never leaving her body. He cupped one of his hands under her ass, thrust her pussy toward his face, then rubbed the inside of her thighs with his fingers, followed by swirling licks from his tongue. He traced his tongue all over the inside of her thighs near and around her pussy. Cara, arms above her head, grabbed the slates of the headboard as she writhed under Hawk's teasing. "That feels so good, honey. I want your cock inside me."

"I know you do, but I'm not ready yet, baby." Hawk looked at her. She placed her feet flat on the bed, pushing her pussy further toward Hawk's teasing tongue.

"Do you want my tongue on your pussy?" he asked between licks and kisses.

"You know I do."

"Beg me for it." His tongue kept stroking around her opening.

"Hawk, you're driving me crazy. Just do it!"

He chuckled, his breath tickling her skin. "Beg me for it."

Cara needed his tantalizing tongue on her right that second. The anticipation was too great. If begging was the only way he'd put his wicked tongue on her clit, she'd beg. "Please, honey, please put your tongue on my pussy. I need the release. Please."

"I'm gonna put my mouth over your sweet pussy lips and taste you."

He did just that, biting her lips tenderly. He spread her lips open with his tongue and put his mouth over her mound. Kissing her wet folds with urgency, his teeth nipped and sucked her pink pussy. As Cara gasped and stiffened her legs, he wiggled his tongue further into her. His stiff tongue darted in and out as she shoved herself toward him, moaning in pleasure. Hawk pulled out his tongue and laved the area around her clit then grasped her ass cheeks and thrust his mouth on her glistening pussy. His chin shone with her wetness as she fisted his hair, pushing his face deeper into her throbbing mound.

"Fuck me, Hawk. I want you inside me. I want you to fuck me hard."

As he unzipped his pants to free his stiff cock, his mouth never left her soaking heat. He caressed her folds with his fingers and flicked the top of her nub with the tips until it was hard and erect. Then the tip of his tongue massaged it as Cara's whole body tingled, and the mounting tension started its ascent to explosion.

"Your pussy is so juicy. I love it that way, babe," he said hoarsely.

He slid his tongue all around her clit, lapping up her wetness. As he sucked on her sweet spot, Cara groaned and writhed, her skin damp from sweat. Slipping two fingers deep inside her, Hawk finger-fucked her while her sex clenched and gripped his fingers. With the other hand, he reached up and pinched her nipples. Cara exploded in a thousand surges of pleasure as her body convulsed, and as she rode the wave of ecstasy, she cried out Hawk's name over and over. He pulled her to him. "I love how you respond to my touches, my sweet wildcat," he muttered.

When her breathing returned to normal, he kissed her shoulders and nipped them with his teeth. She reached down and grabbed his cock, tightening her grip on his hardness while she circled the top of his cock with her thumb. He flipped her onto her stomach and spread her legs with his hands.

"Get on your knees," he rasped.

She complied, smashing her chest on the mattress, her ass high, her pussy splayed open and waiting for his cock. She knew he saw her swollen lips twitch, and she craved him inside her warmness.

"I'm gonna fuck you hard, real hard. Your pussy has been aching for this."

He slid his shaft up and down her folds as her wetness coated his length. She quivered as he kneaded her ass cheeks, bending down to kiss, bite, and lick while he spanked each one to redness. Each slap, followed by his caressing mouth, brought Cara to heightened levels of passion. As she neared climax, Hawk plunged his cock deep into her as his fingers stroked her clit. He pounded in and out, thrusting her forward into the headboard. Reaching over, he put a pillow between her head and the headboard as he fucked her hard. His breath came in pants, and his fingers quickened their strokes on her nub as each plunge brought her further along.

As his legs and ass tightened, her pussy snatched his cock. Cara screamed out, "Hawk!" and her muscles acted like clamps around his squirting dick. He followed with, "Fuck, Cara, fuck!" as all his tension released. They both collapsed on the bed, spent, panting, and tingling.

Hawk rolled off Cara's back then drew her into him so her ass fit against his drained dick. He wrapped his arms around her as she pushed her hair off her sweaty face. Then, reaching behind her, she patted Hawk's butt. He kissed her ear, murmuring, "I love you."

Placing her hands over his, she snuggled back further into him. "I love you, Hawk. I can't imagine my life without you."

"You won't ever have to, babe, because I'm here to stay."

He tightened his hold on her, and her heavy eyes closed. She let herself drift closer to sleep with Hawk's arms protectively around her. In the last moments between wake and sleep, she knew she would never have to go through anything by herself again. Her man had her back, she had his, and they loved each other. Life was good.

KYLIE AND DORIS hugged Cara when she came into the kitchen bearing a platter of sausage and peppers.

"'Bout time you wore Hawk's patch," Doris said as she stubbed out her cigarette.

"I'm so happy for you, Cara," Kylie squealed. "I'd love to meet someone who cares about me."

"You will, Kylie."

"Not if my dad can help it. Guys are terrified of him. I'll die a virgin."

Doris and Cara laughed. "Wait until you go away to college. You'll see how things will change for you," Cara said.

Kylie brought her fingers to her lips. "Remember, my dad doesn't know anything about my plans yet. I'm trying to keep the peace for as long as possible."

At that moment, Banger walked into the kitchen. He hadn't seen Cara since that dreadful night. Smacking his lips when he saw the platter of Italian sausage and fried peppers, he took a taste. "Damn, Hawk's lucky he's got a woman who can cook." He fixed his eyes on her and said in a low voice, "You done good with that situation with the Nomads. I'm proud to have you in the Insurgents family."

"Thanks, Banger. That means a lot to me."

Cara went out to the great room carrying a tray of beef brisket, the steam mixing with the cigarette smoke as she put the tray on the buffet table. One of her duties as an old lady was to prepare and set up food for family get-togethers, normally held on late Sunday afternoons. In nice weather, the barbecues were in the yard, and in inclement weather, they were in the great room.

Cara saw Jax at one of the tables. She went over to him and tapped his shoulder. He turned around and grinned when he saw her.

"How are you doing, Jax?"

"Good as new. Heard Hawk got off his ass and claimed you."

"Yeah."

"Thanks for visiting me in the hospital and checking up on me."

"You're welcome. I'm just glad you're feeling fine. You gave us all a scare."

Hawk came up to her, his arm possessively around her. Her leather vest with his patch was a beacon to all men to stay the fuck away.

"I love seeing you wear my patch," he breathed in her ear.

"I love wearing it and seeing how happy it makes you."

"I never thought I'd have a woman wear my patch, but now that you're in my life, I can't picture it without you."

He kissed her hard in front of all his brothers and Cara kissed him back, happy to be a part of his club, his world, and his life. Standing in the smoke-filled room, with all the brothers and old ladies and Hawk by her side, she realized she was whole for the first time in her life.

Yes, life was good again. It was very good.

EPILOGUE

Four months later

"IT'S ALL OVER?" Cara asked Ralph Bowles, the deputy district attorney assigned to the Nomads' cases.

"Yes, they pled guilty to firearm possession and manslaughter in exchange for us dropping attempted rape, assault with a deadly weapon, sexual assault, and a bunch of other charges that would've gotten them over a hundred years in prison, if convicted. Considering Rot and Beaver were on parole, and Viper is an ex-felon, the weapon charges alone will give them years in prison. They're looking at serving a minimum of twenty-five years. They and other members of their gang are also facing federal charges of drug and sex trafficking along with a slew of weapon charges. You can be sure they'll be gone for the long stretch."

"That's a huge relief. I dreaded a trial. The last thing I wanted to do was see Viper again. Good job."

"The Department of Corrections will notify you whenever any of them comes up for parole."

"Yeah, I know the drill. Thanks for all your hard work, Ralph."

As Cara clicked off her phone, relief washed over her. *It's finished. After all this time, it's over.*

Asher came into Cara's office. "I overheard. I'm glad you have this behind you."

"Thanks, Asher. Hawk, Jax, Chas, and Ruben will be relieved, as well. There's one thing a biker doesn't want to do, and that's cooperate with law enforcement."

"Whatever happened to the dirty cops and detectives who were in cahoots with the Nomads?"

"They got fired and are being prosecuted. It'll serve them right to be in the same prison with the Nomads. We'll see how friendly everyone will be under the same roof. Good riddance to all of them."

"You're taking off this weekend?" Asher asked.

"Hawk surprised me with a weekend trip to Aspen. We're going on his Harley. It should be beautiful, now that spring is finally here."

"I still find it funny when I think of you on the back of a Harley."

"I love it. I'm thinking of buying one for myself."

"That'll kill your mother, for sure. She any better about you and Hawk?"

"Very slowly coming around, and for her, that's huge. I better go to my arraignments. If you want, you can take off early this afternoon. I won't be back until after four."

"Thanks, boss. Have a nice weekend."

THE RIDE ALONG Deer Trail Pass showcased hints of spring as the milder air replaced the colder winter winds. A lone red-tailed hawk flew over an open field near the rocky cliffs. Trees sprouted green leaves with beginning floral buds as the mild temperature opened the door to a flurry of life after the long, frigid winter.

Cara, arms around Hawk's waist, marveled at the beauty of the spring season. It was a short season in Colorado; the newly green leaves could easily be stunted by a freezing, wet snowfall. Just seeing the greenery beginning to fill out the bare branches caused a flutter of elation in Cara. Spring was the time for rebirth. She had come a long way since that horrible night in November. The coldness of the wintry air had matched the iciness in her heart when she found out that her dear cousin was a killer. It had taken her months to come to grips with that realization, and even though she missed the Eric she knew, she breathed easier knowing a cruel, calculating killer was stopped.

She leaned her head on Hawk's shoulder and he turned around to look at her, his hair blowing around his face. Tilting forward, she kissed his cheek. She had been Hawk's old lady since the end of December. For the past four months, she wore his patch. Every time she donned the leather vest or the jacket bearing his patch, his eyes beamed with pride. She loved him more than she ever thought it was possible to love a man.

Through the dark months which followed the awful night in the shack, Hawk had been her patient rock; she never could've done it without his strength and support. He was an amazing man, and she still couldn't believe he was all hers. Whenever women came on to him, which was often, he'd squeeze her hand or put his arm around her shoulders as if to say he didn't want any other woman but her. A funny, warm sensation went through her each and every time. *I love being Hawk's woman.*

Cara adored the quaintness and elegance of Aspen, only an hour drive from Pinewood Springs. Cara used to come to Aspen a lot with her parents when she was a kid, and later with friends, but it'd been four years since her last visit. She was happy Hawk suggested it.

The Harley stopped in front of the historic landmark Hotel Jubal. Located in the heart of the town, the hotel harkened back to Aspen's silver-mining days. Cara adored it, as it blended elegance with mountain spirit.

"I love this hotel," she gushed as she hugged Hawk's arm.

"I know how you like old stuff."

"Guess that's why I'm with you."

He pretended to be insulted as he swatted her butt.

A crackling fire in a large, stone fireplace greeted them when they walked into the lobby. A blend of modern and historic décor made up the large room. Sleek, white couches mixed well with over-stuffed brown couches, and large Native American rugs accented the hardwood floors of the lobby. It was quite lovely.

A short bellman escorted Cara and Hawk to their room, and a beautiful suite welcomed them complete with stunning views of the white-capped Rocky Mountains. The room's floor-to-ceiling windows were like a frame, the spectacular mountain range the painting.

After tipping the bellman, Hawk came behind Cara and nuzzled his face into her neck. "Like it?"

"I love it. Can you afford this?" Worry creased her brow.

He laughed. "Yeah, babe, I can afford it. I have a dispensary, remember? Do you know how much I make with one little dispensary?"

"Enough to afford the room?" she joked.

"Yeah, something like that." He lightly sucked on the tender spot on the side of her neck, right above her collarbone.

"You're going to mark me."

"I plead guilty to that. What are you gonna do about it?" He sucked harder.

"Not a damn thing."

She turned around in his arms and faced him. Brushing his lower lip with her tongue, she unzipped his pants.

"Doing that is going to get you fucked," he rasped.

"Promise?"

Hawk led Cara into the spacious bedroom, and as he sat on the edge of the bed, he tugged her to him and kissed her. Their whispering soon turned to moans of pleasure as they gave way to their desire.

SEATED AT A table for two against the brick wall, Cara ordered a dirty martini with extra olives, and Hawk ordered a bottle of dark German beer. Steakhouse No. 316 was Cara's favorite restaurant in Aspen, and she knew Hawk would love it since his favorite food was steak.

Hawk stared at Cara as she took a sip from her martini, a small drop clinging to her lips.

"What are you looking at?"

"You. You're so damn sexy. I can't get enough of you."

"You're not too shabby, yourself."

Cara slipped off her high heel and rubbed her foot up and down Hawk's leg before she placed her foot on his lap and twisted her heel into his crotch. His cock felt like a thick, hard rod beneath her heel.

With smoldering eyes, he leaned toward her. "Get over here."

She stretched over the table and their lips met in the middle. The sourness of the lime on his full lips was enough to draw her closer. She slipped her tongue inside his mouth—it was cool from her martini. They pulled back when the waiter came over to take their order. Then Hawk placed his hand over hers and gazed at her, and she saw the candlelight reflected in them.

"I can't believe Kylie will be graduating high school in a couple months," Cara said.

"Tell me about it. I never thought Banger would let her go away to college. She has you to thank for that."

Cara had championed hard for Kylie to go away to college. She'd found scholarships and grants for her so when Kylie confronted her dad, she had a lot of ammunition to fight her battle for independence. Banger put up a good fight, but in the end, he acquiesced. Cara was happy for her; Kylie had wonderful experiences ahead of her.

After Cara finished her last bite of filet mignon, the waiter came over with a delectable crème brûlée. He brought two spoons.

"We didn't order this," Cara said.

"The gentleman did," the waiter replied.

Cara looked at Hawk. "When?"

"I know it's your favorite dessert. I ordered it when you went to the bathroom."

"How sweet." Although, she didn't have the heart to tell him she was so full she was ready to burst. She picked up a spoon and broke through the hard, crusty top.

"Yum, this is fantastic. Here, try some." Cara put the spoon in Hawk's mouth. "Like it?"

"It's rich."

"That's what makes it so decadent." A small amount of the cream coated her finger. "Open up," she said to Hawk. He opened his mouth, and she put her finger in it. As he licked and sucked the dessert off, their eyes fixed on each other. She pulled out her finger, put it in her mouth, and licked it. As she withdrew it, Hawk watched with a devilish smile on his face.

"That *is* some good shit," he said.

They ordered two Amarettos on ice for after-dinner drinks. As Cara watched the twinkling lights of the town from the window, Hawk grasped her hand and put something hard into it. Looking at it, she saw a small black box. "What's this?" she asked.

"Open it."

Fingers trembling, she did. Inside, a brilliant three-carat solitaire caught the glimmer of the light. The diamond was set in a fourteen-carat gold band, with six princess-cut emerald stones on each side. It was stunning.

Hawk retrieved the box from her, took out the ring, put it on her ring finger, and said, "Marry me."

Time stood still as Cara's heart burst in a million pieces. *I can't believe Hawk asked me to marry him. I never thought he would. I love him.*

"Oh, yes. Yes, I'll marry you."

Hawk kissed her hand. "I'm so in love with you, you don't even know how much, baby."

As she leapt from her chair, rushing to him, Hawk pushed his chair back. Cara plopped on his lap and kissed him all over his face until her mouth covered his. "Let's go back to the hotel. I want to show you how happy you've made me," she murmured against his lips.

BACK AT THE hotel, Hawk had his pants unzipped before they made it to the bedroom. He unbuttoned Cara's blouse as his hand slid up her skirt, noticing she wore those sexy thigh-highs, the ones which drove him crazy. His fingers grazed across her pussy, above her thong. Hawk's cock grew harder as he fingered the strip of fabric between her ass cheeks. "Fuck, you drive me wild," he muttered between kisses and bites on her lips and neck.

Cara moaned, arching her back and making her nipples brush

against his t-shirt. He fondled her breasts, took each nipple into his mouth and teased it.

Cara pulled Hawk down on the bed on top of her. "I love you so much," she breathed into his ear.

He looked into her eyes. "You're so beautiful." He kissed her, his mouth and tongue trailing her lips, her jawline, her tits, before settling on her stomach. While he licked her belly button, Hawk kneaded her stomach in a circular motion.

"I can't wait to have our baby growing inside of you."

"Whoa, let's slow down a bit. I've been engaged for less than an hour."

"You want kids, don't you?"

"I do, but we have time. Someday, I do want to have your child."

Hawk squeezed her, then spread her legs open and caressed her wet pussy with his fingers. Then he entered her with his hard cock. They rocked back and forth together, their movements increasing in speed as their grunts filled the bedroom. They both reached their orgasm together, clutching each other as sweat trickled down their bodies.

Hawk buried his face in Cara's neck and murmured, "You know, whenever we make love, to me, it's like the first time we've ever made love. I love you completely, Cara."

"I love you so much, Hawk. I'm happy to spend my life with you." She kissed his lips, then pulling out his hair tie, she ran her fingers through his hair. They held each other, listening to their beating hearts and relishing being together.

I finally found what's been missing from my life for all these years. I have my Cara, my wildcat, in my life forever. The moonlight illuminated the couple as Hawk listened to Cara fall asleep.

Fuck, life is incredible.

The End

Make sure you sign up for my newsletter so you can keep up with my new releases, special sales, free short stories, and other treats only available to newsletter readers. When you sign up, you will receive a FREE hot and steamy novella. Sign up at:

http://eepurl.com/bACCL1

Visit me on Facebook
facebook.com/Chiah-Wilder-1625397261063989

Check out my other books at my Author Page
amazon.com/author/chiahwilder

Thank you!

Thank you for reading my book. I hope you enjoyed the first book in the Insurgents MC series as much as I enjoyed writing Cara and Hawk's story. This rough motorcycle club has a lot more to say, so I hope you will look for the upcoming books in the series. Romance makes life so much more colorful, and a rough, sexy bad boy makes life a whole lot more interesting.

If you enjoyed the book, please consider leaving a review on Amazon. I read all of them and appreciate the time taken out of busy schedules to do that.

I love hearing from my fans, so if you have any comments or questions, please email me at chiahwilder@gmail.com or visit my facebook page at facebook.com/Chiah-Wilder-1625397261063989.

To hear of **new releases**, **special sales**, **free short stories**, and **ARC opportunities**, please sign up for my **Newsletter** at http://eepurl.com/bACCL1.

Thank you so much for taking a chance with an indie author and her debut novel. You have made the journey from reader to writer even sweeter. Without your support and love of words, books wouldn't exist. So I thank the *reader* in all of you, and the *risk taker* for picking up books from unknown authors.

Happy Reading,

Chiah

JAX'S DILEMMA

Book 2 in the Insurgents MC Series

Available Now!

Jax, Sergeant-At-Arms of the Insurgents Motorcycle Club, likes his women easy.

Raised in the outlaw biker world, Jax has bedded more women than he can count. The only things on his mind are big ass Harleys, scorching whiskey, and pretty women who can spread on command.

Then he meets Cherri—the stripper with ice blue eyes and white-blonde hair.

He wants her in his bed.

She would rather not.

Cherri has complicated stamped all over her. Jax doesn't need a woman like her messing up his life.

Too bad he can't stop thinking about her.

Cherri ran away from a bad situation back home.

She has secrets she hasn't shared with anyone. Stripping is her means of making enough money to start a new life, and nothing's going to screw up her plans.

Then she meets Jax.

He's gorgeous, sexy, and a cocky bastard. His tattooed, ripped chest and biceps make her drool. She knows she should run far away from him, but her body wants him in the worst way.

Just as she begins to relax, her past collides with her new life. Cherri must navigate a deadly obstacle course littered with outlaw motorcycle clubs and a power-hungry politician.

Jax won't stop until he claims Cherri. He vows to protect and love Cherri no matter what. When put to the test, will Jax betray his family—the Insurgents MC, or will he lose the woman he loves forever?

Excerpt

Jax's Dilemma

PROLOGUE

THE SCORCHING SUN bored into Cherri's skin as she lay among the wildflowers. Vibrant blues, purples, yellows, and pinks carpeted the verdant field. Evergreens stood tall on the mountain range as a gurgling creek lulled her to a state of peacefulness. She could almost feel goose-bumps on her forearms as a light breeze caressed her.

"Fuck, that feels good, hon."

The raspy, male voice brought Cherri back to reality, and she looked at the thirty-something man grunting and sweating as he thrust his dick in and out of her. She stared at the peeling paint in the corner of the ceiling. If only the jerk wouldn't have opened his mouth, she would've been able to stay in her safe place.

"Fuck, you feel good," he said as he squeezed her small breasts too hard. Putting his mouth over her pink nipples, he sucked them like a vacuum.

Fuck, when is this tool going to come? Cherri tried hard to get back to her safe place, but she couldn't; her valley of wildflowers and sunshine was gone, retreating to the far corners of her mind until the next time she needed a protected haven.

She had created her safe place when she was fourteen years old and her life had turned to shit. It kept her sane until she split three years later to make her own way.

Finally, at the age of eighteen, her wildflower valley made the sex tolerable, especially with old men like the one who kept pawing her and pushing his lame dick into her. At least she'd get five hundred dollars for this trick. Even though she normally didn't turn tricks, this guy was different, or so Brandon, the bartender at the gentlemen's club where she danced, told her. The guy was rich and someone important. A councilman, she thought. The money was too good to pass up, so she agreed to be with him. She just wished he'd finish already; she wanted to go back to her apartment and take a long shower to wash off his stench.

"Are you getting close to coming?" He squeezed her breasts again.

"Huh...? Oh, yeah, sure, baby. You make me feel real good. I'm coming now." Putting on one of her better performances, she writhed and screamed as she bucked under him.

"I'm coming now, too," he grunted. He stiffened, exhaled, and collapsed beside her.

It's about fuckin' time. Turning her head toward the window, she could see the blue sky. Tightness covered her chest while her throat grew thick. She wondered if being a whore was her destiny. Saltiness stung her eyes as she squeezed them shut, willing herself to be anywhere but in that mediocre motel room with the tobacco-stained curtains and the peeling paint.

A swat on her butt made her turn her head toward her paying lover. He leaned in close; his sweat was pungent. He kissed her deeply, his tongue thick and wet in her mouth, making her want to gag.

"That was awesome, hon. You and I are going to be regulars. I like the way you make me feel. I know you liked it." Running his eyes over her, he lingered on her young breasts. Wiping his brow with his fingers, he said, "I can be a real generous man. You think you'd like to be my permanent girlfriend? I can set you up real good."

Could I stand him pawing at me all the time? "Would we live together?"

"I'd love that, but no, we'd have to be discreet. You know, with my political position and all. I'd set you up in a nice apartment. I'll use untraceable funds. I'd come see you a few times a week. We may be able to sneak away once in a while for a weekend trip or so, but, for now, we'd have to stay in. I'll give you an expense account, of course."

"So, I couldn't see you every day?"

Dragging her closer to him, he smiled. "I know that's a disappointment, hon, but I'll make every minute count when I come over. Oh, I won't be spending the night, either. I have to stay under the radar, you know? Once things calm down after the election, we can see each other more. What do you say?"

Inside, her body sang for joy. Did this two-bit politician think she *wanted* to be with him all the time? *What an ego he must have.*

"Oh, and I have one condition. You have to quit your job at the bar. You won't need to strip anymore. I'll make sure you're well taken care of, if you make sure I am. You know what I mean?" Winking at her, he leered and twisted her breast.

Wincing at the force of his touch, she nodded. What did she have to lose? Not having to strip for a bunch of sweaty, lecherous men was a dream come true. The possibility of moving out of her roach-infested shithole made her giddy. For once, she'd be in a nice, safe place and wouldn't have to worry all the time about being evicted or attacked. Plus, the proposition sounded a hell of a lot better than the shit life she currently had. Maybe she'd finally be able to save enough money so she could get out of Denver and go somewhere quiet and respectable, pretending her past never existed.

"Sure, why not?"

He hugged her while he rubbed her dry slit. "You're making me horny again, hon."

As he groped her body, she sighed, fixing her eyes on the ceiling.

CHAPTER ONE

Three years later
Pinewood Springs, Colorado

"CHERRI, I NEED your ass out there waiting tables. Miranda called in sick, and we're short tonight," Emma, the club manager, said.

"What about my dance set?"

"I switched you to the last slot. You'll be on in about two hours. You're the only one who's worth shit around here. You can dance *and* waitress. One of your tables will be the Insurgents."

Her stomach lurched. "Can't Liza take it? She likes catering to them."

"They asked for you, and since they're paying your salary and own the club, you fuckin' do what they ask. Go on now. Get your ass out there, and be sure to wiggle it so you can get some big tips."

Cherri peeked out from behind the curtains to take in the room. Yep, there he was, sitting at the front table, his jean-clad legs straddling the chair backwards. He wore a black vest with patches all over it; the left top side had a diamond-shaped 1% er patch, while the right side had one which read Sergeant-At-Arms and underneath it, his name, *Jax*. Tight across his muscular chest, his black t-shirt showed off his well-defined pecs and abs. His sandy brown hair was longer on the top and shorter on the sides in the style of a fauxhawk, and pierced eyebrows framed his hazel eyes. A full sleeve of tattoos decorated his right arm while his other bore various designs of skulls and daggers. He was handsome in a rugged way, his five o'clock shadow giving his face a hard edge. Staring intently at one of the dancers spreading her legs and running her red-tipped fingers over her slit, he leaned forward, his bulging biceps moving with him.

"Come on, Cherri. Get a move on! We got a full house," Emma barked from behind her. Shutting the curtains, Cherri ran to her dressing room, threw on a turquoise t-shirt and a short skirt over her thong, and rushed out to the bar area.

Dream House was utter chaos that night, and she knew her feet would be blistered and sore from standing on her four-inch heels for too long. Even though she was aware she should be grateful to be alive and at the strip club, she was sick of everything. When she had learned she was primed to be the Mountainside Strangler's next victim and had narrowly escaped a tortured death, she shuddered. If the Insurgents hadn't come to the Deadly Demons' clubhouse a couple of months before rescuing her, she'd be six-feet-under.

Choosing to work at Dream House hadn't turned out so bad, and it was a lot better than waitressing at one of the Insurgents' restaurants. She knew the MC wanted to keep her close because she knew a bit too much about what happened that early November morning at the Nomads' clubhouse. What the MC didn't get was she was happier than hell they had eliminated the pieces of shit who'd enslaved her. She'd never squeal, not in a hundred years, but these outlaw bikers didn't trust her, so there she was shaking her ass once again at another strip club.

When she came up to the Insurgents table, her stomach felt queasy. The guys always made her go into panic mode, never knowing when one of them might touch her or, worse yet, force himself on her. So far, they'd contented themselves with just looking and making lewd comments, but she saw the way they fucked the club whores. It was like the whole club, including the women, just wanted to fuck all the time. It was disgusting.

"Come on over here, sweetness," Jax said, looking at her with lust in his eyes.

She had avoided going over to his side, preferring to stand next to Chas and Axe, who were engrossed in watching the dancer play with her big tits.

"What do you want to drink?" she asked.

"I said to come on over by me. Now," Jax growled, his boyish grin gone.

Cherri walked over to him, and his hand squeezed her butt through her skirt. She flinched. He laughed. "Why so jumpy, sweetness? You got a soft ass that is way too tempting." He slipped his hand under her skirt, pinching her cheeks.

"Don't do that! You don't have the right to touch me."

Anger flashed in his eyes. "Yeah, I do. Fuck, we own you. You're Insurgents' property, and I can do whatever the fuck I want." He pulled her toward him.

"No one owns me. Do you get off on forcing yourself on women?"

Jax's jaw clenched, his eyes narrowing into slits. "Don't *ever* fucking say that to me again. I don't have to force any bitch, got it?"

"Then leave me alone." Cherri knew she should keep her mouth shut, but she couldn't. For the past two months she had been with the Insurgents, Jax had been sniffing around her. She had to admit he was good-looking and sexy, but she had no interest in any man. Men wanted a woman for fucking, nothing more. She was *so* not into that. If she had to fuck, she expected to get paid well for it.

She knew Jax wanted into her pants real bad; he made it clear every time he looked at her with his desire-filled eyes. Whenever she was in the clubhouse or at the strip bar, he'd take every opportunity to brush against her, rubbing his firm chest against her small breasts. She hated the way her body would feel all funny, like a million butterflies were flying around inside her when their bodies touched in passing. She didn't need the guy complicating her life, needing to stay focused on her goal of leaving the club and making a better life for herself. Jax was turning out to be a distracting nuisance.

Jax's gaze raked her body, his hands in his lap. He threw her a half-grin. "Bring me a shot of Jack and a Corona, sweetness."

She nodded, took the other members' orders, and went to the bar. Returning with the drinks, she placed them in front of the bikers.

Leaning across the table to give Jax his, she realized too late he had a full-frontal view of her breasts. Hearing his sharp intake of breath, her cheeks flushed as her blue eyes locked with his for a heartbeat. Turning away, she busied herself with the other tables. She didn't like the intensity, the spark of connection that coursed through her body when their eyes met.

For the next hour, Cherri ran her ass off waiting tables, clearing glasses, and fending off advances from many of the patrons while trying her best to avoid getting any closer than necessary to Jax. When she came back to the Insurgents' table to bring more drinks, he didn't call her over to his side anymore. She was grateful, even though his eyes bored a hole into her each and every time she placed drinks in front of the bikers. It was downright unnerving.

As she stood by the bar waiting for her newest drink order, she felt a hand on her shoulder. Glancing sideways, she saw Emma. "Cherri, go ahead and get ready for your dance set. I can take over from here," she said.

Cherri ran to the dressing rooms in the back of the bar, trying not to fall as she dodged the boxes of liquor and napkins littering the floor behind the stage curtains. Freshening her makeup, she teased and sprayed her shoulder-length, white-blonde hair. Her eyeliner and eye shadow made her blue eyes look like two ice cubes surrounded by black smoke. Cursing when her sheer thong sported a run, she replaced it with a silver-colored one, breathing heavily as she tried to get herself together before she was announced. After dusting iridescent glitter over her body, she pulled on a pink metallic short skirt, her heart-shaped ass peeking out from underneath it. The matching halter top fitted tightly over her small, round breasts. She slipped on her five-inch Lucite pumps, checked herself out in the full-length mirror, and waited for her cue to take the stage.

The stage was a decent size, not as big as some of the other strip clubs she had danced for. There were two poles on each side of the stage and a stainless-steel chair in the middle. Sometimes Cherri would use the pole, sometimes the chair, but mostly she liked to dance the old-fashioned way—no props or gimmicks, just relying on the rhythm of her body.

The lights dimmed, and the mist from the fog machine created a web around her and the stage. Throwing her head back, her long hair touched the top of her skirt. The clear, crystal-jeweled barbell dangling from her belly button caught the light, glimmering like chunks of diamonds. Buckcherry's song, "Crazy Bitch", filled the bar as Cherri moved her hips suggestively while licking her full lips slowly. She strutted around the stage swaying her hips, thrusting out her ass, and smooshing her breasts together. Lowering herself to the floor, she began a series of movements she was sure would make any man's cock hard.

As she rolled her head in circles, her hair brushing against the floor, she saw all eyes on her. Some of the guys in the front row had their hands on their dicks as they watched her crawl forward and, leaning in to them, she almost touched her forehead against their oily ones. As she inched forward, her breasts bounced, spilling out of the confines of her halter. Straightening out, she rocked back on her knees, her glittering thong peeping out as her hands played with her breasts.

When she threw her head forward, she looked straight at Jax. He stared at her, his face tight, hands on the table. Even from where she was, she saw hunger in his eyes. Placing a finger in her mouth, she sucked it, dragging it out as her other hand grabbed her sex. Smiling seductively at him, she unhooked her halter and let her high, rounded breasts free. She liked teasing him, and on stage she felt safe; he could look at her but not touch. From the way he stared at her, his eyes crazed with desire, bulge aching to break free, she knew he wanted her. That was what she loved, the power she held over men with her body. When men were wild with lust, they'd do anything to stick their dick in her. That was where she had the control, and no one could take it from her. Amid all the shit she had in her life, knowing she had *some* power, *some* control, made her feel stronger.

She looped her fingers around the waistband of her skirt, pushing downward as she shimmied out of it. When she stood upright once more, the mist swirled around her, the lights glimmered, covering her like a shroud, and the glitter makeup on her body sparkled. Stroking her covered slit with her pink-tipped nails, she licked her lips as she spread her legs wide. Turning around, she bent over, looking at the entranced spectators between her legs. It was at that moment she watched Jax blow a kiss to her; a simple gesture which made her stomach flip-flop. The stage lights went out, and the audience applauded and cheered.

She exited the stage and went to her dressing room to get her robe. As she massaged her sore feet, she heard a shuffling sound behind her. Turning around, she saw Jax standing in the doorway, his eyes glinting with arousal.

"You outdid yourself tonight, sweetness," he drawled.

"Got to pay the bills, you know?" She didn't like him being there, in her space, so close to her. It made her uncomfortable, causing her heart to race, her temples to throb. She didn't know why she had such a reaction to him because she never felt anything in a man's presence except disgust. It was something about this biker that threw her off-kilter, made her think of her childhood dreams of happily-ever-after before they became distorted. She snorted, shaking her head to dispel her foolish thoughts.

Jax came up to her, his hands on her shoulders, pulling her close to him.

"What the fuck are you doing? I'm wiped out and want to get home. I don't have time to fend you off, got it?"

"Shh, calm down, little one. You're always fighting, trying to be so tough. Just relax and let things take us where they will." He cupped her chin and brought his lips down on hers. It was a gentle kiss, like a brushstroke on canvas, and his tongue skimmed over her mouth. She instinctively leaned in closer to him, her mouth pliant under his. "You've got such kissable lips, sweetness," he murmured against her mouth.

Counter to her reason, her body responded, but when he brought his hand up toward her breast, she shut down. She was no longer Cherri, exotic dancer at Dream House; she was a frightened young teen hiding under the stairs of her home. She jerked away from Jax, pushing him backward. "I told you I'm tired. I gotta go. Stop fuckin' groping me."

Looking surprised at the switch in her demeanor, he said, "What just happened? A couple of seconds ago, you loved it, and now you turned into a frigid bitch. What the fuck?"

Her ice blue eyes flashed with anger. "Why don't you leave me alone? What the fuck is your problem? I'm not interested in you or *any* man. I have to do this shit for now, but my job description doesn't include having one of the owners handle me. There are plenty of whores around here who'd love to suck your dick. Go to them and leave me the fuck alone."

"That shit you were doing on stage was meant for me. If you don't want the attention then don't be such a cock tease. And watch your fuckin' mouth when you talk to me. I don't like bitches thinking they can say whatever the fuck they want."

"Well, I don't like assholes thinking they can paw me whenever the fuck they want, so I guess we're even, aren't we?"

Rage filled his eyes as he pitched toward her. She ducked out of his grasp, scooped up her clothes from the floor, and locked herself in the bathroom. The door vibrated as he slammed his fist on it, making the wood groan under the force of his strength.

"Your ass better *stay* in there. You fuckin' need to learn respect, bitch!" he yelled.

"Give *me* respect and I'll give it to *you*," she replied as she put on her clothes.

She waited for about twenty minutes, not sure if he was still outside the door. Weary to the bone, she decided she'd have to deal with him if he were still there since she couldn't spend the night in the bathroom. Opening the door, she peered out, seeing no one. Breathing a sigh of relief, she threw on her jacket, slung her tote and purse over her shoulder, and rushed out the back door.

Outside in the parking lot, the frosty air made her feel alive as it stung her cheeks. The haziness of the night transformed the moon into a blurry orb hanging in the dark sky. While driving to the apartment she shared with two of the other dancers, she replayed the encounter with Jax in her mind. His gentle kiss made her feel mushy and funny inside—funny in a good way—but then he had to go and start his grabbing shit, just like all the men she had ever known. It was like they all wanted a piece of her to devour until she had nothing left of herself. *Why do men have to be such assholes all the time?*

Once she entered her apartment, she went straight to her bedroom, threw her purse on the floor, stripped off her clothes, and flopped on her bed, too tired to take off her makeup. A few minutes later, she was sound asleep.

Other Titles in the Series:

Jax's Dilemma: Insurgents Motorcycle Club Book 2
Chas's Fervor: Insurgents Motorcycle Club Book 3
Axe's Fall: Insurgents Motorcycle Club Book 4

Made in the USA
Middletown, DE
21 June 2016